The Jellyfish Problem

The Jellyfish Problem

Tessa Yang

Berkley
New York

BERKLEY
An imprint of Penguin Random House LLC
1745 Broadway, New York, NY 10019
penguinrandomhouse.com

Book design by Alison Cnockaert
Interior illustrations by Jenni Surasky

Library of Congress Cataloging-in-Publication Data

Names: Yang, Tessa author
Title: The jellyfish problem / Tessa Yang.
Description: New York: Berkley, 2026.
Identifiers: LCCN 2025039776 (print) | LCCN 2025039777 (ebook) |
ISBN 9780593955826 hardcover | ISBN 9780593955833 ebook
Subjects: LCGFT: Novels | Fiction | Action and adventure fiction
Classification: LCC PS3625.A67796 J45 2026 (print) | LCC PS3625.A67796 (ebook)
LC record available at https://lccn.loc.gov/2025039776
LC ebook record available at https://lccn.loc.gov/2025039777

Printed in the United States of America
1st Printing

The authorized representative in the EU for product safety and compliance is Penguin Random House Ireland, Morrison Chambers, 32 Nassau Street, Dublin D02 YH68, Ireland, https://eu-contact.penguin.ie.

For Mom

It is easy to be fooled by jellyfish.

—Lisa-ann Gershwin, *Stung! On Jellyfish Blooms and the Future of the Ocean*

The trick was learning to think like a monster.

—Sy Montgomery, *The Soul of an Octopus: A Surprising Exploration into the Wonder of Consciousness*

The Jellyfish Problem

There was something in the water. There was always something in the water in my mother's bedtime stories: a slimy-skinned *kappa* springing onto land with its life force wobbling in the bowl on its head, a *ningyo* mermaid heralding storms and disasters, a shape-shifting *kawauso* luring unsuspecting humans to the water's edge. This menagerie of knowable misfits had felt like the most incredible gift to a misfit girl from a landlocked town. Dad always worried Mom would give me nightmares, but she never did.

In my favorite story, though, the monster was never truly known. It was whispers and glimpses of lights on the water, rumors of drowned sailors traded secondhand. I think that was why I demanded to hear this tale over and over, my fascination born more of frustration than awe. I craved a neat epilogue with a clear moral, where you understood everything that had happened and why. But that was never the kind of story it was going to be.

"Long ago," began Mom, in the hoarse whisper she used when

trying to sound spooky, "there lived an aging widow whose son had been lost to the sea . . ."

What was loss to me at that age? A misplaced toy? A pet-store goldfish found floating belly-up in the bowl? I remember feeling baffled by the grief-stricken widow as I lay there tucked under my ladybug comforter, trying to understand why she did what she did. Why get in the water against all warnings and common wisdom? Why take your chances with the beast?

I know the answers now.

This isn't the book we set out to write together, but I still think you would've loved it.

Part One

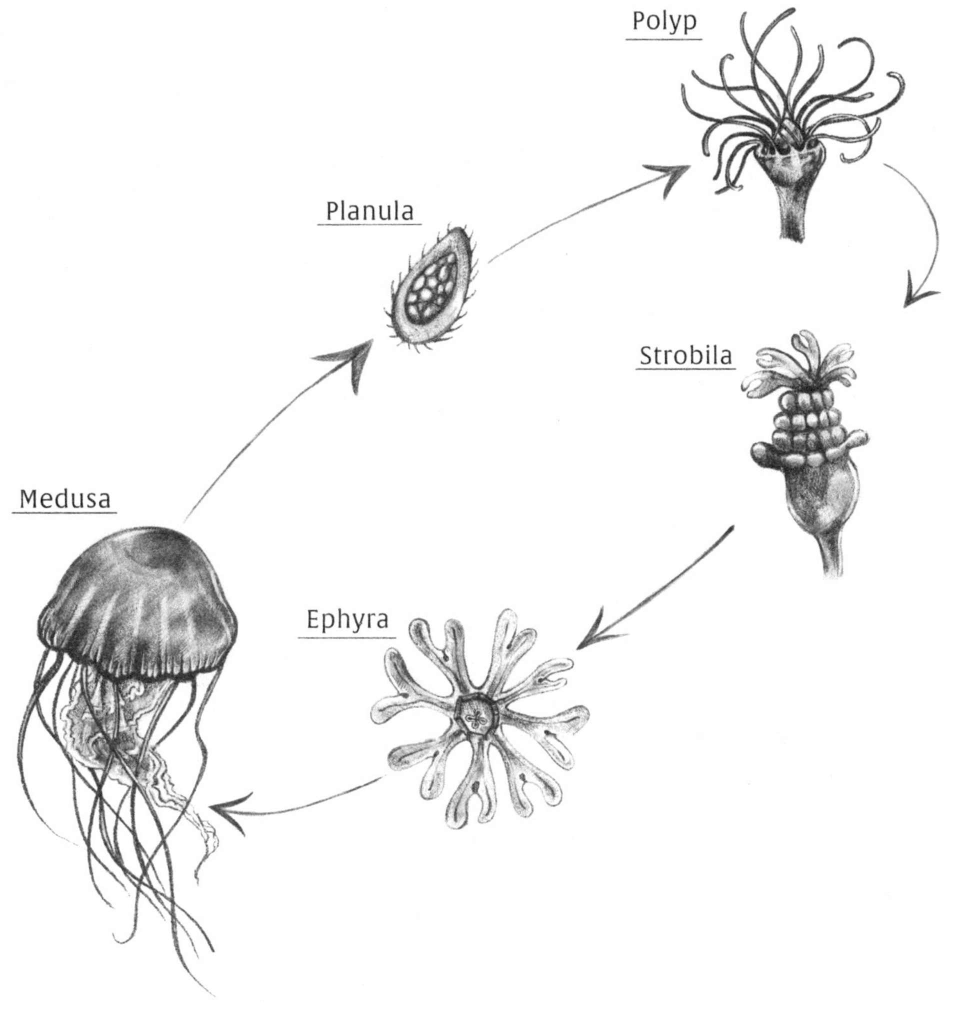

A Jellyfish Problem

Jellyfish is a misnomer. Fish are cold-blooded vertebrates that respire through gills. Jellyfish are bloodless invertebrates that exchange gases directly through their skin. The spinelessness of jellies—their apparent frailness—has led to the word's slang meaning: a weakling or a doormat. A person devoid of a backbone.

We hope this book will prove jellyfish to be anything but weaklings. As we'll show in the coming chapters, you don't need a backbone to inspire awe, to elicit fear, to change the world.

AA: Too much?

JN: Just enough.

There are certain people from your past whom you never expect to resurface. Nadia was one of mine. We'd had a short-lived, intense friendship near the end of college before graduating and heading down our separate paths. Though I thought of her often in the intervening decade—thought of, in particular, the night we'd spent together on the roof of the science building, stars above, Nadia's head heavy on my chest—I hadn't tried to reach out. Why would I? She'd made it clear that whatever existed between us was over, graduation the perfect excuse to sever a connection that had always meant more to me than to her.

I couldn't think of a single reason for her to be calling me from an unfamiliar number at half past five in the morning on a Tuesday in May after eleven years of silence, but that was what happened.

"Hi! Is this Josie?"

I knew it was her immediately because Nadia was the only person who'd ever called me by that name. I had been Jo and Josephine and *Jo-Ness* spit to sound like *Jonas* by a high school softball coach disgusted by my tendency to daydream in the outfield—*snap out of it, Jo-Ness!*—and in the scuba diving class I took to get certified at sixteen, I was even briefly known as Nessie, as in the lake monster, due to having an air consumption rate so low I was presumed to be partially aquatic.

Josie belonged to Nadia because she claimed it, and I let her.

My shoulders screamed out in pain as I straightened from my desk, where I'd fallen asleep over my laptop. The screen had gone black, sparing me the separate agony of confronting the pages of my book manuscript—*The Modern Medusa: A Jellyfish Primer* by Josephine Ness and Aldo Antunes—still covered in unresolved comments: mine, and Aldo's.

As I cleared the gravel from my throat and blinked away the last clinging dregs of sleep, the familiar contours of my office at Seaheart swam into focus. The white wall bearing my framed diplomas and Ocean Conservancy calendar, still open to January's image of spawning corals. The broken filing cabinet whose top drawer rolled determinedly open unless sealed with a piece of masking tape. The desk plastered with a quilt of sticky notes, the oldest so old they'd lost their stick and fluttered around each time I patted down the area seeking whatever item I'd lost track of.

It wasn't always like this. Aldo used to scold me for being a neat freak. Then he died and my world tipped into an entropy I couldn't control. Power cords snaked out of nowhere to trip me. Just-washed mugs reappeared in front of me, silty with the cold sediment of coffee I didn't remember drinking. The voice of an old friend slipped through a cracked-open door, beckoning me into the corridor of our shared past.

"Nadia? Nadia Markov?" I said. "Is that really you?"

It was pleasant spending the next several minutes catching up, filling in with broad strokes our lives since undergrad. Nadia had taught English overseas for a few years, gotten her master's in education, bounced around various districts looking for the right fit, and was now teaching in a one-room schoolhouse on a remote island off the coast of Maine. I told her I worked as the research coordinator at a small aquarium, brazenly perched at the waterless edge of Joshua Tree. *Small* sounded specialized and cozy, which Seaheart was. *Small* didn't necessarily scream short-staffed and broke, which Seaheart also was.

"Oh my god, you're on the West Coast? What time is it there?" cried Nadia. "I'm so sorry, Josie, I thought you were still in the Northeast . . . I was trying to catch you before work."

I reassured her it was okay without adding that I was already at work, because I hadn't left work, because I'd effectively moved into work, converting my bottom desk drawer into an overnight kit complete with a spare set of clothing, deodorant, toothbrush, and a mini tube of travel toothpaste. What had begun as a contingency plan for those late nights when the hour-plus commute back to my apartment in Riverside didn't seem worth it had fast evolved into the new norm. It was all hands on deck for those of us who'd survived the latest round of layoffs. And I slept better on my office's rock-hard love seat than in my own bed. The guilty dreams didn't follow me here.

By now I was in the staff room, trying to wrest a mug from the dish rack without causing an avalanche. The aquarium's cleaner had quit last year, and Elijah Pinsky, Seaheart's director and general curator, refused to replace her, insisting the staff could learn to clean up after ourselves. I felt newly attuned to my untidy surroundings when I compared them to where I imagined Nadia was calling from. I put her in an airy beach house with sea-green walls, gauzy pastel curtains, and handwoven baskets full of beautiful rocks. Her fridge door displayed magnets from her travels, each one pinning a photograph of an adoring friend.

I successfully rescued a mug, then turned in a helpless circle looking for the coffeepot.

"Are you still into jellyfish?" Nadia asked me.

Was I still into jellyfish?

I had an October deadline for the jellyfish book Aldo and I had been writing for three years, which I was helplessly stalled on now that I had to finish it alone. I saw jellyfish everywhere: in the slow-motion shimmy of a plastic bag being shaken open, in the swirl of water around the bathtub drain, in spiderwebs and raindrops, in the scoop of light floating inside a contact lens. Jellyfish were my first thought on waking and my last thought before falling asleep, and their graceful, translucent bodies undulated through the dreams that fell between. Not one but two women had dumped me on the grounds that I liked jellyfish more than I liked people.

I confirmed for Nadia that I was still into jellyfish.

"That's awesome. Because if I'm being honest, that's why I called you. We're having a bit of a jellyfish problem on the island—actually, we're having a really *big* jellyfish problem."

"You mean like a bloom?" I hadn't read anything about a high-density jellyfish swarm in New England, though it wasn't impossible that one had turned up there. Across the planet, blooms were on the rise. Theories as to why varied depending upon whom you asked. Aldo was a proponent of the wax-and-wane theory: jellyfish numbers oscillating as part of a natural cycle, with expected peaks and valleys over time. I countered that climate change created ecological vacuums where jellyfish could thrive like never before. We had butted heads on the subject so often, it nearly derailed our book.

"It's probably easiest if I show you," said Nadia. "Hang on, sending it now."

The turn in the conversation led me out of the kitchen and into the lab. The hum of circulating water was instantly soothing. Half the space was given over to quarantine for newly arrived animals or ones recovering from illness. The rest of the room belonged to my polyp parlor. Jellyfish in their polyp phase were twitching stalks half a centimeter high, capped by a swaying bouquet of hairlike tentacles. My heart swelled with affection for these tiny, stubborn weirdos who grew back with weed-like speediness when you tried to scrape them away.

I redirected my attention from the tanks to my phone as the screen lit with an incoming message. It was a video clip—fourteen seconds of shaky footage taken from shore sometime during the night. Out on the water, bright red tendrils of light squiggled through the darkness.

Nadia's voice lifted from my phone speaker, rapt, excited: "What do you think?"

"I think . . ." I watched the clip again. The tendrils were so bright, they smeared together. Even in the dim lighting of the lab, I had to tip my phone at an angle and squint to make out individual lines. "I think this looks really fake, Nadia."

"Assume that it isn't."

"You filmed this?"

"Someone I trust did. A friend."

I watched it for a third time. The Nadia I remembered from college was smart, but burdened with that particular type of naivete that afflicts the people pleasers of the world: She would believe anything before she believed someone had deceived her.

"Even if it is real," I said, "this isn't anything to go off of. Lots of things in the ocean emit light. Algae, bacteria—"

"And jellyfish!"

"Certain species."

"My friend says it's a jellyfish," said Nadia stoutly. "The biggest in the world."

"But you haven't seen it."

"Would it make a difference if I had?"

"Of course," I said, surprised she had to ask. "Footage can be doctored, but you're the most trustworthy person I know."

The embarrassing scale of this compliment echoed back at me. I couldn't actually see my cheeks flushing in the dark glass of the nearest tank, but I felt the heat flooding my face.

Fortunately, Nadia was still preoccupied with my earlier comment. "I haven't seen it," she admitted. "Not in person. My friend says it's not safe."

There were a handful of jellyfish species whose stings could be lethal to humans—their toxins had been Aldo's area of expertise—but I'd yet to meet one that caused harm just by being *looked* at. I was more convinced than ever that Nadia was being pranked.

"Do you want to?" she asked, after a pause.

"Do I want to what?"

"See it."

It took me a second to grasp her meaning. I was distracted by the sound of a door opening and closing somewhere in the building. That could only be Elijah, whose work hours grew in inverse proportion to the aquarium's funding. The more money we hemorrhaged, the earlier the boss started. I glanced at the time on my phone screen and winced. Not yet 6 a.m.

"You want me to come there?" I asked Nadia. My stomach fizzed with a strange feeling that I identified a moment later as excitement. I hadn't felt truly excited about something in a long time. "Visit you on the island?"

"I know it's a huge ask, you're thousands of miles away, you have your own life—"

I had a mental image of the apartment I hadn't visited in two days, the long-dead snake plant in my foyer, Aldo's ashes in their urn on the mantel, its front emblazoned with a mother-of-pearl sea turtle. No one had fought me for those ashes. His parents were dead, he had no siblings, all his friendships were fleeting. He'd had to die for me to realize how alone he was in this world, except for me.

"—and it's totally weird for me to call you like this out of the blue when we haven't talked in ten years—"

"Eleven," I said.

"Eleven! Even weirder. So, of course, no hard feelings if you say no. But, Josie . . ." A dumb little thrill coursed through me at the second use of my special name. "It's hard to explain. I'm still a newcomer here and the locals can be pretty closed-minded—they're not about to open up to me about their problems, I mean—but from what I can tell, they're scared."

"Of what?"

"*It.*"

I experienced that brain glitch I got sometimes when faced with the nonsense of human emotion. It used to upset me when I was younger, but over the years I'd learned to accept that people didn't make any sense to me, particularly where their fears were concerned. A garter snake slithering past your sneaker wouldn't do you any harm. Thunder was just the expansion of hot air around a lightning bolt. The squeamish terror around insects was especially baffling. Before finding my way to marine biology, I'd thought I would be an entomologist. I used to stalk the playground with a magnifying glass, searching for beetles and centipedes to study.

This hobby didn't endear me to my schoolmates, among whom I was cleverly known as Bug-Eyed Weirdo—an epithet that followed me all the way to graduation, indifferent to the fact I'd shifted my focus to jellyfish in the fifth grade. By the time I fled Indiana for the Pennsylvania college that had dumped a large scholarship in my lap, I'd acclimated to my solitude and even learned to embrace it. Who needed people when I had the dreamy pulsations of the moon jelly, the deep-sea flashes of the atolla jelly, the long swirly oral arms of the black sea nettle—these fragile, gentle beasts incapable of acting cruelly just to make a point?

It was Nadia who reeled me to the shores of human connection. Nadia who taught me that people could be good and kind and fun, and worth taking the time to get to know. That lesson had endured, in spite of the way things ended between us. Without it, would I ever have befriended Aldo? They never met each other, but I imagined he would've liked Nadia, and I knew he would've loved the idea of my dropping everything and flying across the country to pursue a giant, probably mythical jellyfish.

"Can you hang on for a second?" I said.

I put my phone on mute, tucked it into my back pocket, and slipped into the hallway. Elijah's office was still dark, but I knew where to find him at this hour. A heavy white door separated the staff-only area from the exhibits. I pushed it open, and there he stood with his back to me, leaning against Stingray City, forehead pressed to cold glass. He could have been meditating, or praying, or suffering a very quiet mental breakdown. A cownose ray soared in the water above his head, pumping her graceful foot-long wings. I cleared my throat.

"What is it, Jo?" Elijah said without turning. The exhaustion in his voice wasn't a product of the early hour. That was just how Elijah sounded. I was convinced he had come into the world weary, sighing the disenchanted sigh of a newborn who'd already seen too much.

I liked Elijah. We were afflicted with the same curse of loving things no one else cared about. He had three kids at home—freckly teenagers whose faces beamed out of school portraits in his office—but the aquarium was his baby. He was doing everything he could to save it.

"I was wondering if it'd be all right for me to take off the next couple of weeks," I said.

That earned me a turned head and a single arched eyebrow—the closest he got to looking truly surprised. But asking was a courtesy. We both knew I had a backlog of sick days and PTO a mile long.

"Business or pleasure?" asked Elijah.

I wasn't sure. Obviously Nadia had called me so that I could help with the island's supposed jellyfish problem—but a tiny hopeful voice countered that she could've called plenty of other people. The Department of Marine Resources, Woods Hole, a nearby university. She had chosen me because she'd been thinking about me during these eleven years, too.

"Bit of both, I guess," I said.

He nodded. He wouldn't pry for more information. That was another reason I liked him: Elijah was all business.

"Bon voyage," he called mournfully as I headed back into the staff area. I looked over my shoulder as the door swung shut, and for a moment his shadowed figure, blue-lit at the edges from the light spilling from the ray tank, elongated into something else—a distended and otherworldly silhouette, not quite human.

I shook off the illusion, choosing to refocus on my growing sense of excitement. I told myself it was the giant jellyfish that intrigued me here: the possibility, however slim, of witnessing something I had never witnessed before. It was the jellyfish, yes—not the embers of a painful crush I'd thought long extinguished, pathetically rekindled at the sound of Nadia's voice flowing out of my phone. Not the desire to go somewhere new and be a different person for a little while, someone whose workplace wasn't about to go under, someone whose best friend hadn't died because of her stupid mistake. The jellyfish. The jellyfish. The jellyfish.

I swerved into the staff room, unmuted my phone, and asked Nadia, "What did you say the name of the island was?"

Welcome to Shattering

Jellies take on such radically distinct appearances throughout their life stages that scientists once believed juveniles to be a different species altogether. A seedlike planula plants itself to the substrate. The polyp, resembling a tiny watery carrot, blooms from this seed, eventually budding into a stack of pancakelike discs that separate into starry ephyra. Though they float freely through the water, these teenagers bear little resemblance to their adult counterparts. Only when they sprout their telltale curtain of stinging tentacles can the casual observer confidently name what she sees and then swim away in horror at her discovery: jellyfish!

AA: Colorful!

Shattering Point: eight hundred acres of spruce forest and granite shorelines and bracing, choppy waters to deter all but the gutsiest swimmers. Twenty-two miles from the coast, it was the most eastern lying of Maine's four thousand islands, straddled by the Gulf to the west and the Atlantic Ocean to the east. The economy survived off haddock and lobster exports, plus a small tourism industry centered on bird-watching: storm petrels in the summer, razorbills in the fall. Major businesses included a bed-and-breakfast, a souvenir shop, and an ice cream parlor. Year-round residents numbered just under fifty.

I researched the island while packing for my crack-of-dawn flight out of LAX and ran out of information within minutes. The internet did not have much to say about Shattering. The Wikipedia page was six sentences. In a part of the country crowded with vacation hot spots, no one cared about this scrap of rock that made so little effort to appeal to outsiders. But Nadia had always been an adventurer. It did not surprise me in the slightest that she would be attracted to such a far-flung place.

Memorial Day through Labor Day, a ferry voyaged across the Gulf to Shattering Point twice weekly. But as it was still the off-season, Nadia had explained I'd have to take the air taxi. Ten hours, two flights, and one Uber later, I arrived at what looked like a stable fronting a strip of tarmac. The shaggy-haired man inside gnawed a pen cap as I told him where I was trying to get to. He shook his head regretfully.

"Air taxi's got to be booked in advance."

"Can I book it now?"

"Mitch won't be in until this weekend. He's at his niece's birthday."

"Is there no other way out to the island?"

"Mail boat makes a run every Friday," he offered.

It was Wednesday.

I stepped outside to call Nadia. Straight to voicemail. I hadn't heard from her since I texted yesterday afternoon confirming I'd bought my plane tickets and she had responded with a string of yellow heart emojis.

But there was a missed call from my mother. The sight of it made me break out in an agitated sweat.

We'd never had the type of relationship where we talked regularly. But since Aldo died, she'd been calling twice a week. She said she wanted to know how I was doing, but really, she wanted to tell me how *she* was doing, which was poorly. She was taking Aldo's loss so hard. She had liked him so much! She thought we were going to get married—no matter how many times I told her that it had never been like that between us. Aldo and I were research collaborators, dive buddies, and friends. Also, I was *gay*, remember? (No, she did not remember.)

I didn't want to talk about Aldo or my grief—certainly didn't want Mom to know how I still sometimes surfaced from one of my bad dreams and thought I saw him standing in the corner of my bedroom, a lanky figure sheathed in the black neoprene dive suit and lime-green fins he'd died in, dripping water all over my floor. My mother had an affinity for the paranormal you wouldn't have expected from an accountant who could recite tax laws like they were inscribed inside her eyelids, and the last thing I felt like entertaining was her smug certainty that I was being haunted by a vengeful *yōkai*.

I fended her off now by texting a fib that contained a kernel of truth: Traveling for work. Might be off-grid for a while.

I tucked my phone away when the shaggy-haired man called me back to the stable. He was excited. He said he had a solution.

We walked across the tarmac and into the trees. The man slightly favored his left leg—arthritis or an old injury. *If he's lead-*

ing me away to try to kill me, I thought calmly, *I'll kick that leg out from under him, then swing my duffel into his face.* The bag was heavy thanks to my bulky old laptop, which I'd packed for the unlikely possibility I got inspired to work on my book on the island.

We emerged into a small harbor. The Gulf stretched into the distance, studded with the bright bobs of lobster buoys. *Cyanea capillata,* the lion's mane jellyfish, a record holder for size, was native to these waters. One specimen discovered off the coast of Massachusetts had a bell with a diameter of seven feet. If there really was a giant jellyfish hanging out around Shattering, it was probably a lion's mane.

The shaggy-haired man approached a woman stacking lobster traps at the edge of a dock. She was fiftyish and wore a pair of bright yellow fisherman's overalls. Wiry gray hairs poked out from beneath her baseball cap.

"Hey, Pamela. Think you could take this young lady out to Shattering? She's stuck here till Mitch gets back."

Pamela lobbed a quick, cutting glance at the man before her gaze latched onto me. I knew that look: as if I were a plateful of alien hors d'oeuvres dropped onto the table, not at all what had been ordered. Though my father was a gangly red-haired Scotsman with Midwestern roots stretching five generations back, I took after my Japanese mother in appearance. There were lots of stares in the fussy Indiana suburb where I'd grown up, stares more inquisitive than hostile, a swift, invisible calculus taking place behind people's eyes.

Pamela sucked her cheeks. "Fifty bucks."

"She's kidding," said the man.

Pamela looked at me again. She was not kidding.

I dug my wallet out of my bag. "I only have forty."

"Plumb out of luck."

"For Chrissake, Pam," said the man. She wouldn't bend. He produced his own wallet and spotted me a ten.

Pamela showed her teeth as she tucked the bills into the front pocket of her overalls. "Welcome aboard. *Miriam*'s down at the end there on the left."

I turned to the shaggy-haired man. I didn't feel bad about scheming to attack him two minutes ago. It was always better to expect the worst from people. "Thank you for your help."

"You betcha. Can I ask what you're headed out there for? We don't get a lot of folks going that way this time of year."

"I'm visiting a friend." That seemed the simplest way to explain it.

"A friend?" He raised his eyebrows. "Well, now, didn't think those islanders had any friends."

"You ever been out there?"

"No reason to. Funny place, Shattering, way out there on the edge of things. Easy to forget it exists. You hear stories, though . . ."

He peered at me hopefully, and I humored him: "What stories?"

"Strange accidents, early deaths. Fishermen going out there and never coming back. My old man used to say the place was cursed."

I absorbed this claim without comment. This guy was like my mother: a dreamer, a reveler in fantasy. I preferred it down here on planet Earth, where everything always had an explanation, provided you had the right tools to see it.

Pamela had retreated to the end of the dock and was waving at me.

"You better get going," said the shaggy-haired man wisely. "Before she changes her mind."

I carried my duffel to the end of the dock, where a boat was bobbing between pilings, the words *Miriam's Smile* emblazoned across the hull in cursive font. It was small. Really small. I stood there looking at that small, small boat as coldness crept up my legs and a bad taste flooded my throat.

Pamela stuck her head out of the cabin. "I don't have all day."

The engine coughed to life. I clutched the starboard railing as *Miriam's Smile* swung into the Gulf.

I didn't know where to look. The nearness of the ocean sent dizziness swerving through me, but closing my eyes was worse. I hadn't been in or on the water since that final nightmarish dive with Aldo. I wasn't avoiding it. There just wasn't any need. My last voyage on a ship was for a research cruise last summer, two weeks chasing jellyfish blooms across the Mediterranean with an international team of biologists and oceanographers. Aldo hadn't participated in that expedition. He was jetting out of the grubby halls of academia and into the promised land of industry. Most recently, he'd partnered with a brilliant materials engineer to design a jellyfish-sting-proof swimming and diving suit colorfully named the Nematoskyn. There was a job at the bioengineering company for me, too, Aldo had insisted, better paying than my "shitty little aquarium gig." But I had no interest in leaving Seaheart, my polyp parlor, the absurd freedom Elijah granted me to study whatever I pleased.

Now I really wished I'd exited the lab and tried getting on the water before coming to Shattering. What a terrible time to discover this problem, trapped on a boat with a stranger, on my way to reunite with a friend whom I hoped to charm with all the wisdom and maturity I'd gained in the past eleven years.

Sunlight sparkled crazily on the water. With every second, the seabed slanted away from us, the light dimming to perpetual dusk. The Gulf was over three hundred meters at its deepest point—the pressure equivalent of thirty additional atmospheres. My lungs squeezed painfully. The ocean was everywhere, sloshing, gurgling, rising over my head.

I stuck it out as long as I could before opening the door and sliding inside the cabin. Pamela gave me a skeptical once-over.

"If you're gonna hurl, don't do it in here."

"I'm not gonna hurl," I said, with more confidence than I felt.

"What is it that you do, anyway?"

"I'm a marine biologist. I study jellyfish." The word alone was soothing. I focused on my breathing. In through the nose, out through the mouth. A glowing blue *Aurelia aurita*, a moon jelly, drifted into my mind's eye, the pulsations of its bell matching the rhythm of my breaths.

"A marine biologist who don't have her sea legs," scoffed Pamela. "How's that work?"

"It's mostly lab work." It was a common misconception that Aldo and I whiled away our workdays submerged in shark cages or floating around with dolphins. The fact that we spent so little time in the water was one of the reasons we continued to meet up for dives each year, despite our hectic work schedules.

I was thinking about water again. Water that pulled you into its gullet, flooding your nose and lungs. Water that reduced your friend to a drowned husk of the man he'd once been.

"Don't like jellyfish," announced Pamela. "Nasty little buggers. No manners. Got a bad sting once as a kid."

"There are over two thousand species of jellyfish. Most of their stings you wouldn't even notice."

"I noticed this one, didn't I? Left a scar that lasted months."

Aldo was covered in scars, a testament to his unofficial title as the World's Most Envenomated Man. He claimed to have been bitten, stung, clawed, or otherwise toxified by over two hundred venomous animals. Aldo made a lot of claims. The guy was a champion bullshitter who'd say anything for a reaction. But even I couldn't deny he had a rare resistance to poison. It was this unlikely quality that had led him to study jellyfish in the first place.

My own origin story was a lot less exciting. My parents and I had been on vacation in South Carolina with my father's extended family. I dreaded the trip and the enforced playtime with my semi-feral boy cousins whose hobbies included soccer and trying to kill each other. Cousin Theo—a bullish nine-year-old who stalked me at holiday gatherings, ready to yank my ponytail or plunge a saliva-slicked finger into my ear—alerted us to the presence of the jelly on the beach. I joined my other cousins in gawking at the raw gray thing slouched on the sand like an angel's lung dropped from the heavens. The wobble of sunlight on its gelatinous membrane mimicked movement, and we did not at first realize it was dead.

The boy cousins entered a deliberation on who would be tasked with touching it, and the answer, of course, was me. I was more than happy to do so. Now that I'd recovered from my initial surprise, I could see that the lung possessed an alien beauty. I wanted to scoop it up and whisk it away to admire it privately, but settled for stroking its squishy dome with two fingers while my cousins looked on in fascinated disgust. The membrane bounced gently, something like petting a water balloon. As soon as I got back to my parents' house, I would commandeer the family computer for an hour and a half, ultimately identifying the creature as *Stomolophus meleagris*, the cannonball jellyfish, an abundant species in the waters of the southeastern US.

"Grooooossss," whined one of the cousins, while another tried to goad me into licking it. Theo had a different idea. Starstruck by the jelly, I failed to heed the gasps and giggles that warned of imminent mischief. I looked up only when Theo's shadow landed across my lap. My cousin's eyes were blank and shiny. The stick—had he been hiding it behind his back this whole time?—swung down like an ax, clobbering and bursting the watery bell of the jellyfish. He swung again and again, and I leapt to my feet as the lovely, fragile corpse was obliterated into a slimy mash that wept into the sand.

I forgave Theo long ago for the wet willies and the ponytail yanks, but I never forgave him for smashing my first jellyfish.

There was no way to convey any of this to Pamela. Few people could appreciate the romance of a jellyfish pulsing through the water, let alone a half-deflated one on the sand. So instead I said, "Jellies are some of the most ancient organisms on the planet. They predate the dinosaurs. They're older than trees, older than sharks. They have a lot to teach us." My eyes were still closed, *Aurelia aurita* shining like a friendly lamp.

"Hmm," said Pamela, unconvinced. And that was all she said

for the remainder of our journey. If I was hoping for a distraction in the form of additional conversation, my reluctant chauffeur was not going to provide it.

It was at least better to be inside the cabin, away from the sight of the water. My breathing gradually evened out. My thoughts turned to Nadia, what I would say to her, what she would see when she looked at me, how I'd ease us into the subject of our decade-plus estrangement without seeming needy or desperate. When I next looked out the cabin windows, a light fog was lifting from the ocean, and land was reappearing in pieces: the jagged outlines of evergreens first, followed by rooftops and power lines and a quick flash of a tall spire I identified as a lighthouse, poking up from the other side of the island.

Pamela pulled up alongside a narrow dock whose end disappeared into the fog. She showed her teeth again. "Good luck, Jelly Girl."

The last of the dizziness left me as I stepped uneasily onto the dock and hurried toward shore, passing the humps of other boats docked and bobbing in their slips. There didn't seem to be anyone around, though the fog was so thick, congealing over the earth like clotted custard, I could've missed someone standing ten feet away. The thought chilled me. I liked observing. I hated being observed.

The dock led me into a small grassy area, where a single vacant bench seemed to hover on its cloud of mist. I walked through wet grass and onto a wide road marked with a faded sign: BEACH STREET. I tried to call Nadia again but didn't have any service.

I kept walking inland, hoping for a cell signal. Buildings loomed blurrily where I squinted. They looked like storefronts, each entry overhung with a striped awning in a different shade of pastel. Beach Street must be what passed for the main drag around here. I heard soft voices, a door opening with a high-pitched chime that split the stillness unnaturally. I had the impression of people stirring at the boundary where vision faded, tracking my progress up the potholed street, and I sped up, trying to outrun the silly drumbeat of paranoia in my temples. I did not want to talk to anyone before I talked to Nadia. If I only kept going a little farther, I'd find her hurrying down the street to meet me. There was a good explanation for why she hadn't met me at the dock, just as there was a good explanation for why she blew me off all those years ago. Once we cleared the air, we could be friends again. Maybe more than friends.

Then I crested the top of the hill, and something moved sharply to my right, sending a bolt of adrenaline coursing through me. My phone slipped out of my hand and landed face down on the ground. The figure—*thing*, whatever it was—continued its flailing as I stooped to recover my phone, the screen now webbed with hairline cracks I barely registered because *it* was breathing, too, huffing and grunting with the effort of a person running out of air.

I crept closer, jaw clenched and trembling, and saw, to my embarrassment, that it was just a dog, an old German shepherd roped to a stake outside someone's house. To the left of the house, a fairy-tale garden rose up behind a picket fence, sprawling bushes and droopy fronds beaded with moisture and a dry fountain with a smirking cherub and a constellation of bulbous pink flowers dangling from toothpick-thin stems. The fear fell out of me. The whole display reminded me of the lovely chaos of my father's vegetable garden, which he'd maintained with painstaking tenderness until the day he died.

The pink flowers looked a little like the bells of *Drymonema larsoni*, also known as pink meanies, another big whopper of a jellyfish found along the Gulf Coast. I extended my fingers over the fairy-tale garden's fence to graze one of the blossoms. The dog emitted a single warning bark.

"Hey! Get away from there."

A man's voice boomed like a foghorn through the suffocating silence. A moment later, I spied him marching through the garden toward me, trailing tendrils of fog and brandishing a dirty trowel. He was in his late fifties or early sixties, white, short, his bald head spotted with sun damage.

"I wasn't doing anything," I said.

"Betty says otherwise." The man angled his head at the dog, which was on its feet, straining at the end of the rope.

"I was just admiring your flowers," I said.

"They're not for your admiring." Up close, the man had eyes just like the shepherd's. Glossy brown and watchful. "Who are you?" he asked. "How did you get here? What do you want?"

"That's a lot of questions."

"I got a right to ask 'em. You people are always causing trouble."

"What people?"

"People from away," he sniffed. "Foreigners."

I glanced past him into the garden. "I wonder how many of your precious plants are foreigners."

"None. Native species only."

"Point me to Nadia Markov's house, and we'll never have to see each other again."

"The schoolteacher?" He flicked the trowel carelessly. "She ran off."

The surge of dislike I felt was not quite powerful enough to settle the little rumble of panic in my stomach. Nadia, jetting off so soon after calling me here. Blowing me off, abandoning me, when I'd come all this way. She would never . . . Except, of course, that she'd done it once already. At the end of college, at graduation—I saw again her body turning from me, an unfamiliar, steely expression clouding her features, shutting me out.

"I talked to her yesterday," I said, managing to keep my voice neutral.

"It's happened before. This life ain't for everyone. People come here, expecting some kind of New England postcard fantasyland. It's rough going. No hospital, no movie theater, no Walmart. Only got the one paved road. You have to be self-sufficient. You have to know how to survive."

"Where's her house?" I asked.

The man's scowl deepened. But before he could answer, a woman's voice warbled through the garden, high and carrying: "Who are you talking to out there?"

The man flinched as if he'd been struck. "No one! Go back inside!"

A pear-shaped white woman around the same age as the man with the trowel was already wading through the rows of plants toward us, her egg-yolk-yellow skirt dragging in the dirt behind her.

She halted a few feet from the man and gave him a look of mild revulsion. Then her gaze found me, and she brightened.

"Oh! Hello there. And who might you be?"

"Josephine Ness, ma'am."

"Ness: *From the headlands.* Josephine: *God will grow.* But grow what, I wonder?" She looked at me thoughtfully. I had the impression I was being scanned, measured, the sum total of my personality and appearance stripped to its skeleton and carefully stored for later analysis. The man had sunk into a slouch, the trowel dangling limply.

"I'm Margaret Sloan." The woman extended a hand covered in chunky rings over the fence. There was a queenly flourish behind the gesture that made me think I was supposed to kiss it. "Margaret, from the Greek, meaning *pearl.* Friends call me Margo, which, of course, you are."

I settled for shaking the hand.

"You're extremely interesting-looking, Josephine," said Margo warmly. "Has anyone ever told you that?"

"Um—"

"It's your aura. Something mysterious there. A kind of scaly thing, like a scab." She squinted. I resisted the urge to take several steps back. "I'm an empath. And an artist. My latest project is portraits. I'd love to paint you! How long are you in town?"

"She was just leaving," said the man.

"Actually, I'm looking for someone," I said, hoping the woman would be more helpful. "Nadia Markov. Can you tell me where to find her?"

Margo Sloan had uncannily wide blue eyes, which widened still further at the mention of Nadia's name. "Ohh! You're *Josie.* Nadia's friend. Of course, of course. We heard you'd be coming."

News must spread fast in a town of under fifty people. It pleased me to think of Nadia ricocheting around this grim little outpost, informing anyone who would listen that her old friend Josie was flying in for a visit.

My pleasure died when the man cut in, stubbornly, "I *told* you: She's left the island."

Margo swatted him in the rib cage. "Don't be ridiculous." To me, she added, "I'm sure she'll be along soon, dear. I can sense these things, you know—the comings and the goings. Wouldn't you like to come in and have some tea while you wait?"

"She's not interested," snapped the man. "Can't you tell by now no one's interested in your damn drawings?"

"I asked her for tea. *Tea!*" Margo leaned into his face and screamed this last word. Her coif of ginger hair—which I recognized now as a wig—wobbled ominously.

"No one's interested in that, either."

They fumed silently. The dog shifted and whined. I sensed a storm coming. Before it made landfall, I pleaded, "Will one of you just tell me how to get to her house?"

It was the man who finally relented and rattled off directions: Up this street, left at the rooster sign, go halfway up the hill till you see the green house with the white shutters.

"But I'm telling you," he called after me, determined to get the last word, "you won't find her there. That girl is long gone."

Missing

In their mature form, jellyfish are known as medusae, their rippling tentacles apparently reminiscent of that ancient Greek monster with living snakes for hair. But just as Medusa has been reclaimed by modern feminists as an icon of women's agency, so jellyfish may yet be rescued from their unsavory reputations. They, too, may be victims of a bad PR job, summarily cast as villains when their story is more complex.

I wasn't completely off the mark when I imagined Nadia's home. The boxy green cottage with the white shutters did resemble a beach house. A coir welcome mat in the shape of a rabbit sat lopsided on the front porch. I hammered at the door.

As the seconds piled up, my bad feeling intensified. Margo Sloan had to be right: Nadia was obviously around here somewhere. She wouldn't just leave, not when she was so determined to show me this giant jellyfish. But what if she got sick? Injured?

I suddenly remembered something else from college: the little black box clipped at Nadia's waist, which she'd consult from time to time with a bored expression and fiddle with before meals. She was diabetic. What if there'd been a delay getting her insulin delivered to the island? What if she'd slipped into a coma and collapsed right on the other side of this door?

I set my hand on the knob.

The door swung inward, and I snatched my hand back just in time to avoid being dragged inside with it.

The man staring down at me reminded me of a lumberjack. He was tall and tan with broad shoulders that strained against his orange flannel. All that was missing was the beard. His cheeks were as smooth as a ten-year-old's.

"Who are you?" I asked, startled.

"Who am I? You're banging at my door."

"I'm looking for Nadia."

Recognition flickered in his dark brown eyes. He was about my age or a little older. "You're Josie Ness."

I didn't like the sound of that name in his mouth.

The lumberjack reached up and squeezed the bridge of his nose. "Shit. I didn't think you were coming so soon . . . I'm Roger. Roger Alvarez. Nadia's husband."

Husband.

The word rattled through me like a rock through a well.

"You're . . . what? Where is Nadia?" I asked.

"I don't know, I'm sorry. Do you . . . want to come in?" He didn't move out of the doorway. I had to scoot right past him, inhaling a whiff of his overbearing pine-scented cologne.

I stepped into a cluttered foyer. All of the curtains were closed. Roger walked into a living area full of rustic furniture and just stood there looking at me. I realized the invitation to come inside had been an empty one, a ritual of politeness. He wanted me gone. But I wasn't going anywhere until I got some answers.

"Where is Nadia?" I asked again.

"I don't know." He sounded annoyed now. "She went to work yesterday like usual. She never came home."

The reality settled into me, turning me cold: Nadia was really missing. "And that doesn't worry you?"

"Not really, no."

I was appalled by his nonchalance. What kind of husband acted like this when his wife went missing? How did I even know this guy *was* Nadia's husband? She would've said if she was married. It would've come up.

I set my duffel on the floor and folded my arms across my chest. "She called me. She invited me here. I know she wouldn't just leave before I arrived."

"I thought you guys hadn't talked in, like, ten years."

His words rang like an accusation. A challenge. "What's that supposed to mean?"

Roger gave me a pitying smirk I wanted to knock off his baby face. "Look. I don't know what Nadia was like a decade ago, but what you have to understand about Nadia *now* is that she gets on these kicks, okay? She gets caught up in stuff. It's why we move around so much. It's how we landed here, on this ridiculous island. Yesterday she was passionate about international education, today it's rural schools, tomorrow she'll want to move to Hollywood and tutor child actors on movie sets. It's not unlike her to get some idea and run off to chase it."

"Out of the blue," I said. "Without telling anyone. Without telling *you*?" I raised my eyebrows. Roger's smirk died. I didn't like the dismissive way he was talking about Nadia. Sure, I remembered how she'd antagonized her adviser by changing her major every semester, but I saw her roving interests as a strength, not a flaw. She wasn't afraid of failure. She saw potential everywhere, in everyone. "I met a guy who told me Nadia left the island for good."

"What *guy*?" said Roger.

"Bald. Xenophobic."

He made a scathing sound in the back of his throat. "You must mean Norm Sloan. I'm sure he does wish Nadia is never coming back, but he doesn't know what he's talking about."

"Did you call the police?" I asked.

"There are no police on Shattering. And anyway, there's no crime here." He shook his head in exasperation. "She just got distracted. She'll show up tomorrow with, like, an industrial ice cream maker, or a Vespa, or a bunch of chickens . . ."

"How would she even get to the mainland?"

"I assume she took my boat. It's missing."

It was an infuriatingly neat explanation. Seeing no way around it, I speed-walked into the kitchen, like I'd find Nadia sitting at the table, sipping a cup of tea. Back in college she used to guzzle buckets of bitter black tea with sprigs of mint leaves. It was what her parents used to drink in Russia. Nadia said she had an ancestral hankering for the stuff, that it flowed through her veins instead of blood.

I didn't find Nadia, but I did spot a photograph of her and Roger on the refrigerator, his arms wrapped around her waist, her head resting on his chest. A swell of pettiness brought a bitter taste to my throat, and I choked it back.

"You can still spend the night here if you want to." Roger slouched in the doorway behind me. Something in him had deflated. "We've got a spare bedroom upstairs. I feel bad you came all this way. It's never cool when she does this. But to do it to someone who traveled thousands of miles to see her . . ."

I refused to be lumped into the same sorry category as this man. "I didn't come to see her," I said. "I came to see the gigantic jellyfish."

Roger blinked, his bushy eyebrows knitted into a frown. I felt a flash of triumph.

"She didn't tell you about the gigantic jellyfish?"

"I don't know what you're talking about."

I took out my phone. Service was back. Roger held the screen close to his face as he watched the video Nadia had sent me. The squiggly, glowing lines must've looked even less convincing through the busted glass.

"That could be anything," he said, passing the phone back to me.

I had expressed similar skepticism to Nadia, but fueled now by a powerful need to disagree with Roger, I found myself floating closer to certainty.

"Did Nadia tell you about my work?" I asked.

"You're some kind of scientist."

"I study jellyfish. I'm writing a book about them. I'm going to find this thing, and then I'll decide what it is or what it isn't."

"All right," said Roger cautiously.

We'd hit an impasse. He moved aside, and I returned to the living room to retrieve my duffel.

Before I left, I pulled up maps to locate the bed-and-breakfast I had read about online. There was no way I was spending the night here. With Nadia's *husband*.

"If you hear from her," I told Roger curtly, "tell her to call me."

• • •

The fog was burning off in a spill of evening sunlight, washing Beach Street in misty gold. I had blundered right past the bed-and-breakfast, a tired-looking Victorian house with purple turrets and a wraparound front porch, on my blind journey in from the dock.

Inside, I rang a bell placed on an antique desk at the foot of the stairs. The chime seemed to carry through every crevice of the old building. A dining room opened out on the left side of the foyer. I tried to imagine it packed with activity: a pair of newlyweds poring over an island map, a group of retirees chomping toast, a small child peering out through a forest of chair legs, a server edging their way through the chatter to pour coffee and collect plates. The scene just wouldn't click. The dining room at Retreat-by-the-Sea cradled its emptiness as if it were designed for it.

It took so long for anyone to show up, I started to wonder if the B and B was still closed for the season, the front door accidentally left unlatched. Then a floorboard creaked, and I looked up to discover a woman staring down at me from the landing. She wore a denim shirt over leggings, the sleeves cuffed at the elbows to reveal brown forearms thickly roped with black-and-white tattoos. I guessed she was in her late twenties.

"Help you?" she asked.

All the moisture had vanished from my mouth. For a panicked second, I forgot what I was doing there. "Uh. Looking for a room. For the night?"

The woman strode down the stairs and stepped behind the

desk. She was strikingly tall for a woman, close to six feet, made even taller by the messy knot of dark hair piled on top of her head. As she pulled a leather-bound book from one of the drawers and flipped to the next available page, I zeroed in on her tattoos and saw they depicted flying things, an intertwined universe of them, honeybees swarming a blimp that bled seamlessly into the rings of Saturn, itself encircled by the looping tail of a kite. They were beautiful.

"Name for the reservation?" she asked.

"Jo Ness."

"Jonas—?"

"No, Jo like Josephine. Last name Ness."

She looked at me, *really* looked at me, hard, like I'd uttered a joke and she was trying to work out the punch line. Her eyes were a lighter shade of brown than mine, freckled with gold and amber. I felt pleasantly warmed by the heat of that stare but also judged. Cornered. I stood taller, refusing to blink. Then the woman bent her head again, and I watched her write my name in the book in impressively neat cursive.

"Welcome to Retreat-by-the-Sea, Jo Ness. My name's Tony Newell. I run this esteemed local establishment. Any problems, let me know. You can have your pick of rooms at this time of year. There's Montana, Alaska, Texas, Rhode Island, Tennessee—"

"Montana will be fine."

Tony opened a different desk drawer and passed me the key—an actual old-fashioned metal key attached to a pink ribbon—and said she'd be up with my linens.

I traipsed up the staircase to the second floor. The room marked MONTANA was small and tidy, with sponged blue walls and a canvas print of wolves and pine trees over the bed. Vacuum lines crisscrossed the floor. A wrinkled Montana state flag covered the nightstand like a tablecloth. I puzzled for a minute over the pirate's chest on the bureau, heaped with gold plastic medallions. The answer came to me only after I'd plugged in my phone and tossed my duffel on the floor.

The Treasure State.

I drew back the curtains on a bank of floor-to-ceiling windows. The room overlooked Beach Street, which was empty but for a man ambling down the sidewalk with his dog. I looked closer: It was cranky Norm Sloan and Betty the German shepherd. I watched them slip from a stretching pool of shadow cast by a building and into a band of weak sunlight, then back to shadow, as if blinking into and out of existence. My body was still on California time, but here on Shattering Point, it would be dark soon. It had never crossed my mind that I would have to spend a night in this unfamiliar place without Nadia.

Roger's words needled at me: *I thought you guys hadn't talked in, like, ten years.*

What did he know about anything? Nadia hadn't even trusted him enough to tell him about the jellyfish. As for why she hadn't told me about her husband, obviously things weren't going well between them. She was frustrated with Roger. Embarrassed. She hadn't wanted to get into it over the phone. We would talk about it once she came back from wherever she'd gone, as we'd once talked through all our challenges and dilemmas.

Three solid knocks landed on the door I'd left ajar.

Tony Newell entered the room and began stretching the sheet over the mattress without saying a word. She worked efficiently, like someone who'd done it a thousand times, her fingers smoothing and tucking, the muscles on her long arms rippling. She plucked the folded top sheet and flapped it open, and a fresh laundry smell sailed through the room. The sheet drifted and settled onto the mattress, and she set to tucking its edges, too, until the bed was as tight and clean as a new trampoline.

"Thanks." The word thunked out of me and sat awkwardly between us.

"Oh, my pleasure," said Tony. She had one of those flat voices that made it hard to tell if she was being sarcastic or not.

"You seem young to run this place all by yourself." I cringed inwardly at how patronizing the words sounded.

"I'm just babysitting," said Tony, shrugging. "My aunt's the owner. She had to leave town to take care of something back home."

"You're not from here?"

"Hell no. I grew up on the rez. Aunt Maya, too."

"What brought her here?" I wished I could shut the hell up. It was as if my vocal cords had been hijacked by a gay ventriloquist who was very determined to keep this attractive person trapped in the room with me.

Tony looked only a little surprised at my interest, before continuing. "She always wanted to open a B and B. No one's vacationing on Indian Island, so she came here, about a decade back. I followed. She was, like, the cool renegade aunt. I thought I'd stay here a few years, make some money, then try to get into vet school . . ."

I managed to silence the ventriloquist and avoid asking whether she'd ever applied: It was none of my business.

Tony ran her hand across the bedspread, smoothing invisible creases. "I recognize your name now. You're Nadia's friend, right?"

Hearing Nadia's name brought me back to myself: I had come to Shattering for a purpose, and it was not to stumble through chitchat with the hot innkeeper. "You know her?"

Tony huffed out a hard breath that could've been a laugh. "Everyone knows everyone around here."

"And do you know where she is?"

"I heard she had a doctor's appointment. She should be back soon."

I nodded, as if this answer satisfied me completely. But I was acutely aware that I'd now been handed three contradictory explanations for Nadia's absence: She'd finally had enough of island life, she was off chasing one of her silly whims, she'd ducked out for an appointment. Which was it? And if she really had departed Shattering for civilization, then why wasn't she answering her phone?

I jolted when my own phone started vibrating on the nightstand. I lunged toward it, certain that it had to be Nadia. I had already decided to forgive her, so determined was I to wring some success out of this cross-country journey, to have the old Nadia back again—

MOM.

"Ugh!" Tony didn't miss the sound of annoyance I made as I flinched back from the nightstand.

"Need to take that?" she asked, raising an eyebrow.

"It's just my mother," I mumbled.

She tilted her head. "Are you two close?"

It was my turn to make an aborted laugh sound. "I wouldn't put it that way. I'm an only child and she just—she worries."

The phone went on vibrating for what felt like forever, Tony staring at me all the while. There was judgment in that stare again, and I didn't like it.

"You should call her back," said Tony as the phone finally fell silent.

I felt a flicker of annoyance, some combination of having my hopes of reuniting with Nadia dashed yet again and having a complete stranger tell me what to do. "Thanks for the advice. But you don't know anything about me."

Tony's features tightened with a look of true anguish that startled me.

"You're right," she said quietly. "I don't."

She moved back toward the door, and I felt a confusing need to apologize.

But when Tony looked at me again, she wore a tired customer-service smile that was as good as a door slamming shut between us. "Breakfast starts at seven, if you're interested. For dinner, try the Urchin."

The Urchin

Jellyfish are remarkably fragile. Their bodies are almost entirely water, bound by a layer of tissue just a single cell thick. They bash themselves to death on any sharp object. Remove them from the water, and they turn into graceless blobs that dry out and die within minutes.

Jellyfish are stunningly resilient. The acidic seas that dissolve the skeletons of other marine animals have little effect on their boneless bodies. They can endure low-oxygen environments and are largely unaffected by common pollutants. As the oceans succumb to the effects of human-induced climate change, these frail-looking invertebrates emerge as unlikely victors. A poisoned sea may yet teem with millions of indifferent jellyfish.

AA: No evidence of causal relationship btw climate change and jelly numbers!

JN: Fight me.

The Urchin was a murky-windowed building set back from the road behind a chest-high brick wall, its only identifying feature a spiny echinoderm painted on a swinging sign above the door. A stale, mustardy smell blasted me when I walked in. It looked like an amalgam of every dive bar I'd ever patronized: a shallow, basin-like room with green lamps suspended on chains, shredded bar stools, scratchy music of unknown genre, and a big pool table in the corner, harshly lit, like a surgical table in an operating theater. The one concession to originality was the fishing nets sagging from the ceiling. By way of food, they served fried fish sandwiches, fish tacos, fish and chips, fish stew, fish pie, fish pie mac and cheese, and Caesar salads.

I ordered at the bar, then settled into a booth in a corner. I tore a napkin into halves, then quarters, then confetti. It felt like ages since the lunch I'd scarfed during my layover in Chicago, but I wasn't hungry. Nadia's absence loomed, clouding out every physical need.

I could call the police myself, but what would I say? Nadia had been missing for barely twenty-four hours, and there was no evidence of foul play. But the conversation with Tony had left me feeling off-kilter. I was beginning to think these islanders knew more than they were letting on.

I was still brooding several minutes later when the door to the Urchin opened, admitting a wisp of salty coolness. Nadia's husband scanned the room. There was only one other customer—a muscly blond guy in a puffer vest chatting up the blue-haired waitress at the bar. I shrank into the shadows, but Roger Alvarez spotted me and hurried over.

"How did you know where to find me?" I asked sullenly.

"Well, it's dinnertime, and it's not like there are a ton of places to eat around here. I've been thinking"—my arms tightened as he slid into the opposite booth—"about what you said. About why Nadia called you." Roger folded his hands on the table and fixed me with a squint that was probably supposed to be intimidating. He just looked like he needed glasses. "What exactly did you tell her about this jellyfish?"

I hid my surprise. I'd always had a strong poker face. But I couldn't believe *this* was what Roger had spent the last hour thinking about: not concern over his wife's disappearance, not fear for her well-being, but a giant jellyfish whose existence he hadn't even seemed convinced of. "Why do you care?"

"Because of the timeline," said Roger. "She calls you yesterday morning, she disappears later that afternoon. Don't you think that's a pretty big coincidence?"

"So she's *disappeared* now?" I said dryly. "Not on an impromptu quest for chickens?"

"Did you tell her to go looking for it?" His words had a pressurized quality, like he was struggling not to yell. "Because if you did—I mean, jellyfish are crazy dangerous, aren't they?"

"No," I said, annoyed. "They're not."

"I read that box jellyfish kill a hundred people each year—"

"And mosquitoes kill a million. Also, box jellyfish live in tropical water. You might want to dig a little deeper on your next Google search."

Roger squeezed his hands together. He was getting angry, and I was glad for it. "I just want to know what you told her."

"That I didn't think the jellyfish was real, but I would come take a look anyway."

"Why would you come if you thought it was a hoax?"

"Because she's my friend and she asked for my help."

"Is that all?" said Roger, studying me closely.

I wondered what, if anything, Nadia had divulged about our night on the rooftop. It wasn't inconceivable a married couple would talk about that sort of thing. Past flings, college hookups. Maybe Nadia had written me off as one of her "kicks"—a quick flurry of superficial interest, there and then gone. Maybe she'd made me out to be that most tragic of gay stereotypes: the pitiful lesbian pining after her straight best friend. Maybe that's exactly what I was.

The blue-haired waitress brought my haddock sandwich and a basket of onion rings. I hoped the interruption would get Roger away from this line of questioning, but he only let me get one bite in before continuing, his voice pitched now at a furious hiss:

"If Nadia went looking for this thing and got hurt, that makes *you* responsible."

"And if she ran off because her husband keeps infantilizing her, whose fault is that?"

He seemed genuinely shocked, as if the idea had never occurred to him. "Nadia wasn't running away from me. She's not—we're not—" He quit sputtering and glared. "You don't know anything about us."

"I know you keep talking about her like she's some hyperactive kid you're sick of dealing with." It was as good a theory as any: Nadia fled Shattering not because she'd grown sick of the place, but because she'd grown sick of Roger. I'd known the guy for two hours and was ready to be done with him.

"I *love* Nadia!" he bellowed. "She's not perfect, but I would never do anything to—"

"'Scuse me, miss." Roger and I both glanced up to find the muscly blond guy from the bar towering over us. It was tough to gauge how old he was. He had the weathered look of a young man who was aging prematurely, his small pink eyes sunken in bags, his yellow hair thinning. He jerked his chin at Roger. "This guy bothering you?"

"We're fine, Emmett," said Roger flatly.

"Was talking to the lady, not you." Emmett stared at me with the predatory patience of a snake that would wait all day for its quarry to emerge from hiding. Roger slumped in his seat with his arms folded, his jaw tight. I realized, too late, how loudly we'd been speaking.

I took a breath. "No. We're good."

"Glad to hear it," said Emmett. But he didn't move. He swiveled his stare over to Roger. Some tug-of-war of male antagonism was being waged between the two. Emmett's end proved the stronger.

"I need a beer," grumbled Roger, and stormed off to the bar.

Without hesitation, Emmett swung into the empty seat. He smiled at me. He had dimples, and his lips were badly chapped. "Josie, right?"

"Jo."

"Emmett Beckendorf. I manage the island's scallop farm." He hovered his hand playfully over my basket of onion rings, and when I didn't swat him away, he took one. "So," he said, chewing, "I couldn't help but overhear . . ." He leaned closer. Little crumbs of fried batter were stuck to the cracked skin of his lips. "You're interested in that big jellyfish we got around here?"

I looked at him with renewed interest. He didn't blink. He barely seemed to be breathing. "You mean it's real?"

"Oh yeah," he said, wiggling his eyebrows. "*Very* real. And I know just where to find it. I can take you there, if you want."

I weighed the offer. I was seriously tempted. This was the first confirmation I'd gotten from any of the locals that Nadia's jellyfish might actually exist.

But for as much as I loved jellies, I wasn't willing to cast off the common sense that told me not to wander into the darkness of an unfamiliar island with patchy cell service, my only guide a shady guy I'd known for less than five minutes.

"Can't you just tell me where it likes to hang out?" I asked.

"But I have to make sure—I mean, it's not the easiest thing to find," he fumbled. "I have to *show* you." There was a desperation in his voice I didn't understand. He had stretched his arms so far over the table, his fingers were dangling inches from my torso.

"I don't think so," I said.

Emmett's smile dropped like lead. "But it's what you're here for, isn't it? It's why you've come all this way. It's why Nadia called you. Don't you want to help us—*her*?"

"How do you know why she called me?" The skin between my shoulder blades was prickling with suspicion. I was liking this guy less and less with each passing second. "She didn't even tell Roger."

"Roger doesn't know shit," snarled Emmett. His charming facade was crumbling. "And the best thing for you and Nadia and everyone else is to keep it that way—"

"What did you say?" Roger had crept up on us. He stood ten feet away, a beer bottle clutched in his fist. The Urchin's greenish lighting had drained him of color. I saw the blue-haired waitress look up from the bar, her eyes flickering over the scene.

Emmett jolted to his feet. "Nothing, man. Josie and I were just talking—"

"Jo," I said.

"We were just talking," Emmett repeated, as if this were the magic phrase that would absolve him of all wrongdoing.

Roger advanced slowly. "Were you talking about my wife?"

"No, I—"

"What did you say about her? *Where is she?*"

"Roger, calm down." I was on my feet, too, looking warily between the two men, wondering what the hell I'd started. Roger had never indicated he thought another islander could be responsible for Nadia's disappearance. He'd completely denied that a crime could've taken place. Then I'd come along and suggested it was *his* fault, and he couldn't have that. Any theory was preferable to that.

Roger strode forward until Emmett was backed against the booth. I waited for Emmett to explain we had only been talking about the jellyfish—the one Roger scarcely believed in.

Instead, an ugly expression closed over his features. "Get out of my face, man."

He shoved Roger back with both hands, and that was all it took.

The waitress yelped as the two men fell onto each other. Everything was happening slowly, as if underwater. I was there and not there, watching as Emmett's hand glided back, his fist soaring into Roger's jaw. Roger was bigger, but the way he was thrashing around made me think he'd never been in a fight in his life.

Time sped up. Before I had a second to think, I scooped Roger's fallen beer bottle from where it had rolled under a table, and whirled to face the wrestling pair. It was an easy decision. I'd always favored the underdog. I channeled my softball days and swung the bottle, clocking Emmett Beckendorf across the back of the head.

"Emmett!" screamed the waitress as he collapsed onto the floor. She surged forward, shoving me out of the way. My pulse was clattering in my ears, the neck of the bottle still gripped in my sweaty hand.

Roger sat up, clutching his face. He seemed stunned to find himself on the floor. I tugged his shirt.

"C'mon. We have to get out of here."

"Not till he tells me about Nadia!" protested Roger, his words slurred.

"Let it go, Roger! He doesn't know where she is!"

Emmett was in no state to confirm this, though he was at least stirring, his legs twitching as the waitress murmured reassurances and attempted to inspect the back of his head.

Her gaze snapped onto me as I coerced Roger onto his feet. "What the hell is wrong with you?" she hissed. "He was just trying to give you what you want!"

Roger leaned on me, almost toppling me, as we tripped outside onto the sidewalk.

We made our slow, shuffling way back to his and Nadia's house. Dusk had engulfed the island, bringing with it a chill. I had forgotten how winter clung in these parts, springtime reduced to a half-hearted wheeze of green. I kept glancing into the shadows behind us to see if anyone was following. The waitress's words echoed back at me. Why did she think she knew what I wanted?

When we got to the cottage, I made sure all the doors and windows were locked while Roger staggered upstairs. I heard water running. I waited until the bathroom door opened and his heavy footfalls dragged down the hall before I tiptoed up to the second floor. I found him in the bedroom, sitting up in bed. The one he shared with Nadia. The room was full of her clothes, her smell. How could it be that Nadia's smell hadn't changed in eleven years? Was it possible she still used the same shampoo, the same bodywash? Or was it the smell of her skin that I remembered, something chemical that remained constant through a lifetime?

"My head's thudding like a drum," groaned Roger.

"You'll be fine," I said. But I was starting to worry he had a concussion.

I raided the medicine cabinet for Tylenol and brought him two pills with a glass of water.

"Thank you. And thank you for helping me out back there. It was really badass." He tossed back the pills and set the glass on the nightstand. The skin beneath his left eye was starting to swell. "Jesus. What a day."

He could say that again. It felt like I'd been on Shattering for a week already.

Roger hesitated, his hands clenching and unclenching around the blanket. "You really don't think Emmett knows anything about Nadia?"

I didn't know what I thought, but I wasn't about to hand Roger any ammunition to go charging back to the Urchin for a second round. I settled on the answer that would end this conversation the fastest. "I think he would've said anything to get me to go with him."

"But why?"

"Gee, I don't know, Roger. Whyever would a man try and get a woman to wander off to an undisclosed location with him?"

He shut his mouth.

I picked up one of the cardigans from the floor, carried it to the open closet, and slotted it onto a hanger. I did this with three more articles of clothing, then moved on to tidying the lotions and jewelry cluttering the bureau. I saw that Nadia still had the pendant necklace her grandmother had given her for her birthday senior year. And the tacky polka-dot dish holding three mismatched earrings was familiar to me, too: I had made it myself, during the ceramics class I took to satisfy the arts requirement at Gladstone. It was lopsided, unevenly glazed, ugly as hell. Nadia had rescued it from the garbage can in my dorm room, chiding me for being too hard on myself. I hadn't realized she'd saved it, and I picked it up now, running my finger along the chipped rim, flush with a pleasant ache of nostalgia that fled as soon as Roger started speaking again.

"Maybe you're right," he said heavily. "Maybe Nadia was tired of me constantly doubting her. I didn't tell you this before, but . . . we had a fight earlier this week."

I replaced the dish on the bureau and turned to face him. "What about?"

"This place." He twirled his hand to indicate the island as a whole. "I agreed to try it for five months. Well, we're coming up on that, and I want out. But Nadia's got a soft spot for these people.

Don't ask me why. Bunch of hillbillies and racists. She said she's not ready to move on."

"I thought she was a flake who couldn't commit to anything?"

"She is!" Roger exclaimed, and then winced, touching his fingers to his head. "*Except* when I want a change," he added in a softer voice. "Then she digs her heels in. Anyway, we argued. It was dumb. I didn't think she was that upset . . ."

"If your fight was about Nadia wanting to stay, why would she take your boat and leave?"

"To teach me a lesson?" He sighed and pulled the blanket up to his chin.

I was probably supposed to comfort him or apologize for making him think he was such a terrible person. The truth was, I didn't really believe Nadia would bail on her marriage like this. If I'd rattled Roger into turning on Emmett, it was only because he'd managed to rattle me first: He'd touched a nerve when he said I was responsible for Nadia's disappearance, because I could see his point, and I didn't want to admit it. What if my dismissiveness at the video had motivated Nadia to try to find some firmer evidence of the jelly's existence before my arrival? What if she *had* gone looking? I remained unconvinced this animal actually existed, but that didn't mean some other calamity hadn't befallen her during her search. The ocean could be a dangerous place.

I saw a flash of Aldo's body as it had looked when the rescue divers pulled it out of the water, his staring eyes and marbled skin, the black airless hole of his mouth. A cold lump of dread formed in my stomach.

Roger rolled around on the bed. I finished tidying and settled into a blue recliner in the corner, still chewing on my fears.

"You don't have to stay," he said.

"I know." I kept telling myself I'd get up and start the walk back to Retreat-by-the-Sea, but as the silence thickened around us and one minute stretched into five, I recognized that I didn't want to leave. It was comforting to be here in Nadia's space, a little slice of familiarity on otherwise strange and hostile terrain. I opened the recliner and leaned back, wondering if this was where she had sat yesterday morning when she called me.

"Tell me a story," said Roger. His eyes were open, and he was looking at me.

I almost laughed; it was such a ridiculous request. "Are you kidding me?"

"I think you're not supposed to sleep right after hitting your head. Tell me a scary story. Something to keep me awake."

"I think that's a myth. And I don't know any scary stories."

A lie. My mother had doled out her ghost stories each night before bed like they were cupfuls of warm milk.

Roger studied me expectantly over the edge of the blanket, like he knew I'd come through for him. And to my surprise, I discovered I did have a story prepared—one I hadn't heard in at least two decades but that swam to the surface of memory the moment I saw Nadia's video in my lab at Seaheart. I saw that it had been lurking there for the past two days, waiting to be hauled dripping into the light.

When I opened my mouth, my mother's words came pouring out:

"Long ago there lived an aging widow whose son had been lost to the sea. He was a fisherman, and a wild summer storm had passed through while he was bringing in the day's catch. The waters had reared up and pulled him under. There was no body for the widow to bury beside her husband, and this she could not accept.

"Every night she went to the seashore and yelled at the ocean to give her boy back, and the waves roared their uncaring music in reply. The villagers began to suspect that grief had turned the widow mad, but she maintained that her son was out there because she could hear his voice, calling to her from the darkness."

Roger widened his eyes. I couldn't tell whether he was riveted or just pretending. Mom was always trying to win a reaction out of me, her frustratingly dispassionate child. A gasp, a shiver, a blurted question that she shushed because questions were not permitted until the end, and even then, she never had any answers.

"One night in late autumn," I continued, "the widow's vigilance was finally rewarded: Lights appeared on the waves, dancing like pale flames. She knew this was her son lighting the path for their reunion. But grief had hollowed her out; she was too frail to row the boat herself, nor could she count on any of the villagers to help her, for rumor had it the lights were *ayakashi*, the great sea beast whose body burned with the floating fires of the drowned. None wished to approach those unhappy spirits. But the widow was clever and recruited a blind priest who dwelled in seclusion in the mountains and had heard none of these rumors."

Roger's eyes were closed. Either listening deeply, or falling asleep.

"Now, the next part of the tale is uncertain, because we have only the descriptions from the priest, who'd been deceived into thinking he was helping a poor old woman recover her husband's crab pots. The priest and the widow embarked on the seas the following evening. He was her arms and she was his eyes, telling him which direction to row. They were journeying a long while before the widow called out for the priest to stop. A hush fell over the sea. It was a silence such as the priest had never heard before, as if their little boat had sunk right into the grave. The boat began rocking from side to side. He did not dare shatter the evil quiet with his voice, but mentally he chanted the heart sutra to preserve himself from fear: *Form is emptiness and emptiness is form. There is no eye, no ear, no nose, no tongue, no body, no mind.*"

Mom always paused right there after the recitation of the sutra, inviting the perception that this time, maybe, it would end differently. The monster in the water would lose interest and slither off to the seafloor. The widow would realize the folly of her quest and instruct the priest to turn back.

"The priest heard the widow cry out. Cold water rushed into the boat, and borne on that swell was a wet, reaching thing that seared pain into his flesh. At sunrise, a fisherman found him drifting on the water, the oars torn free and the widow nowhere in sight. The priest was alive, but his body was blighted with many burns. He returned to his temple in the mountains and never visited the sea again, but for the rest of his days, he was often roused from sleep by the final words of the widow, as if she were squatting in the room beside him, shouting in rage and fear: *You are not my son.*"

Roger's breathing was slow and heavy. So much for my terrifying tale to keep him awake.

I sank into the recliner and shut my eyes, too. My mind cast itself out of the cottage and down the hill and along Beach Street, following the curve of Shattering's one paved road counterclockwise around the island until I hit a rocky shore. I kept going: out past the frothing surf and into open ocean, where the drama of the planet's largest migration was taking place, a mass vertical movement of billions of organisms from deep to shallow waters, an ancient game of hide-and-seek between predators and prey.

I realized I was asking the wrong question. It didn't matter whether the jellyfish was real, or whether it was as made-up as the *ayakashi*. All that mattered was whether Nadia believed.

And with that, I had my new hypothesis: If I went looking for the jellyfish, then I'd find my way to her.

The Schoolhouse

If you've been seeking a model for a minimalist lifestyle, look no further: Jellyfish are nature's ultimate minimalists. Brainless, boneless, and bloodless, they're comprised of two ultrathin layers of tissue that sandwich the mesoglea, the gelatinous substance that gives jellies their name. The innermost layer, the gastrodermis, lines a digestive cavity that functions as both stomach and intestines. Jellyfish even have a single opening for consumption and excretion—a kind of mouthbutt where food enters and later exits as waste.

JN: CUT.

AA: THAT'S WHAT IT IS!

The dream released me slowly.

I was swimming in the ocean, water streaming past my gills. Thousands of jellyfish bobbed and shimmered like wobbly, fallen moons. They parted as I passed, and closed ranks behind me, forming a tunnel of light.

A rope appeared in my hands. The tunnel solidified into stone, and the light died. I strung myself along the rope as I searched for the way out of the cave, my breaths becoming shorter, harder, each one slicing like a blade.

A sharp pain lanced through my hand. Green blood smoked from the gash and spiraled up toward a chink of skylight slashed into the rock. I frog kicked toward it, but there was a heavy weight dragging me down, a second body clamped to my torso. I pried Aldo off, hating my selfishness but knowing this was the only way out.

I sat up and threw Roger's arm off me. At some point during the night, my lower back protesting the recliner, I must've staggered over to the bed.

Sunlight needled through the blinds, casting bars of sunlight onto the floor. Heavy breaths gusted from Roger's open mouth. The swelling under his eye had darkened into what my father would've called "a proper shiner." I struggled to put the pieces of the past twenty-four hours together: the ride into Shattering with Pamela, the introduction to Margo and Norm Sloan, meeting Roger, checking into the B and B, the fight at the Urchin. They seemed like events that had befallen someone else—especially the part where I'd whacked a guy with a bottle. I thought it was unlikely Emmett Beckendorf would press charges, not least because of what Roger had told me about Shattering's lack of police. All the same, the speed with which I'd made myself an enemy on a small island infused a new urgency into my mission. Track down the jellyfish, track down Nadia. Get out.

Beach Street was silent but for the distant roll of the tide and a metallic *snip-snip-snip* coming from behind the Sloans' garden fence. The German shepherd, Betty, turned her head to follow my progress as I walked down the road and up the porch steps into Retreat-by-the-Sea. The dining room was as empty as it had been yesterday evening, but there was a carafe full of hot coffee on the sideboard and a metal tree hung with sunflower-splotched mugs.

I filled one almost to the brim and sat in a chair at the dining table, absently rubbing the scar on the back of my hand. It was from my dive knife, the one Aldo had given me for Christmas back in grad school. The cut hadn't been deep and probably wouldn't have left a scar if I hadn't insisted on peeling the scab off before it was ready. Ripping and bleeding, the new skin breaking and knitting itself together over and over, a private punishment ritual that did nothing to ease my guilt.

I had sat with the truth for seven months, but here on Shattering, the comforting diversions of Seaheart stripped away and no Nadia to distract me, the pain of it was sharper: It was my fault Aldo had died. And now I had possibly put another friend in danger.

A floorboard creaked. I glanced up, heart leaping, and there was Tony Newell, watching me from the doorway. A green sweatshirt hid the tattoos on her arms, and her dark hair cascaded almost down to her waist.

"Good morning."

"Good morning," I said. My voice was raspy. They were the first words I'd spoken since last night.

Tony strode into the kitchen and returned a minute later with a platterful of scones. I was surprised, though not displeased, when she sat down to eat with me.

"You didn't sleep here," she observed.

I wondered why she'd noticed that. It was both disturbing and thrilling to imagine her laying her ear against Montana's door, maybe even using her key to peep inside.

"I was with Roger," I said, and then, hearing the subtext, hastened to add, "I mean, not *with* him with him. We didn't—you know—I'm not into men."

"Good for you," said Tony.

I thought my face was going to explode.

She fetched the carafe and poured herself some coffee. I drank mine as fast as I could, scalding my tongue, as if I'd find a repository of charisma waiting at the bottom of the mug.

What was wrong with me? I'd never been attracted to anyone this fast before. With Nadia the feelings had built organically, over the months we spent together, friendship melding into romance so effortlessly I still didn't know at what point the shift had occurred. I couldn't recall feeling this flustered about my last girlfriend, either—a software engineer whom Aldo had branded the Indexer because she loved personality assessments. On our first date, alarmed I could divulge neither my Myers-Briggs profile nor my Hogwarts house, she messaged me a list of links to online quizzes, which I dutifully filled out and allowed her to interpret on date two. I admired her enthusiasm for shrinking humanity into ever smaller and more arbitrary boxes.

Then, as always, things fizzled, the relationship devolving into a frazzled push and pull of neediness and resentment. I thought she was being juvenile and unfair, bitter at having to share me with my work. Aldo concurred. *Cut her loose*, he'd said. And I had, without misgivings or regret.

Tony settled back into her chair, blowing lightly into the coffee mug. "Heard there was a fight last night."

I searched her tone for disapproval and found none. "Some guy named Emmett attacked Roger."

"Emmett's not usually a brawler," remarked Tony. "Roger must've provoked him."

I felt an unwelcome need to defend Nadia's husband. "He's just worried about Nadia. Emmett said—" I struggled to remember the menacing words he'd spoken as Roger blundered into the conversation. "He said that Roger didn't know anything. And it was best to keep it that way." I looked at Tony, who was inspecting a scone, seeming like she was barely listening. "What do you think he meant by that?"

"I have no idea." She bit into the scone and grimaced. "God, these are awful, aren't they?"

I tried one, and it crumbled to sand in my mouth. "Uh, yeah. They're pretty bad."

"I swear I'm a decent cook. It's baking that screws me over. I don't do well having to follow all those specific measurements."

"What's that saying? Cooking is a feeling, baking is a science?"

"You must be a good baker, then," said Tony. "Being a scientist and all."

"I'm terrible," I said. She smiled for the first time. It sent dopamine crashing through me like an avalanche.

Tony stepped back into the kitchen and returned with scrambled eggs and toast and potatoes that, as promised, were very decent.

But the meal and Tony's company, welcome though they were, couldn't wrestle my thoughts away from Nadia. This afternoon would mark forty-eight hours since her disappearance. My mind flooded with horror-movie images of a tentacled thing reaching over the side of a boat and dragging her into the watery darkness. Why did I have to tell Roger that stupid story?

"I still haven't heard from Nadia," I said, setting down my fork.

"Cell service can be tricky around here," said Tony.

But I seemed to have service at Retreat-by-the-Sea, and I'd had it at Nadia and Roger's house, too. I felt a recurrence of the same doubt I'd grappled with at the Urchin last night. Had Tony been honest with me or not?

"What did you say she went to the mainland for again?" I asked, testing.

"She, um . . ." Tony moved potato cubes around her plate without attempting to eat any of them. "She mentioned an appointment. Look, don't take this the wrong way, but—" She looked up at me, her lips pressed tightly together. "I think you should leave."

"What? Why?" It galled me how hurt I was by her desire to get rid of me.

"Like you said, you still haven't heard from Nadia." She put her fork down, then picked it back up and tapped it on the side of her plate. "And word's going to get around about what happened at the Urchin last night. People look out for their own around here." The vague threat hung in the air around us like smog.

"I can't leave," I pointed out, remembering what the shaggy-haired man at the airstrip had told me. "The air taxi's down."

"Can you drive a boat?" Tony stood and went into the foyer. I heard the wooden scrape of the old desk drawer as it opened. She returned and placed an object on the table between us: a square-topped key on a blue float shaped like a whale.

I stared at her. "You're just going to loan me your boat? You don't even know me."

"You seem pretty trustworthy."

"I'm not going anywhere," I said firmly, pushing the key away. "I need to find Nadia. Actually, no—I need to find a giant jellyfish. Do you know anything about that?"

A brief ripple of emotion passed across Tony's features, too fast for me to read it. She swept some scone crumbs off the table into her other hand. "That's just a silly rumor."

"Emmett said—"

"Emmett's full of shit. Stay away from him." There was no mistaking her tone now: She was angry. I was momentarily crushed at the thought I'd upset her. Then my own anger lifted onto its hind legs to match hers, and we were like two rival bears sizing each other up in the woods.

"How did you know I was a scientist?"

"What?" Tony's hand spasmed open, and the gathered crumbs trickled into her lap. I'd caught her off guard.

"I never told you I was a scientist. So how did you know?"

She paused, seeming to scrabble after her composure. "Nadia mentioned it. Nadia said her college friend was coming, and that you were— Oh, what does it matter what she said? I'm trying to *help* you, Jo." She reached out and squeezed my arm, and the pleasant jolt of electricity at the contact faded quickly. There was something sharp and unforgiving in Tony's grip. Like a warning, or a plea.

I shook her off and stood. "Are you kicking me out?" I would swallow my distaste and go stay with Roger, if that was the case.

"No, no. Of course not." Tony sounded defeated as she tucked the boat key into her fist and pulled her hand into her lap. "You can stay as long as you want."

"Thank you," I said stiffly.

"You're welcome."

And then there was nothing more to say.

• • •

I took a shower, bending under the hot spray, knuckling the knots in my lower back. I felt unsettled by the conversation with Tony and suspicious of my own need to keep her in my good graces. I'd been lonely since Aldo died—I could admit that. What I couldn't do was let that loneliness propel me into placing unearned trust in the first attractive person who smiled at me. I had to stay focused, for Nadia's sake. It would be smarter not to believe anything I couldn't confirm on my own.

And so, after returning to Montana, dressing in clothes still furrowed with suitcase creases, and trying Nadia yet again (straight to voicemail), I opened our text messages to review the one concrete piece of evidence I had.

I was even more exasperated by the video this time around. I'd seen better footage of the Loch Ness Monster. The red lines—the jelly's alleged tentacles—morphed in and out of focus as they fanned across the water. A prankster equipped with even amateur video editing skills could surely generate something like this.

But according to Nadia, a friend had taken the video for her. A trustworthy one. That person didn't seem to be Roger, or Tony, and I seriously doubted Emmett Beckendorf would count among her friends—not that I was an expert on friendships. Nadia had been my first real friend, and Aldo my second, and in both cases, the gravity that pulled us toward each other resisted all efforts to make sense of it.

But sometimes, I thought, sometimes people were friends with their coworkers.

When Nadia said she taught in a one-room schoolhouse, I thought it was just a turn of phrase. I saw immediately on arrival that I was wrong: Shattering's schoolhouse was literally one room, a squat barnlike building plucked from another era. An American flag flapped from a short pole out front, and a rusting weather vane rotated on the roof. Someone had taped a sign to the door, handwritten on a sheet of pink construction paper.

CLASS CANCELED UNTIL FURTHER NOTICE.

The door was unlocked. I stepped into the classroom, which was packed with crooked rows of student desks, the kind with rickety wooden chairs attached by metal poles. A woodstove crouched in the corner, its pipe disappearing into the wall. I traced my finger through the ghosts of recently erased words on the chalkboard: Nadia's last lesson.

We had met in a classroom: Professor Hano's Intro to Japanese, Monday and Wednesday, 7 to 9 p.m. It was senior year, and we'd both let our foreign language requirement go until the last minute. I thought the class would be easy. I had a working knowledge of the language already from my mother. But she'd never bothered to teach me to read or write. I was forever confusing 目 with 日, 人 with 入, 午 with 牛. Hano was a madman who tasked us with learning five hundred kanji before the end of the semester—"Just five a day!" he cried on repeat, flashing five fingers in our faces whenever we started to fall behind.

Nadia had a knack for the characters but struggled with the grammar. Handing back our first exams one evening, Hano commented that if the two of us could only figure out how to share a brain, we'd both finish the class with a 4.0.

Nadia looked at me, and I looked at her. I wasn't in the habit of paying too much attention to my classmates beyond perfunctory exchanges needed to complete a project or write up a lab report. What I saw was a red-haired girl wearing a Gladstone College tank top, glasses, and an expression of surprised intrigue, as if I were a fascinating curio rescued from a bin at a tag sale—a stumbled-upon treasure, its worth too long unappreciated. Though I would come to learn she shone that light of curiosity on just about everything, it made me feel special. I wasn't used to that, either.

"Wanna share a brain?" she'd asked.

I understood she was suggesting we study together, even as my imagination leapt to the strangely intimate image of our brains intertwining, ropes of fatty matter braiding together, transforming us into an unstoppable superorganism.

I picked up the chalk from the tray in the one-room schoolhouse and carefully traced out the kanji for *kurage*, "jellyfish," which Nadia had taught me, not because it was one of Hano's five hundred but because she thought I'd like to know. Two characters: 水母. "Water" and "mother." As if jellyfish were the originators of water, the oldest guardians of the sea.

I set down the chalk and looked around the empty classroom. Obviously there would be no coworkers here for me to interrogate. Teaching on Shattering was a one-woman show. This made me more certain than ever that Nadia would not have just walked out without warning, abandoning her students before the end of the school year.

A door at the back of the classroom opened onto a square of overgrown grass. Beside a swing set with a bright red slide, a child was spinning in wide circles with his arms thrown out. As I watched, he lost his footing and crash-landed on the grass, giggling. He spotted me and waved dizzily.

I crossed the yard and he got to his feet, still wobbling. He was five or possibly six or eight—I wasn't good at estimating kids' ages—with a tuft of electrified-looking hair. His T-shirt was streaked with rainbow colors designed to look like paint streaks, and the chubby legs poking from his basketball shorts were grass-stained at the knees.

"Hey," I said.

"Hi!"

"What's your name?"

"Sidney Anakin Oliver Bernet."

"Wow, that's a mouthful."

"I have two middle names. My mom's dad's name was Oliver," he explained. "But *my* dad really likes *Star Wars*."

"I'm Jo," I said. "I was named after my grandpa, too. He was called Joseph."

Sidney made an appalled face. "That's a boy's name!"

"They went with Josephine for me," I said. "Is that better?"

He took my hand and pulled me over to the swings.

"You go. I want to push."

"In a minute. I need your help with something."

I crouched down so we were eye to eye. Sidney placed a palm

on my shoulder, deadly serious. He smelled like grass and sunscreen—the premature smells of summer. "Can you tell me the last time you saw your teacher?" I asked.

"Ms. Markov? She was there . . ." Sidney lifted his hand from my shoulder and pointed at the schoolhouse. "She taught us about—ummm—what are they called? Like an elephant trunk but also the kind on a tree?"

I had no idea what he was talking about.

"Rocks!" he shouted, getting frustrated. "You throw them sometimes but you're also in a rock band?"

"Oh. You mean—let's see—are they called—homonyms?"

He did a little victory shimmy. "She taught us about homonyms."

"How many students are in your class?"

"It's just me and Lila, my cousin. She is one year, three months, twelve days younger than me."

I quietly absorbed this new horror of island life. My saving grace as a bullied child had been the hundreds of other public school children in whose masses I could safely camouflage.

"What happened after the homonyms?" I asked.

"We ate our snacks. I had Goldfish, Lila had peanut butter crackers, and Ms. Markov had a cheese stick."

"And after that?"

I reached deep inside myself for patience as he described every detail of the school day: the afternoon's math lesson, the chalk art they drew outside, how it started to rain so they had to move recess inside and play Guess Who? instead (Sidney was on Ms. Markov's team. He was always on Ms. Markov's team).

"And then," he said, drawing a deep breath as he arrived at his finale. I tensed, waiting for the big reveal. "And then Lila and I went home."

"That's it?"

"We go to Grandma's after school. It stopped raining, so she let us play outside. Lila saw a rabbit and wanted to name it Hash Browns, but *I* said—"

"And Ms. Markov stayed at the school?" I pressed. "You didn't see her after?"

Sidney shook his head no. I didn't know what I'd expected from this child, but I was disappointed. I lowered myself into one of the swings. The whole construction creaked, and for a second I worried the beam was going to collapse.

Sidney seemed to be wrestling with his own sense of letdown. He settled into the second swing, his eyes on his sneakers.

"I miss her," he said gloomily. "She was the best teacher we've ever had."

"I bet," I said.

"Mr. Andrews used to call me and Lila the Terror Twins. Even though we aren't twins. He said we were the reason he lost all his hair. Ms. Markov was different. She was—she was my friend!" His lower lip quivered. He seemed moments away from tears.

I was hung up on his last word, hearing it now in Nadia's voice.

"Did she say that?" I asked. "That you were friends?"

Sidney nodded again.

I took out my phone. He watched only the first three seconds of the jellyfish video before turning his face away.

"You took this, didn't you?"

He became very interested in yanking up blades of grass beneath the swing.

"It's okay, Sidney. You can tell me. I'm Ms. Markov's friend, too."

"Do you know what her middle name is?" he asked slyly.

It was a test. I needed to answer correctly, or this conversation was over.

I thought back to college, to Nadia's email address: nymarkov. It was something Russian. Something related to her father's name. I met the man at Family Weekend. He had a small round head, gold spectacles, and a hanging belly that he hitched his hands around like a pregnant woman. Nadia introduced us. *This is Josie. Josie, this is my dad . . .*

"Yuri—Yurievna," I stuttered. "Nadia Yurievna. Right?" I was sure that was right.

Sidney opened his palm and let the breeze carry the blades of grass across the yard. "She told us we had unique visions," he whispered. "She said even on a little island, there were things here that didn't exist anywhere else in the world. She had us do a show-and-tell. Lila brought a mushroom she found in Grandma's garden . . ."

"And you brought the video," I finished. "How did you record it?"

"I used Grandma's phone. She's always losing it."

"Can you show me exactly where you saw the jellyfish?"

He blanched and shook his head.

"How come?" I asked.

"It's not—you won't—" His lip began quivering again.

I gave up. The last thing I felt like doing was defusing some kid's meltdown. Besides, Sidney had given me enough already. I knew now that the footage he'd captured was authentic. Nadia was right: He was utterly trustworthy. He lacked both the deviousness and the technical skills to contrive a hoax.

I felt again that fizz of excitement in my stomach. Shattering's giant jellyfish was real, and I was going to find it. I would track down Emmett Beckendorf, fake an apology, try to get him to divulge in daylight what he'd been on the cusp of revealing last night . . .

"Wait!" wailed Sidney.

The momentum of my plan had pushed me to my feet and halfway to the schoolhouse door. I turned to find Sidney chasing after me.

He halted, panting. "Don't hurt her."

My brain glitched as I tried to comprehend where this fear was coming from and, as usual, came up empty. "I wouldn't hurt Nadia. I'm just trying to—"

"Not Ms. Markov. Clementine."

I stared at him blankly. He poked the phone still clutched in my hand.

"The jellyfish's name is Clementine?"

He bobbed his head yes.

"And how do you know Clementine is a girl?"

"I just *do*." He drew back from me, pouting. I got the sense he'd had this argument before. "We're friends," he added stoutly.

"Okay, well, I'm not going to hurt her, either." I lowered myself to the ground again, and he met my stare uncertainly. "My job is to study jellyfish. I just want to see Clementine, maybe write some things about her."

He squinted, as if he'd spot the lie squirming across my forehead. "You're *not* going to kill her?"

"Of course not."

"You're not gonna poison her or stab her or shoot her or blow her up with a bomb—?"

Grandma was letting this kid watch too much TV, I thought.

"I'm gonna use my eyes to look at her," I said. "That's all."

He backed away, still looking at me doubtfully. Nadia would've been able to get through to him. Sidney had known she was someone to trust. Other people, you peeled away their superficial niceness to find the stinking selfishness lurking a few layers down. Not Nadia. It was why that scene at graduation had bothered me all these years—why I was so determined to set things straight between us.

"Clementine lives by the lighthouse." Sidney galloped back to the swing set, scrambled up the slide, and stood facing me from the top of the platform, like a captain in the crow's nest, the breeze stirring his hair, hands slotted authoritatively onto his hips. "And she only comes out in the dark!"

The Lighthouse

Bioluminescence is widespread among jellyfish. Around half of all species are capable of producing their own light. The main function of this light emission appears to be deterring predation, with the bright, startling flashes of color broadcasting the same message as a lighthouse positioned on a rocky coast.

AA: i.e., stay tf away from me if you know what's good for you.

I went back to Retreat-by-the-Sea, to Montana, to gather my materials for the evening's jellyfish stakeout: binoculars, rain gear, waterproof field notebook, camera, a fistful of the same granola bars I kept in my desk at Seaheart and ate for dinner with embarrassing frequency. I saw that packing all this in the first place had been an act of hope: Despite my healthy skepticism of the video, I had wanted Shattering's jellyfish to be real.

But there were still hours to go until nightfall. With no other way to spend them, I reluctantly pulled out my bulky laptop and opened my book manuscript.

Though Aldo was a coauthor, it had always felt like my book. Most of the chapters were mine. Aldo was a better-known name in the field, but I was a better writer, and he kept getting pulled away to address snafus with his sting-proof suits. More than once, I had debated kicking him off the project altogether.

That prospect became unthinkable after he died. I saw that Aldo was all over these pages. And that was a problem. On her read through the most recent draft, the editor had said our voices were too distinct. She wanted the book to read as friendly, approachable, scientifically sound but informal. That had been the pitch: a jellyfish primer for the general public, with the aim of destigmatizing these animals that incited so much revulsion and fear. Basically, it was a PR scheme, like what sharks had been undergoing for the past twenty years. If a great white could be redeemed in the public eye—transformed from a bloodthirsty killing machine to a graceful apex predator worthy of our respect—why not jellyfish?

But in cultivating our "approachable" voices, the fullness of our personalities came out. The manuscript did read as a jerry-rigged mash-up of Aldo and then me, Aldo and back to me. My final task before submitting the book to the publisher was to smooth this out, blur the lines between us, and I couldn't do it. It felt too much like erasing him.

I scrolled through each chapter. I stared at the blinking cursor. I took the commas out and put them back in again, eyes glazed, mind preoccupied with thoughts of Clementine. At one point, a gentle tapping sounded on the other side of Montana's door, so light I wouldn't have recognized it as knocking if it hadn't come again. *Tap-tap-tap.* I sat up straighter, caught between contradictory responses: *Come in! Go away!* I hadn't seen Tony since breakfast and didn't especially want to see her now. What if she'd changed her mind and wanted to kick me out after all?

I stayed quiet, until the soft creak of a distant floorboard told me she'd retreated.

At half past six, I packed my laptop away, slung my backpack over my shoulder, and stole out of the silent building, aiming in the direction of the lighthouse I saw on my way in yesterday.

Beach Street circled the perimeter of the island. Beyond the seawall, small gravelly patches were bared by low tide. A stoop-shouldered woman slopping seaweed into a metal bucket glanced up as I hurried past. *People look out for their own around here.* Tony had been trying to unnerve me with that warning, and the annoying thing was that it had worked. I braced for a hurled insult or vicious glare.

Instead, the woman flashed a gummy smile and waved. "Path on your right, with the berry bushes!"

I smiled tensely and sped up, so spooked by the unexpected friendliness I barely absorbed her words. Then I came upon the exact landmark she'd described: a narrow trailhead half swallowed by scraggly bushes studded with shining berries. How the hell had she known where I was going?

I jogged down the path, where I was halted by a wire fence. There was a sign on the gate, black letters on yellow, more official-looking than the one on the schoolhouse door: BEACH CLOSED. But in direct defiance of this message, the gate was ajar, beckoning me like an outstretched hand. I glanced once over my shoulder before pushing my way through.

The beach was wide and rocky, all gray waves and rough

edges. There were no picnic tables or firepits or garbage cans—none of the man-made conveniences that encourage a person to sit down and stay awhile. The scarred cast-iron tower of the lighthouse loomed on a bluff overlooking the water, surrounded by crumbling outbuildings. Even with its beacon dark, its cupola smeared with guano and grime, it commanded a forlorn majesty, like the vacant palace of an overthrown regime.

A squat two-story cottage was attached to the tower by a covered tunnel, its roof threaded with dead ivy. It was here that the lighthouse keeper would've once lived, though a faded sign informed me the place now served as Shattering Point's lighthouse museum. I pressed my face to a dark window until I made out a shadowed dining room, a circular table with the chairs pulled out as if the family had just stepped away from their dinner.

The wind picked up as I approached the edge of the bluff. The air smelled of salt and sulfur. I peered down the sheer face of the cliff, where waves frothed and slammed against a landscape of granite chunks and ledges. Dizziness surged through me, and I stumbled back, blinking spots out of my eyes.

If Nadia had slipped and fallen while trying to get a glimpse of Clementine, there was no way she had survived.

I forced myself to peer over the edge again, seeking the bright clash of a hat or jacket against all that black and gray. It occurred to me I might be staring at the inspiration behind the island's name. *Shattering*: the fate that awaited any unlucky person or thing that tumbled into the breakers. A narrow staircase was carved into the side of the cliff, providing access to a gravelly shore that would be entirely underwater once the tide came in.

I lingered at the top of the stairs, waiting for the old me to materialize and muscle her way into the body of this coward I didn't recognize. It wasn't the risk of falling or even the prospect of finding Nadia's broken body that deterred me from making the descent. It was the stretch of darkening water rolling out to the horizon. I felt the ocean's presence like a stalker breathing down my neck.

Cowardice won, and I retreated back to the bluff. Huddled beneath the slanting overhang of one of the outbuildings, I stuffed my freezing fingers into my armpits, waiting for the jellyfish to appear.

It was hardly an unfamiliar state. Sometimes it felt like I'd spent half my life wedded to the uncooperative timetables of jellyfish, whose boom-and-bust cycles remained mysterious even to those who studied them closely. We weren't even sure where they came from. We knew jellyfish started their lives as little stalks that hitched themselves to hard surfaces underwater, but these polyps that grew so enthusiastically in the lab were hard to find in the vastness of the sea. Wild jellies sprang onto our radar as adults, in their medusa form, when their free-floating bodies and stinging tentacles created hazards for fisheries and swimmers.

Glittering shards of sunset clung to the sky behind me. A bright white moon, just past full, struggled to show its face through the clouds. The wind that threw me against the wall of the shed was accompanied now by a spray of chilly rain. I saw I'd been stupid to think I could spend the whole night out here exposed to the elements, but if I ducked inside to warm up, even for five minutes, who knew what I'd miss?

I crawled out from under the overhang, holding the hood of my raincoat to my head with both hands, and let my squinting gaze travel up to where the lighthouse's cupola met the denser darkness of the sky.

The door set in the base of the tower opened at my touch—another stroke of serendipity I didn't question. The circular room beyond was empty except for the dusty rubble of a piece of broken-down furniture and a spiral of metal stairs that corkscrewed up and up. The climb reacquainted me with the limits of a body that spent most of its days hunched over a microscope or computer: I was out of breath within seconds, a stitch knifing through my side. I paused at the halfway point to suck in some air, thinking of the lighthouse keeper who would've made this journey several times daily, burdened with barrels of oil in the era before electric lamps. I wondered when the lighthouse had been decommissioned, whether Nadia had walked this path, whether I'd find her waiting for me at the top.

A short ladder ascended through a trapdoor into the lantern room, which was far from the grand atrium I'd imagined. It was small and shabby and smelled strongly of birds. There was no Nadia—no anything except for the lens, a big glass-and-metal beehive that squatted in darkness in the center of the floor. The encircling windows gave the impression of being suspended in a very small greenhouse sixty feet above sea level. Chilly ocean air pulsed through a broken pane of glass. But it was dry, and the wind was muted.

I settled the trapdoor back into its frame and stationed myself in front of one of the windows, looking down over the indifferent darkness of the sea.

I could stand there all night if I had to. It was like that when I got really focused on something. Aldo, too. In grad school we used to spend long nights in the lab, impervious to boredom and fatigue. At some point I'd do the math and point out that it had been eight hours since dinner. Aldo would reach into the malign depths of his bulky, faux-leather man purse and produce a bag of Mike and Ikes or Milk Duds. He liked the crappy candy they sold in movie theaters. *Hit me*, he'd say—my signal to wing a Milk Dud at him so he could catch it in his mouth. Then, as with all things between us, it became a competition. Who could catch the most candy in a row? Who could stuff the most Junior Mints in their mouth without laughing and spewing chocolate all over the floor?

As the last of the sunlight faded, the hard edges of the world smeared away. Though I hadn't dived in seven months, the sensations came back to me easily. I felt pleasantly dreamy and unmoored, alone in my lightless capsule floating high in the night.

Suddenly, brilliance: I almost toppled from shock as light blasted the little room. The electric bulb must have been on a timer. The beam spun a circle around the lantern room, paused, and swung itself out again. The lens purred as it rotated on its stand. I felt unsettled by the light, and by the realization the lighthouse wasn't decommissioned after all. It felt too much like entering a room you thought was empty, only to discover a stranger had been crouching in the shadows, watching you all along.

The patter of rain died. Starlight drizzled through the clouds. A smell slid out of nowhere, a sweet-sour stink like cut flowers left in a vase for too long. It slithered through the broken window, flooding my nostrils, scalding the backs of my eyes. For a moment I feared I'd be sick.

Then a blast of red light broke across the dark water, and I forgot about my body entirely.

This light on the water's surface was of a different species than the one pulsing from the bulb inside the lens. It possessed a liquid quality no machine could generate. A viscousness like blood. Giddiness burned through me. When divers descended into deep-enough waters, inert gases built up, causing a dreamy drunkenness known as nitrogen narcosis. It made you feel ecstatic and powerful. It made you want to do dangerous, impossible things.

The rising light paused, then lifted, crashed, and shattered, a million red diamonds raining onto the ocean where they sank and reignited, more brilliant than before, caught in the swirling body of a vast thing, an ancient brainless thing, its glowing tentacles fanning net-like over the black water as it reached and spread its magnificent length toward me.

The jellyfish resembled the thing in Sidney's video the way a living, breathing human resembled a hasty tracing of their photograph. Or the way sound resembled the description of sound. The video was a mockery, the poorest attempt at an approximation.

There was nothing unconvincing about Clementine in real life. She was gargantuan, rivaling the colossal squid for size. She had no bell that I could see—the domed structure that gave jellies their classic umbrella-like appearance. She was all curl and sinew, a floating curtain of sinuous hair. Her bioluminescence ran the spectrum from crimson to carnation, undulating across her body in rhythmic waves.

The light hurt my eyes, but it was the kind of pain I craved more of. I pushed onto my toes, leaning through the broken pane and into open air. The tentacles swayed closer. The red glow pulled me into it, and the lighthouse beam brushed my spine, goading me on. Only the frailest thread of common sense kept me from punching through the rest of the glass and throwing myself into the night.

I felt the camera strap digging into my neck and raised the viewfinder to my eyes, barely aware of where I was aiming.

Hours compressed themselves into moments. Clementine's light paled and released me. The most unsettling thing about nitrogen narcosis was the speed with which it switched off. There was no comedown. One second you were a god. The next, a regular dumbass who'd been fooled into feeling special. I reeled back from the windows, dry-mouthed and newly aware of twin cramps knifing through the backs of my calves.

No trace of the sweet-sour reek lingered. The stretch of ocean beyond the cliff had extinguished itself into darkness. Clementine was gone. I felt stunned, betrayed by her absence. I fumbled for the camera, and my sense of betrayal deepened: The images were as faulty as Sidney's video, the jellyfish's majesty muted into so many fuzzy lines.

I took the camera off my neck and threw it much harder than I intended. It hit the lantern room floor with an awful sound and broke into bits of glass and plastic. I crawled around trying to collect them, and they scattered, evading my touch.

Then my hand brushed something cool and rubbery. The texture was familiar. The lens rotated, the lamplight ghosting over my hand and illuminating a lime-green diving fin. I looked up, and my wooziness sharpened into a fear so dense and cold it froze me in place.

I was no longer alone in the lantern room. Black-suited, hooded, his expression obscured by a full face mask and the fat plug of the regulator protruding from his lips—it was Aldo Antunes as I'd seen him last. The lighthouse beam passed over him and flung him back into shadow, leaving his silhouette painted across my vision. When the light rotated again, he was still there. Standing right above me.

How long had this specter been lurking there, silently sharing my vigil? I waited for him to do something. Say something. He never spoke in my dreams, but this was no dream. I could feel the hot blood rushing in my ears, and the cold glass of the windows as I staggered to my feet and scrabbled behind me for something—a handhold, a weapon, a clue that would teach me to make sense of what I was seeing.

"You're dead," I whispered.

Aldo seemed to weigh these words. There was something wrong with my vision. The lighthouse beam had dimmed to a hazy white, singing out at random intervals I could no longer track.

But I could see his gloved hand with perfect clarity: It lifted with eerie slowness, as if he were about to wave or salute.

The feeling shot back into my body. I tore my eyes away and hurtled down the spiral stairs.

Ayakashi

Color doesn't just serve to make jellies beautiful. Like every component of these simple yet efficient invertebrates, color serves a purpose. Blue may function as a form of sunscreen against ultraviolet light. In the deep sea, where red light is filtered out, scarlet stomachs camouflage jellies as they digest their fluorescent meals. The green fluorescent protein in *Aequorea victoria* has revolutionized the study of cell biology. Used in everything from cancer research to host-pathogen interactions to gene expression, it has helped achieve countless scientific breakthroughs. What other superpowers are jellyfish hiding?

AA: Telekinesis, necromancy, time travel, invisibility, superstrength.

JN: The ability to keep you on task for five minutes.

I ran, pebbles sliding out from beneath my feet, cold sweat slicking down my back. I hardly knew where I was going, except away from the water, away from the awful vision of Aldo in the lighthouse.

But I was on an island. There was only so far you could run from the ocean before you ran into it again.

I blundered through the fence and up the slope onto Beach Street, where I finally stopped and slumped against the seawall, winded. I thought I'd been in the lantern room only a couple of hours, but a soft light tingled in the eastern sky, tinting the water silver. Somehow, it was nearly dawn.

I clasped my hands, and the answering pressure reached me through layers of numbness. I recognized it as my response to panic, a kind of deactivation, like a device powering down all but its most vital functions in order to preserve battery. It was like that when I resurfaced from that final dive without Aldo, as I tripped my way out of the sinkhole and up to the ranger station, yelling for help while feeling curiously removed from the whole performance. Who *was* that woman, making such a fuss?

He had only ever appeared to me in the foggy seconds after waking, an apparition easily relegated to the vestiges of a bad dream. In the lantern room he had been so solid. So real.

I cast around for a rational explanation. Could the interplay of harsh light and deep shadow in such a small space have played tricks on my eyes? (But I'd *felt* the edge of his fin under my hand.) Had the appearance of the gigantic jellyfish sparked some form of grief-stricken wish fulfillment, and I had simply imagined he was there with me? (But I would never have wished to see him like that: wet and dead and steeped in a monstrous silence, his facial features all sealed up behind the mask.)

My mind twitched around that other explanation, the one that made perfect sense of everything but that I would resist accepting until every alternative had been ruled out: After seven months of crawling through an Aldo-less world, gamely mimicking the motions of a woman who'd managed to move on, I had finally, fantastically unraveled. I was losing my mind.

I pressed my hands into the top of the seawall as I tried to take stock of my situation. The bag with my field notebook and binoculars was still huddled in the lantern room with what remained of my camera. It could stay there forever; there was nothing in it that couldn't be replaced.

Nadia was still missing. A shiver passed through me as I relived how close I'd come to flinging myself off the top of the lighthouse. What if she hadn't been able to resist the siren call of Clementine's light? It was seeming more and more likely that something really bad had happened to her, and I couldn't face the reality of another dead friend. I wouldn't.

As for Clementine—*what could she be*? Not a lion's mane, or anything I'd laid eyes on before. In spite of my fear that I was actually going crazy, I felt a powerful kick of curiosity. I wanted to see Clementine again, and I would. I just needed to get away from the island for a little while, get my head on straight, and I'd come back better equipped, ready to learn more.

Norm, Roger, and Tony had all told me Nadia was on the mainland for one reason or another. Maybe it was time to believe them.

This was not running, I thought with conviction as I started running again. This was part one of a well-ordered plan. I had been a sane person before I got to Shattering: I would chase that sanity back to the mainland, look for evidence of Nadia there, then regroup and figure out how all the pieces came together.

I banged on Nadia and Roger's door for over a minute before he answered, looking rumpled but alert.

"I have to get off the island," I said.

"Now? Why? What's going on?" Roger watched me warily. I realized how crazy I must look. My eyeballs strained in their sockets, as if they'd swelled to twice their natural size, and my face stung from what must've been small cuts left by the broken window. I fought the feeling that something had changed inside me, a crucial switch flipped on or off as I stood in the lantern room, watching Clementine bleed her glow all over the water.

"Did you find out something about Nadia?" Roger asked.

"Not exactly."

"*Not exactly?* What the hell does that—?"

"Please, Roger." My head soared with exhaustion. I didn't have the energy to fight with him. "I don't know where she is, okay? I just—don't think she's on Shattering anymore."

Roger's anger passed quickly. He looked tired, too. "I called the cops," he offered.

For a second I thought he was talking about the fight with Emmett at the Urchin, before remembering how I'd nagged him about getting the police involved in Nadia's disappearance. "And?"

"They said they'll file a report."

"A report. Great. So helpful."

"What did you expect them to do?"

The truth was that I didn't really expect the police to do anything, especially if Roger was going to divulge the part about his and Nadia's fight and the missing boat; she was too easily cast into the role of the resentful runaway wife. But as long as I urged him to make the call and he didn't, I could tell myself he was a bad husband to Nadia.

I'd lost that particular advantage now. Roger sagged in the doorway, looking much smaller than he had when I met him two nights ago.

"She's been gone over forty-eight hours," he murmured. "No call, no text. What if she's—?"

I recognized the lull I was supposed to fill with reassurances: *We'll find her, she's fine, there's an innocent explanation here, she's fine* . . . But I was no longer convinced of any of those things, and I wasn't interested in testing the universe's screwed-up sense of humor by blurting overconfident platitudes.

"Come with me," I said instead. My motives were selfish: I didn't trust myself to drive a boat twenty-two miles, not after what had happened on the ride in.

Roger raised his eyebrows. "Where?"

"Anywhere. Just not here."

He hesitated. "What if Nadia comes back?"

"She knows how to get in touch with you. There's something off about this place, Roger. It'd be better if we both left. Maybe talking to the police in person would help."

It was a useless suggestion, but one that I could see appealed to him nonetheless. He wanted off this island as much as I did.

"My boat's gone," he reminded me.

"I've got that covered. Meet me at the dock in ten."

I turned and bolted down the brightening street without giving him a chance to protest.

It took only a few minutes to gather the rest of my belongings from Montana. I'd barely had a chance to settle in. I went downstairs and poked my head into all the rooms on the first floor, looking in vain for Tony. She'd told me to get in touch with her if I had any problems, but it was only now occurring to me she hadn't provided a phone number.

I returned to the foyer and hesitated for a grand total of five seconds before rifling through the drawers in the antique desk. It wasn't stealing, I reasoned, as I slid the key on the blue plastic whale float into my pocket. Tony had all but begged me to borrow her boat yesterday. I was just taking her up on her offer a little late.

There was no fog cloaking the western shore today. The Gulf stretched into the distance, flat and gleaming like a sheet of metal beneath the rising sun. To my relief, Roger was waiting for me on a bench, a camping backpack slung over his broad shoulders.

"Good day for travel," he commented.

I made a noncommittal noise and handed him the key. "Tony's boat?"

"I think it's this way . . ." He clomped off toward the dock. I kept my gaze pinned to his back, the water surging at the edges of my vision. The familiar dizziness gathered in the center of my forehead and spread.

Roger slapped his palm onto the hull of a scuffed white motorboat: *The Phantom Maiden*. It was even smaller than *Miriam's Smile*. He twisted the key in the ignition, and the engine started with a growl. Here was my ticket off Shattering, away from the awful specter of my dead friend in the lighthouse, but I found I couldn't move. My knees had locked. My vision boiled with little black pinwheels.

"Leaving so soon?"

I managed to turn my head, and Emmett Beckendorf's face swirled into view. He was in tall brown boots and yellow overalls like the ones Pamela had worn, a big wad of fishing nets draped across his arms. He looked unscathed from the fight at the Urchin, but from the way he was glowering at me, I intuited that he was sporting a good-sized knob on the back of his head.

I should've been relieved that he hadn't suffered any serious damage. Instead, the sight of Emmett coiled my dread tighter. I was gripped by a premonition that he was here to prevent us from leaving.

Roger flung the last of the mooring lines into the boat. He was pointedly not looking at Emmett. "Let's go, Jo," he said, his voice curt.

Emmett's hand clamped onto my shoulder. I was already shaky; the added weight almost buckled me. I forced myself to hold his stare, to look cool and unafraid.

His glare dropped away. He met my gaze with an expression of surprise. His little pink eyes searched my features, as though he didn't recognize me.

I was having the opposite experience: It was as if I suddenly realized I knew Emmett Beckendorf from a past life. A mask had fallen away from him. His face, newly bared, glowed with an uncanny familiarity that I could neither place nor resist. It was maddening, like having just one bar of a melody repeating in your head as the whole song drifted out of reach. Was it really possible we'd crossed paths before? I felt strangely drawn to him, yanked by a magnetism that had nothing to do with sex.

Then Emmett laughed, loud and mean, and the spell was

broken. He released me with a gentle push. It was enough momentum to cut through my paralysis, and I stepped into *The Phantom Maiden*, clutching my bag to my chest.

"Go on, then," said Emmett. "Safe travels. Don't hurry back." He laughed again.

Roger guided the boat away from the dock. The prow cut a clean white line through the water as we sped into the Gulf. The western sky was still lightless, streaky with dark clouds. The shore shrank, and Emmett with it, the fishing nets piled at his feet, his hand arcing back and forth in a jaunty wave.

"My god, I'm so glad to get off that rock!" Roger called over the grinding of the motor. Some tension had poured out of him. He sat in the cockpit with one hand flopped over the wheel, looking like a man jetting into a badly needed morning of leisure.

I felt worse than ever. Every foot of distance gained from Shattering seemed to stretch something inside me to the point of breaking. I was abandoning Nadia—abandoning Clementine—just as I'd once abandoned Aldo in the cave. I made the mistake of glancing behind me, just once, where the lighthouse jutted into pink-stained clouds like a skeletal finger raised in judgment.

Dizziness roared through me. The soothing image of my moon jellyfish remained elusive. All I could see was Aldo.

I choked and the world flipped. This was worse than what I'd experienced on the trip to the island, worse than what I'd felt peering over the edge of the bluff and into the breakers. My joints burned. My skin was being flayed from my skeleton piece by piece. The air had curdled into something dense and unbreathable.

A distant pain bloomed across my skull, a whisper compared to the rebellion exploding inside me, every cell rioting for air. Like a stuttering movie reel, I saw flashes of still-living fish flopping in sagging nets, finned sharks ribboning blood as they spun into the depths, an octopus stranded at low tide, dried out and deflated as an empty balloon.

Blackness closed in, then unfolded like a hand.

I was staring at a small dirty pond, its surface ropy with algae smears. Cypress trees leaned over the water as if straining for a glimpse of their reflections.

"Like pea soup full of alligators," said Aldo.

I laughed. He was right: The sinkhole didn't look like much of anything. Certainly not the gateway to a system of breathtakingly vast underwater caverns. Aldo had been nagging me to join him at this notorious Florida dive site for years.

We slopped off the makeshift dock and into the shallows. The sinkhole dropped off steeply. We sank a few feet down, checking our airflow and our weights. Aldo curled his thumb and forefinger into the *Okay?* sign. I mirrored it back at him. Then his thumb twisted, pointing down. The diver's signal to descend.

We descended, and a feeling of tranquility settled over me. Before my father died, he had been an avid meditator. He'd tried to induct me into his morning ritual, calmly reciting the directives to home in on my breathing as I squirmed on the floor, my mind seething with jellies and bugs and the discomfort of my legs contorted into a half-lotus position. I loved him and I wanted to please him, but the state of heightened awareness he retreated into each morning continued to elude me—until that summer day I completed my first open water dive. As our group had descended into the old quarry in Kentucky, the sunlight slanting through the water in muted rays, a slender-bodied catfish drifting past my head, close enough to touch, there it was: the yawning eye of the storm around which my thoughts tumbled freely. I never could bring the feeling back with me onto land.

Aldo plunged into the shaft that led to the cave system, and I followed. The caverns were strung with a system of guidelines to help divers find their way. The passages were tight, but the testimonials I'd studied online promised a succession of larger chambers around eight hundred feet in, each bestowed with an ostentatious name. The Chapel. The Ballroom. The Gallery. The Armory was the grandest and biggest of the caverns, the one we'd traveled all the way from the West Coast to see.

A craggy ceiling pressed overhead, and slick rocks studded the floor below. There was no one around but Aldo and me, which was how I preferred it: as if we were the last two humans on earth. Our dive lights seemed less to illuminate the space around us than to call it into existence. Aldo released the guideline and floated upward, inspecting something near the ceiling. As I watched, a cloud of brown sediment rolled gently through the chamber, filling the space between us.

Silt-outs were a known hazard in cave dives and wreck dives—any enclosed space where disturbed particulate had no current to disperse it. The silt hung out in the water column, taking hours or days to settle. Visibility shrank to zero. Your dive light reflected off the grainy particles, revealing nothing. You became a blind animal spinning in a watery gloom where up and down ceased to exist.

Aldo strung his way along the guideline toward me and tugged my arm through the wet suit, the gesture's meaning unmistakable: *This way.* He was always so certain he was right, as was

I—a friendship founded on mutual pigheadedness. I resisted him. Aldo was a skilled diver, but the silt-out had him disoriented. He was trying to lead us deeper into the cave. I pulled him in the opposite direction. We engaged in this useless tug-of-war for several minutes, wasting air. I felt annoyance and impatience—not yet fear.

Aldo's hands framed my head and pulled me inward. We were inches away, mask to mask, posed like lovers about to kiss. A wordless miscommunication passed between us. He released me, and I swam away from him until the beige cloud swallowed me whole.

For the next several minutes I frog kicked solo through the silt, squeezing around tight corners I didn't remember from the journey in, the sickening realization slowly dawning on me that Aldo had been right: I was going the wrong way. I rotated, and my fin clipped a wall. Rotated again, another wall. The clicking of my regulator created a happy music in my ears. I felt woozy and unstoppable. I was three hundred feet down. My dive knife was in my hand, though I had no memory of reaching for it. I'd cut my way free! The blade scraped against rock, and then a starburst of pain ignited across my hand, bringing me back to my body.

Divers rationed their air based on the golden rule of thirds: a third of the tank pressure for the journey in and a third for the journey out, with the final portion reserved for emergencies. I was well into my emergency allotment. I reversed course, straining to keep my breathing slow and measured, but the panic had finally found me. My fins smacked the cave floor, stirring up more sediment. The vision that haunted me was not of suffocating or drowning but of being trapped there forever, swimming in circles in the dark. I was so convinced this would be my fate that even when the silt thinned and I was out of the cave and ascending at dangerous speed, I didn't really believe I'd escaped—not until my right hand broke the algae-smeared surface, followed by my head, and I flung off my mask, dazzled by the sun.

But I saw now that a part of me had never escaped.

A part of me was still down there, rising toward the surface even as something else was rising with me. I felt it stirring in the water, lifting itself with the smooth-edged patience of a machine. The body of the *ayakashi* from my mother's story was beaded with ghostly lights, and the light burning brightest belonged to Aldo, furious at me for leaving him behind. If he went the right way, why did I make it out of the cavern and he didn't? Did nitrogen narcosis have him as bewildered as it did me? Or did he turn back when he realized I wasn't following?

I wouldn't ever know the answers to these questions. I kicked, my legs like concrete pillars, but the *ayakashi* had me in its tentacled grip. It reeled me down into the darkness and I surrendered to it. I was nothing to this many-minded creature. A speck. A short-lived bubble that flitted and popped. There was relief in being made so small.

Venom Guy

Earth has undergone five mass extinction events. The Ordovician-Silurian extinction killed off 80 percent of all marine life. Some seventy-five million years later, the Devonian extinction spared most terrestrial species while wreaking havoc on the seas, eliminating major reef builders and wiping out the entire placoderm class. The Permian-Triassic extinction, also known as the Great Dying, represents the largest mass extinction in our planet's history, leaving only 10 percent of the world's species unscathed.

The mass terrestrial die-off of the Triassic-Jurassic extinction paved the way for dinosaurs to dominate the planet—at least until the infamous asteroid crash-landed and triggered the Cretaceous-Tertiary extinction, and *T. rex* breathed its last.

We tell you all this in order to emphasize what the jellyfish has survived. It will go on surviving, years after this book has shriveled to dust and both its authors are long gone.

AA: Speak for yourself. I'm gonna live forever.

I didn't like Aldo, in the beginning.

I met him in Oregon, in the early days of grad school, at a meet and greet held at a sports bar a mile off campus. I went in spite of my better judgment. College was three months in the past. I was pursuing my dream of studying jellyfish. I could be a new person here: confident, open-minded, caring.

I knew as soon as I walked in that I'd made a mistake. The room boomed with overlapping broadcasts from half a dozen TVs and the drunk, happy chatter of too many strangers packed together. I tried for a quick exit, but my adviser, Dr. Colling—a wiry blond woman and fire coral expert who looked like she'd be more at home on a surfboard than in a lab—materialized out of nowhere and flung a freckled arm over my shoulder, dragging me into the chaos.

I drank a G&T, then another. The booze dulled the edges of my anxiety but stopped short of transforming me into an extrovert who could navigate the competing streams of conversation with anything approaching grace. I answered direct questions. I tried to smile. The glass sweated all over my hand and dribbled condensation down my wrist. I wished Nadia were there. I mourned her as if she'd died, as if she weren't just a text message away. But as the months marched past, our silence felt increasingly unbreakable. And I was stubborn. I wanted *her* to reach out to *me*.

Suddenly, like a lamp shining through the dark, a single word penetrated the background noise and pulled me irresistibly toward it: *jellyfish*.

A lanky dark-skinned guy a few years older than me was holding court at a corner table. I hadn't really understood what that term, *holding court*, meant until this moment. His hands whipped and slashed in an aggressive display that the captive eyes of his audience followed as if he were weaving magic out of thin air. He would not have seemed out of place pontificating behind the pulpit, or striding across the floor of a car dealership, selling you on an impractical model you didn't want or need. I recalled from Dr. Colling's introductions that he was a second-year doctoral student from Brazil, though I couldn't summon his name.

The man stopped his flailing in order to show off a rubbery oblong scar in the crook of his arm. The audience leaned in to admire it.

I spoke up: "That's not from a jellyfish sting."

Heads swiveled in my direction. I couldn't read their expressions. Annoyed, surprised, or merely curious? The man with the scar tented his hands under his chin and flashed me a bright smile. "Yeah, it is—I was just telling these guys. Ran into a box jelly in Queensland last month."

"That looks more like a burn to me. And stinger season in Australia runs October to June."

"Maybe this one was a late bloomer." His easy smile never slipped. I disliked him instinctively.

A bespectacled guy in my cohort whose name was either Hank or Frank put in, "Aren't box jellies some of the most dangerous ones out there?"

"You got that right!" cried the charlatan, smacking Hank/Frank fondly in the ribs, and the man blushed like a cartoon character. "Fatality rate is around forty percent."

"That's a gross exaggeration," I said. "The latest research shows—"

"Wouldn't faze you, though, would it?" interrupted a woman

whose name I also couldn't remember. She wore dangly fish skeleton earrings and sat so close to the charlatan she might as well have crawled into his lap. She bumped her shoulder with his and shot me a smug glance. I gathered that I was supposed to be jealous. "Aldo holds the world record for venomous animal encounters," she explained. "He's in the *Guinness Book* and everything."

"Wait, seriously?" said Hank/Frank.

Impressed looks were traded around the table. Was everyone under this idiot's spell?

The charlatan—Aldo—drank deeply from his glass. "They tell me I have a natural resistance to most organic toxins."

I slouched my weight onto one hip. There would've been a spot for me at the table if people shifted their chairs. "*They.* Meaning—?"

"Doctors," said Aldo.

"Doctors," I repeated. "Yes. Right. Of course."

"It wasn't always like that." His voice became wistful. I just managed to avoid rolling my eyes as, with great emotion, Aldo went on to explain that at twelve years old, while hiking with his cousins in a national park, he'd been bitten by a venomous snake—a species that was not supposed to exist outside a tiny island off-limits to the public. He was clinically dead for sixteen minutes. "A few months later, this researcher tracked me down at my mom's place. He couldn't believe I'd survived. He wanted to study me. He found me fascinating."

This time I didn't manage to avoid rolling my eyes, though nobody was looking at me.

"So now you just go around getting bitten and stung by venomous animals?" Hank/Frank asked.

"A man must make sacrifices for science," said Aldo gravely, and everyone laughed except me. "My current research focus is lionfish venom. But from time to time, I still get study requests. There's a team in Costa Rica trying to use my blood to make a new type of rattlesnake antivenom."

"Give me a break," I said, more loudly than I meant to.

This time there was no mistaking my colleagues' expressions. They were irritated. Maybe they accepted this harebrained story, maybe not, but they were enjoying themselves, and I was ruining their good time.

"You think I'm lying?" said Aldo. I'd finally killed his con man's smile. The woman with the fish skeleton earrings squeezed his arm and whispered something in his ear: a fangirl's reassurance. He twitched his head away from her. He sipped from his glass and lowered it slowly, his eyes never leaving mine. "What would it take to convince you?" he asked.

"How about a demonstration?" I said. "Oh, wait." I mimed patting myself down. "I left all my rattlesnakes in my other pants. Too bad."

I walked away, my face burning from alcohol and from the painful awareness that I'd just torched several potential friendships. What else was new? Josephine the buzzkill, Josephine the know-it-all dork. Bug-Eyed Weirdo. I had been stupid to think it could ever be any other way.

I didn't expect to talk to Aldo again. Oregon State was ten times the size of Gladstone. It took a concerted effort not to walk around with my head on a swivel like a tourist in Times Square. As a second-year student, Aldo spent most of his time at the marine station an hour away on the coast, and my experience with braggy liar types was that they tended to avoid people who called them on their shit.

He surprised me by seeking me out, just a few weeks later. I was in the library on the main campus, in one of the glassed-in study rooms on the sixth floor, making my way through a stack of readings for my physical oceanography class. How had he found me? Before I could ask, Aldo flung a leather purse onto the table and pulled out a Tupperware container. Inside was a spider. Large, black, the distinctive scarlet hourglass splashed across its abdomen. I had been fascinated by black widow spiders when I was little and had often scoured my parents' woodpile seeking a specimen. I never found one, just a whole lot of wood roaches and pill bugs that I dutifully inventoried in my observation notebook.

"Entomology lab," said Aldo, answering my unasked question. I wasn't even surprised. It was obvious to me that Mr. Venom was the type of guy who could sweet-talk his way into anywhere, get his hands on anything.

Aldo peeled the lid off the Tupperware. The spider scuttled to the edge of the table. He trapped it between his hands before it could leap onto the floor.

"Are you crazy?" I asked.

"You wanted a demonstration."

Except the widow wasn't cooperating. Aldo tried to entice it onto the bare skin of his arm, near where the oblong scar fanned out beneath his elbow. The spider fled, and he trapped it again.

"C'mon! Bite me, you bitch!"

"Stop it. You're scaring her."

When the widow scampered away the next time, I reached across Aldo, scooped her up, and deposited her back into the container. He looked at me with an expression teetering on the edge of respect.

"Not many people would've touched that thing."

"Mortality rates from black widow bites are less than one percent."

"Still. You could end up with some nasty symptoms. Swelling, cramps, vomiting."

"Not you, though," I said. "You're *invincible*."

"I never said I was invincible. I said I had a natural resistance." His lips protruded in a boyish pout. I was pleased at how much my skepticism irked him.

Aldo tipped back in his chair. His hair was mussed into an unruly hedge that somehow suited his face shape perfectly. Dark stubble covered his cheeks and jaw. He was handsome, I conceded, if you were into guys who looked like they'd crawled out of the woods.

"What's your name?" he asked.

"Jo Ness."

"You study jellyfish, right? Beautiful animals. I've been enchanted by them ever since I saw a swarm of Atlantic sea nettles as a boy. Amazing how something so physically fragile can be so ecologically powerful."

I stuck my face behind an article like I was waiting for him to go away. But I was warming to him in spite of myself. Even in a marine science program, it wasn't every day you met someone who spoke fondly of jellyfish.

"You should see if you can get a slot in the toxicology lab," said Aldo. "Lots of opportunities to study jellies there."

"Are you trying to poach me from Dr. Colling?"

"I'd be doing you a favor. Colling's getting fast-tracked to dean. That lab will be low priority for her starting next semester."

"I'll think about it."

Aldo let me go on pretending to read for another minute before adding, stubbornly, "I really have been stung by a box jelly."

"Not there, you haven't," I said, pointing to the scar.

He hesitated. "You're right. Not there. That's from when I burned myself on a teakettle last month. Happy?"

I laughed. He'd folded much easier than I thought. Not such a formidable salesman after all. "I'll be happy when you stop telling that dumb story about the snake."

"The snake was real!"

He jumped to his feet and stood over me, fuming. The black widow stretched its jointed front legs toward the roof of its prison, pedipalp twitching.

"You should take her back now," I said idly, returning to browsing the article. "Someone's going to miss her."

By way of response, Aldo whipped off his belt and slid his pants down to his knees.

"Whoa there, dude," I said, also getting to my feet. "That was *not* an invitation."

"Don't flatter yourself. I want to show you something." He rotated and jabbed at a spot on his left thigh. I leaned forward to inspect a golf-ball-sized patch of flesh that was gray and spongy, the texture of a rotten peach.

"I suppose you're going to tell me that's where the snake bit you."

"Yes," said Aldo. "It changed my life. I was clinically dead for—"

"Sixteen minutes, yeah. I remember. Let me guess: You ran away from the white light?" I still thought this guy was full of shit, but I felt a scientific curiosity to discover how far the shit reached.

"Oh, there was no light." Aldo's eyes had gone flat. "I was in a cave. Inside was a giant anaconda with horns on its head and fire in its eyes. It said it could take my vision, my life, or my sanity."

I raised my eyebrows. "Which did you choose?"

"I didn't answer. But when I woke up in the hospital in São Paulo, I wasn't dead, and I wasn't blind."

"So you're saying that you're crazy."

Aldo pulled his pants up to his waist and sat down again. "I've read about other people who've had near-death experiences. They talk about having a renewed sense of the value of their lives. For me, it's the opposite. I don't value my life anymore, and this frees me to live it without fear. So if that's what you mean by crazy, then yes: I am crazily indifferent to what happens to me." He laid a finger against the side of the Tupperware container, shaking his head disapprovingly at the uncooperative widow. "I've never told anyone that part of the story before."

"Oh, come on."

"Contrary to what you seem to think, I'm actually committed to building a career for myself. No one's handing out postdocs to the guy who says he's been visited by a malevolent snake spirit."

"You probably just hallucinated from the venom."

He grinned and snapped his fingers in my face. "So you *do* believe I was bitten!"

I scoffed. "Why do you care what I believe?"

Aldo didn't answer right away. He refastened his belt, tucked the Tupperware back into his man purse, and moved toward the study room's door. With one hand on the knob, he replied, finally, "I don't know."

It was the first thing he'd said that I took for truth.

• • •

Mysteries persisted: Why did we like each other? Why did we continue hanging out even as we butted heads over everything? (The most cost-efficient jellyfish deterrents, the best type of scuba diving mask, whether Sour Patch Kids were a delicacy or disgusting.) Why did I bring him home for Christmas that first year of grad school to meet my mother, who appalled me by gushing over him like he was the son she'd never had?

I stirred through theories as Aldo sat digesting Mom's mirin-glazed salmon in my father's old easy chair, which still smelled like his aftershave if you tucked your nose into the frayed cushion and sniffed. Aldo and I were both only children and functioned as surrogate siblings to each other. We shared a madness for our work that was of a magnitude unusual even for grad school. Despite his superficial bravado, Aldo was, at his core, as socially awkward as me: I evaded, he performed. Contrasting approaches to the same set of insecurities. I had watched over the past few months as our colleagues who'd been so fascinated by Aldo at the meet and greet peeled away from him, settling into more enduring friendships. His charisma was for the short term. Even the woman with the fish skeleton earrings had moved on.

"People find me insufferable," he'd said to me once with a shrug. It wasn't hard to imagine why. His stubbornness was extreme, and his bluster tipped easily into arrogance. Then there was the whole I-don't-value-my-life thing. How were you supposed to care about someone who couldn't be bothered to care about himself? Somehow, I was able to put those flaws aside, to zero in on Aldo's best qualities: That he was attentive and funny and fun to be around. That he seemed to like being around me as much as I liked being around him.

I recognized, on some level, that I was using Aldo to replace Nadia, who still hadn't reached out. Not on my twenty-second birthday, not on Thanksgiving, not even today, on Christmas, her favorite holiday, when I was sure she'd texted a flurry of festive well-wishes to every friend and relative who celebrated. Was she thinking about me at all? Had she already deleted my number? Things were so much easier with Aldo. There wasn't some quivering lump of tension between us, waiting to be recognized. We were friends, pure and simple. I had never had that before.

His hand stretched lazily toward the recliner's lever. The chair shot open, jolting him backward.

"Your mom's nice."

She was in the kitchen, cleaning dishes, having shooed away our offer to help. Over the sound of water running, I caught traces of her tuneless singing. My visits home had rarely been so frictionless.

"She thinks we're going to get married," I said.

"Did she tell you that?"

"She doesn't need to." I had spent enough time around my mother to recognize the predatory gleam in her eyes as she looked him up and down at the airport. My friendship with Aldo fed her fantasies that my purported gayness was just a phase that would dissolve in the rearview once I met the right man.

"In that case," said Aldo.

He closed the chair and went for his man purse on the table. I felt a moment of panic as he dropped to a knee, bearing an item behind his back.

"Josephine Ayumi Ness. Will you . . ."

The seconds stretched into eternity. My mother banged pots together in the sink. Aldo's expression was as serious as I'd ever seen it. Was it really possible he'd miscalculated our friendship so badly?

"Go scuba diving with me?" he finished, revealing his gift with a flourish.

The anxious blush drained out of my face as fast as it had appeared. He was holding a dive knife in a slim black case. I accepted the knife and unsheathed it.

Though Aldo and I talked scuba diving a lot, we'd yet to embark on a trip together. It was an expensive hobby on a grad student's stipend. But there were ways to keep costs down. Driving instead of flying. Lugging our gear to avoid rental fees. Crappy motels.

"It would be my genuine honor," I said, matching his solemn tone.

My mother stepped into the living room as Aldo was getting to his feet. Her gaze oscillated frantically between the two of us, her hands frozen in a dish towel.

"What's happening?" she demanded.

I laughed, knees buckling, and almost dropped the knife blade-down into the hardwood.

"The start of something beautiful," said Aldo.

Part Two

Cannonball jellyfish
Stomolophus meleagris
Portuguese man-of-war
Physalia physalis
Sea walnut
Mnemiopsis leidyi
Lion's mane jellyfish
Cyanea capillata
Moon jellyfish
Aurelia aurita

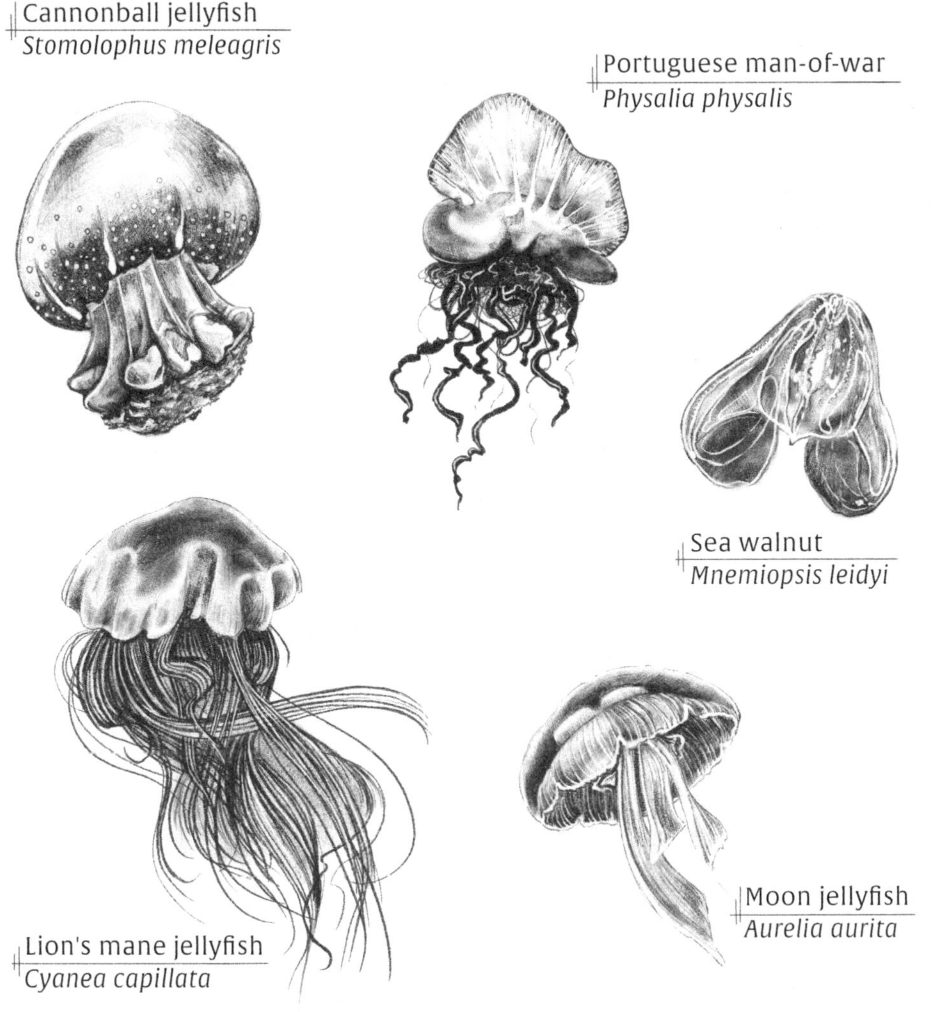

The Tunnel

The diverse forms and bold colors of jellyfish have inspired a host of creative common names. A selection of this author's favorites includes: the purple people eater, the sea tomato, the bitey whitey, the flower hat jelly, the long stringy stingy thingy, and the noodle goon.

JN: You made this one up.

AA: Just checking to see if you're paying attention.

The smoke detector blinked its red light every thirty seconds. I lay there for a while, drowsily watching it through slitted eyes. I was on a bed, a really comfortable one that conspired to coax me back into sleep, but I resisted it. Memories were limping into focus. The lighthouse. The jellyfish. Aldo in his dive suit. Roger and the dock and the boat and the cave, the goddamn cave that kept pulling me back no matter how many times I told myself I'd escaped it.

For a second I believed that all the events of the past seven months had been nothing but a hypoxia-induced hallucination: I'd just been hoisted from the sinkhole by rescue divers. Aldo, too. He was resting in a bed down the hall, charming all the nurses. If only my aching limbs would cooperate, I could get up and go see him and apologize for almost getting both of us killed.

I ran my tongue around my gums and discovered my mouth was still working. "Where am I?"

"Texas," a woman's voice replied.

I lifted my head a few inches off the pillow. The blanket on top of me was emblazoned with a big white star. The long-horned skull of a steer was affixed to the wall over the bureau, glaring through empty eyes.

Dread trickled through me. I was back on Shattering Point, in one of Retreat-by-the-Sea's themed guest rooms. Tony Newell stood to the left of the bed, proffering a plastic cup that I refused, even though my mouth tasted like I'd been gargling with swamp water.

"We were leaving. We were on a boat!" I yelled this last part like an accusation. The effort made my head throb. Tony set the cup on the nightstand, settled into a chair by the bed, and produced a penlight that she attempted to shine into my eyes.

"What are you doing?"

"I'm trying to see if you have a concussion."

This was such a sensible answer that I stopped squirming at once. Beyond the circle of stabbing brightness, I watched Tony's eyes narrow in concentration.

An invisible line between us tightened. It was like what had happened with Emmett on the dock, but the pull was brighter, hotter, harder to resist. I was filled with the desire to reach out and wrap my arms around her, which I repressed by balling my hands into fists beneath the blanket.

If Tony registered our newfound closeness, she didn't show it. She clicked the penlight off and leaned back. "Pupils are nice and reactive. My expert opinion is that you're going to live."

"Are you some kind of doctor?"

"I'm an EMT."

"You're an innkeeper and an EMT?"

"Small town, everyone wears more than one hat. I'm also into wildlife rehabilitation."

She handed me the cup again. This time I accepted it, swishing the cold water between my teeth.

"We were leaving," I repeated. There was a stubborn gap in my memory after Roger and I boarded *The Phantom Maiden*. "How am I back here?"

"Roger turned around when you collapsed."

Collapsed. A melodramatic word I didn't know what to do with. I flashed back to a house I'd seen once as a kid, pulverized by a tornado, chunks of brick and furniture spewed all over the lawn.

"Where is Roger now?" I asked.

"He's just outside." Tony rolled her eyes. "He's been hovering over you all day."

"All day? What time is it?" I glanced at the window, but the curtains were drawn.

"Nearly three. You want something to eat?"

"I want to talk to Roger."

Tony weighed this request silently. I shifted my limbs uncomfortably on the bed. My skin felt tight around my body, the blood pulsing too close to the surface. I imagined I could sense Tony's blood rushing around inside her, too.

She disappeared into the hallway, and a minute later Roger burst inside, wild-eyed with his shirt untucked.

"Oh my god. I thought you were going to *die*."

I was surprisingly touched by his obvious relief that this was not the case.

Roger sat in the chair Tony had vacated, and he leaned forward to inspect me. I assumed I looked even worse than I had when I arrived at his house that morning. The hair against my neck felt as though it hadn't been washed in weeks, and there was an itchy crust around my mouth. Someone had dressed me in an overlarge cotton pajama shirt that gapped at the collarbone. My hands felt too big, and my fingertips buzzed. I resisted the feeling that I'd woken into a borrowed body that belonged to someone else.

At least Roger looked the same to me. He was who he'd always been: Nadia's annoying husband.

"It was so scary . . ." he murmured.

I took a deep breath. "What happened, exactly?"

"One minute you were just standing there. The next you were on the floor."

"A seizure?"

"I don't think so. One of my brother's kids has epilepsy. I've seen seizures before. This was more like you ran headlong into a brick wall. You just . . . dropped." He fixed me with a reproachful stare, as if asking how I could possibly do such a thing to him.

"I told you we had to get off Shattering," I said. "Why did you turn around?"

"We were a half hour out from the mainland! You would never have made it."

"You don't know that. I fainted, okay? It was anxiety. It happens sometimes when I'm on the water. I just needed a few minutes to come around . . ." I clung to the anger, which felt life-giving. It was Roger's fault I was back here, on this island full of secrets and ghosts.

The thought called up the memory of Aldo in the lighthouse—so clear, so sharp, knifing through the core of me. I shivered and darted my gaze around the room. There was no one in Texas but Roger, and Tony, who'd reappeared in the doorway, arms folded across her chest.

"Where's my phone?" I whipped my head around, looking for my duffel, and winced as pain lanced through the back of my skull again. "The air taxi will be running tomorrow. Let's book it now." Water was my problem; flying over it would be my way out.

"Trying to leave again is not a good idea," said Tony.

I bristled at the challenge. "You were the one trying to kick me out!"

"That was before. I tried to spare you, Jo." She sounded, for a moment, genuinely upset. "But you just had to go sticking your nose where it doesn't belong. Now you can't go anywhere."

Roger's expression was blank. "What is she talking about?"

"I don't know," I said. "She's crazy." Tony raised her eyebrows, and heat crept up the back of my neck. "I want to leave. I'm leaving," I told Roger, raising my volume again to a level just below shouting. "Give me your phone."

"I—" Roger sputtered and shrank back in the chair. He glanced—infuriatingly—at Tony. I sensed his loyalty slipping, his growing conviction that *I* might actually be the crazy one.

I wasn't used to being thought of as unstable. Unfriendly and awkward, sure—these were charges I'd borne all my life. They were like weird birthmarks you wished you didn't have but got used to over time, because you'd always had them and you always would. But my mind was my mainstay. My one offering to the world. Even from a young age and despite my unconventional fascinations, I was still the girl with a good head on her shoulders.

What if Aldo's death had broken something inside me permanently? After his body was recovered, I insisted for days that it wasn't him. It was a counterfeit, a dummy with my friend's lime-green fins slotted onto its plastic feet.

"You can't leave," Tony repeated, her voice rigid now with urgency. "Like, physically. It's not going to work."

I glared at Roger, even though I could tell he was as baffled by this statement as I was.

"I don't believe you," I told Tony.

She sighed, as if I were exhausting her. She stretched her arms until something in her back popped, and I jumped, certain I'd felt the tendons sliding over my own bones.

Tony lowered her arms and leveled her gaze at me. "Would you believe Nadia?"

• • •

My legs trembled after so many hours in bed. Tony tried to help me out Retreat-by-the-Sea's door, and I batted her away. I was still mad at her. It felt good to be mad at somebody.

The sky was overcast. We piled into a junky gold car that looked like it should've been driven by a tiny old man. I sat in the back, watching Tony's eyes flicker in the rearview mirror. The car prowled down Beach Street, the wipers cutting uneven streaks through the rain. I was full of questions, as, I assumed, was Roger, but we both remained quiet, bewitched by the spell of forward motion: We were finally getting somewhere. Further demands or protests risked undoing the progress that we'd made. It wasn't difficult to imagine Tony turning the car around like an exasperated dad plagued with one *Are we there yet?* too many.

The rain slowed to a drizzle by the time the gold car veered off Beach Street and started bumping down the path hemmed in by berry bushes. Tony parked in front of the gate, which yielded soundlessly at her touch. I slotted my hand over my forehead and squinted through the mist as we proceeded up the empty beach on foot, not at all happy to see where we were headed.

But Tony didn't lead us to the tower where Aldo had been lurking. Instead, we halted outside the attached cottage I'd peeked into last night: Shattering Point's lighthouse museum.

"Nadia's in there?" said Roger. He craned his neck to survey the top of the tower. "She's been in there this whole time?"

Could that be possible? As Aldo and I stood in the lantern room last night, watching Clementine rise from the depths, was Nadia sequestered just below us, held against her will, praying for Roger and me to come find her?

Tony pressed a doorbell. There was no answering chime from inside. Roger planted himself six inches back from the threshold as if preparing to rush whoever greeted us.

At least a full minute passed before the door opened. The woman in the cottage commanded a formidable presence despite being dwarfed by Roger's height. Long white hair waterfalled down her back beneath a dirty bucket hat. Her blue windbreaker was ripped at the sleeve, and her small, scornful eyes gleamed under the ridge of a heavy brow. It was hard to guess her age. Her skin was whorled with wrinkles, and from certain angles she appeared frail, but there was an undeniable strength about her, like a gnarled tree that you knew would outlive you.

Adding to the woman's intimidating aura was the walking stick she clutched, its brass handle twisted into the shape of a beady-eyed eagle.

Roger waffled. I saw that he'd mentally prepared himself for a face-off with a muscular foe, another Emmett Beckendorf he could meet with both fists raised. This grandma had thrown him for a loop. "Oh, um. Hello there, Sylvia—"

She lifted a hand without looking at him. Roger instantly quieted. Then the old woman shifted her eyes onto me, and for the third time, I felt that weird tug behind my sternum, the certitude that this stranger and I had met before.

"Has it happened, then?" Sylvia was still looking at me, but it was Tony who replied.

"Despite my best efforts. Jo, meet Sylvia Steele—museum curator, town clerk, unofficial president of Shattering."

Sylvia crushed my hand in a calloused grip. "Pleased to meet you, Dr. Ness. We've been looking forward to your arrival. I s'pose you've got questions . . ."

"They want to see Nadia," added Tony.

Roger relocated his courage. "What have you done with her? She's been missing *three days*! If you hurt her, I'll—"

"Oh, quit your blubbering. Your wife's fine. I'll take you to her now." Sylvia turned and lumbered inside, leaving Roger gaping after her.

We filed into the cottage. The place had been either impeccably preserved or studiously restored to capture a bygone era. In addition to the dining table I'd glimpsed last night, there was a large brick hearth, a vintage chandelier containing twelve cobwebby candles, and a desk with a scarred hutch. Framed photographs and laminated placards lined the walls. A few artifacts rested inside display cases: a compass, an oil lamp, a stack of shabby green books. Nadia was nowhere in sight.

Then Sylvia shifted one of the boxes and flipped up a corner of the dusty rug: There was a trapdoor in the floor, not unlike the one I'd climbed through to access the lantern room last night.

Roger peered down into the square hole with a grimace. It really did look like the entrance to a prison.

Sylvia descended the steps first, followed closely by Roger, then Tony. I was left in the cottage's living room by myself. A bad feeling was wafting out of the open trapdoor. *He's not down there,* I told myself sternly. *He died a thousand miles away. You saw the body. You have the ashes.* I shuffled forward and aligned my toes with the edge of the opening, thinking of the sea turtle urn on my mantel back in California, trying to summon its cool cylindrical weight. The urn was a bad joke: Aldo despised sea turtles, as he did all the ocean's charismatic megafauna. Those flagship species, universally beloved, remained utterly tedious to a man who favored the venomous and the slimy.

A scuffle of footsteps, and Tony's face appeared below mine. "Are you coming?" she said impatiently. "Or what?"

The tunnel sloped downward. The ceiling was low enough that I could extend a hand and graze the buzzy yellow lights. I decided that the best thing to do was to go as fast as possible—a plan that was foiled ten seconds later when I rounded the next bend and almost collided with Roger. Just ahead of him, Sylvia proceeded at a measured pace, her walking stick thudding the stone floor.

"How much farther?" I sounded high-pitched and trembly and not at all like myself.

Sylvia didn't answer. The tunnel was just wide enough that I could've squeezed past Roger and overtaken her, but I didn't like the idea of venturing onward alone. It would be just my luck to sprint ahead of the group only to hit a fork in the passage. One branch led to fresh air and freedom; the other, hours of panicked scrambling as the walls got tighter and tighter.

We pressed on for another few minutes. I tried to keep my thoughts on Nadia and nothing else. I was holding it together pretty well until, all at once, I wasn't.

I dropped to my knees, digging my fingers into the wall. This tunnel wasn't built to accommodate four bodies, all greedily sucking oxygen. There wasn't enough air.

Roger's face appeared at the end of a tiny aperture. "Are you all right? Is it happening again?"

"Nah," replied Tony's voice. "This looks like a good old-fashioned panic attack."

I wished she wasn't right. I wished I could blame these sensations on something beyond my control. Then it wouldn't be my fault. I wouldn't feel like such a failure.

"Have to get out of here," I mumbled, knuckling my sweaty forehead.

"You will. Just breathe," said Tony.

She told Roger to keep going. When I glanced up seconds or minutes later, the passage was empty. The shock of this latest abandonment rattled through me. First Nadia, then Aldo, now Roger. Why couldn't I keep people in my life?

But Tony was still here, close enough now that I could actually smell her—a clean, laundry-like fragrance with notes of coconut that might've come from her shampoo. A warm weight descended on the back of my neck. For a frightening, disembodied moment, the scene inverted: I was suspended above myself, and my fingers were Tony's fingers, smoothing the knots of tension away.

The vertigo broke as soon as she started speaking.

"It's really not far. We're just headed down to the water."

The prospect of being near the ocean did nothing to relax me.

"There's a harbor," Tony went on, her voice steady, more soothing than I'd ever heard it. "Small, tucked away. This whole setup came about during Prohibition. Rumrunners brought booze down from Canada. The last lighthouse keeper made a fortune off it. If you really want to get Sylvia riled up, mention how her granddaddy dearest was a big-time smuggler."

I was aware that she was telling me this history as a distraction, and I was grateful for it. "Sylvia's grandfather was the lighthouse keeper?"

"Old Gus loyally maintained the light for twenty-two years—right up until he was found dead in his bed one morning. Shady circumstances."

"Poison?" I asked, thinking of Aldo.

"So the rumors said. He was in business with some bad dudes."

The air in the tunnel was flowing a little easier. This grim story was having the same paradoxically comforting effect as my mother's gruesome tales: a tragedy held apart from me, where I could study all its jagged edges without worrying I'd get cut. I wondered how Tony had known it was exactly what I needed.

She lowered her hand from my neck, but the warmth of her fingers lingered. I released my hold on the wall and rose to my feet. We stared at each other in the close space of the tunnel. As the last of my anxiety siphoned away, a feeling of awkwardness set in. I was torn between wanting to thank Tony and wanting to forget this humiliating episode ever happened.

"Onward?" she said finally.

I nodded. "Onward."

• • •

The tunnel spit us out on a scoop of gravelly beach. The bluff we'd just passed through arced out in a long forested promontory, forming a small cove. It was raining still, but the afternoon sun showed its face through a twisting veil of clouds. At the end of the beach, I could make out a boathouse with peeling red paint, a few muddy skiffs stacked with tools, and a couple of larger boats moored to a floating dock. The languid water of the cove made for such a stark contrast with the lashing waves beneath the lighthouse, it was as if the tunnel had transported us to a different island altogether.

The lighthouse itself was out of view, blocked by trees. Even from the vantage point of the lantern room, there would be no way to see what was going on down here, and the tunnel seemed like it was the only access point from land. The cove was perfectly camouflaged. A smuggler's paradise.

Sylvia led us to a large cabin squatting in the mouth of the forest, spruce branches sprawled across the roof.

"Shoes off," she ordered, and blocked the doorway with her walking stick until Roger and I pried off our muddy sneakers.

Sock-footed, we followed the old woman down a wood-paneled passage, Tony bringing up the rear. The hallway terminated in a nondescript door. Sylvia removed a brass key from a nail next to the frame. Roger was visibly struggling to contain his impatience now that it seemed a single door separated us from his wife, but in the seconds-long pause before it opened, I felt a flicker of doubt. What if this was all a trap? There was no Nadia—just a small bare room in which Roger and I would be confined until the islanders decided what to do with us.

The room we entered was small, but not bare. It contained a large table, several chairs, a couch, and a wood cabinet with a built-in sewing machine. Perched in one of the chairs with an expanse of green yarn draped across her lap and a skein resting at her feet was a small red-haired person I recognized.

"Nadia!" Roger sprang across the room with the agility of a much smaller man and wrapped his arms around her. My whole body tensed with the urge to drag him away. "Nadia, my god, you're alive, I've been so worried. Are you all right? How did you—? What are you—?" He ran out of words and settled for planting his nose into her neck.

"Told you she was fine," grumbled Sylvia.

The Rooftop

Jellyfish are not known as social creatures. The vast jelly blooms that make headlines are a strategy for reproduction, rather than an indication of true gregariousness. These r-selected species do not rear or have any relationship with their offspring. If jellyfish communicate with each other, they do so in a language we cannot comprehend.

JN: Yet.

The heavy metal door swung shut with a thud, knocking against the brick used to wedge it ajar. Nadia strode briskly across the roof toward me. Gladstone College's science building faced east, where the quarter moon was brightening over the glossy blackness of the football field. The whole campus was steeped in the suffering quiet of finals week. I could hear the white light draining from the long-dead stars overhead, and my own thoughts, pounding away inside my skull with drumlike intensity.

I had scooted right to the edge of the rooftop, legs hanging, flip-flops dangling off the ends of my toes. Nadia sat, as always, to the left and a little behind me, not quite so indifferent to the forty-foot drop to the pavement below. But she never told me to move back. Ours wasn't that kind of friendship. Neither of us played mother hen. The closeness born of our caffeine-fueled late-night Japanese study sessions had spread into other realms. We took rambling walks around the athletic fields and cooked meals together in Nadia's off-campus apartment. She had plenty of options for company—an eclectic collection of friends pieced together from her many extracurricular activities—but she guiltlessly blew off other social engagements to spend time with me. She confessed to feeling lonely in her usual crowd: Everyone was settling into their postcollege groove, defining themselves by their plans for the future or lack thereof. Anxiety and bragging abounded. Nadia had no idea where she was headed and didn't view this as a problem. Wasn't the potential of the adventure always more exciting than the adventure itself?

She liked hanging out with me, she claimed, because I was both totally grounded and totally liberated from the straitjacket of social niceties. I could not schmooze or grandstand if I tried. I cared about what I cared about; the rest could go to hell. "People like that are the ones who save the world," she said. I doubted there would be any world saving in my future as a jellyfish scientist, but I admired the ruthless, ambitious person I was becoming in Nadia's eyes.

The rooftop was our special place. The custodian kept the door propped for his smoke breaks and looked the other way when I came up here to stretch my legs or give my eyes a rest after working for hours in the lab. Nadia thrilled at the view and the illicitness of being up high in a forbidden place. She liked to recline on her back and trace her fingertip around the constellations her grandpa had taught her the names of. Boötes, the herdsman. Virgo. Cancer. Hydra, the sea serpent, of which only its orangey alpha star was visible.

There were no constellations named after jellyfish, an injustice Nadia remedied by making one up for me. I dubbed it *Stygiomedusa*—the great phantom jellyfish that dwelled in the deep seas. It swam in the spring skies somewhere near Ursa Minor, and I could never find it without Nadia's help.

Tonight, after a minute of silence had passed, Nadia said, "I've been worried about you. You disappeared. You weren't answering my texts. What happened? Where did you go?"

"My dad died," I said.

"Oh, Josie . . . I'm so sorry. Why didn't you say anything?"

"I didn't want to bum you out right before finals."

"You wouldn't have bummed me out. I would've helped you."

It was nice of her to say—Nadia was always saying nice things, which she meant sincerely—but if my recent passage into the country of grief had taught me anything, it was that you wandered those shores alone. Even my mother, who shared this loss with me, was shrouded in her own private and mysterious anguish. They had known each other so long before I was born, their miraculous late-in-life child. My father was a year younger than me when he embarked on the exchange program to Kyoto, an old city full of old temples and rock gardens, his flame-red hair turning heads wherever he went. I had known the facts of my parents' unlikely love story since early childhood, but it upset me now to imagine them young and unburdened with their whole lives ahead of them.

"Was he sick?" asked Nadia.

"He'd had some heart issues. Nothing that made us think he'd drop dead. My mom found him on the kitchen floor."

"How awful . . ."

"There was a big fight about the funeral. His brother wanted him buried in the same cemetery as their parents, but Mom said he wanted to be cremated."

"Who won?"

"Mom, of course. There's no convincing her of anything. We're going to take a trip to Kyoto this summer and scatter the ashes where my parents met."

"That'll be nice."

I nodded, but the truth was I feared any extended time with my mother without my father as a buffer. He'd always played peacekeeper between us. It was likely that the trip would devolve into sniping and huffy, drawn-out silences before we'd landed in Haneda.

"Maybe there's something we can do for him here," said Nadia.

"What do you mean?"

"Like a way of honoring him. What was he into? What did he like?"

"Being outside."

"Check," said Nadia, spreading her arms to embrace the summer night.

"Gardening, cooking, fishing, camping . . . He read these cheesy detective novels where it was so obvious who did it. He said it relaxed him. He watched basketball games. He meditated every morning, even on Christmas. I used to do it with him sometimes when I was little."

"That's it!" cried Nadia, her voice catching with excitement.

"What's it?"

"Let's meditate. I've always wanted to try. You can teach me."

It was just like Nadia to express gleeful enthusiasm for what amounted to sitting and doing nothing. "It's been a long time," I cautioned. "And I was never any good at it. I'm going to be a really bad teacher."

"That's okay. I'll be a bad student. We'll match. I close my eyes, right?"

"You can." I rotated on the rooftop to face her. There was just enough of a glow leaking from the floodlight by the door for me to make out the shine of her glasses, the big white G on her Gladstoners sweatshirt. I never got into all that school spirit stuff. Gladstone was just a place where I found myself, a dot on a map. I never intended to take away anything from college except my degree. Until I met Nadia. "It's really about doing whatever is comfortable," I said. "Whatever will help you concentrate."

Nadia closed her eyes. I kept mine open, not even trying to follow my own instructions as I coached her to focus on the solidness of the rooftop beneath her, then home in on the sensations of her breathing. The coolness of the air entering her nostrils, the warmth as it exited. Nadia breathed steadily. I felt like a voyeur, but I couldn't pull my stare away.

We'd be leaving each other soon. The thought should not have surprised me, but I was sore with grief, newly sensitive to all life's casual cruelties. Graduation was in four days. In a month I'd be moving to Oregon to start grad school, and wherever Nadia was going, it was not there. Not with me.

When I estimated ten minutes had passed, I told Nadia she could open her eyes. She wiggled and stretched her arms.

"Wow. That was—"

"Relaxing?"

"Nerve-racking. I'm not used to being quiet with myself like that."

"It's impressive you were able to find any quiet at all. Usually people's thoughts are way too loud the first few times. Dad called it 'taming the monkey mind.'"

"You're a better teacher than you think," said Nadia, smiling.

There she was, being nice to me again.

We settled into a comfortable quiet. I resumed sitting with my legs sweeping the empty air, and Nadia flopped backward to look at the stars. I felt hollow, scraped raw, as I had ever since my phone woke me last week at five in the morning and I answered to hear my mother screaming in mixed English and Japanese, sounding less distressed than angry, as if Dad's death were all my fault.

Then I felt a slight tug on the end of my foot. A laugh rang out of the empty hole in my chest.

"What?" said Nadia.

"One of my shoes fell off."

She sat up. "Should we go get it?"

By way of answer, I kicked off my second flip-flop. There was no sound of it hitting the pavement below.

"Hang on, let me do mine!" Nadia wrenched off her Converse and winged them into the night.

I balled up my sweatshirt and tossed it. She shimmied out of her jean shorts, then flung both her socks. We were giddy with laughter as clothing rained off the rooftop. Nothing had ever been so funny before.

At last, as sobered by the prospect of dashing down the brightly lit stairwells of the science building in our underwear as we were by one another's near nakedness, we stopped laughing. Light illuminated the right side of Nadia's body, gathering in the scoop of her collarbone, the hollow of her hip. She scooted closer, and when we kissed, pleasure rippled through me like a caffeine jolt. Nadia was tense, careful. The hard bumpy surface of the roof grated against my shoulders as I leaned back and hoisted her on top of me.

I felt pinned between two contradictory certainties—that if I didn't have sex with Nadia, I would regret it for the rest of my life, but that I would also regret it if I did.

She sighed, and I didn't know what to make of the sound, which could've signaled pleasure or exasperation, boredom or relief. The whole of Gladstone College held its breath around us, the whole of the world. I felt cradled in the center of a vast and awesome stillness.

We made our decision simultaneously. We were sharing a brain, like Professor Hano had suggested. It was thrilling to be joined with someone like that. Nadia brought her face down to meet mine, her hand tightening around my waist. I felt her shiver as the breeze pulled the night air across our skin. It was still too cold to be lying around without clothes on, and I was a little worried the custodian was about to appear for his next smoke break. But I didn't even think of moving.

Reunion

Computer modeling plus good old-fashioned field ecology has allowed scientists to better predict when and where jellyfish blooms will occur. In Hawaii, a decade of research has revealed that the shoreward migration of box jellies corresponds to the lunar calendar, with the biggest spike in numbers occurring eight to ten days after the full moon. "Jelly forecasts" may soon become a standard feature of the local meteorological report in coastal cities, as routine as precipitation and humidity.

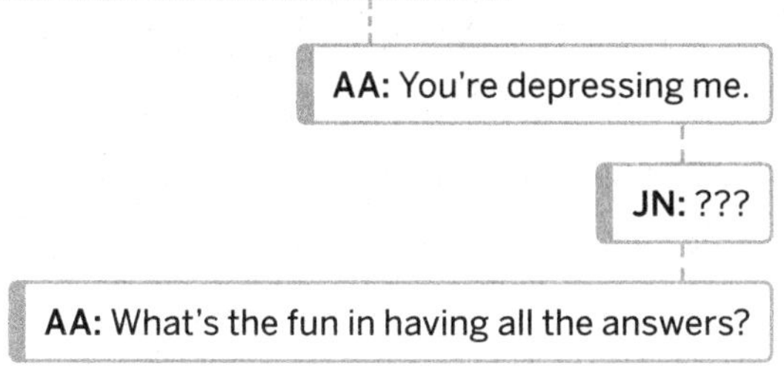

Nadia seemed as shocked to see us as we were to see her. She rose with difficulty—Roger's arms were still latched around her—and let her knitting needles tumble to the floor.

"Josie, you came." Her voice sounded different from how I remembered now that I was finally hearing it in person—deeper, more grown-up. It was exhilarating to be in the same room as her, finally, after over a decade apart, yet somehow the ten feet of faded linoleum stretching between us seemed vaster than the thousands of miles that had separated us during our estrangement. I'd envisioned this moment too many times, and now all I could focus on was the ways it did not live up to fantasy. Nadia's glasses were wrong, the black square-framed pair from our college years upgraded to a round, frameless style that made her face look too naked. Tony and Sylvia stood clustered in the doorway, and Roger went on clinging to Nadia like she was a human life preserver. The couple's size difference struck me as ridiculous. The top of her head barely reached his breastbone. I wished everyone were gone, that it could just be me and Nadia.

I forced down these disappointments and hitched a smile onto my face. "Of course I came. You asked me to."

I'd been hoping for a display of gratitude. Instead, Nadia looked like she was going to cry.

She turned away from me, toward Roger, and that hurt more than anything I'd endured on Shattering Point so far.

"What happened to you?" Nadia tipped Roger's chin up and traced a finger around the outline of the yellowing bruise.

"Nothing. That doesn't matter. What happened to *you*?" There was anger in Roger's voice now, the kind that was twinned with relief.

Nadia offered a weak smile. "I've been safe and sound, if a little cooped up." She gave Sylvia a hard look that lacked heat. Nadia had never been the glaring type. "I'm not thrilled about how this played out, either, but I know Sylvia has the whole island's safety to think about . . . and she's been taking good care of me. She even taught me how to knit. Look!" She snatched the length of green yarn from the chair and displayed it with a kind of desperate cheer: the lumpy beginnings of a scarf. "It's for you. It'll go great with your winter coat, won't it?"

Roger took the scarf and held it limply, at a loss for words. I couldn't think of anything to say, either. I'd fretted over so many possible explanations for Nadia's disappearance the past few days, and here she'd been the whole time, locked in some old lady's sewing room. She didn't even seem that angry about it. This was more than people-pleasing: Nadia had been Stockholm syndromed.

"Let's go outside," suggested Tony, breaking the awkward silence.

We gathered at a picnic table between the cabin and the boathouse. The rain had halted. The spring air was misty and cool. Sylvia brought out a canister of stale cookies and glared at me until I took one.

"I don't understand," Roger said. He had eyes only for Nadia, was looking at her like he'd never seen her before. "You just took off for three days to stay in some random cabin and take knitting lessons? Without telling me? This whole time I thought you'd been injured or fallen off a boat and drowned . . ."

The distress in his voice annoyed me. "You didn't think any of that," I reminded him. "You were convinced she got caught up in one of her schemes and ran off to the mainland, remember? *I* had to tell *you* to call the police." It was essential that Nadia know I'd never bought into her husband's dismissiveness, that *I'd* been the one who cared.

"It wasn't like that, Rog," Nadia said. She cast a nervous look at Sylvia, as if asking for permission. The old woman shrugged.

"It's none of my concern how you want to explain things. This was never about him."

My pulse fluttered as Nadia finally looked at me. "So, then—you saw it?" Her voice was hushed and trembling.

"Saw what?" demanded Roger.

"What's the kid call it again?" Tony asked. "Caroline?"

"Clementine," grunted Sylvia. "Damn stupid name, if you ask me. One of us should've gotten in there earlier, come up with something better . . ."

"Saw *what*?" Roger was working himself into a frenzy.

"The giant jellyfish," I said. So Nadia had gone searching for it after all.

Everyone was looking at me now, awaiting my confirmation. I hesitated to give it to them. Whether it was a side effect of smacking my head on the boat floor or a more willful sort of amnesia, the memory of what I'd witnessed in the lantern room had taken on a surreal and fragmented quality, like the recollection of a dream. I wanted Clementine to be real, but her appearance had become fused with the nightmarish vision of Aldo. My mind would not permit me to have one without the other.

I sat in silence, paralyzed, until Tony answered for me:

"Of course she saw it. Can't you tell, Nadia? Just look at her. Look closely."

But Nadia had glued her eyes to the picnic table, refusing to glance up at me again. It was so like that afternoon at Gladstone's graduation—the averted gaze, the stubborn press of her lips, my full-body horror at becoming repellent to the person I cared about most—that I nearly jumped to my feet and bolted. Only my desire for answers kept me in my seat.

"Can someone *please*," I said, glaring around the table at everyone but Nadia, whom I vowed to ignore for as long as she was ignoring me, "tell me what's going on here?"

Sylvia aimed her stare out past the boathouse, into the smooth waters of the cove. "The jellyfish first surfaced in October, on the full moon." Her voice was deep and steady; I experienced a dizzying falling-through-time sensation, as if I were a child at bedtime again, listening to one of my mother's stories. "It was exciting, in the beginning. Shattering's very own sea monster. All the locals came out to see it. Hell, even Norm Sloan left his garden to come up to the bluff. Everyone wanted a piece of it, wanted to feel special. And it did make you feel special. It was almost like—" She broke off, searching for the right words.

"Like it was talking to you," supplied Tony. "I know that sounds crazy, but . . ."

It was not crazy. Or maybe it was just a kind of crazy I could understand. I had long felt that the cadence of a jellyfish moving through the water was a kind of secret language, one we humans were just too obtuse to comprehend.

"There was talk of monetizing the thing," added Tony. "Monster tourism. Make an Instagram, sell T-shirts. Then the holidays rolled around. Folks were planning on leaving the island to see family on the mainland. That was when we realized . . ."

"Something funny happens when you try to leave Shattering," said Sylvia, her face hard and unsmiling. "A mile out, you start to feel a little queasy, even if you've never been seasick a day in your life. And it only gets worse from there."

"We've been calling it the barrier," said Tony. "Its exact borders seem to fluctuate, but it circles the whole island, and it always extends farther on the seaward side. That's how the fishing boats can still get out."

"Small miracles." Sylvia crunched through a cookie, the sound unnaturally loud in the stillness beneath the trees.

Roger lobbed a baffled look among the four of us. "You're saying you can't leave? You're trapped here?"

Sylvia winced.

"We try to avoid using the T-word," said Tony. "It really bums people out. But in essence, yeah. There's just no going past a certain point. We obviously had to ditch the monster tourism idea after that. Can you imagine the slogan? *Come to Shattering Point . . . the island that never lets you go!*"

"But what—how—?" Roger had lost his capacity for language again, and for once I was with him. None of this made any sense.

"Took us a while to work it out." Tony looked toward the water, too, her fingers tightening around the edge of the table. "But it's the jellyfish. No one who's laid eyes on Clementine can get more than a few miles off the island."

A pronounced silence fell, which I took it upon myself to break:

"That's impossible." My voice was flat and cold.

"It's not, though," said Tony sharply. "You saw yourself what happens."

Roger darted a terrified look at me. *Like you ran headlong into a brick wall.*

I remembered his description of my collapse, too, but unlike Roger, I refused to be cast in whatever insane fable these people had constructed.

"That's *impossible*," I repeated. "I know jellyfish. I've spent half my life studying them. What you're describing goes beyond anything that's ever been—"

"You don't know this one," said Sylvia.

"Why didn't you warn us?" Roger had recovered from his shock and sounded angry again. "Nadia and I moved here after you already knew. All of this could've been avoided if you'd just been honest!"

"*I* wanted to tell you guys about Clementine as soon as you got here. We held a town meeting the day after Christmas. I was outvoted." Tony flicked her eyes at Sylvia.

"Now wait just a second there, Roger," said Sylvia, silencing his next protest. "Think that through. You and Nadia arrive on Shattering in January. Someone sits you down, explains we've got a possessive sea monster on our hands. What would you have done?"

"Gotten the fuck out of here," said Roger.

"You sure about that?" Sylvia was looking not at Roger but at Nadia.

Nadia pressed her hand on top of his. "C'mon, Rog. Be fair. You know I never would've quit my job on the basis of some urban legend. And you never would've believed it in the first place. Not without proof. One or both of us would've gotten curious and gone looking. And then—"

"You'd be exactly where we are now," finished Sylvia. "Except you'd both be stuck."

Roger was silent. Nadia withdrew her hand and tucked it into her lap.

"After Sidney showed me his video and I talked to Josie, I came down here on Tuesday to try and get a peek at the jellyfish. I got lucky—or unlucky, depending on your perspective."

"Clementine only surfaces on the full moon," explained Sylvia. "And for the two days after. We keep the beach fenced off during those nights."

"It was open," I said. It felt reassuring to state an objection grounded in material reality, one nobody could reasonably dispute. "Last night when I came to the beach—the gate wasn't locked."

"Well, no," said Sylvia irritably. "We were trying to make it easy for you. Although not easy enough. You were supposed to see Clementine on Wednesday night. This one was supposed to take you." She jerked her head at Tony, who twisted her mouth in a grimace. "After she got cold feet, Emmett stepped in, and you know how that ended. My god, girl, for someone who supposedly loves jellyfish, you sure as hell made it hard for us to take you to ours! But it all worked out in the end . . ."

It was my turn to shoot a confused look around the table. "You *wanted* me to see Clementine? Why?"

"Isn't it obvious?" Sylvia smiled, and through the deep wrinkles on her face, I could suddenly discern the shape of her skull, the cavernous hollows of the eye sockets, the violent jut of each cheekbone. "We need your help, Dr. Ness," she said. "We need you to help us kill it."

Her words snapped something in me, and it was a blessing. I felt freed from any need to entertain the remainder of this ridiculous conversation, any need to regain Nadia's affection or force these people to see sense. It had been a mistake to let Tony talk me into coming here.

I'd had enough of all of them. I'd had enough of Shattering Point.

I turned and stalked up the beach, already resolving to take the tunnel at a sprint.

"Jo, wait—!" Footsteps skidded on gravel behind me. It was not Nadia but Tony chasing after me. A gull erupted from the top of the boathouse, squawking.

Tony overshot me and stopped, arms extended, palms out, as if trying to placate a wild animal. We faced each other at the boundary where gravel turned to patchy grass. The entrance to the tunnel loomed ahead of me, and silence stretched behind—Sylvia, Nadia, and Roger still clustered around the picnic table, watching our little drama unfold. Somehow, I had become Tony's responsibility to manage. Tony's problem to solve.

"I know this is insane. I know you don't want to believe us." The words tumbled out of her in a breathless rush. "We tried to call someone from the state, and they wouldn't believe us, either. They thought it was some kind of prank. And then this week when Nadia saw it, she told Sylvia she'd called you, and you were this jellyfish expert, and you were *already on your way . . .*"

"Move," I said. Clearly, I had misjudged Tony. She was as deranged as the rest of them. I would escape this island with or without her blessing, with or without Roger's support. I had found my way out of the cave where I'd lost Aldo. I would find my way off Shattering Point.

It was as if the memory summoned him.

His stretched-out silhouette loomed over Tony's shoulder, so close she would've felt his exhalations against her neck were he still breathing. This time, there was no disorienting light show on which to blame the illusion. Aldo was really here, arrayed in all the scuba gear he'd been wearing in the lantern room. The useless gear he'd had on him when he died.

Tony didn't miss the way my mouth had fallen open, my gaze fixed on a point behind her. She whipped her head around—they were face-to-face now, she and Aldo, her eyes staring unseeingly into the murky screen of his mask. By the time she looked back at me, wearing a nonplussed frown, dread had turned my knees to jelly, and I'd sunk right onto the ground.

"This isn't happening," I muttered. "Not happening, not happening . . ."

Aldo's hand lifted into the air just as it had last night, and I dropped my stare, clinging to the juvenile certainty that if I just avoided looking at him, he would go away.

Tony sank down beside me, her hand on my back. "You're overwhelmed—I get it. I didn't want it to happen this way. But it did, and you're here, and, well—would it be the worst thing to try and help us?"

A strangled laugh died in my throat. Help them? I was losing it. I could barely help myself.

"Josie?"

Nadia's voice was the only thing in the world that could've wrenched my stare from the ground. She stood a few feet away. There were tears in her eyes. This was turning into a really shitty reunion.

"I'm sorry," she whispered. "I swear I didn't know when I called you. I thought it was a regular jellyfish, just a big one. But it's true—Sylvia took me out on the water, and you can't go far, you'll get really sick. It's like—like your body's being pulled out of itself, and your skin hurts, and you can't breathe." A cold recognition pooled inside my stomach. I fought the sensation that I was back aboard *The Phantom Maiden*, the air thickening around me. "I wanted to call you and warn you, but they wouldn't let me. I was so, so angry with them, Josie, I really was. All I could do was hope that when you couldn't find me, you'd turn around and go back . . ." Her voice cracked. I realized she was pleading.

I wasn't sure who Nadia was to me anymore, but I took no pleasure in seeing her reduced to tears on my behalf. And I did not believe she was a liar.

I took a deep breath and got to my feet, careful to keep my back to the tunnel and the Aldo specter that seemed as determined to stop me from leaving as Tony was. Tony and Nadia both scrambled back, as if expecting me to strike them. But that frightening calmness had settled over me again. It was only with a scientist's detached logic that I could continue to hold myself together.

"How many people are stuck here?" I asked coolly.

"Including you?" Tony took a moment to do the calculation. "I think we're at forty-seven."

"What about flying over this barrier?"

"Doesn't work."

"What about swimming—?"

"Nope. Took three of us almost drowning to work that one out."

"It's got to be killed!" called Sylvia. She and Roger were walking up the beach toward us. Roger immediately seized Nadia's hand, like she'd disappear again if she weren't glued to his side.

I was staggered by Sylvia's ignorance. Her arrogance. "If even half of what you're saying is true, Clementine is the most incredible cnidarian to ever be encountered by humans. And you just want to *destroy* her?" I shouldn't have been surprised. It was the same old hatred, the same old popular disdain that Aldo and I had been trying to reverse with our book. It was Pamela still harping on a jellyfish sting decades later. It was Cousin Theo swinging his stick.

"Why would you even need help killing a jellyfish?" Roger demanded. "Aren't they, like, all water?"

"This one's different. We've tried killing it," said Tony. "Over and over. Nothing works."

Roger threw up his arms, so exasperated he momentarily relinquished his grip on Nadia. "Then how hard can you possibly have been trying?"

"Listen, you little wiseass," growled Sylvia, knocking the beak of her eagle-headed walking stick against Roger's sternum; it took some stretch of the imagination to think of Roger as *little*, and he puffed up against the challenge, squaring his shoulders and glaring down his nose at the old woman. "You have no idea what we've been through. We tried our damnedest to keep you and Nadia out of it. How about a little gratitude for that?"

Roger laughed hollowly. "You'll have to forgive me if I don't feel especially grateful to my wife's kidnapper!"

They argued. Tony tried to reestablish order by outshouting them both. Nadia looked stricken. I remembered how much infighting among her Gladstone friends had upset her, how badly she'd always needed everyone to get along.

While everybody was distracted, I snuck a glance over my shoulder. The mouth of the tunnel was dark and empty. My vision of Aldo had disintegrated. If the real Aldo were here, what would he have done? Not fled from what he didn't understand. Not condemn the most amazing jellyfish he'd ever seen to whatever fate these people assigned her.

I still didn't know what I believed, or what I trusted myself to find out. But one thing was for sure: Something highly unusual was happening on Shattering Point, and a giant jellyfish was at the center of it. I needed to fend off the islanders long enough to start gathering answers, figure out how Clementine's nature worked and what the implications were for jellyfish everywhere.

"Maybe," I said, pitching my voice so as to be heard above the bickering, "maybe there's another way."

Roger paused mid-retort, his mouth open. Sylvia lowered her walking stick and looked at me.

"Maybe there's a way to get off Shattering *without* killing Clementine," I clarified.

Tony and Sylvia traded glances.

"You think you can figure out a way for us to, what, outsmart this thing?" Tony asked.

"Of course she can," Nadia interjected passionately. "Josie's incredible, okay? She's an absolute genius where jellyfish are concerned. She'll know how to help us. She's going to figure this out!"

She flitted me a hesitant smile, which I didn't return. Her words had the cringey quality of obvious hyperbole. She was trying to flatter me, without bothering to address any of the things she'd done wrong: ditching me at Gladstone; failing to mention her freaking *husband*; inviting me here, on an extravagant whim, without having the slightest idea what she was getting me into.

"I don't know what I can do," I corrected her. Nadia deflated at the rebuke, and it sent a petty satisfaction soaring through me. I faced Tony and Sylvia, trying to look like a sane, trustworthy person who definitely wasn't hallucinating her dead best friend. "But I do know that I need more time to understand Clementine."

"Time, sure." Sylvia chuckled, and we all followed her gaze to the just-risen moon, dangling above the tree line like a pale gray apple with a sliver cut from it. "You have twenty-six days," she said.

* * *

This time I led the way through the tunnel beneath the lighthouse, moving at a pace just short of actual running. Sylvia stayed behind in the cove. Nadia, Roger, and Tony were soon lost to the twists and turns behind me. I didn't want to talk to any of them. They had all, in their way, deceived me—except Roger, whose mere existence was betrayal enough.

With every step, I felt my scientist's logic ebbing away, leaving a slippery panic in its wake. I had bought myself some time, and I had no idea how to use it. I was trapped here. Helpless. Alone. The smuggler's tunnel closed in on me, pinning me in place even as I hurtled through it.

I could sense Aldo around every bend in the passage like it was one of my dreams, but it wasn't until I'd burst through the trapdoor and spilled out of the lighthouse keeper's cottage onto the bluff that I saw him again, a solitary figure posed on the bitter edge of Shattering Point. He stood facing me on the cliff, half a step from toppling over the edge, untouched by the cold wind blowing off the Atlantic.

Form is emptiness and emptiness is form. There is no eye, no ear, no nose, no tongue, no body, no mind. I never understood why the blind priest in my mother's story reached for those cryptic words as the monster moved toward the surface. But I got it now. What a gift to be scraped clean of selfhood at the moment the knowable world split open and nightmares slithered out.

Monster in Motion

Contrary to popular belief, not all jellyfish are drifters, pushed about by the whims of wind and tide. The steady contractions and pulsations of a jelly's bell in fact make for a highly efficient form of swimming. They can lift and lower themselves in the water column as they avoid predators or hunt for prey. They can move with a purpose.

AA: They got places to BE, baby!

Twenty-six days. A lot could happen in that time: an entire body's worth of skin cells regenerated, an entire bloom of jellyfish gathered and dispersed. In twenty-six days, the short-lived male black widow could father a thousand baby spiderlings and then die in the jaws of its hungry, cannibalistic mate. Wars could be launched. Relationships formed and ruined.

Three days in, my biggest achievement was getting really drunk.

I wasn't alone, and why would I be? The people of Shattering Point had been trapped on this miserable rock for months. At the Urchin, after the sun went down, the island's facade cracked open, and the frustration came fountaining out. Here at last was the town as it truly existed, pretty performances melted away. Men with long beards and leathery skin cackled at the counter. A waif-thin woman tottered past on her way to the bathroom, arms thrown out like a tightrope walker straining to keep her balance. A shoving crowd gathered around the pool table, cue sticks clacking as a red-faced couple fenced their way across the floor. A second group was engaged in a raucous game that involved pitching items into the fishing nets that dangled from the ceiling—coins and bottle caps first, then their own shoes, hats, and someone's glasses yanked right off his blotchy nose.

The blue-haired waitress moved through the masses with ethereal grace, keeping us all hydrated with cupfuls of watery beer. I feared mine contained a healthy dose of spit; I remembered how friendly she'd seemed with Emmett Beckendorf and how she'd screamed at me when I struck him with the bottle. I drank it anyway. I hated the taste, but it was doing the trick. I hadn't encountered Aldo since he'd materialized on the bluff. Even my bad dreams had stopped, drunken slumber smacking me like a blow to the back of the head.

I couldn't bear to see him like that again. A twisted version of the thing I desired most in this world. Hard evidence of my slipping grasp on the real. I was afraid, but I was also angry at myself. I had never really mourned Aldo. I'd never let myself weep and break down and rail against the injustice of the universe. I'd never reckoned with my guilt, or even told anyone I felt responsible for his death.

I was paying for all of that now. Seven months of suspended sorrow had crashed into me, leaving me dumb and broken in its wake. I wanted to be better than this, but I didn't know how.

A cheer went up from the bar as someone scored a point in the net-throwing game. My eyes landed on a man sulking on a stool in the corner, alone, like a boy who'd been excluded on the playground. Roger recognized me at the same moment I recognized him.

He slumped into my booth without asking, just as he had my first night on Shattering. Since I'd last seen him at the cove, the bruise under his eye had faded to a dull smear, barely noticeable in the bar's dim lighting. Maybe it was the beer, but I felt awash in unexpected sympathy for him.

"Cheers," I said, lifting my cup.

Roger frowned, and then, seeming to interpret the gesture as the peace offering it was, clunked his cup against mine.

He sipped. I guzzled.

"You want to maybe slow down there?"

"Nope." I set my cup down on the table, scattering a group of ants that were clustered around a sticky spill. "Why aren't you home with Nadia?" I recognized that I was fishing for more evidence of marital problems—a consolation prize to help dull my lingering sense of abandonment. After her passionate soliloquy on my "genius," Nadia had yet to reach out to me.

But Roger wasn't going to give it up that easily. "I got my boat back," he offered instead. "Sylvia asked Emmett to move it out to the cove after Nadia saw that thing. They were all in on it together. They really wanted me to think she'd left me."

"But she didn't." Annoyance creased the edges of my buzz. There he went again, making this whole situation about *his* feelings, when he was the only one who'd been spared. Sylvia had said it herself: Sequestering Nadia was never about Roger. It was about getting me here, baiting me into seeing Clementine so I'd be coerced into helping destroy her. Now I was stuck on Shattering Point. If anyone got to feel resentful about the way things turned out, it was me.

Roger wasn't going to lose his job when he failed to reappear after his two-week vacation.

Roger still had a way off this island if he wanted it.

Roger still had Nadia.

Someone laughed loudly by the pool table, and the noise drove a spike through my brain.

I took another drink, feeling the cold beer pool in my stomach.

Roger bowed his head closer to mine, and I saw from his glassy stare that for all his efforts to pace himself, he was drunk, too.

"So what's the plan?" he asked.

"Plan?"

"For getting past the jellyfish. I want to help. Please. I'm going crazy just doing nothing." He dug his fingers into his hair, which was so sweaty it maintained its tousled shape even after he dropped his hands back into his lap.

"I'm working on it," I said.

In my few sober moments, I had in fact shot off a dozen very weird emails to colleagues who'd authored papers on subjects related to what I knew of Clementine's behavior. Abyssal gigantism. Vertical migration. The lunar cycle's impact on marine spawning events. I kept my wording in these communications deliberately vague. I knew how I'd reacted to this so-called barrier, and I was afraid of being branded as crazy.

Another part of me feared the opposite: that I *would* be believed.

The terror and confusion of the past few days hadn't quite managed to snuff out my ego, which chafed at the thought of some other scientist showing up here and taking all the credit, shoving me away from the most exciting discovery of my life.

It was late May, the time when academics fled campuses for conferences and fieldwork. My inbox was promptly inundated with stiff little autoreplies. *I am out of the office until . . . I will have limited email access . . . Please expect a delayed response . . .* So far I'd only managed to get one guy on the phone, an Australian biologist I met during last summer's research cruise, an expert on light in the deep sea. I asked him whether there was any precedent for a long-term human reaction to marine bioluminescence—say, a rare type of paralysis, where one couldn't move past a specific geographic point? He listened to me talk for a while, then politely asked in his charming accent whether I was taking any drugs.

"What do we do, Jo?" persisted Roger. "How do we make Clementine let Nadia—let everyone—go?"

My annoyance deepened. The truth was I had no idea what to do, and I hated him for asking. How did you make sense of an animal that would be submerged in the depths of the ocean for the next twenty-three days? An animal that was unknown to science? An animal that defied all knowledge of what that animal should be capable of?

"You want to know what to do?" I flattened my palms against the table, feeling my arms tremble. "Move on with your life."

"Nadia *is* my life."

"Oh, Jesus, spare me the loyal husband act. We're not in a

fucking rom-com. We're in a horror story, and you're one of the lucky ones. So go on and get out of here. Isn't that what you've wanted all along? To get the hell off Shattering?"

"You'd like that, wouldn't you? Having her all to yourself."

A sneer had entered his voice. I felt a ripple of answering defensiveness pass through me.

"Don't be stupid. It's not like that."

"I *saw* the way you were looking at her."

I trusted my boozy glow to conceal the heat rising in my face. "It's not like that, Roger." And it wasn't. I was just a means to an end to Nadia. Once I solved the island's jellyfish problem—*if* I solved the island's jellyfish problem—our eleven-year estrangement would pick up right where it left off. I'd been so stupid to drop everything and come running here, thinking she cared about me, thinking she wanted to make amends.

"Well, I'm not abandoning her," Roger snapped. "So you can put that idea out of your head."

"Do what you want." I was done with this conversation. I staggered over to the bar for another beer, and when I got back to the booth, he was gone.

• • •

I didn't stay at the Urchin much longer. The encounter with Roger had stolen what peace I could find there. My legs autopiloted me down Beach Street, toward the shore. The sight of the water had always been a comfort to me. Too late, I remembered I wasn't that person anymore.

I halted on the dock, my throat constricting as I took in the flat blackness of the Gulf. The wooden posts were topped with small lamps, half of them dead, but I could still make out the boats, a dozen of them bobbing tauntingly in the water. In a sleepy town like this, a town where everyone knew everyone, surely it was custom to keep a spare key taped under the outboard or stashed in the glove box.

Do it, I urged, as I'd been commanding myself every waking hour since leaving the cove. My legs stayed stubbornly locked in place.

It wasn't a sense of loyalty or responsibility or my steadfast belief in what I'd been told that prevented me from trying to escape. It was fear. Nadia had described with perfect accuracy the physical symptoms I'd experienced while attempting to leave Shattering: the queasiness, the burning, the suffocating pain. But it had been more than that. I had relived my final moments with Aldo. I had felt his rage at me for abandoning him to die—not a preset constellation of unpleasant physical sensations, but a punishment so cruel, so personal, that whatever entity had concocted it was banking on my absolute refusal to risk a repeat experience.

It wasn't wrong. I didn't want to feel anything like that again. Ever.

Defeated, I turned to start trudging back up Beach Street—and startled at the sight of a human figure leaning against a lamppost. Panic cut through me before my eyes adjusted and I recognized it was Tony.

She'd also kept her distance from me since the cove. Or maybe I'd been keeping my distance from her. But I was hyper-attuned to her presence in Retreat-by-the-Sea at all times: the lingering whiff of coconut, the muffled pulse of her music, the screech of an ironing board as it opened.

And she'd been leaving me breakfast, too, these past couple of mornings: a thermos of coffee, a small plate of eggs, and two triangles of toast with a paper towel over the top to keep everything warm. I had wolfed down these offerings without gratitude, without thought.

"I see the research is going well," said Tony. I had shuffled into the cone of light shed by the streetlamp, and her eyes were slowly appraising as they took in my flushed face, unwashed hair, and rumpled clothes.

"What are you doing here?" I was trying not to sound rude and had no idea whether I'd succeeded.

She stepped forward, closing the gap between us. She had a jacket on, which was smart. The night air remained chilly. Now that I'd extricated myself from the Urchin's muggy press of bodies, I was starting to shiver.

"I've been instructed to keep an eye on you," Tony said, "in the event you get any ideas about hijacking a boat and throwing yourself against the barrier again."

I attempted to arrange my features into an expression that suggested I hadn't been thinking about doing exactly that.

"Instructed by who?" I asked sourly, slumping against the lamppost.

"The president herself, of course," answered Tony. "Sylvia Steele says 'jump,' we all say 'how high.'"

But that wasn't true, I thought. "She told you to take me to see the jellyfish," I said slowly, concentrating on not slurring my words, "and you didn't."

A cacophony of voices clattered down the street toward us. It must've been later than I realized; the Urchin had closed, expelling its patrons onto the sidewalk. Tony glanced briefly in their direction before her stare resettled on me.

"I guess, once I saw you, it really hit me: that we were potentially changing your life forever. Taking you away from your family, your friends, your job." She sighed. "I saw you and I felt bad for you."

I resisted the pity, which only deepened my sense of uselessness. "I don't need anyone to feel bad for me."

"No? You've been slouching around for days, drowning your sorrows, acting all pathetic—"

"I am not pathetic!"

"Prove it," she challenged.

I straightened too quickly, stumbling over a seam in the sidewalk. Tony reached out to steady me. I didn't pause to think about it: I put my hand on the back of her neck and pulled her lips to mine.

She tensed, then leaned into me hard. Shock at my own boldness fizzled into a delight that crackled to the ends of my hair. Tony tasted like the ocean and moved with its fluid power, her body contouring perfectly into mine. She propelled me backward into the lamppost, and I slid my fingers up the hot skin of her lower back, feeling her tremble. Or was I the one who was trembling? Elation bore down on me when I realized I couldn't tell where Tony ended and I began.

Precious seconds slipped by unnoticed before she withdrew. I floundered and tripped, coming to rest in a dazed pile at the foot of the lamppost.

Tony looked down at me and shook her head. "You smell like a backed-up drain."

She turned on her heel and marched toward the B and B.

* * *

The rejection had an instant sobering effect. I picked myself up off the ground and blundered into the street. The drunken mob had dispersed. The road lay bare and quiet beneath a sky smeary with stars, and the waning face of the moon watching silently. A ticking clock counting down Clementine's return.

My lips buzzed with the memory of the kiss. Had I really just thrown myself at Tony like a drunk, overzealous teenager at a homecoming dance?

Unable to bear the prospect of reencountering her just yet, I strode past the B and B and up the hill. I had no destination in mind, but it felt good to move my body. In addition to scuba diving, Aldo had been an avid runner. He was always trying to get me to train for races with him. I never told him, but I thought he looked funny when he ran: long arms pumping, elbows jutting. But in the water he was like a seal, all his land-bound ungainliness melting away.

I found myself wondering again: If Aldo were here, what would he do? I was sure he'd come up with something. He was open-minded in a way I was not. He thought outside the box, whereas I lived inside it. If ever there was a time for a touch of ridiculousness, it was here on Shattering Point, where my reasoning brain had failed me.

If I hadn't gotten him killed, I could've called him and asked for his advice.

But if Aldo were alive, would I have even ended up on Shattering? I had once used Aldo to try to replace Nadia. I had come to the island in an effort to do the reverse. Now I had no one.

Tony was right. I really was pathetic.

At the top of the hill, I paused. Norm Sloan's fairy-tale garden whispered beyond the picket fence. A light on the back of the house brightened slim pathways of white stone that wound between the plants, which nodded their heads agreeably in the night breeze. Despite the late hour, the gardener himself was on his hands and knees, packing slimy brown ribbons of what looked like seaweed into the dirt. I watched him lower his face until his nose brushed a striking yellow flower with a sunburst of scarlet at its center. The sight was strangely intimate, as if I'd burst into his bedroom while he was undressing.

I tried to peel off without being seen, but the German shepherd, Betty, gave me away again, charging down the white path toward the fence, barking her head off.

Norm startled as if waking from a trance. He rose stiffly to his feet and smacked his thigh. "Heel, girl." Betty fell back at once, dropping onto her haunches and gazing up at her master for approval.

Norm stared at me over the fence, and it was exactly like our encounter a few days back, except the now-familiar layer of uncanny recognition pulsed between us. I wondered what could explain this sensation, which Tony had referenced in the cove, too. *Of course she saw it. Can't you tell, Nadia? Just look at her.* Was it possible Clementine had coaxed a subtle new pheromone to the surface of our skin, enabling those of us who'd witnessed her to perceive this sameness in others? There was a clue there, but I couldn't pin it down. It didn't make any sense.

"You're still here," said Norm, without surprise.

"So is Nadia," I felt compelled to point out. "You lied when you said she'd left the island."

"Didn't lie. Didn't *know*." He wiped his hands on the front of his jeans. "I keep my distance from all this sea monster nonsense. Whatever's going on out there is none of my concern."

"Even though it means you're trapped here."

Norm showed no signs of agitation at my use of the forbidden word. "Who's trapped? I've got everything I need." He turned to survey his plants with pride. "When we bought the place, wasn't nothing here but a field full of sandy dirt and woodchuck burrows. It was three seasons before I got it looking the way I wanted. Had to fight with frost, drought, fungus . . ."

The odd thought struck me that Norm and my father would've had a lot to talk about. Though he was otherwise a man of few words, Dad never could resist the opportunity to wax poetic on compost and plant zones, soil drainage and root rot.

"I've got everything I need here," Norm repeated smugly. The front door opened suddenly to my right, swinging a triangle of light across the ground. "And just one thing I don't," he grunted.

Margo Sloan, the artist, the *empath*, stood on the front stoop, wrapped in an elaborate green dressing gown spotted with white cranes. The ginger wig she'd worn the day we met had been swapped out for a silky black bob.

Déjà vu yanked at me. Margo had seen Clementine, too.

"Josephine? Is that you?"

She said it like she'd been expecting me.

Norm retreated into his garden as I let Margo fling an arm around my shoulder and sweep me inside. It wasn't like I had anywhere else to be.

"How are you, dear? Have you been eating enough? Sleeping? Your aura is very cloudy." She guided me down a narrow hall and into a room easily identifiable as an artist's studio by the stacks of canvases and folded-up easels. A pungent odor of citrus lingered. I thought it was paint until Margo stuck a mug under my nose and the smell intensified. "Tea?" she asked brightly.

"No, thank you."

Margo waggled the mug, insistent. "It's my own blend. Good for digestion, good for opening the third eye. Do you know I'm sixty-two years old, and I'm not on a single prescription? A cupful of this after every meal, and you'll never need a doctor again."

I relented and sipped. The tea tasted like boiled oranges.

"Do you always stay up this late?" I asked.

"I'm a night owl. After midnight is when the creative juices really get flowing. Besides, I knew you'd be coming. The first time I laid eyes on you, I felt our energies intertwine. I'm an empath—did I mention? But with some beings, the connection is especially strong."

She steered me into a plain chair in the center of the room, then settled onto a second chair behind an easel.

"Oh," I said, uncomfortable. "I'm not really here for—"

"*Shhh!*" Margo flapped her hand in annoyance and then proceeded to spend an interminably long time staring at me.

I scrubbed the soles of my shoes against the floor, feeling painfully self-conscious. When was the last time I'd brushed my hair? So many little daily rituals had died with Aldo. A massive inertia built up around the simplest tasks, until they just didn't seem worth the energy.

"What are you doing?" I asked finally.

"Looking," stated Margo. "The artist's first task is to see."

Slowly, dramatically, she pulled a paint palette toward her and wetted a long brush in a glass of murky water.

I had never been painted before. I didn't even like to be photographed. There was something unpleasant about seeing myself represented. I never felt like it was me the image had captured but a sly doppelgänger, her intentions unknown.

But I couldn't bring myself to leave. It was quiet here in the studio, peaceful and easy, the silence broken only by Margo's brushstrokes and her little hums of contemplation. No one was asking anything of me. I felt like I could finally expand my lungs in a full breath.

I relaxed into my chair, letting my gaze travel around the studio. Incomplete sketches were tacked to the walls at uneven heights: the bulge of a naked shoulder, a face with just a nose, a pair of eyeballs squinched shut. I counted no fewer than seven teacups, stashed on end tables and windowsills.

Then I became aware of a painting facing outward from the corner of the room—a stretched-out, nebulous, organic thing composed of scarlet feelers. From this angle I could only see a portion of it, but even that limited snapshot made my breath stall in my chest.

"Is that—?"

Margo turned her head to follow my pointing finger. She smiled. "Our jellyfish is glorious, is she not?"

"She is," I said, grateful to meet someone who understood. I should not be so quick to dismiss weird people. I was a pretty weird person myself.

"Do you know, in the beginning, I was resentful?" Margo turned back to her canvas, adding more brushstrokes as she talked. "I was supposed to move to Portland in January, with my dear sister. So many more opportunities for the artistically inclined in the big city."

"What about Norm?" I asked.

"What about him?" Her voice crinkled with annoyance. But she recovered within moments, her dreamy tranquility jerked back over her face like a mask. "Of course I take the vows of marriage *very* seriously," she said, eyes fluttering closed, two fingers pressed to her heart, "but there comes a point in life where one must take stock of one's choices—choices made when one was, possibly, quite young, a little foolish, a little too easily smitten by a strapping young fellow who still had all his hair . . ."

She opened her eyes and sipped her tea.

"But since those early moments of bitterness, I have arrived at a different conclusion: We have been *honored* by Clementine's presence. She has bound us to this beautiful place, and to each other, through the only force in the universe strong enough to withstand every effort to destroy it."

"Which is?" I asked.

"*Love*," murmured Margo, her blue eyes wide and shiny.

"Right . . ." I rescinded my earlier generosity: Margo was just *too* weird.

She worked in silence for the next half hour. I was starting to doze off in my chair when she declared our first session complete.

"I'll need you to sit for me a couple more times before I've captured everything. But it's coming along quite nicely. Perhaps you'd like to see—?"

"No, thanks." I stood, shaking off my drowsiness as I forked my stiff arm over my shoulder in a stretch. There was only one thing I wanted to see.

I walked to the corner of the room and beheld Margo's Clementine painting in its full glory. I didn't know anything about art. Maybe to someone who'd never laid eyes on the jellyfish, it wouldn't have looked like much. But to me, it was transporting: I was back in that lantern room, watching the dark ocean ignite.

Margo had painted the giant jellyfish from a bird's-eye view, as if she'd been stationed in the lighthouse, too. Clementine took up the full frame, captured mid-dance as her tendrils rippled out to meet the edges of the swirled black canvas. Using softer and deeper shades of red, the artist had re-created the undulating movement of Clementine's bioluminescence, the way the light had rolled over her body in gentle waves.

But it was more than the accuracy of the portrait that stunned me. There was an impression I had no words for, something that went beyond the visual. It was as if the painting were emitting a chord at a pitch just above or just below the level of human hearing—the same chord that had thrummed through me as those glowing tentacles stretched shoreward, and I'd fought the urge to go plunging out the lantern room window to meet them.

"Perhaps you've noticed our Clementine is camera-shy?" Margo sidled up beside me, blowing contentedly on a fresh cup of tea. "She requires a different medium to show off her full grandeur."

"It's remarkable . . ."

Margo simpered at the praise. "I'm working on a series. *Monster in Motion.* I consider it to be my greatest artistic challenge yet."

"A series?" I managed to pull my eyes away from the portrait and look at the artist. "You mean you have more of them?"

Citizen Scientists

In 1909, the biologist Jakob von Uexküll popularized the term *umwelt* to describe an animal's unique sensory realm. The umwelt of a bat includes the visual and auditory spectra made possible by echolocation. The umwelt of a dog includes olfactory receptors that allow it to perceive smells undetectable to human noses. What exists within the umwelt of a jellyfish?

Specialized sensory structures called rhopalia hang from the margins of a jelly's bell, allowing it to perceive light and shadow. In place of a central nervous system, two nerve nets distribute information across the body, allowing different parts to work in harmony. A recent study has even shown that box jellyfish can engage in associative learning, modifying their behavior based on experience.

Our assessment of animal complexity is biased, shaped by the limitations of our own umwelt.

AA: We can't appreciate what we can't perceive.

Margo was happy to let me borrow her Clementine portraits—a set of eleven in total. I took my prizes back to Montana and sifted through them one at a time. I couldn't stop looking at them. Every other item in the room seemed flat and grayscale by comparison. I wanted to live inside those paintings. I wanted to drench myself in Clementine's brilliant red light.

Margo's determination to document the giant jellyfish, to observe and appreciate and understand, had humbled me. I saw I had been going about this the wrong way. The foremost jellyfish experts in the world would not help me make sense of an animal they'd never experienced. My experts were here, on the island—firsthand witnesses who'd observed, hypothesized, and experimented in their desperate quest to understand the reach of Clementine's strength and discover any of her weaknesses. The residents of Shattering Point were citizen scientists. It was time for me to become a student again.

It was comforting to drift off with the giant jellyfish watching over me, beaming her gentle majesty into the room. The following morning, I fended off my hangover with Tylenol and a shower and the usual thermos of coffee awaiting me in the empty dining room. I sent an email to Elijah, requesting an extension to my vacation, saying I needed to stop by Indiana to see my mother on my way back. I hoped he'd supply the subtext himself: aging parent, obvious emergency, nothing I could do.

Elijah was passive, and I was Seaheart's longest-serving employee. He wouldn't push me. He wouldn't want to risk losing me altogether. Not yet. If I could figure out an exit from Shattering Point by the time Clementine surfaced in June, there was still a chance my job would be waiting for me on my return.

Powered by a new sense of determination, I gathered my courage and went in search of Tony.

I found her vacuuming Alaska. She had her back to me, a pair of blocky headphones clamped over her ears. I lingered awkwardly in the doorway, waiting for her to notice me.

Last night's scene played out in my memory on a cruel and unstoppable loop: pulling Tony toward me, kissing her, the slightly salty taste of her lips against mine. What if she didn't want to help me? What if she thought I was a creep? What if she decided to banish me from the B and B? Where would I go then? My calves tightened with the desire to run far, far away.

Tony turned and blanched at the sight of me. She flipped the vacuum off and slid the headphones down around her neck. "Jesus Christ. How long have you been standing there?"

"Just, like, a minute or two." Which now struck me as far too long a time to be watching someone.

Tony ran a hand through her hair, which was down again today. It looked soft and heavy. I imagined wrapping it up in my arms like a bundle of fresh towels, burying my face in its coconut-smelling depths.

I cleared my throat. "I just wanted to apologize. For last night. I shouldn't have—I was in a bad place."

Tony leaned her hips against the bureau, which was stenciled with tiny moose. "It's me who should apologize. I shouldn't have been so hard on you. Your entire life's been put on hold. Everyone went a little nuts when we realized we couldn't leave. I think, all things considered, you're doing great."

"Thanks," I said, heartened.

"Also." She shrugged. "I kissed you back."

I suddenly had no idea what to do with my hands. Had they always been so big and stupid?

The unbearable silence stretched on until Tony broke eye contact by stooping and yanking the vacuum plug from the wall.

"So, then," she said, in a forcibly casual tone, "have you come up with a way to get us all out of here without murdering your beloved jelly?"

"Is that what you want?" I asked.

"What I want . . ." Tony hesitated, then began roughly looping the cord around the vacuum handle, shaking her head. "What I want is to get out of here, Jo. Whatever it takes."

I wasn't sure that was true. It was Sylvia, not Tony, who'd insisted Clementine had to die. But there was a tightness around Tony's mouth that told me not to go poking at a sore spot. There was enough friction between us already.

"I've decided that I need more information," I said. "And also that I—need help." The foreignness of the words nearly gagged me. I went to absurd lengths to avoid asking people to help me. Even as a child I'd been obstinately independent, wanting to do everything on my own.

"Okay," Tony said. "But I should warn you: Marine biology isn't really in my skill set."

"I need to interview the locals," I said. "Anyone who's had contact with the barrier, anyone who's gotten close enough to try and kill Clementine. Could you help me get the word out?"

She smiled. "Sounds better than ironing curtains."

• • •

I set up on the first floor, in the sitting area opposite the dining room, its walls papered with green fleurs-de-lis, its shelves stacked with Tony's aunt's kitschy knickknacks: smiling animal figurines, snow globes encasing national landmarks that whirled in pink glitter storms when shaken. Perched on a velvet tufted sofa in front of the empty fireplace, my laptop resting on an end table draped in lace-trimmed cloth, I felt ridiculous, like a child playing at royalty.

I saw movement out of the corner of my eye: Tony, in the hallway, wearing a smirk as she pressed something to the doorframe. She disappeared a second later, and I got up to discover a handwritten sign: *Jelly HQ*, with a passable drawing of a jam jar underneath it.

The islanders responded to Tony's invitation faster than I'd anticipated. My first customer wandered in within the hour: a soft-spoken man with salt-and-pepper hair and a matching beard and dark, doleful eyes. He introduced himself as Lawrence Fleming, one of Shattering's veteran lobstermen. I was pretty sure I remembered Lawrence from the Urchin, where he'd been among the hard-drinking patrons flinging his shoes into the fishing nets. I declined to mention this, and if Lawrence recognized me as the dour outsider quietly unraveling in the corner booth, he did me the equal favor of keeping this to himself. What happened at the Urchin stayed at the Urchin.

Lawrence explained that he'd been part of the crew that had attempted to poison Clementine last month. And he had a video to show me. As with Sidney's footage and the shots I'd grabbed from the lantern room, little of Clementine's splendor had transmitted. I could've been looking at an algal bloom, or a glow-in-the-dark oil slick fanning out across the water. *Camera-shy*, Margo had called the jellyfish. Tony's Instagram idea would've never taken off.

But Lawrence's video wasn't completely useless. The crew of would-be Clementine killers was easy to see: three of them, plus whoever was holding the camera, silhouetted by the deck lights on someone's fishing boat, working together to wrestle a big, sloshing barrel toward the water.

"What is it?"

"Sodium cyanide," said Lawrence.

I gave him an annoyed look. Cyanide fishing was still used in the aquarium trade despite being illegal. The poison destroyed coral reefs and damaged the organs of fish so severely, the majority of them died in transit.

Lawrence held my stare, refusing to be chagrined. "Desperate times."

"And it didn't work."

"See for yourself."

I went on watching the phone screen. The men and their barrel had reached the stern. Bile rose in my throat at the prospect of the cloud of poison spreading over the water, blotting out Clementine's brilliant light.

But they never got that far. The men halted. Someone in the video cursed. It was as if they had simply stopped, stayed by a collective misgiving. The giant jellyfish oozed away, out of reach, carrying her rippling bands of bioluminescence with her.

I looked back up. "I don't understand."

"You've seen it," Lawrence said solemnly. "It takes you outside of yourself. You forget where you are. *When* you are. It's like being paralyzed."

When Tony had said they'd tried killing Clementine over and over, I'd envisioned outrageous, death-defying stunts: bullets repelled from tentacles as if they were wrapped in Teflon. Or, more sensibly, Clementine might have the ability to regenerate, as had been documented in at least one jellyfish species, recovering from physical damage at record speed.

This was even more incredible. This was a defensive strategy that infiltrated the predator, arresting the threat at its source.

"It's amazing," I breathed, poring over the video again as it replayed.

"That's one word for it," said the lobsterman, eyeing me uncertainly.

More locals trickled into the B and B over the course of the day, lending credence to Lawrence Fleming's story: Clementine could not be so much as lightly prodded with a fishing rod. The islanders had tried shooting the jellyfish. They had tried chopping her up with a boat's propeller blades. They had tried grabbing her up with a trawlnet. They had tried wearing blindfolds as they carried out these assaults, hoping to insulate themselves from the dizzying spell of Clementine's bioluminescence. Nothing worked. "It won't *let* us," whined the jowly woman who owned the souvenir shop, as if Clementine were a stern mother who'd suspended TV-watching privileges.

For a few of the islanders, the giant jellyfish had taken on the status of myth. They spoke of her with hushed voices and awe in their eyes, and if they didn't go as far as Margo Sloan in describing themselves as *honored* by Clementine's arrival, they could appreciate that they were in the presence of something incredible.

But for the most part, the giant jelly was like an infestation of roaches that wouldn't be stamped out. "That thing," my interviewees called her, and "the beast," and sometimes even "*your* beast," happy to consign Clementine to an outsider, happy to make her my problem to solve. I typed notes and asked follow-up questions and looked at their lousy recordings, withholding all judgment. But through it all I burned with secret pride for Clementine, my stubbornly unkillable jellyfish.

Questions around her nature were piling up inside me. Where did she come from? What role did she play in the food chain? What environmental factors had compelled her into waters she'd never visited before? How did her defensive strategy work, and could it be deployed against nonhuman predators, too? Was she venomous? God, Aldo was going to be so jealous when I told him—

I kicked back from this thought like a repelled magnet, clenching the sides of my laptop to steady myself. I'd thought I was past the stage of forgetting he was gone.

Near the end of almost every interview, there was a strange and unwelcome pivot. Without my prompting, the islanders opened up about all they longed for beyond the barrier, everyone and everything they feared they'd never reach again. Distant relatives. Dream vacations. Favorite restaurants. The goateed guy who owned the ice cream parlor wouldn't stop talking about the incredible éclairs he'd eaten at a hole-in-the-wall bakery in Paris as a teenager, how he'd always sworn he'd go back once he was grown and had his own money.

These disclosures filled me with a crawly sense of shame. Why couldn't people keep their feelings to themselves? I wiggled with discomfort on my velvet throne. I tried and failed to resist thinking about my own life, a stalled and hollow life since losing Aldo, but a life all the same. My apartment, bare as a bachelor pad. My mother, whose calls and texts I could not dodge forever. My fussy jelly babies in their polyp parlor at Seaheart.

Tony floated back and forth in the hallway, pretending to clean, eavesdropping. I wondered who or what awaited her off Shattering. A long-distance girlfriend or boyfriend, probably—very attractive, thoughtful, loving, in possession of normal interests and a hairbrush.

And yet, she'd kissed me back.

I hauled myself out of my daydreams as Mr. Éclair thanked me for my time and trooped out of the room. Tony materialized in the doorway, ready to escort in my next interviewee.

"*You're not gonna like it*," she mouthed.

I didn't like it.

The person who stepped into the room next was Emmett Beckendorf, blond hair plastered to his scalp in the imprint of a hat, shoulders thrown back like he was ready for another fight. He wore the same tall brown boots he'd had on that morning at the dock—the morning when we'd locked eyes, and he recognized the subtle change that indicated I'd seen Clementine, and let me go crashing into the barrier anyway.

"You almost got me killed," I snarled.

Emmett dropped into the armchair on the other side of the hearth. "Roger was there. I knew he'd get you back. I would've stopped you if you were on your own."

"Yeah, right."

"It's the truth. You can believe it or not."

"How's your head?" I asked pettily.

Emmett didn't rise to the provocation. "Do you want to hear what I've got to say about the jellyfish, or not?"

I swallowed my rage and sank back, drumming my fingers on the sofa arm.

Emmett scratched the side of his neck, which was peeling with sunburn. The swagger he'd performed at the Urchin was gone. His eyes roved over the shelves full of knickknacks. He seemed uncertain how to begin.

"I told you what I do here on the island?" he asked.

"You said you run the scallop farm."

He nodded. "It's been slow going, getting it up and running. Start-up costs are high. Some of the old-timers think I'm crazy. Me, I say they're in denial. Cod stocks are crashing. Water's getting too warm for lobsters. Scallops are the future. Landings were worth over five hundred million last year."

Now it was my turn to sigh, loud and bored.

Emmett flushed but pressed on.

"I've got my nets hung about two miles west of the island. I drive out to check 'em every day. Lately it's gotten . . . harder. I can still get out there, but I don't feel so good. I like to get back as fast as I can."

I suppressed a shiver when I caught his meaning. "You think it's moving," I said. "You think the barrier is moving in?"

"Is that possible?" he asked, his tone as purposely flat as mine.

I watched him, trying to gauge his motives. Was he lying to me again? Trying to scare me?

Then Tony was in the doorway, gripping a Swiffer duster like she was going to brain someone with it.

"What the hell, Emmett? How long have you known about this?"

Emmett had the decency to look abashed. "Just a coupla days.

I told Sylvia. She said not to spread it around, said it might make folks panic. But she thought the scientist should know . . ."

Tony was gnawing ferociously at one of her thumbnails, and it unsettled me. I hadn't seen her truly distraught before.

"You said the barrier fluctuates," I reminded her. "In the cove. You said its border changes—"

"Twenty, maybe thirty feet." Tony shook her head. "Not like this."

Sitting still was suddenly impossible. I moved my laptop aside and got to my feet. Emmett stood, too, his hands tensed into trembling fists at his sides. He didn't like me, and I didn't like him, but just then our shared apprehension, layered on top of our weird magnetism, wrenched us so painfully close I could feel my lungs inflating with his shallow inhales.

"I'm going to move my nets in," he said decisively. "I should've done it already."

"No," I said. "You have to leave them where they are. It's our best landmark. It's how we'll know if things get worse."

"Easy for you to say! This farm is my entire livelihood. I can't risk not being able to reach it."

"If the barrier moves any farther, you're going to have much bigger problems than your livelihood!"

"So move the nets," said Tony, "and drop a buoy where they used to hang."

I clammed up. Emmett, too. It was a simple compromise, and an obvious one. I should've thought of it myself.

"I can do that," he conceded. He stuffed his hands in his pockets and glared at me, his fear vanished, gobbled up by animosity. I preferred it that way. There was a cleanness to our mutual dislike, a welcome contrast to the strange jumble of crossed wires I'd felt before.

"Will you tell me if anything changes?" I asked.

Emmett looked for one moment like he was going to refuse. He glanced at Tony, who gave a barely perceptible nod.

"Fine," said Emmett. He turned and plodded out of the sitting room. I heard Retreat-by-the-Sea's screen door squeal as it closed.

I braced my hands against the cool wood of the fireplace mantel and shut my eyes. The hours of talking—trying to buttress myself against the islanders' hatred, pain, and confusion—had rekindled my hangover. I felt achy and exhausted. And though I had more information now than I did before the interviews, it only presented new obstacles.

The barrier was moving in a way it had not moved before. This news, if it ever got out, would only induce the islanders to double down on killing Clementine. So far they hadn't been successful, but that didn't mean they never would be. Desperation could provoke striking creativity in a person. In only twenty-two days, Shattering's giant jelly would resurface, and the islanders would have a new plan. I needed to have one, too.

I lowered my head until it thunked against the mantel. "Okay, that's enough. Jelly HQ is closed for the day."

I heard the sound of tape coming unstuck, and then Tony was beside me, proffering her jam jar sign with a serious expression.

"For your scrapbook."

"Ha ha."

She crumpled the paper into a ball and tucked it in my back pocket.

As one, we rotated out to face the empty room, and I wondered if Tony, too, was gripped by the illusion of the walls shrinking inward. I felt the press of stone against my body, the scrape of my fins against rock as I tried to wiggle free.

"What do you think?" asked Tony. She was worrying at that thumbnail again.

I rubbed my face with both hands. "I think I should've taken your boat and gotten the hell out of here when I had the chance."

"Probably. What do you think about what Emmett said?"

"I don't know." It was the only honest response. "Are we sure he's trustworthy? You said he was a liar."

"I only said that to try and get you to leave. Emmett's all right. Once you get to know him," she added, in response to the face I made. "I really can't imagine anyone lying about a thing like this. But if you want, we could take a little trip out to the scallop farm and see for ourselves."

My chest tightened at the thought of being on the water again.

"Or I could go," said Tony.

I was half-flattered, half-disturbed at her ability to read me so accurately. My whole life, I'd been told I was inscrutable. Here was this woman I'd known less than a week, able to translate the thinnest scrawls of emotion flitting across my face.

"Only if you wouldn't mind," I said gratefully.

"You asked for my help. I'm here to give it to you."

She squeezed my arm in a friendly, reassuring way. A we're-in-this-together sort of way. It was not at all the type of touch I craved, but I wasn't going to throw myself at Tony again. Tony wasn't the person I wanted. The person I wanted was married and ignoring me.

But maybe Nadia staying away was for the best. The desire to see her again had gotten me on the plane, but now that I knew what was really at stake on Shattering Point, it was better not to have the distraction. Let her stay in her cottage with her husband. Let her stay away from me for the rest of our lives.

The screen door squealed open. Tony retracted her hand, and we both turned to face the newcomer standing on the threshold.

It was Nadia.

All my empty resolve disintegrated in a burst of pleasure that momentarily lifted me out of my body.

"Hi, Josie." She wiggled her fingers in a meek wave. "How are you doing?"

Reunion, Part 2

Watching a jellyfish swim is a viscerally soothing experience. The next time you're having a bad day, park yourself in front of an aquarium, or just pull up a video on YouTube. Witness the fluid pulsing of the bell as it tows a trailing curtain of tentacles through the water. Feel your heart rate slow, and your stress melt away.

I didn't want Tony eavesdropping on this conversation, so I took Nadia upstairs to Montana—a decision I regretted as soon as I turned on the lights and appreciated what a mess the place had become in the past seven days. My wet towel from that morning's shower lay puddled at the foot of the bed. Margo's Clementine portraits were stacked on the dresser, the treasure chest displaced to the floor where it had tipped, scattering plastic coins. The few personal items and articles of clothing I'd brought with me from California had multiplied and flown to every corner of the room.

Nadia commented on none of this. Instead she threw her arms around me and pulled me into a tight hug. I inhaled, and there was her smell, in her neck, her hair. She tucked her chin into my shoulder, and for a second we were twenty-one years old again, secreted in the library basement with our hiragana workbooks.

"I should've done that when I first saw you," Nadia murmured into my shoulder.

"You should've," I agreed.

"I was distracted. There was so much going on. Roger was so angry—"

Her husband's name pierced a hole in my fantasy. We were in our thirties; she was married. Eleven years of life squatted solidly between us.

I made a half-hearted effort to straighten the covers on the bed before sitting. Nadia joined me, arranging herself cross-legged with her back propped against the wall. Now I really regretted bringing her up here. The scene was too intimate, too reminiscent of those hours-long conversations we'd once had in my dorm room. I studied Nadia and realized I couldn't even tell if she'd changed in the manner of Emmett and Tony and everyone else, maybe because there'd always been a thread of magnetism between us.

"How are you doing?" she asked me again.

"You know." I made an empty sweeping gesture with one hand. It was an impossible question to answer.

"I would've checked on you sooner," said Nadia, toying nervously with the edge of the blanket. "Roger said you were mad at me. That you needed space."

I *had* been mad at Nadia, but it annoyed me that Roger would make himself the messenger.

"I would totally understand if you were," she said earnestly. "I asked you to come here, and you did, and now you're stuck . . ."

"You had no way of knowing what was going to happen," I said. Even in my most self-pitying moments, I'd never believed that

Nadia had intentionally trapped me here. She'd called me in good faith.

And yet.

I saw again her turning from me, the shadow of the silly graduation cap slanting sideways across her face. The crowd outside Gladstone's field house didn't suck her up—she vanished into it, deliberately. And then nothing. For eleven years. No apology, no explanation.

Nadia peered at me keenly. "You're really not mad?"

I didn't want to get into it at that moment. I really didn't. I wanted to enjoy our first encounter without Roger hanging on to her. I wanted the warm reunion I'd been imagining ever since she called me last week. But the words just exploded out of me:

"Why did you leave me?"

Nadia flinched, but the fact that she knew what I was talking about confirmed she'd been thinking about our time at Gladstone, too. "I didn't leave you, Josie," she murmured. "We graduated. It was time to move on."

"Bullshit. You avoided me that day. We were supposed to get lunch together with our families."

She dropped her face into her hands. "You're right. I'm sorry."

I sagged. It was no fun fighting with someone who caved so quickly.

"That night we spent together was a mistake," Nadia said, her words muffled. "I didn't know how to undo it. I knew that you were . . . And I was worried you thought *I* was . . ."

"Don't flatter yourself, okay?" My voice sounded cold and distant. "I knew it was just a stupid hookup. It's not like I was in love with you or anything." It was the most bold-faced lie I'd ever told.

Nadia looked up, the lenses of her glasses smudgy with fingerprints. "You were so sad after your dad died. I just wanted to make you feel better."

"You can't go around having sex with people to make them feel better, Nadia!"

She flinched again. Her lips quivered. For one horrifying second, I thought she was going to burst into tears.

Then she was laughing, and so was I. I tried to suppress it, but it just kept coming. Nothing was funny. It was simply a release, borne on a flood of tamped-down feeling eleven years in the making. God, I had missed Nadia. I had missed her in her own right, and I had missed the person I was when we were together.

Our laughter faded at the same instant. It was just like that night on the rooftop, only this time I knew where we stood with one another. It made me a little sad, but also relieved. So Nadia had never loved me, not in the manner I'd loved her. She'd loved me more like how I'd loved Aldo. The idea would take some getting used to. But it didn't have to be a bad thing.

I wiped the tears from my eyes and lay back on the bed, pressing my hands against my stinging abdominal muscles.

Nadia nudged my knee. "How come *you* didn't reach out after graduation?"

"I don't know. I guess I thought I'd offended you somehow. I kept waiting for you to reach out to me."

Hearing it out loud, it all seemed so dumb. A few minutes of awkwardness followed by eleven years of silence. What would my life have been like if we'd stayed connected? I would've gone to her and Roger's wedding. I would've sent her photos from my dives with Aldo. I would've leaned on her for comfort after he died.

Even if she couldn't have eliminated the burden I'd been living with for the past seven months, she would've eased its weight. She would've found a way.

The urge to open up to Nadia about Aldo rose within me. But she had known me before his loss had broken me. I wanted to cling to that worthwhile version of myself for as long as I could.

I sat up painfully, clutching the edge of the mattress as the room reeled. "God, I'm hungover."

"You, too? Roger's also been overdoing it." Nadia's grin faded. "He's taking this whole thing pretty hard."

"Making it all about himself, you mean."

"Everyone makes everything about themselves," said Nadia sagely. "It's part of being human."

I rolled my eyes. Good to know her exhausting generous streak hadn't faded in the past decade.

"He told me how you helped him out that night at the Urchin," Nadia added. "When Emmett came after him. I really appreciate that, Josie."

"It was the right thing to do," I muttered. But what I was thinking was that I should've let him get his ass kicked a little longer.

Nadia sighed. "I know you two don't really like each other—"

"Why? What'd he say?"

"—but you're both important to me, and if we're all gonna be stuck together on this tiny scrap of an island for the time being . . ."

She was asking me to play nice. She should've known me better than that.

I got to my feet under the pretext of hunting for my water bottle. Nadia's words had reminded me of my impossible task, from which I'd been briefly and blissfully liberated by our reconciliation.

I found the bottle on the windowsill and downed the little bit of plastic-tasting water that remained. Somehow it only made my throat feel drier.

Another shiver passed through me as I looked down over Beach Street. Was it my imagination, or could I actually *feel* the moving barrier? Not around me but inside me—a warning itch like the pressure that boded a sneeze.

"It's getting worse," I said. I couldn't look at Nadia. I screwed the lid back on the empty water bottle with shaking hands.

"What do you mean?" she asked quietly.

I swore her to secrecy before explaining what Emmett had said. Sylvia was right: More people panicking was the last thing we needed.

But Nadia wasn't panicking.

"The barrier always moves around a bit. Maybe this is as far as it's ever going to go."

"Tony said—"

"Tony doesn't know everything there is to know about Clementine, Jo," said Nadia reasonably. "You said it yourself: Nothing like this animal has ever been documented before. None of the other fishermen have noticed anything new with the barrier, have they?"

As far as I knew, they hadn't.

Nadia joined me at the window. Her chronic optimism had sometimes irked me in college, divorced as it was from the reality that things didn't always work out for the best. But worst-case-scenario thinking had its pitfalls, too. If I let myself brood over the vision of the barrier suffocating us all in our sleep, I was going to end up right back at the Urchin.

Nadia gave my fingers a light squeeze, and I squeezed back.

"I don't believe we're going to be trapped on Shattering forever." Her voice rang with a confidence that would've sounded false coming from anyone else. "We're going to figure something out."

"You mean *I'm* going to figure something out."

"No, Josie," she said, jostling my arm in playful reproach. "*We*. When I told Tony and Sylvia that you could help us—it's not fair to put all that on you. You don't have to do it on your own. Everyone wants the same thing here."

"No, Nadia. Some people want to wipe Clementine off the face of the earth."

"Everyone wants to get off Shattering!"

"Not Norm Sloan . . ."

She shook her head fondly. "I forgot how you have to make everything an argument."

Her eyes drifted past me, to the stack of canvases on the dresser. "What are those?"

She was probably trying to distract me, but I didn't mind. If Nadia had found something to admire in the shitty little ceramic dish I'd made at Gladstone, she was going to be really wowed by Margo's Clementine portraits.

I moved the pile to the floor, where Nadia went through the paintings one at a time, oohing and aahing appropriately.

"I know she's a little cuckoo," said Nadia, "but you have to admit, Margo's got talent. And how cool that she's been painting Clementine since the very beginning!" She gestured at some text scrawled in the bottom-right corner of the canvas, which I had taken to be the artist's signature.

But kneeling on the floor beside Nadia now, I saw that I was wrong. It wasn't a signature. It was a date.

Goaded by an intuition I didn't question, I reshuffled the paintings so that they were arrayed chronologically, the oldest on the left and the newest on the right. Nadia scooted out of the way to make room. When I was done, the portraits formed a crooked path from Montana's door to the foot of the bed. Instead of studying each one individually as I'd done last night, I let my gaze sweep across them, trying to relax my eyes like I would with an optical illusion, trying to see past the surface.

And just like with an optical illusion, when the old hag leaps out of the young woman and you're forced to wonder how you ever could've missed her, it seemed so obvious to me now: The paintings on the left were the ones where the jellyfish's tentacles sprawled languidly, luxuriously, right to the edge of its prison. As you proceeded down the line, it shriveled to a red heartbeat dully thudding in the center of the canvas.

"What do you see?" I asked.

Nadia's eyes swept from left to right and right to left. I stayed quiet. I still didn't totally trust my mind—not as long as it was going to jump scare me with periodic visions of my dead best friend. I needed the corroboration from someone I trusted, and Nadia had become someone I could trust again.

She glanced up at me, her forehead puckered with a frown. "Clementine is getting smaller."

Stressed

All true jellyfish are equipped with stinging cells called nematocysts. When activated, they fire at a speed of one millionth of a second—the fastest type of movement in the animal kingdom. There is no stopping a sting once it's been triggered.

JN: Are we trying to redeem jellyfish, or are we trying to freak people out?

AA: Can't we do both?

"The jellyfish is stressed-out?" said Sylvia Steele.

It was the morning after my interviews at Jelly HQ. We were in Shattering Point's lighthouse museum, in the old stone cottage, its door propped open with a statue of a bulbous toad. Raindrops plunked onto the roof. Tony had given me a ride in the junky gold car and was now stationed in one of the dining chairs, knees tented, feet propped on the table. Town clerk Sylvia Steele had kept her back to me as I spoke, scratching a straw broom in agitated jerks across the floor, but she turned to face me now that I was done, her expression slack and unimpressed.

"The *jellyfish*," she repeated, her tone dripping disdain, "is stressed-out."

"It's called degrowth," I explained. "Some jellyfish species can shrink in response to external threats like reduced water quality or starvation. It's a survival trick. They make themselves smaller to minimize resource needs until conditions have stabilized."

"And you're basing all this off some artwork?" scoffed Sylvia. "Doesn't sound very scientific to me."

I was already regretting mentioning Margo's portraits. It would've been more convincing to say I'd noticed something in the video footage. But blurry footage didn't do justice to Clementine, and Margo's paintings were so compelling, so clear. I believed she'd captured something significant, and the strength of that belief embarrassed me.

I glanced at Tony, hoping for words of support. She'd said she was here to help me. She had already made good on her offer to take *The Phantom Maiden* out to the scallop farm, where she'd confirmed Emmett Beckendorf was neither paranoid nor a liar: The familiar queasiness had crawled through her within seconds of cutting the engine. It seemed the barrier really was creeping steadily inward from the west. It had probably been doing so for some time, undetected.

But the easy camaraderie that had existed between Tony and me yesterday in Jelly HQ had evaporated overnight. She'd seemed almost chilly toward me on the drive over, the silence freighted with a heft that felt personal. All she did now was lift and lower one shoulder in an apathetic gesture that seemed to say, *What can you do?*

Sylvia set her broom aside and moved toward one of the glass display cases, clutching a rag and a spray bottle. I followed, forcing her to keep me in her sight line.

"It's not just the paintings. Have you noticed that rotten smell, when Clementine surfaces? Sea anemones emit an odor when stressed. Certain species of coral, too."

"So maybe you're right," said Sylvia with a shrug. "Maybe our sea monster is stressed-out. That sounds like a good thing to me. We keep hitting it each month, maybe it'll shrivel down to nothing. Problem solved."

"Or maybe we'll cause the barrier to shrink faster. We shouldn't operate under the assumption that destroying her is the right move. Not until we know more."

Sylvia sighed and faced me. "I know you think I'm some sort of brute, trying to kill this thing. I've lived by the ocean twice as long as you've been alive. My granddad, God rest his soul, taught me to respect the life that lived there." She lifted her eyes to a black-and-white portrait over the fireplace: a square-jawed, stocky man in a sailor's cap. "I'd wager Gus preferred animals to most people. You remind me of him. But this beast is older and stronger than you're giving it credit for," finished Sylvia grimly.

She walked to a different display case and extracted the stack of shabby green books. They were slim and identical and looked like journals. She took a minute to sort through them before handing me one. It dropped into my hands with more force than I expected. The words *Lighthouse Keeper's Log* were embossed on the cover, and beneath that, in smaller type: *Augustus James Steele, 1932–1935*.

"I've been digitizing my granddad's records," Sylvia explained. "Sort of a pet project of mine. When Clementine surfaced in October, it reminded me . . ."

She flipped open the keeper's log to a page she must've memorized, about a third of the way through. Augustus Steele's handwriting was abominable. It took a second for the faded, spidery letters to transform into decipherable words:

October 22, 1934

9:07. Daily inspection. Moderate cloud cover. Rain from north. Fog signal operating normally. 11:17. Rain persists. Polished lenses. 14:58. Mail arrived. My request for asst. keeper goes unanswered. 16:20. Glimpse of lightning. I have a cold.

It was the sort of first-person account historians lived for, but I felt myself going cross-eyed from the tedium. I mentally revised my portrait of lighthouse keeping as a noble and romantic occupation. What a dreary life Augustus Steele must've lived, forced to catalog every dull minute of the long, dull day.

Then I reached the bottom of the page and saw what Sylvia wanted me to see:

22:18. Lights on the water. Scarlet, burning. Something surfaces from the deep.

I looked up. "You think this is the same animal?"

"It's possible, isn't it?" said Sylvia.

It should not have been possible. This entry was penned almost eighty-five years ago. In their polyp phase, jellyfish could persist for years, delaying their strobilation until environmental conditions were right. But a fully mature medusa like Clementine was a different matter. The trade-off of gaining tentacles and movement was increased fragility, increased exposure to predation. Most jellies in the wild lived less than three years.

But since arriving on Shattering, I'd learned a lot about what I didn't know. I'd scoffed at Sidney's video, which turned out to be real. I'd dismissed the notion of a jellyfish that could keep a group of people trapped on an island for seven months, and here we were.

Plus, there was something distinctive about Augustus's description: *Scarlet, burning.* Most marine bioluminescence was blue, the color that traveled farthest in the water. I remembered the feverish warmth that had blazed through me in the lantern room. Maybe Clementine really had been around for decades. I had to keep in mind that this was a jellyfish that broke all the rules.

"Does your grandfather mention these lights again?"

"Not that I could find," replied Sylvia. "But if it's not the same animal, it's got to be the same species."

"What makes you so sure?"

She took the logbook from me and cradled it against her torso. "Granddad had a certain reputation on Shattering."

I glanced at Tony, recalling the story she'd shared in the tunnel about the rumrunners. "I heard he was a smuggler."

"Not that," she snapped. "I mean that he was nervous, fearful. Kept to himself. Well, lots of folks did, and still do, but he took it a step further. Round the time I was born, he stopped leaving the island. Didn't set foot on the mainland between 1934 and the day he died. He said just the thought of leaving Shattering made him sick. Always thought he had the agoraphobia. But now—"

"You're saying he couldn't leave? You're saying the barrier existed, even back then?"

"It'd sure explain some things."

"Or it's just what you said: He was nervous and fearful."

Sylvia seemed not to hear me. Her eyes were on Augustus's portrait again, her gaze cloudy. "It was my grandmother who found him. He slept late when he could, being up minding the light most of the night. By the time she checked in on him that morning in '43, he'd been dead for hours. Already cold."

A chill rippled through me as I thought of my own mother coming across my father on the kitchen floor.

"They said he'd been poisoned by one of his business partners." Sylvia shook her head slowly, some heat gone out of her at the memory. "Never made any sense to me. Prohibition had ended years before. At the time he died, Granddad was just a lighthouse keeper. No more, no less. Who'd want him dead, huh? And how would they have arranged it? It's not like someone could've crept in here on the sly. Wasn't hardly anyone on Shattering in those days."

Tony shifted at the table. Her expression was unfazed. Did she think the old woman was rambling? Did I?

I took a deep breath. "If you're saying Clementine was somehow *responsible* for your grandpa's death—"

"That is exactly what I'm saying." Sylvia's eyes were off the portrait and back on me, her tone icy once more. "If the barrier existed back then, if it moved back then just like it's doing now and he got caught on the wrong side—"

"That's a lot of ifs."

"You don't know this island like I do, girl. You don't know the stories."

She narrowed her eyes and clutched her grandfather's logbook tighter. She had her theory, I had mine. Where did that leave us? Was Shattering Point's giant jellyfish an ancient and invincible monster that had been stalking these shores for decades, one that had already taken a human life and was poised now to take forty-seven more? Or was she an animal like any other, struggling to adapt to a degraded ocean, her pulsating light less a signpost of danger than a cry for help?

In the silence I became aware of the distant thunder of the waves bashing the rocks beneath the lighthouse. Clementine was out there somewhere, dimmed and resting in the oceanic dark. The jellyfish held all the answers. The challenge was to convince her to share them.

And just like that, I knew exactly what Aldo would do.

"Clementine surfaces for three nights, right?" I said. "Give me the first one."

"To do what?" asked Sylvia.

"Get in the water with her." I managed to keep my voice steady, but the lines of my palms were greased with sweat.

For the first time since I'd met her, Sylvia Steele looked startled. "You want to go swimming with this thing?"

"Not swimming. Diving. I want to see Clementine up close, in her natural habitat." Margo Sloan had said as much: The first task was to see. Whether you were trying to understand the workings of a tiny bacterium or the migration patterns of a humpback whale, you weren't going to get very far without finding a way to observe your subject. "If she's stressed, she might be showing other symptoms. Symptoms that could point us to the real problem. She could be contracting unevenly, or producing unusual amounts of mucus—"

"Gross," said Tony.

I was careful not to look at her so she would not spot the fear I felt twitching all over my face.

Sylvia went on watching me, as if she were waiting for me to backpedal. When I said nothing—less out of determination than because my tongue, absent all moisture, had superglued itself to the roof of my mouth—she remarked, sounding almost impressed, "I've got to hand it to you, Doctor: No one's thought of doing anything like *that*."

Sylvia replaced the logbook in its display case with the others and then ambled over to the dining table to sit, using her walking stick to swipe Tony's feet out of the way.

"We do everything by majority vote around here. You want Emmett to hold off, you'll have to make your case at our town hall meeting next week."

I found my voice: "Emmett Beckendorf?"

"He's got another scheme he's cooking up for June."

The bottom dropped out of my stomach. I didn't have to ask for details to know Emmett's plan would be bad news for Clementine.

"I look forward to hearing all about it," I said, pleased at how fearless I sounded. Maybe if I playacted at confidence for long enough, the real version would find its way to me.

• • •

After leaving the museum, I strode toward the edge of the bluff, testing myself, my joints liquefying with every step. The ocean opened up before me, a rippling sheet of gunmetal gray. Raindrops pummeled the surface. Sharp rocks boiled over with long ribbons of white foam. The tide was racing in, flooding all the crannies that had been bared on my last visit. Limpets and sea stars would be anchored in place by their muscular feet, barnacles anchored by the brown cement seeping from their heads.

What was anchoring me? I felt feeble and transparent, like I was barely tethered to the earth. I scanned for Aldo and didn't see him. But I would not be fooled into thinking he was gone.

The junky gold car was idling, headlights glaring through the gloom. I slid into the passenger seat drenched and shivering. Tony obligingly blasted the heaters, and then we started bumping up the path toward Beach Street.

Possibilities clattered through my mind. That Clementine, or her ancestors, had been living around Shattering Point for nearly a century. That we were all in more danger than I'd thought.

If Nadia were here, she'd be encouraging me to look on the bright side: We had no way of knowing whether Sylvia's interpretation of events was true. Even if it was, nine years had elapsed between Augustus's alleged sighting of Clementine and his mysterious death; the jellyfish had been surfacing this time around for only seven months. As for the stories Sylvia had mentioned, she must have been referencing those "strange accidents" the shaggy-haired man had been so eager to tell me about back on the mainland—urban legends, tall tales, like my mother's spooky stories. They had nothing to do with Clementine. Nadia would tell me to put them out of my mind.

But it wasn't Nadia in the car with me. It was Tony, and I had no idea what was going through her head.

In the end, she spoke first. "What is it with you and jellyfish, anyway?"

It was a question I'd been fielding most of my life, and I lapsed automatically into my scripted response: "They're amazing animals, outwardly simple but deceptively complex. They're older than sharks, older than trees—"

Tony cut me off. "Lots of animals are old and amazing. What is it about jellyfish, specifically?"

I hesitated. There was no judgment in Tony's voice, only a determined curiosity. She glanced at me out of the corner of her eye every few seconds, then back to the road, blurry in the downpour.

"People don't give them enough credit," I said finally. "People don't see them for what they are. They're underdogs. Misunderstood."

Tony's lips quirked upward in a half smile. "Like you?"

I settled for shrugging, uncertain whether I was being mocked or not.

Her expression darkened as we started following the curve of the shore back to the B and B. "What if Clementine is poisonous?"

"Venomous," I corrected.

"God, you're a dork."

Was that exasperation tinged with affection, or just exasperation? I wasn't sure, but I thought I felt our iciness thawing, some new appreciation warming the air between us.

I smiled as I pressed my forehead against the window, watching my breath plume across the glass.

"I think I've got a work-around for that," I said.

• • •

The brilliant materials engineer with whom Aldo had been working on his sting-proof suit was named Ha-Yun Kim. We'd met once at a research symposium in Santa Monica three years ago. I fired off an email to her after returning from the lighthouse without much hope she'd remember me. She surprised me by writing back straightaway and agreeing to set up a video call first thing Friday morning.

I brought my laptop into the dining room after breakfast, my camera showing a view of the chintzy lighthouse painting over the sideboard. The storm had cleared out. Sunlight spilled through the big picture window and splashed across my lap.

There was no point in mincing words.

"I need the Nematoskyn," I said as soon as Ha-Yun's image popped into view and we confirmed that we could hear one another.

"You and me both," she said. She was in her mid-forties, with chunky tortoiseshell glasses and a spiky hairstyle that kept phasing into her blurred background, turning the top of her head into a smooth brown egg. "There's been a manufacturing delay. We won't be able to bring it to market for another six months."

My stomach simmered with a complicated feeling: part dismay, part relief. Six months from now, it would be winter, Beach Street pillowed with snow, icicles dangling from the roof eaves. How much closer would Clementine's barrier have moved by then? My mind supplied a grotesque image: forty-seven corpses cold in their beds like Augustus Steele. I didn't know if Sylvia's theory about her grandfather's death was right, but I couldn't wait half a year to find out. Nor could Elijah be placated with excuses for that long. I'd be fired, my poor jelly polyps starved to death and dumped down a drain.

"Okay, never mind," I said. "Have a nice d—"

Ha-Yun cut me off: "What I *do* have are the prototypes. The ones Aldo was testing." The sound of his name in someone else's mouth gave me a stomach-swooping sensation, like when you miss a step on a staircase. Ha-Yun's head swiveled to the left, and I wondered if the suits were hanging there on a rack in her office, just out of my view. "Of course, I can't go handing those out to anyone," she said, looking back at me.

I locked eyes with my own vacant expression. I wasn't good at this game: bargaining, subtext, strategy.

"How about . . . an official testimonial for your website?" I tried.

Ha-Yun wagged a finger. "Not a testimonial, an endorsement."

"Fine. Whatever."

"*And* you're going to come on board as a consultant for my next project."

I opened my mouth. Shut it. It was the same offer Aldo had been nagging me with for half a year, but coming from Ha-Yun's lips, it felt more like an order. "I'm no consultant."

"You haven't even heard what the project is."

"Jellyfish-proof flip-flops?"

"Oh, apparel is very *last year,*" said Ha-Yun. "We're branching out. Working on the Nematoskyn, I kept bumping into all kinds of bioengineering potential. I'm planning a whole line of jellyfish-inspired products, beginning with"—she dropped her voice dramatically—"the Jellybot."

"Is that a robot made of jellyfish or a robot that tracks jellyfish?"

"Neither. It's a robot that harnesses jellyfish propulsion mechanics to maneuver itself through the water. Low-power, maximum efficiency, nearly noiseless. That's the plan, anyway."

"Why me? I don't do hydrodynamics."

"Aldo always spoke highly of you, Josephine—"

"And you thought highly of Aldo?"

"Actually, I thought he was crazy," she said lightly. "But it was a type of crazy that worked for me. See, I'm a results-oriented person: I'm willing to overlook a lot of personal quirks if someone can get me where I want to be. Aldo said you looked at jellyfish and saw possibilities where everyone else saw problems. That's the kind of mindset I need around here."

"I already have a job," I said, annoyed.

"At your rinky-dink aquarium?" She raised her eyebrows. "Yes, Aldo mentioned that, too. That place'll be closed in a year. You know it, I know it."

I had never met someone who'd so mastered the art of sounding smug and pitying at the same time.

"My company, on the other hand, is thriving. The Navy's already interested in the Jellybot. You'd be well compensated for your efforts, and you'd get to redeem jellyfish in the eyes of the public. Isn't that exactly what you want?"

This arrogant woman had no idea what I wanted. Even if the aquarium wasn't thriving from a business standpoint, Seaheart had been a perfect professional home for me all these years. It had kept me afloat after I'd lost Aldo, gifting me with a sense of purpose that carried me through those empty days. I was loyal to it, and to Elijah. What was the point in trying to escape Shattering if it wasn't to get back to the things I loved?

"I'll consider it," I said.

"Aldo also said you were a stubborn pain in the ass."

"Yeah, well, he would know."

She whipped off her glasses and leaned into the screen, so that I could see the smears of concealer not fully blended beneath her eyes. "My condolences, by the way. I was sorry to lose him. I heard that you were with him when he—"

"You heard wrong."

I didn't want to get into Aldo's death with a person I barely knew—a person who'd only valued him because his was the kind of crazy that enhanced her company's productivity.

"Ah. Well, never mind, then." She replaced her glasses and leaned back in her chair, all business again. "Tell you what. Take the long weekend to think about it. I'll have my assistant draw up a consulting contract for you to review. Soon as it's signed and returned, he'll ship you the prototype—and not one second before."

"Aren't you going to ask what I need the suit for?" It was dumb to hand her a question I didn't want to answer, but I felt the need to remind Ha-Yun that, despite her money and her brilliance, she didn't know everything.

"I assume it has something to do with a jellyfish," she said breezily.

Her square vanished. I was left blinking at a full-screen version of my own face.

Haunted

The pain from a jellyfish sting ranges from mild discomfort to widespread burning agony. Compare the sting of an Irukandji jellyfish—said to be so painful its recipients beg for death—to the sting of a moon jellyfish, a warm and pleasing tickle that this author has had the pleasure of receiving a half dozen times.

JN: Could you please sound less turned on by the moon jelly?

AA: You're one to talk.

Ha-Yun's reference to the long weekend should've clued me in, but it didn't: I was astonished to walk into Retreat-by-the-Sea's dining room the next morning and discover a stranger drinking coffee at the table. Sitting in my chair.

"Good morning!" he hailed me in a too-loud voice. He was round-cheeked and balding with big ears and small, fast-moving eyes—an overgrown mouse of a man. He smiled, and his smile was like a bright light stunning me out of sleep. Two more strangers, an elderly man and woman costumed in clashing floral T-shirts, had taken their mugs into the sitting room, where they were chuckling over something on one of their phones. The sound of their easy laughter made the hairs on the back of my neck prickle.

The end of the month had crept up on me. Shattering Point's tourist season had begun.

"Good morning," I managed.

The man introduced himself, offering a name I instantly forgot.

The kitchen door swung open. Tony ferried a platter of scrambled eggs into the room, looking every bit the hostess in her striped apron with the metal serving spoon protruding from the pocket. The elderly couple meandered in from the sitting room and joined the mousy man at the table, all three chorusing their thanks before diving into their breakfasts.

I sat and ate with them, because I was hungry, and I didn't know what else to do. Their pleasant chatter seethed in my ears like a pot that had overboiled. All three were birding enthusiasts, called to Shattering by the promise of nesting plovers.

When the conversation came around to me, I faltered.

Tony, who was doing something over by the sideboard, replied with a speed that betrayed her fear I might answer truthfully: "Jo's visiting a friend of hers, our new schoolteacher."

"Aah! So it's your first time?" crowed the elderly woman. "We've been coming every spring for, oh—what is it now, Tom? Six years?"

"No place like it in the world, Shattering," the elderly man said with a smile. "You're in for a real treat, Jo. How long are you staying?"

I coughed out a maniacal laugh.

Tony's grip landed on my shoulder. "Jo, darling, could you help me out with something in the kitchen?"

The tension whooshed out of me the second the door closed behind us. I hadn't realized I was clenching all the muscles in my arms.

"Are you gonna be able to keep your shit together?" Tony asked. Her face looked different. I realized it was because she was wearing makeup.

I leaned against the refrigerator, feeling weak. "I can't believe people are still visiting here."

"Of course they're still visiting. What d'you think I've been cleaning this place for—fun?" She unscrewed the lid to the carafe and poured fresh coffee from the pot, splashing some onto the counter. She was nervous, I realized—the first day of her first season running the business on her own. "My aunt put everything into Retreat-by-the-Sea. She trusted me to keep it going for her. And that's what I'm going to do."

"She really wants to keep the business going?" I said, stunned. "Even with what's happening on the island?"

"Maya left in September before any of this started."

"And you *didn't tell her*?"

"Keep your voice down!" hissed Tony, casting a worried look at the kitchen door. She replaced the coffeepot and then looked back at me, still frowning. "She has enough on her plate, okay? I can handle this myself." She paused, mouth tensed into a defiant grimace, daring me to challenge her.

I stood straight and folded my arms across my chest. "What happens if any of those people out there see Clementine?"

"They'll be long gone before the next full moon. And we keep the beach fenced off, remember?"

"What about the moving barrier?"

"Hasn't moved any farther. We overreacted, Jo. For all we know, it could stay right where it is for years."

Nadia had basically said the same thing, yet I wanted to go on arguing with Tony. In light of the possibility that Clementine had caused Sylvia's grandfather's death, populating the island further, even with temporary guests, seemed to be asking for trouble. There was still a lot about Clementine we didn't understand.

I also recognized that I had less selfless reasons. The tourists put me on edge. I wanted them gone. They didn't belong here, and their wrongness cut through me like a stitch.

Tony pulled in a slow breath as she mopped up the coffee spill with a paper towel. I hadn't meant to admonish her. She was trying to make the best of an impossible situation. I was the one who was supposed to figure out Clementine, not Tony. None of this was her fault.

"On a related subject," she said, "I'm gonna need Montana back."

"Oh." Another outcome I should've seen coming. There were only six rooms in the B and B. Of course Tony would need all of them.

A charged quiet fell between us, broken by the scrape of cutlery and hum of chatter in the dining room.

"I can stay with Nadia," I volunteered, at the exact same moment Tony said, "You can stay at my place."

"What?" I said.

"Oh, no. That makes more sense," Tony said quickly, turning from me to drop the paper towel into the garbage.

"No, I just—I wanted to make sure I heard—"

"You guys have known each other a long time," she continued, still with her back to me, "plus she and Roger have more space."

"Oh, okay . . ."

"Okay," said Tony. She looked at me, through me, and then she walked past me into the dining room.

• • •

Nadia was ecstatic at the prospect of our "sleepover," emphasizing her *yes* with a dozen yellow heart emojis, plus the one of two girls holding hands. A week ago, this reply would've sent my heart tripping down a very tall staircase. Now I only felt sorry at having turned down Tony's offer, if in fact that was what I had done. What was implied by that offer? That she liked me? That she was still thinking about that kiss, too? I shook off the possibility. I had to resist falling into that trap again, the same one I'd fallen into with Nadia eleven years ago. Nadia had only wanted to be nice to me. Tony was just doing the same thing.

The act of packing up my belongings filled me with a sadness I hadn't expected. Montana, with its dopey treasure chest and pervasive odor of lemon furniture polish, had evolved into a safe haven for me this past week and a half, a place where I could stew through my hopes and doubts in comfy solitude. It was where Nadia and I had reconciled. And my vision of Aldo hadn't followed me here, either.

My laptop was on the nightstand, still open to Ha-Yun's contract. I could've sworn I'd closed out of it last night before going to bed. I didn't want to work for someone who cared more about money than science. I didn't want to abandon Elijah as Seaheart was crumbling around him. But if I said no to Ha-Yun, what alternative did I have?

I stooped to collect a sock that had slithered under the bed.

That was when I saw Margo's Clementine portraits, neatly stacked in the corner where I'd left them after examining them with Nadia.

I tottered up Beach Street with the canvases stacked across my arms like pizza boxes. The elderly birders had finished their breakfast and were talking on the sidewalk with the goateed owner of the ice cream parlor, the one who longed for his Parisian éclairs. He was all smiles today, every trace of glumness hidden behind a veneer of hospitality that was almost spooky in its convincingness. I tuned them out, zeroing in on my footsteps and trying not to drop any of the paintings. It felt good to have a simple task I couldn't screw up.

The Sloans' door knocker was shaped like a Celtic Green Man. It followed my hand with steely eyes as I rapped three times, knocking again when no one answered. I felt a strange loyalty to those portraits and was reluctant to abandon them on the front stoop.

Margo Sloan finally appeared, wearing the same ginger wig she'd had on the day we met, and a black beret pinned at a lopsided angle. She sounded groggy, as if I'd woken her.

"Ah, Josephine. Have you returned for your next portrait session?"

"I'm just dropping these off. Thank you again for letting me look at them."

Margo beckoned me into the foyer with a warning: "Watch your step, dear."

She tipped her head toward the kitchen, which was a battlefield of ceramic fragments and glass shards. The wreckage was so substantial, it had spilled into the hallway. It looked as if a cabinet's worth of dishes had been hurled onto the floor.

I edged my way around a splintered plate. "What happened?"

"Marriage, dear," said Margo, "is not for the faint of heart."

I trailed her into the studio, where she took the portraits from me one at a time and slid them into a large wardrobe between sheets of waxed paper. Beneath her beret, I thought her color seemed off, her face tinged with a grayish pallor.

"Are you sure you're all right?" I asked.

"Oh yes, dear. Don't worry. It was me doing the lion's share of the throwing. Irish temper. It's my one flaw."

"Can't you move out? At least go to a different house?" The other islanders had spoken of everything they stood to lose beyond the barrier. Here was evidence of the opposite: a rotting marriage compelled to fester past its expiration date.

"I'm not going anywhere," said Margo, her voice sharpening with reproach. "This is my home. I'm the one who picked it out for us fifteen years ago. And *he* won't abandon his precious flowers. Have you ever met anyone who values *plants* more than they value *people*?"

She shut the wardrobe doors and faced me.

"Wouldn't you be willing to sit for me, Josephine?" she asked sweetly. "Just one more time?"

I sat. I knew better than anyone the pleasure of losing yourself in your work when the rest of your life was falling to pieces. I could give Margo that.

But the atmosphere in the studio felt different, tainted, the aftereffects of the couple's fight lingering in the air like a bad smell. The sketches on the walls leered in arrogant judgment. I stiffened at every creak, thinking it was Norm, a snarling Betty at his heels. I resisted the unintended implication of Margo's words: that her miserable, misanthropic husband and I were somehow alike. I would never put a jellyfish before a human being.

Margo also seemed agitated, shifting around on her chair like she couldn't get comfortable. She sipped from her teacup. I was grateful not to have been offered another taste of her homemade brew. She picked up her paintbrush again, and the breath gusted out of her in a frustrated sigh.

"Would you *please* stop your squirming?"

"I'm not squirming," I said, startled.

"Not you, Josephine," said Margo. "You're doing fine. But your friend's got ants in his pants."

"My—what? What are you talking about?"

She waved her paintbrush in my direction. "Tall fella in the silly black suit. Dancing around, dripping water all over my floor . . . There, now. He's settled down right behind you. That's perfect. Don't move, either of you."

Fear ran through me in icy trickles. I didn't turn around. I barely breathed. I gripped the edges of the chair until the skin beneath my fingernails stung. *Form is emptiness and emptiness is form. There is no eye, no ear, no nose . . .*

Memorial Day

The most venomous animal on the planet is a jellyfish.

The air was warming. The tendril of breeze that slipped through the window of Nadia and Roger's spare bedroom smelled uneasily of summer. The room was stuffed with boxes of books and board games and picture frames that had never been unpacked—Nadia too flighty to commit to the task, Roger too optimistic that their stay on Shattering Point would be a short one. She had cheerfully shoved all this into a corner as she showed me around my new accommodations, seeming so happy to host me that I could do nothing but return her smile, try to be grateful, and try not to think the one thought that hadn't left my mind since I'd fled Margo's studio yesterday morning before she could offer me another chance to look at the portrait.

Other people couldn't see your hallucination. That meant my vision of Aldo was something *other* than a hallucination. Something like the ethereal *yōkai* that had populated my mother's scary stories.

It was a term that defied easy translation. Apparition, monster, demon, ghost—*yōkai* were all of these and none of them, the wily, spectral presences that stalked the borderlands between known and unknown. My favorite *yōkai* were always the creatures, but monstrous forms could borrow human shapes, too. A disturbed spirit might latch onto the physical world and linger, pummeling still-living relatives with terror and misfortune. Even as a kid, I had never actually believed any of it.

At least I wasn't losing my mind. I clung to that silver lining, the only one I could spin out of this increasingly nightmarish scenario.

I was not losing my mind. I was *not* hallucinating my dead best friend.

Instead, I was being haunted—*hunted*—by a thing that wore his face.

Was that better, or worse?

I wanted to talk to Nadia about it, but I could never get her alone. Roger was always right there, sitting on the couch beside her, washing dishes in the next room, hovering over her shoulder in the hallway when she stuck her head in the spare bedroom to tell me good night. If I hadn't been so annoyed, I might've been flattered by his apparent concern that I was beguiling enough to steal her away from him.

Roger was, at least, trying to be civil with me. I suspected Nadia had also asked him to play nice. He asked questions about my research, and gamely endured our many nostalgic stories about Gladstone, laughing at Nadia's spot-on imitation of wacky Professor Hano and his five hundred kanji. I tried to match his efforts, for Nadia's sake. I tried to catalog Roger's best attributes: He clearly doted on Nadia, he seemed like a good listener, he was an amazing cook. I tried to suppress my bitterness when they touched in the thousand effortless ways of a couple blithely accustomed to shared proximity—her arm grazing his torso as she reached past him for the saltshaker, their legs pressed together on the couch.

But my patience had frayed by the second night of the "sleepover." It had been a mistake to come here. I should've accepted Tony's invitation when she first offered. There was no way to do so now without hurting Nadia's feelings, or giving Roger the satisfaction of having pushed me away. I tossed and turned and only managed to fall asleep by fantasizing minor calamities that might befall him: a case of food poisoning that confined him to the bathroom for the day, a busted tooth that forced a trip to a dentist on the mainland.

Monday dawned bright and clear, the hot sun blasting through wispy clouds. Nadia had explained that the annual Memorial Day cookout would take place in the town square, followed by a fireworks display at the lighthouse, celebrating the official start of Shattering's tourist season. I didn't want to go. Tomorrow was my deadline to get back to Ha-Yun Kim. I had the idea that I would spend the day researching state-of-the-art underwater drones. There had to be a device out there sophisticated enough to capture clear footage of camera-shy Clementine. If I could get a hold of something like that, it would spare me having to dive, which in light of Margo's discovery, I was even more desperate not to do: The *yōkai*, I'd deduced by now, only showed up when I neared the water's edge.

Nadia wouldn't take no for an answer.

"You don't need to be working *all the time*, Josie."

"You do understand I'm trying to figure out how to spring us all out of here, right?"

"And you can keep doing that tomorrow," she said firmly. "Today is a holiday. Everyone's gonna be there. Plus, Roger's bringing his *abuela*'s famous coleslaw!"

"Just give up, Jo," advised Roger, waving a mayo-covered spatula at me from the sink. "Her goodwill is a force of nature. Resistance is futile."

I helped Nadia load up a cooler with some cans of beer and soda from the fridge. Maybe she was right. Maybe it would be good for me to be around other people. The town square was well inland, with no view of the ocean. I could always sneak back to Nadia and Roger's house before the fireworks display.

As we were walking out the door, I felt my phone buzzing in my pocket. I withdrew it and stared hard at the name floating on the cracked screen.

"I'll meet you there," I told Nadia.

"You better," she said.

I stepped back into the foyer, took a deep breath, and answered the call.

"*There* you are," said Mom.

"Here I am."

She sounded exasperated, which was typical. I was her exasperating daughter, whose needs had not made sense to her since infancy. Without my father to mediate between us, we were lost to one another, jabbering at frequencies that only rarely intersected.

"Where are you?" asked Mom.

"I told you. I'm traveling for work."

"Why don't you answer my text messages?"

"I've been really busy," I said. "And the cell service around here isn't great." Neither was a lie. As we were talking, I roved about the house in pursuit of a fleeting signal, Mom's voice now booming through my phone's speaker, now shrinking to a crackly whisper.

"*Where?*" she pressed.

"Maine," I said.

"Maine . . . Dad and I went there once. We got on a boat to see whales, but they didn't show up. This was many years before you were born. Maybe if we went back now, the whales would show up for you."

I settled in the kitchen, where a fly was buzzing over the slivers of grated carrot Roger had left on the cutting board.

"So how are you doing?" Mom asked, the sly emphasis placed on *you* alerting me to the fact that her thoughts had once again turned toward Aldo.

I hesitated. Experience taught me not to go to my mother for comfort. She had a unique way of stoking my anxieties and making me feel even worse. But she'd been the one to tell me stories about *yōkai* in the first place. If there was anyone who knew how to banish a tenacious ghost, it was my mother.

"I'm—a little overwhelmed," I hedged.

"I think maybe you work too hard," said Mom shrewdly.

I heard a loud squeal through the phone as a door opened. Something about that squeal—its familiar two-tone whine—set my teeth on edge. I thought of the kitchen cabinet in my apartment whose rusty hinges defied all my efforts to lubricate them.

"Ma, where are you?" I asked slowly.

"What do you mean?" she said, with the defensiveness of the guilt-ridden.

"Oh my god. Are you *in my apartment*?"

"What! You weren't answering me. I thought you were dead. I called your aquarium. They said you were out of town, didn't know where. What was I supposed to do?"

"Not break into my home! How did you even get inside?" I had a terrifying image of my ninety-pound mother clad in a black tracksuit, jimmying a window lock with a screwdriver and slithering over the sill.

"No break-in," she said sulkily. "I found your spare key. You really need to make a better hiding spot for that."

"Oh my god, Ma . . ."

"So when you coming home?"

"I don't know. Please leave now."

"I'll just wait for you here. It's so dirty. I've been cleaning."

"Don't clean. Don't touch anything." My skin crawled at the thought of my mom sweeping a dustrag over my shelves, clucking her tongue in disapproval at the number of expired condiments in my fridge. This was a whole new level of invasion, and there was nothing I could do about it. "Please go back to Indiana. I promise I'll come visit as soon as I'm done here, okay?"

"But *when*?"

"I don't know!"

My inability to answer the question only calcified my panic. What if I never figured this out? What if I was stuck here with Nadia and her husband for the rest of my life? What if the barrier kept moving, shoving me closer and closer to the water, where the *yōkai* was waiting?

What if Clementine never let us go?

I made a swipe at the fly, whose buzzing had crescendoed to chainsaw levels. It flitted easily out of reach.

"I can hardly hear you," Mom complained.

"I'm not saying anything."

"You should do something with these, you know." She did this often on the phone, talking as if I were in the room with her and could see what she was doing. She could've been gesturing at anything. The pair of sneakers with the shredded soles I'd been meaning to toss or repair. The beautiful set of titanium cookware she'd sent me for Christmas, which I'd yet to take out of the box.

But what I saw in my mind's eye, clear as a video recording, were the backs of my mother's fingers skimming the sea turtle urn where Aldo's ashes rested.

"I'll call you as soon as I can," I said, and hung up, switching my phone to silent for good measure.

• • •

Shattering's town square was a small plaza next to the post office, just a stretch of concrete slabbing with weeds tufting up through the cracks. The single mail truck parked out front was the lusterless white of a T-shirt that had been washed too many times. Round metal tables dragged over from the ice cream parlor were covered in paper plates and side dishes. The smell of charcoal wafted from a line of grills. On a makeshift stage fashioned from wooden crates lashed together, an old lobsterman plucked a banjo while the Urchin's blue-haired waitress chanted experimentally into the mic. "Testing one . . . testing two."

I observed all this from the post office stairs, where I'd secreted myself with a fish burger I had taken three bites of and no longer wanted. The conversation with my mother had left me feeling nauseated. People stood around talking in small groups as they ate. Nadia and Roger chatted with the woman who owned the souvenir shop. Emmett Beckendorf was hacking into a watermelon. Tony flipped burgers at a grill. Nadia's student Sidney Anakin Oliver Bernet swung from the hand of a woman with flyaway white hair whom I took to be Grandma. Even the tourists were here, leaking their wrongness into the plaza with every word and gesture.

The whole party struck me as desperately sad. The islanders had to be so sick of this place and of each other, yet here they were, putting on a display of summery merriment, pretending everything was okay.

I thought I was well concealed on the post office's stairs, but the kid's sharp eyes picked me out. Sidney detached from his grandmother and beelined toward me at such speed I braced for impact.

He came to a dramatic, panting halt inches from my legs. He wore a T-shirt with a lobster on it. A speech bubble above the lobster's head announced, *I Am Number One!*

"You're still here!" exclaimed Sidney. "What's your name, again?"

"You remember," I said. "It's a boy's name."

"Michael!" Sidney grinned and leaned into me. The audio had finally been figured out. The man with the banjo twanged a fast-paced melody while the waitress crooned a song about dirt and sunsets and finding your way back home.

"Ms. Markov is back. You found her," said Sidney, looking at me with such adoration I couldn't bring myself to correct him.

"She was just taking a little vacation," I said. "She missed you and Lila very much."

Sidney grew serious, cupping my cheek with his palm. Why were children's hands always so *damp*? His eyes flickered across my face, his mouth slightly open, and I knew he was tracking those magnetic threads stretching between us.

"You saw her," he breathed. "You saw Clementine."

"I did."

"And you didn't hurt her?"

Pity squeezed at me. I knew now why he'd been so fearful of my intentions back in the schoolyard. Month after month, he'd been forced to endure the grown-ups' efforts to destroy his friend Clementine, conducting his own anxious countdown to the full moon, a cycle of looming terror and fleeting relief as she defied the odds, again and again. I could suddenly see myself in this kid, his weirdness and his loneliness. What must it be like to grow up on a tiny island with a younger cousin as your only playmate? You learned to strike up friendships wherever you could find them—with a teacher, a stranger, a giant bioluminescent jelly.

"I'll never hurt her," I promised.

Sidney beamed, showing the rectangular gap of a missing tooth.

"Hey—want to know the Japanese word for jellyfish?" I asked.

"No, thanks." He'd tuned in to the music, twisting his hips and wiggling his arms. "Dance with me, Michael!" He tried to tug me off the stairs.

Over the kid's head, I glimpsed Norm Sloan swipe a hot dog off one of the grills and glare at it as if inspecting for contaminants.

A fresh wave of nausea gripped me. Where there was a Norm, there was surely a Margo nearby.

I made a quick retreat behind the mail truck, leaving Sidney to frolic off in search of a more enthusiastic dance partner. I felt better the second I was screened from view of the square—at least until I realized this hiding spot was already taken.

Tony coughed in surprise, unleashing a cloud of sweet-smelling smoke, then relaxed when she saw it was me. "Oh, hey. You want a hit?" She pulled a pretty orange-and-blue pipe out from behind her back.

"No, thanks. It makes me paranoid." More paranoia was the last thing I needed. I peeked around the edge of the mail truck, keeping my eyes peeled for flowing skirts. I was sure Margo would try to corner me into another portrait session given the chance, and I wasn't looking forward to fending her off. She had glimpsed something she wasn't supposed to see, a bit like eavesdropping on a private conversation. I resented her for it. And I was afraid.

I glanced back at Tony, who was slouched against the truck's door. She wore the same apron she'd had on in Retreat-by-the-Sea, its stripes now splashed with droplets of burger grease.

"Who're you hiding from?" I asked.

"My responsibilities," said Tony dryly. "I don't know how Aunt Maya did it. Forty-eight hours in, and I'm so goddamn tired. I'm never gonna make it to Labor Day." She raised her eyebrows at me. "Who're *you* hiding from?"

"Margo," I admitted. "She, uh, keeps trying to paint me."

"Let me guess. She said you were interesting-looking? That's code for *not white*. She keeps pestering me, too."

I smiled thinly. I would've vastly preferred if Margo's interest in me could be attributed to my fascinating ethnic ambiguity, rather than the thing she'd discerned leering over my shoulder. Just the thought of the *yōkai* made me shiver.

"But you're in luck," Tony added. "She's not here. Norm said she has a stomach bug."

I relaxed slightly. But I wasn't in any rush to rejoin the party. It was nice to be back here with Tony, encased in the cool square shadow of the mail truck.

She tipped her face and exhaled a stream of smoke downwind. "How are things at Château Nadia?"

"Château *Roger* and Nadia."

Tony laughed. "He's kind of a dweeb, isn't he?"

I smirked, then immediately felt guilty. It was one thing to harbor my own private frustrations about Roger. Shit talking him with someone else felt like a betrayal to Nadia, who just wanted the two of us to get along. "He's all right," I amended. "It's just—it would be nice to have some one-on-one time with Nadia."

"Mind if I ask," Tony said, with the air of someone who was going to ask regardless, "what the deal is with you two?"

A few days ago, I wouldn't have known how to answer that question.

"We're friends," I said carefully, and was relieved to find no traces of internal resistance. If Roger aggravated me, it wasn't because I longed to be in his place. I just wasn't any good at sharing my friends. Aldo and I had had each other, and no one else.

But that wasn't a fair standard to impose on loving, gregarious Nadia, who would always have other relationships. If I wanted to keep her in my life, I'd have to find a way to accept that.

Tony snorted. "Friends who fucked, maybe."

I felt myself flush. Had I really made it so obvious? Tony had barely seen Nadia and me together. "Why would you say that?"

"That day she came to see you at the B and B, you were in your room for ages."

"We were just talking!" My tone was exasperated, but inside, I felt a hopeful twitch of doubt. I remembered how aloof Tony had seemed with me the day after Jelly HQ, and then again in Retreat-by-the-Sea's kitchen when I'd suggested staying with Nadia over her. I was historically bad at picking up on signals. My ex, the Indexer, had had to practically climb on top of me before I understood she wanted to go out. I'd been so fearful of displacing my feelings for Nadia onto Tony and getting myself hurt again. I was still fearful. But I was also curious.

"Why do you even care?" I asked.

"I don't," said Tony. Her voice was cool and measured, the pipe dangling in her left hand. "I just don't like drama. This place is too small for it. You can't get away from anyone."

"Well there's no drama. Nadia and I really *are* just friends." I'd always hated that phrase, *"just" friends*—how it automatically demoted friendship to a lower rung on the ladder of human connection, a bond defined by its lack. But I'd had to reach for it more than once to explain my relationship to Aldo, and I would grudgingly accept its utility now, because I needed Tony to understand.

I couldn't tell whether it was working. Tony wasn't an open book like Nadia. She was more like me. Blank, careful. She tucked the pipe away and swept her stare over me. Her eyes had gone a little pink from the weed. I held myself still, waiting.

"Do you like birds?" Tony asked.

Be Careful What You Wish For

Though it's their stingers that tend to capture the public's fear, jellyfish's true destructive potential goes much further. Consider the USS *Ronald Reagan*, the nuclear-powered supercarrier—over one thousand feet long and costing over $4 billion to build—whose maiden voyage was abruptly halted in Brisbane in 2006 when over 1,700 pounds of jellyfish were accidentally sucked into its condensers. An environmental mishap, or an act of jelly war? You decide.

JN: Cut.

Stupidly, I realized I had imagined Tony living in one of the guest rooms in Retreat-by-the-Sea. But she had her own place—a small gray bungalow perched on a slope above the B and B that looked like it was about to lose its footing and slither down the hillside. Inside, the living room radiated warmth and clutter, sweaters slung over every chair back, a patchwork of frames covering the walls, and a multiscreen gaming system spewing cords all over the floor.

I examined a framed photograph hanging near the door: a lanky prepubescent Tony arm in arm with a middle-aged woman in lavender scrubs.

"Is this your aunt?"

"Mom." Tony sidled up next to me and studied the photo. "Those were the days. Before I broke her heart by leaving."

Tony frowned at the photo before beckoning me into the kitchen.

It was the sort of room that would've outraged my mother. Racks and baskets were crookedly hung from the walls and crammed with pans, spoons, oils, paintbrushes, sponges, mismatched mugs, and unlabeled mason jars full of grains and spices. I barely had a chance to take it all in before a blur of incoming motion made me duck and clap my hands to my head.

"Don't mind Scoot," said Tony. "He's a real show-off."

The bird—small, brown, some kind of sparrow—scrabbled its tiny claws into the row of thin scratches already carved into the back of a chair.

"He lives here with you?" I asked.

"The goal is to release them back into the wild. But every once in a while they get too soft. Too attached." She shook her head as if in disapproval, but I could see the fondness in her eyes as Scoot flapped and alighted on her outstretched hand. She let him rest there for a moment, then dropped her arm and sent him launching toward the curtain rod above the sink.

We entered a room that a normal person probably would've used as a home office or a second bedroom. For Tony, it was the bird hospital. Half a dozen cages of different shapes and sizes were stacked against the wall. A rolling metal workbench sat in the corner, stacked with supplies. Though both windows were thrown open, the air smelled like a mix of disinfectant and a sweet animal musk.

Only one cage was occupied. I lowered my face to the bars and watched the seagull wobble around its enclosure, overbalanced by the yellow wrapping around one of its wings.

"Does it have a name?"

"Seagull Number Seven," said Tony.

The sight of Seagull #7 ambling in clumsy circles flooded me with a sadness I didn't understand. I had seen plenty of animals in captivity before. My fingers twitched with the desire to undo the latch and open the cage door, but it wouldn't make any difference. The bird was too injured to fly away.

Tony settled onto a stool behind the workbench and produced several ziplock baggies. "I make my own feed. There's too much filler crap in the manufactured stuff." I watched her pinch seeds from the baggies and sprinkle them into a metal dish. Her large hands didn't look like they'd be suited to the delicate work of splinting bird wings or pipetting water droplets into baby bird beaks. I remembered how those fingers had felt as they massaged the knots in my neck, bringing me back to my body when I'd spiraled far away.

"I never thanked you," I realized.

Tony glanced up. "For what?"

"For calming me down that day when we were in the tunnel."

She dismissed my gratitude with a wave of her hand. "Don't mention it."

"It's not like I'm—I mean—" I twisted a corner of newspaper that was poking from one of the open cages. Tony went on mixing her bird feed with her back to me, but I could tell by her posture that she was listening. "I just want you to know I haven't always been like this. I lost someone last year and it's got me a little messed up."

Tony tilted her head in a decidedly birdlike manner. "Aldo?"

My guts flipped at the sound of his name. "How do you know that?"

"You were talking in your sleep, that day you collapsed."

"What did I say?"

"Not much. Just the name, over and over. Sounded like you were looking for him."

I should've been mortified at the thought of mumbling pitifully in front of a near stranger, and I was. More surprising was the current of relief running side by side with my humiliation. So few people knew what had happened to Aldo. My mother and Ha-Yun Kim were the only people who'd spoken his name to me since he died.

"He was my best friend . . . my only friend. He died last year when we were scuba diving. It was my fault. I got turned around. I think he ran out of air while he was trying to find me."

Tony rotated on the stool to face me. "You think," she said. "So you don't know."

"I know that if I'd gone the way he wanted me to, he'd still be alive." There was an aching sense of release in saying it out loud. Yes, Aldo was dead because of me. Maybe the more comfortable I got admitting this fact, the more its cruelty would congeal into a more bearable form—a little dried-out husk I could slip into my pocket and learn to carry without stumbling.

Tony sealed up the bags on her workbench. Seagull #7 stopped circling and shuffled toward the cage door as she approached. I wondered if gulls, like crows, could recognize human faces. Did it know Tony as its healer and caregiver? Would it be another one who lost touch with its wildness and lived out the rest of its life indoors?

The full scale of my entrapment on Shattering slammed into me without warning. I would never again witness the splendor of a coral reef. Never sag into the cushions of my father's easy chair. Never walk into a movie theater and see Aldo's favorite candy arrayed in glossy spotlit rows under the counter. Never return to my childhood home, where I'd been so unhappy in such an unremarkable way.

There was no room called Indiana in Retreat-by-the-Sea. If there had been, what would have awaited me behind that door? A bedspread emblazoned with the white horseshoe of the Indianapolis Colts. A framed print of the official state poem we'd been required to memorize in elementary school, of which I could now recall only two lines: *I must roam those wooded hillsides, / I must heed the native call.* My parents huddled over a crossword puzzle, twin strands of steam curling from mugs of matcha and fogging up their reading glasses.

Tony was watching me closely. I got the feeling she knew exactly what I was thinking, because she'd thought through her version of it, too. All the islanders had.

"I don't want Clementine to die," she said.

The words sent warmth humming through me. "You don't?"

"I don't even want this dumb bird to die." Tony lowered into a squat to stare at Seagull #7, who stared calmly back. "I wasn't lying when I said it felt like Clementine was talking to me. Like she *knew* me. Honestly, I think she might be the most amazing animal in the world."

My attraction to Tony was solidifying by the second. "But?" I could smell the complication dangling in the air between us.

She sighed and looked up at me. "My mom's really sick. That's why my aunt left. To help take care of her. It was supposed to be me. But we've always had a—challenging relationship, me and Mom."

I nodded. I knew all about challenging mothers.

"So I bargained with Aunt Maya: 'You go, I'll stay and manage the B and B.'" Tony's voice was smaller and tighter than I'd ever heard it. "I made it sound like I really wanted to try my hand at running the business. The truth is, I was just happy to have the excuse to stay. Then Clementine came around, and it felt like some kind of cosmic punishment, or one of those be-careful-what-you-wish-for fairy tales." She laughed briefly and without humor.

"How's your mom doing now?" I asked.

"She's stable. They're taking it day by day."

I felt that uncomfortable squeeze of pity again.

I joined Tony on the floor, which was speckled with spilled birdseed. Her shoulders relaxed, almost imperceptibly. I wouldn't have noticed if we hadn't been scooched so close, our arms pressed together, her skin bleeding warmth into mine.

When she kissed me, every thought dropped away. My head was perfectly empty, and it was bliss. I felt the thud of Tony's heart, fast and loud, not against my body but inside it, crowding out the space where my own heart had been. And the hair brushing my neck was her hair, and the blood streaming through my veins was hers, too.

• • •

The summer afternoon lingered. Evening moseyed in late and lazy, spilling long shadows across the floor. Tony swung an arm out of bed to switch on a curtain of string lights that thrummed with a lilac glow. When her hand dropped and crawled along my thigh, I visualized it as a starburst of bioluminescence exploding across my skin.

It had been over a year since the Indexer dumped me. I wondered what moniker Aldo would've assigned Tony. The Innkeeper. Bird Girl. I imagined bringing her on one of our dive trips, Aldo at first balking at the incursion, playing the wounded party until Tony disarmed him with a deadpan one-liner and all his pique melted off him in a laugh. He was like that. Quick to sulk, quicker to forgive.

Tony lay still and quiet beside me, the purple lights playing across her closed eyes. She was not Nadia, I thought with conviction—she was not even *slightly* like Nadia, and this came as a relief. I laid a hand lightly against her cheek. She didn't stir. But even in sleep, her jaw was tight and twitching. She was going to grind her teeth to dust.

I must've dozed off, too, because the next thing I knew, I was swimming.

The jellies flickered like dying bulbs as I traveled deeper into the cave. The passages tightened, and the ceiling dropped until I was reduced to wiggling on my belly like a worm. Every survival instinct I had was screaming at me to turn back, but I was so close: He was just ahead of me, the water still shivering where he'd eased his body through it.

With one final, wrenching twist, I tore free from the tunnel and launched myself into open space. But I wasn't in the Armory with its field of towering stalagmites. I was in the same chamber where we'd started. I spun in a dismayed circle, wondering how I could've gotten so turned around.

I wasn't alone.

The snake uncoiled itself, stretching to fill the cavern until the walls seemed to be crawling. It was so big, I couldn't see all of it without turning my head. Its unblinking eyes were like two blazing coals just plucked from the fire. It held me in its stare for a moment, its forked tongue lapping the odor of my fear.

I felt my lips moving, a squeak of a protest traveling up my throat: "You're not Aldo."

"Am I not?" said the serpent. It spoke Portuguese, but I could understand it perfectly.

The snake dipped its head and opened its jaws, revealing four rows of curved teeth. Its breath smelled like charcoal and cooking flesh.

"Your life, your sight, or your sanity."

A heated burst of anger dissolved some of my fear. "Tell me where he is, and you can take whichever one you want." The version of Aldo that had been haunting my waking hours was just an echo, I knew now. A copy. The real version was down here somewhere, right where I left him.

"A bargain striker. How quaint." The snake reared up, the horns on the top of its head scraping the ceiling. "Once upon a time," it said soothingly, speaking now in Aldo's voice, "there was a boy who thought he could cheat me with his silence. But I found him in the end, as I always do. It was in this very cave where we reunited. I gave him his options. This time, he didn't hesitate."

"He gave you his life."

The snake's tongue flickered. "He was careless with it anyway. I, on the other hand, am very careful with my lives. Each one is precious, not to be flung away or wasted."

"Then he is in here. Somewhere. You haven't gotten rid of him." I glanced back at the impossibly tight tunnel. Dread sank through me at the prospect of having to crawl through it again, but I knew that I would do it. I'd struggle my way through the whole cave system over and over, scraping into walls and going blind in the dark, if it meant there was a chance Aldo was waiting for me at the end. "Tell me where he is," I said.

The snake's skin was patterned with black diamonds that shimmered and merged as it shifted. I thought it was lowering down to me, to whisper in my ear or close its jaws around my head. Then I realized it was the cave: The ceiling was dropping, and the floor was rising, the two surfaces swinging slowly together like the hinged valves of a clam.

When we were only a few feet apart, the snake spoke again.

"No need." It didn't sound like Aldo anymore, or any human voice I'd ever heard. "You'll be together again soon."

* * *

My eyes flew open. I was so soaked in sweat, it felt as if I'd just climbed out of the ocean. The ceiling light in Tony's bedroom was on, blaring a harsh yellow that drowned out the softer glow of the fairy lights. A voice was talking: Tony, on the phone with someone while she hopped around, yanking a pair of blue jeans over her hips.

The dream wouldn't leave me. I could still feel the whisper of the snake's scales against my skin, see the fire dancing in its eyes. What did it mean, *You'll be together again soon*? That I would make it back to California and the sea turtle urn on my mantel? That I would find the real Aldo waiting for me somewhere on Shattering? Or was it death that I would find waiting for me instead?

"There's been an emergency."

It took me a second to realize Tony was off the phone and talking to me. A set of keys on an orange lanyard landed in my lap. "Start the car," she said.

A low half-moon was rising in the east. Tony threw herself into the passenger seat of the junky gold car, arms fastened around a red medical bag, and I gunned it as instructed, swerving out of the hilly side lane and skidding onto Beach Street.

"What happened?" Shattering's one paved road was pitted with potholes I didn't know how to avoid, and the rattling bounce of the car had chased away the last of my grogginess. I felt exhilarated and slightly nauseated.

"Roger got hurt," said Tony.

"What? How?" I had a vision of him blowing off one of his hands with a firecracker.

"Not sure. Sylvia found him outside the museum, passed out."

My queasiness intensified. I pressed the accelerator as hard as I dared, not letting up until Tony told me to turn down the path that led to the beach.

The gate remained open, the BEACH CLOSED sign whisked away and stowed until the next full moon. The little car protested as we scraped our way up to the lighthouse, where Sylvia stood in her ripped blue windbreaker, waving her arms.

Tony rolled out of the car before we came to a full stop. I followed more slowly, the keys slipping in my sweating palm. Nadia was crouched on the ground over something that looked like a bundle of sacks carelessly tossed from the lantern room gallery above.

"Roger," said Tony urgently. "Can you hear me?"

In the light falling from the open museum door, the bundle of sacks clarified into Roger, his curls flat and slick against his forehead, lips gaping like the mouth of a netted fish choking on air. But it was his hand I couldn't look away from, his right hand, grotesquely swollen to twice its normal size and looped all around with a rope of angry, dark pink blisters.

"He's been stung." The realization transported me back to a world I understood. I used to track how many times I got caught on the wrong end of a jellyfish's nematocysts, but lost count within a few months of starting at Seaheart. It came with the territory. The stings of the species we kept in captivity were not all that painful, and never lethal.

This was different. Roger's hand seemed to go on ballooning the longer I stared. Tony unzipped the red bag and removed a cylindrical, orange-tipped object. I winced as she plunged the EpiPen into Roger's thigh.

"Did you call for evac?" she asked Sylvia.

"Half an hour at least," the old woman answered stonily. "You know how it is."

It was a tense minute before the straining muscles of Roger's throat relaxed.

"What happened?" asked Tony.

Nadia rose shakily, clamping my arm in a viselike grip. "We came early to help set up the fireworks. He said he wanted to go for a walk . . ." She broke off with a cry as a shudder ran through Roger and he started convulsing.

Tony rolled him onto his side. Nadia was shouting incoherently, her nails digging into my arm hard enough to draw blood. Memories heaved over me in sickening swells. Aldo's limp body ferried onto shore by the rescue divers, the useless, empty air tanks still attached to his back. Someone bending over him to start chest compressions. The awful flare of false hope inside my own chest. He'd been medically dead once before, after the snakebite. He was tough. He'd survived things that would've killed most people. They would bring him back. They had to bring him back.

That was the worst part—when I still thought they could bring him back.

Roger stopped twitching. He was so pristinely still, I knew he was dead. Tony was shaking as she groped for his hand.

"There's a pulse."

Nadia moaned.

"You've got to get him to the airstrip," said Sylvia. "They can't land here."

It took three of us to heave Roger into the back seat.

"Josie." Nadia clawed for me again as I stepped back from the car. "Please—" She wasn't crying. She seemed barely alive, her lips clownishly bright against the whiteness of her face.

The right thing to do was go with Nadia—hold her hand, hold her up, offer whatever comfort and strength she needed. That was what she would've done for me if she'd been with me when I lost Aldo.

But I also knew Roger hadn't been wet. That meant whatever stung him had gotten him on land. It might be out there still, lurking in a tide pool, waiting for me to find it.

"I'm sorry," I said. "I'll be with you soon."

Nadia had no strength left, making it all too easy to pry her fingers off my wrist.

Tony jumped in front. The car swung around and shot down the bluff, small stones spraying from beneath the tires and Nadia's pale face still watching me from the back seat.

Then it was just Sylvia and me and the distant crashing of the waves over the rocks below.

"He'll be fine," said Sylvia.

I didn't look at her. I didn't want to see the lie in her eyes.

"If Roger saw Clementine, they're not going to get very far," I said.

"We're two weeks out from the next full moon."

"She could've changed her behavior."

"I've been here the whole night," Sylvia insisted. "I would've known if that thing turned up early. You can always tell when it's here."

I thought back to the uncanny silence that had fallen over the night before Clementine's red glow appeared, and the sweet-sour smell that flooded every cranny of my skull, even sealed high inside the glass capsule of the lantern room. Sylvia was probably right. But "probably" wasn't as reassuring as I wanted it to be, given the stakes.

"Have you got any flashlights?" I asked.

We both turned our heads in the direction of the water, a swath of churning shadow under a darkening sky.

Sylvia retreated into the museum and returned with a pair of industrial flashlights. The powerful beams swished over gravel as I trailed her to the edge of the bluff and to the perilous staircase, keeping one hand planted against the rock throughout the descent. Sylvia climbed down with the quick, sure gait of someone who'd made this journey many times before.

I was panting by the time we reached level ground, and not just from the effort of the journey. This was the closest I'd been to the water since trying to flee Shattering with Roger. My pulse roared in my ears. The rugged shore stretched out before us, pocked with pools and crevices where anything could be hiding. It was a lot of ground to cover.

"Did he say anything when you found him?" I asked.

"Just nonsense. He was wheezing something awful. Keeled over right in front of me. It's a miracle he made it up those stairs." For all her stoicism, I could tell Sylvia was rattled.

"What sort of nonsense?"

"Something about strands. Or was it strings?"

Maybe Roger had been hallucinating that the stingers were still on him, a burning coil of flame he couldn't shake loose.

We fanned out. My heart was still thundering, and I felt at any second as if I might bend over and vomit onto my shoes, but a pressing sense of urgency kept the worst of the dizziness at bay. The tide was racing in. Whatever we were looking for might soon be washed out to sea.

I inhaled deeply through my nose, held it for five seconds, and released.

The lighthouse lamp switched on automatically. The rotating beam of light swung out over the shore in an illuminated salute, and in the intervals between, the darkness intensified. No one appeared for the fireworks show. Tony must've gotten the word out to the islanders still at the square. Every few seconds I glanced up, tracking the progress of Sylvia's flashlight, semi-concerned the old woman was going to fall and break a hip. Then my shoe hit a slick patch and my own feet shot out from under me. I landed hard on my side, cursing.

The rumbling whir of a helicopter reached my ears as I staggered to my feet. So Roger was finally being transported off island—assuming he was even alive.

I had not wanted this.

I just wanted Roger gone for a day or two. I had never envisioned him dying or dead, and Nadia weeping, Nadia the thirty-three-year-old widow, bereft of the only family she had with her on Shattering Point. I could not be blamed for this. I had not wanted this.

Guilt spread its suffocating bulk through my chest.

The lighthouse beam saluted again. This time it caught a tall human figure standing on the rocks twenty feet away.

I shut my eyes. When I opened them, the *yōkai* was gone.

I picked my way across the shore and pulled up just short of the place where the figure had vanished. There, plastered over a flat shelf of rock, was a severed tentacle, ribbon-thin, gelatinous, iridescent in the glow of my flashlight. It stretched across the shoreline in the direction of the water—twenty feet, thirty, farther than the light could reach. Every time I observed something about it, my focus shifted and I realized I was wrong. The tentacle was covered in tiny spines or hairs—no, it was smooth as a strip of satin. It was wine red in color—no, translucent; no, black, tilting into forest green when I squinted. A gluey secretion pooled around it until I blinked again and that was gone, too.

I felt drawn toward the tentacle's shape-shifting beauty, as Roger had been, powered by a longing to feel its texture against my skin.

"What is it?" cried Sylvia, who must've noticed the beam of my flashlight frozen in place. I was startled to see my outstretched fingers inches from the tentacle, and I yanked my hand back as if burned.

Sylvia was silent when she saw my discovery.

"Don't touch it," I warned.

"Wasn't planning on it." She sounded revolted. Could she not feel the grandeur, the *wisdom* radiating from this rogue limb? It was alive still, loaded with venom and neurons and instinct. Even now, detached from its host, it was hunting. "You think it's Clementine's?" Sylvia asked.

"I do." It was impossible to conceive of this remarkable appendage belonging to anything else. Fear and guilt parted, and a sense of possibility swept in as I contemplated this gift: an offering from Shattering's sea monster herself. "Can you get a bucket, a knife?" I asked Sylvia. "Gloves, too, if you have them."

She hurried back to the staircase.

I searched for a stick to see if I could get a head start on removing the tentacle, but there wasn't one nearby, and I was afraid to stray too far with the water swallowing up more of my prize with each passing minute. The tide threw up a spray that coated my skin in a salty mist. I shivered, but it wasn't from fear. I felt shaky but liberated, like a just-healed arm after a stiff cast is removed.

The feeling emboldened me. I sensed the *yōkai* still lingering close by. When I turned to face it, and it lifted its arm, the beam of the lighthouse blinking over its head like the eye of an indifferent god, I didn't look away.

The *yōkai*'s gloved hand halted and slowly tipped, with the thumb extended and pointing downward.

I felt my own hand moving as I mirrored the gesture. It was instinct, one dive buddy communicating to the other. Even when the approaching bob of a flashlight heralded Sylvia's return, the *yōkai* and I stood together in the darkness, silently confirming our intentions. It felt like a forecast, or a promise.

Thumbs-down. The diver's signal to descend.

The Tentacle

Jellyfish possess radial symmetry. Picture a wagon wheel with evenly spaced spokes, or a tulip with petals symmetrically unfurling from the central pistil. Unlike a wheel or a flower, however, jellyfish are capable of maintaining their symmetry: When a tentacle is ripped or chewed off by a predator, jellies will rearrange their anatomy to ensure equal spacing between the tentacles that remain. This incredible process of self-repair can occur in as little as a day.

There was nothing approximating a lab on Shattering. My priority was to preserve Clementine's tentacle so that it could be studied at a later date. Sylvia drove me back to town in a mud-splattered Jeep. The tentacle we'd triple-wrapped in garbage bags and stuffed inside a cooler. Even through these protective layers, I sensed a coiled slickness, a quickening of the blood like the twitch of a cockroach startled by the kitchen light. Sawing through the tentacle on the beach with the knife Sylvia had provided, racing to save what hadn't already disappeared below the tideline, I'd had the queasy sensation I was hacking off my own numb limb.

The *yōkai* had led me right to it. But for what purpose? To punish me? To make me suffer like Roger? I knew now what it had been trying to tell me all along, but it only wound my fear tighter.

Thumbs-down. Descend.

This thing that was not Aldo wanted me back in the water. The question was why.

Sylvia dropped me off at Retreat-by-the-Sea. Night had fallen heavily onto the island. A winged thing flitted by in the darkness overhead. The sky was starless, the breeze soothing against the sunburn on my neck. The island had slipped into that deceitful season of warm days fading into still-chilly nights.

"Tell Nadia I said . . ." Sylvia trailed off before the thought was complete, her hands rigid around the steering wheel. Neither of us had yet to hear anything about Roger.

"I will," I said.

"I'll walk the beach again when the tide goes out, make sure we didn't miss anything."

"Be careful."

"You, too." She eyed the cooler warily. The Jeep took off, expelling a cloud of exhaust.

The windows of the old Victorian were all lit up. I wondered if the tourists had heard the helicopter that came to take Roger away, if they'd speculated among themselves or wandered outside, hoping for a slice of the drama. My destination was the big chest freezer I'd glimpsed in the kitchen, but the cooler resisted, growing heavier as I trudged up the steps of the B and B, straining my shoulder at the socket. Clementine did not want to be taken inside and abandoned in a building full of strangers.

At the last second, I veered around back and up the hill to Tony's house instead.

The bungalow's door was unlocked, but there was no answer when I called Tony's name. I peeked into the bedroom. The fairy lights were still on, the blankets twisted in a pile at the end of the bed. The smell of sex sent a bolt of desire crackling down both my legs. I felt completely unsteadied by the memory of Tony and me in that bed—half of me desperate to repeat it, the other half fearing it was only our shared desperation that had pushed us together.

I entered the chaotic kitchen, where I discovered an equally chaotic freezer that necessitated several rounds of *Tetris* before I'd carved out sufficient space among the towers of Tupperware and ice cream pints to carefully wedge the bag-wrapped tentacle. Then I started opening junk-crammed drawers until I located a Sharpie and a ring of masking tape.

VENOMOUS!! DO NOT OPEN!!

I stepped back from the freezer, making sure my homemade label was visible. Cold air flowed from the open door. The tentacle was slumped on the bottom shelf. It was happier here than at Retreat-by-the-Sea, but it still struck me as sad, neglected. I could practically hear it calling out to me, like Clementine had when she surfaced below the lighthouse. I hesitated again.

Just a quick peek before I went to check on Nadia and get an update on Roger. Just five minutes.

I cleared off Tony's kitchen table and lined the surface with several sheets of waxed paper. The little brown bird, Scoot, hopped around on the curtain rod, emitting cheeps of interest. After donning a pair of latex gloves I'd discovered in the bird hospital, I held my breath, peeled back the garbage bags, and eased the tentacle onto my makeshift work surface.

The segment Sylvia and I had managed to rescue was just under two feet in length, thicker than the wispy tentacles of the moon jellies we kept in captivity at Seaheart. Its visual mystique had faded—it resembled a strand of chewing gum stretched across Tony's table—and yet there was no frailness to it. It seemed tough and muscular, adhering to my gloved fingers with a sticky grip and only grudgingly releasing.

Sweat gathered in the small of my back. Though Clementine's stinging cells were too tiny to see with the naked eye, they were all over the tentacle, ready to discharge on contact. A microscopic tear in the latex, or a stray droplet of jelly mucus sliding onto the exposed skin of my wrist was all it would take. I imagined my hand swelling like Roger's, the walls of my throat winching shut.

Even this disturbing vision was not enough to persuade me to wrap the tentacle back up. Excitement buzzed between my ears, and the tentacle seemed to vibrate in reply, equally excited to show off its secrets.

I brought my face as close as I dared, squinting hard in the glow of the overhead light. A cloying, fruity odor reached my nose, like a milder version of Clementine's sweet-sour reek. The tentacle was covered in tiny nodules that seemed to twitch beneath the current of my breath. They were clustered unevenly along the tentacle, the smallest smaller than a grain of rice, the largest half the size of my pinkie fingernail. I thought they might be photophores—light-emitting organs—like the ones that studded the underbellies of lantern fish.

I wrenched open more drawers, seeking Tony's sharpest knife.

My hand was steady as I sliced through the biggest protrusion I could find. It resisted, then gave like a popped zit, emitting a sludgy brown liquid. The fruity odor intensified.

That was how Tony found me: holding a steak knife and sniffing a jellyfish tentacle at her kitchen table.

"Where the hell have you been?"

I managed not to drop the knife, though she'd startled me. I hadn't heard her come in. Scoot soared down to greet her, and she shooed him away.

"I've been *calling* you," said Tony, advancing.

"I'm sorry. My phone is—" I looked around the kitchen. All of the drawers were still hanging open. I had no idea where my phone was. "How is Roger?" I asked anxiously, turning back to Tony.

She didn't answer right away. She'd noticed what was on the table. Her eyes moved from the tentacle to me and back again. She took a breath that seemed like it required a lot of effort. "He's alive," she said finally. "That's all I know."

She sank into a chair three feet back from the table, elbows tucked flat against her torso.

"This is what got him?"

"Yeah. Here, smell this—"

"I'm not smelling it!" But she leaned in and sniffed the streak of sludge on the edge of the knife blade. "That's disgusting."

"What does it smell like to you?" I asked.

"Like old cheese in a dumpster."

"Like decay, right? I think Clementine has some sort of infection."

"Excellent. Now it's in my kitchen."

"Jellyfish diseases aren't contagious to humans." Doubt pulled at me even as I spoke. The islanders talked about the barrier as if it were a physical obstacle, but approaching it felt a lot more like contracting an illness. Could some type of zoonotic pathogen explain what was happening on Shattering?

Tony sighed as I bent to saw off another protrusion. "Can any of this help Roger?"

I shook my head no, eyes still fixed on the tentacle. "It takes years to develop a targeted antivenom."

"Then what you need to do," said Tony, "is put all this away, and go take care of Nadia."

I looked up, and she looked back at me, not unkindly.

"She's been asking for you. She needs you, Jo. That's your job right now. To be a good friend."

My insides squirmed. Tony was right.

It took fifteen minutes to clean up and sterilize everything. Tony didn't protest when I replaced the tentacle in her freezer. The knife she directed me to throw straight in the trash.

On my way out of the kitchen, I paused. "You were really amazing before, with Roger," I said. Because she had been. If Tony hadn't shown up, he never would've even made it onto the helicopter. At least now he had a chance.

"Never had to deal with anything like that before," said Tony quietly. "Dehydration, burns, sprains . . . One time Margo threw an easel at Norm. Cut his head open." She frowned and rubbed her jaw. "I feel terrible about Roger, but the thing is, we got lucky: He never saw Clementine. If it had been anyone else, we would've been really screwed. There are huge limitations to what we can do here without any doctors or hospitals. I've been begging people to be careful. But eventually, someone's gonna get really sick and not be able to get past the barrier to reach the treatment they need."

She stood at the counter, shoulders rounded, eyes downcast. I thought of crossing the room and wrapping my arms around her, but I didn't want grief to always be the thing that pulled us to one another. And Nadia was waiting.

"Try to get some sleep," I said.

• • •

The closer I got to Nadia and Roger's house, the more tormented I was by visions of her curled into the fetal position in a dark corner, crying, alone. But the cottage turned out to be full of people: Nadia's neighbors, mostly older women, had descended on the place when word of Roger's fate reached them, a battalion of comfort armed with hot beverages and soothing voices and slabs of homemade bread. I was surprised and touched by this network of care. On the phone Nadia had told me she was an outsider still, subject to stigma and suspicion. It seemed that was the case no longer.

Nadia herself had just retired upstairs, a broad-faced woman in a yellow flannel explained to me. Trying to get some rest.

"Don't wake her," the woman chided as I stole up the steps. Nadia and Roger's bedroom was empty. But the door to the spare bedroom where I'd slept for the past two nights stood ajar.

She was awake, sitting up on the edge of the bed, gazing vacantly at the ceiling. All the lights were off, except for a small lamp on a corner table.

"Josie." Her voice was dull. It frightened me to see her so lusterless.

"Hey," I said softly. I edged farther into the room, stepping over my duffel bag. "I'm sorry. I should've come sooner."

"You should've." She patted the bed. I folded myself around her and pulled the blanket over us both.

It was warm and cozy in our shared tent, but I could feel Nadia shivering. I thought back to the last time we were wrapped together like this, another night in May eleven years ago, when she'd done her best to comfort me after my father died.

"Sorry for taking your room," Nadia murmured. "It felt wrong to be in the bed without him."

"I understand."

"The hospital called. They had to put him in a coma. Do people survive this sort of thing?"

"Yes," I said, thinking of Aldo. But Aldo had been unusual when it came to toxins. It was safe to say Roger didn't share his natural resistance.

"It was so awful," said Nadia, her voice breaking. "They loaded him into the helicopter, and I couldn't go with him. I couldn't even come up with an excuse. I just stood there and *watched* while they took him away."

I tightened my grip around her, and she snuggled into me. I wondered if this was how Roger held her at night as they fell asleep.

"How did you two meet?" I asked, realizing I'd never heard the story.

Nadia sniffled loudly. "Teach for America."

"Roger's a teacher, too?"

"Yeah. But he's terrible at it."

I smiled. Of all the moments for Nadia's pathological generosity to abandon her.

She made a wheezy sound that was either a laugh or a sob.

"He's really smart and creative and organized. But he doesn't have any patience. He thinks kids should just do what you ask them. When I took the job here, the plan was that he'd use the time to figure out what he wanted to do next. Go back to school, learn a trade. We're still young. I kept telling him he could reinvent himself if he wanted to. He had time."

She fell silent. A teakettle whistled downstairs and was quickly removed from the burner.

Nadia mashed her face into the pillow. The hard edge of her insulin pump was digging into my hip. I would have to stay on top of her about that. I wasn't used to having to worry about someone, and the weight of the new responsibility felt crushing.

I hoped she would fall asleep, but after a few minutes, Nadia spoke again.

"I have to get off Shattering. If Roger never wakes up, if I have to make a decision . . . I couldn't bear it, Josie. Not to be in the room with him. Not to hold his hand." She shuddered. "Tell me everything's going to be okay."

I'd once refused to comfort Roger out of fear I was tempting fate. But this was Nadia. And she needed me.

I tucked my chin into her shoulder. "Everything's going to be okay," I said.

Part Three

Gastric cavity
Exumbrella
Epidermis
Subumbrella
Mesoglea
Gastrodermis
Circular canal
Tentacle
Radial canal
Rhopalium
Gonad
Mouth
Oral arm

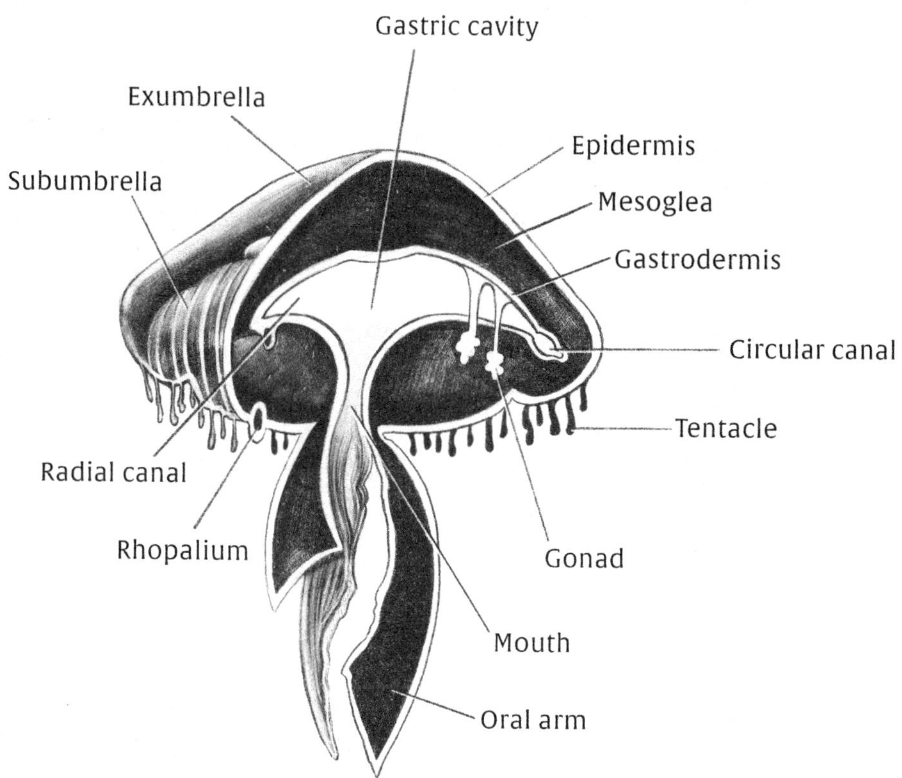

Town Hall Meeting

Another key to jellyfish's long-term survival has been their indiscriminate palates. As opportunistic feeders, they will try to eat just about anything that fits in their mouths, from seaweed to algae to fish eggs to shrimp. Even fellow jellies can appear on the menu.

AA: I think you mean mouthbutts.

JN: I miss you.

On Wednesday morning, Sylvia Steele assembled the town hall meeting in the schoolhouse, which boasted the only room on Shattering big enough to hold fifty-odd people. Every desk was occupied by an adult with their legs awkwardly crammed to fit. Tony was seated to my left, and Nadia was on my right, looking drawn and pale. She'd barely eaten the past two days, despite the mountainous casseroles that were being dumped at her doorstep around the clock by the comfort battalion. Roger remained in the hospital, his chance at recovery uncertain.

As this news percolated through the island, it acquired the obscene gravity of a private misfortune made public. I could feel people looking at Nadia, and though they were looks of pity and compassion, I wanted to throw myself in front of her to shield her from the stares.

I leaned in. "Are you sure you want to be here?"

She nodded. "I want to be part of the solution."

I glanced down at the bullet-pointed sheet of notes I'd drafted in Nadia's kitchen last night, outlining my plan for Clementine. The time had come to make my case before the islanders. I turned in my chair and spotted Emmett Beckendorf leaning against the schoolhouse's back door with his arms hanging loose at his sides. He was relaxed, confident in whatever execution scheme he'd come up with.

He caught my eye over the crowd of seated people and winked. I spun back to face the front of the room, swallowing my revulsion.

Sylvia smacked the leg of the teacher's desk with her walking stick, and the chatter died.

"So here we are again," she said, her voice swelling to fill the room. "There's two weeks to go till the full moon, so now's the time for anyone who's got an idea to share it with the rest of us. I expect you're all getting as tired of this as I am. But we've got a newcomer now. Someone who can give us a fresh perspective." She flicked her stare at me, and I rose and joined the town clerk at the front of the classroom.

Sweat prickled my hairline. I had given plenty of public presentations before, but I wasn't used to speaking in such a high-stakes situation. The faces of the islanders peered back at me, pinched with fear and hope. They were familiar faces to me now, and not just because of the strange aftereffect of witnessing Clementine.

There was goateed Nico, owner of the ice cream parlor, who longed for his Parisian éclairs.

There was Lawrence Fleming, the lobsterman who'd tried to poison Clementine, standing beneath an American flag with three more men I'd also interviewed at Jelly HQ.

There was the Urchin's blue-haired waitress, seeming either anxious or bored as she clattered her fingernails against the desk.

There was Tony, and Nadia, and there were Nadia's neighbors who'd rallied around her after the helicopter took Roger away.

Two faces were conspicuously absent: Neither of the Sloans had made it. I wasn't surprised that curmudgeonly Norm hadn't deemed the town hall meeting worth the hour-long intermission from his garden, but I had hoped Margo would show up. My fear that she'd want to talk to me about the *yōkai* was offset by my hope that the artist would be a vocal supporter of my nonviolent approach to Shattering's jellyfish problem. I hadn't met anyone else on the island who said we were honored by Clementine's presence.

I looked out over the classroom and gripped my notes. "Hi, everyone."

An awkward silence met me, broken by the delighted screams of Sidney and his cousin Lila, who'd been banished to the swing set outside.

"I'm Josephine. Jo. Um. Most of you probably know that already." My ears burned. Tony caught my eye and nodded. I straightened my spine and raised my voice. "Even though Clementine is exceptional, and not like anything I've seen before, she's still an animal—one that's behaving very strangely. When animals do things they've never done before, it's worth looking at their environment to see what's changed. In other words, I believe the barrier could be a stress response. And I believe I've identified the stressor."

I described the nodules I'd found on the tentacle that stung Roger—not photophores, I knew now, but some type of infectious lesion. I looked at Sylvia, still leaning against the teacher's desk with her eagle-headed walking stick clutched in both hands.

"I know you think Clementine's been around a long time. Maybe she has. But that doesn't make her invincible. The ocean is a different place now than it was ninety years ago. The water is warmer, which allows different kinds of bacteria to thrive. Clementine is sick," I said, turning to face the room again. A blurry face peeked through the schoolhouse's back window, ducking away when we made eye contact. The swing set couldn't compete with the allure of a roomful of grown-ups talking sinister secrets. "And if you allow me some time to figure out how to treat her, the barrier could ease up. Maybe even disappear altogether."

There was another silence, during which I dared to hope my appeal had worked. Perhaps, collectively, we really could devise a solution that saw Clementine not killed, but cured. I could already envision the case study in my book, the sensationalized headlines in newspapers all over the country. Saving Shattering's giant jellyfish would be a win for jelly-kind everywhere: a PR stunt so flashy even Aldo never could've imagined it.

Then a small voice spoke up. "We can't wait that long."

It took a second for me to locate its source: Nadia, sitting up straight in her chair. My fleeting hopes solidified into a hard stone in the pit of my stomach.

"I'm sorry, Josie," she said. She didn't sound sorry. Her voice was clipped, completely un-Nadia-like in its cadence. "I know you love jellyfish. But this one is too dangerous. And what you're saying about treating her—how long will that take? Weeks? Months?"

The room filled with creaks as bodies shifted uneasily in chairs. I swallowed past the dryness in my throat. I had expected resistance, but not from her.

"Science moves slowly," I conceded. "But trying to kill Clementine hasn't been working. Isn't it worth trying something new?"

"There's no time," insisted Nadia. "Especially with—" She hesitated. I knew what she was going to say before she said it, but it still sent another shock blistering through me when she blurted the news she'd promised not to share: "Especially with the barrier moving in."

The air in the schoolhouse thickened. I could almost see Nadia's words as they made landfall—the mouths dropping open, the ears pitching toward her as if to be certain they'd heard right. It seemed Emmett really had kept his discovery to himself. Maybe he or Sylvia had been planning to publicize it today anyway, and Nadia had simply gotten the jump on them. It didn't matter. She'd deployed the secret weapon, she'd said the magic words. There was no going back now.

Sylvia widened her stance and stiffened her arms like she was bracing for a blow.

Then several people began speaking at once.

"What is she—?"

"Why didn't you—?"

"But does this mean we'll have to—?"

"How long until someone's caught on the wrong side?" fretted Nico. He was looking at me, eyes wide, as if I alone could answer this impossible question.

Tony gnawed at her thumbnail. The blue-haired waitress dropped her head into her hands. An argument had broken out among the lobstermen, which Lawrence was gamely trying to referee, his palm thrust out to keep one of the men from advancing. As strange and claustrophobic as the situation on Shattering had become since Clementine surfaced last fall, the islanders had adapted to it. They'd learned to make sense of the insensible. Now this wrench had been thrown into their shaky world order, plunging them back into that gulf of terrible uncertainty.

Nadia slumped in her seat, as if the act of betrayal had sucked all the air out of her.

Sylvia stood her ground against the barrage. When the first round of questions and protests had petered into a wounded silence, she flashed a gnarled finger in warning.

"One at a time."

The woman who owned the souvenir shop threw her hand into the air. "Has it moved on the seaward side, too?"

"Far as we can tell," said Sylvia, glancing at Emmett for confirmation, "it's only come in from the west."

"We should set a watch," declared a lobsterman with a pendulous orange mustache. "Twenty-four-hour surveillance. So if it moves any more, we know right away."

Sylvia started sketching out the schedule on the blackboard. Voices called out, and hands lifted into the air as people volunteered for shifts. Almost without my noticing, the mood in the schoolhouse had swung from panic to a grim calm. I recalled what Norm had said to me the day we met: *You have to be self-sufficient. You have to know how to survive.*

As a conversation wrapped up regarding moving all the fishing boats to the other side of the island, Emmett swaggered to the blackboard and shot me a look that said, *Sit the hell down.* I returned the look and stayed where I was.

"So now that everyone's up to speed," he announced, "I think you'll agree with what I'm about to propose. June's full moon could be our last chance. Nadia's right. We have to *act*."

He picked up the piece of chalk Sylvia had abandoned and drew a vertical line down the center of the board, studded with *x*'s every few inches. "Here's the plan. We'll attach explosives to a chain like this and lower it down just before the beast is due to surface."

"How is that different from anything else you've tried?" I asked irritably.

"Because this time," answered Emmett, "me and the boys are going to rig up a remote detonation system with a timer. We'll have two teams, one on the water and one onshore. The water team handles the chain, and the land team flips the switch. The people who actually launch the killing blow will be so far from the beast, it won't be able to stop them. Ten seconds later—*boom*!" A few people actually jumped. "Nothing can survive that," said Emmett with satisfaction.

I kept my face neutral, but I got what he was going for: Clementine had proven impervious to direct assaults. What Emmett was proposing was more like a trap, with added distance and a built-in delay to confuse the jellyfish about where the threat was originating. Would it be enough to overcome her defensive strategy? I had no idea, but it was a clever scheme, and more ambitious than anything the islanders had tried before.

"There are some kinks to work out," Emmett admitted, rotating to face the board again. "The blast range of this type of explosive is small. The beast has basically got to be on top of the barrels when they go off. Detonate too early or too late, and we might miss our window to kill it once and for all . . ."

"*Nooooo!*" The schoolhouse's back door crashed open. Everyone jolted as Sidney galloped inside, still yelling. He tore to the front of the room, trailed by a whiff of sunscreen and a pudgy girl in braids whose loyalty propelled her as far as the teacher's desk, and no farther. Lila hung back, surveying the roomful of adults with an awed expression, three fingers wedged into the corner of her mouth.

Sidney was unintimidated. He swung a furious look around the schoolhouse.

"No," he pronounced crisply.

"Sidney." The white-haired woman from the cookout stood wearily and extended a hand toward him. "Stop this right now. You and Lila need to go back out—"

"No! You can't kill Clementine. I won't let you." A tremble had entered his voice. He looked around the room again, this time with the desperation of a cornered man seeking allies. His gaze landed on Nadia. "Ms. Markov. You said all life is sacred, from the teeniest bug to the biggest redwood tree."

The color rose to Nadia's cheeks as several dozen pairs of eyes swiveled toward her again. "I—I did say that, Sidney," she confessed. "You're right. But this situation is extreme. Human lives are sacred, too, and Clementine is putting us at risk."

Sidney pressed his lips and rotated to face the white-haired woman next. "Grandma. You said Clementine was the most exciting thing that had ever happened on Shattering!"

"That was *before*." The grandmother's voice rang with exasperation. "Before we knew what it was up to, what it was doing to all of us." She beckoned him again. Sidney shook his head and back-pedaled until he bumped the blackboard. Sylvia was on the right side of him, Emmett on the left. A silent exchange was unfolding between the two adults, each nominating the other to grab the kid and turf him out of the room.

Then Sidney saw me.

Neatly ducking Emmett's outstretched arm, he closed the distance between us in three bounds and fastened his arms around my waist.

"You won't let them kill Clementine, right, Michael?" He craned his neck to look at me, his expression buoyant with hope. "You said you'd never hurt her."

The stone in my stomach sank a few centimeters deeper. I empathized with Sidney more than he could ever know. But I'd promised myself I wouldn't put a jellyfish before a human, and I'd promised Nadia everything was going to be okay.

She wanted Clementine dead. So did just about everyone else. No one was going to hear me out now that they knew about the barrier. Fear was too powerful a motivator, killing too simple a solution.

The fight in me was weakening. I accepted in that moment that I wasn't going to win. But maybe I could still snatch a small success from the defeat.

I forced myself to look away from Sidney and back up at Emmett.

"You said timing was an issue. Let me help. I'll get in the water and cue you when Clementine's within thc blast radius. It's going to be tough to gauge her exact position from a boat."

Emmett narrowed his eyes. "Why would you—?"

"Because I'm getting something out of it, too," I said. "You want her dead; I want to see her up close before she's gone forever."

He still seemed skeptical.

It was Tony who cut across his next protest: "This plan of yours might not work, Emmett." She unfolded her long legs and stood. "And if it doesn't," she said levelly, looking around at the silent islanders, "we'll have wasted a night we can't afford to waste. Jo's our plan B. I vote we let her get in the water and at least start gathering some observations. It can only help us in the long run."

I saw heads nodding, heard a murmur or two traded between neighbors. No one spoke up against her. Tony commanded an easy authority, and she was using it to help me still.

Sylvia clanged her walking stick against the desk for a second time. "All in favor of moving forward?"

Hands shot into the air. Emmett's was the last, uncurling stiffly from his side and halting at shoulder height. Sidney's arms dropped from my waist in defeat.

No Friends, Just Jellyfish

Jellyfish are short-lived as individuals, and long-lived as a species. This makes them the opposite of humans, who are remarkably long-lived relative to other primates but whose modern form evolved just three hundred thousand years ago—a mere blink in geologic time. One must question which species has gained more wisdom about the world.

JN: Are you there? Can you hear me?

After the town hall meeting, I went straight back to Nadia's house and signed Ha-Yun Kim's contract. There was no other recourse. After what happened to Roger, a sting-proof dive suit was a must-have. Though I was past my deadline, the contract was countersigned and returned before the end of the day, alongside promises from Ha-Yun's assistant that the Nematoskyn prototype was on its way.

The loss and outrage walloped me as soon as I closed out of my inbox. I'd been cornered into taking a job I didn't care about, working for a woman I didn't like, leaving behind my freedom and abandoning my polyps to wither and die—all so that I could acquire a dive suit that might help me kill the most remarkable jellyfish I'd ever seen. None of this was what I wanted. How had it come to this?

I didn't hear Nadia approach. I wasn't sure how long she'd been lingering in the doorway to the guest bedroom, watching me.

"Thank you," she murmured. "I know you're doing this for me, and I really appreciate it."

"I'm doing it for all of us," I said shortly.

I wasn't ready to accept her gratitude, even if I could understand why she'd turned on me in the schoolhouse. And it was the truth: I was going to help kill Clementine so Nadia could reunite with Roger, but also so Tony could visit her ailing mother, so Margo could escape her marriage. Hell, so Nico could eat some éclairs. And I was doing it for me, too. I had not made it out of the cave alive so I could be stranded on Shattering Point, watching my world get smaller. I wanted to visit my mother and eat a cucumber from my father's garden. I wanted to scatter Aldo's ashes. I wanted to dive in tropical waters again.

None of that could be possible until Clementine was gone, and so I would do as legions of my species had done before me: I would kill the thing that threatened me in order to save myself and the people I cared about, even if it killed a part of me to do it.

I had my eyes on my laptop. Nadia was a persistent smudge in my periphery, still standing in the doorway. She felt like a stranger to me. The old Nadia would've been falling over herself apologizing for betraying me. The old Nadia never would've betrayed me in the first place.

"I would understand," she said quietly, "if you want to stay somewhere else . . ."

I looked at her head-on. She'd taken to wearing Roger's clothes around the house. His T-shirt was a dress on her, its hem dangling to the middle of her thighs. Tony had forwarded me the tiny story about Roger's incident that had appeared in yesterday's edition of the *Midcoast Herald*: "Stinging Creature Washes Up on Maine Beach, Injures Local." He wasn't named in it. He was just a victim, a short-lived sensation, like Aldo had been in the handful of articles that covered his death.

I thought, again, of telling Nadia about Aldo. Maybe it would bring us closer. But dredging up the story of my dead friend wasn't what she needed to hear right now. Roger wasn't dead yet. Roger still had a chance.

"I'm not leaving you here alone," I said instead.

It wasn't actual forgiveness, but Nadia hadn't actually apologized. She swallowed and nodded, teary-eyed, and shuffled down the hall. I didn't go after her. Grief had hardened both of us. I wasn't the same person I'd been eleven years ago, either.

• • •

With the Nematoskyn on its way, I had another important transaction to take care of. Though shipping my scuba gear cross-country would be only slightly less expensive than buying new gear altogether, it wasn't a hard decision. If I was going to dive in unknown waters, I wanted to do it with familiar things.

"Where are you?" I asked, the second my mother picked up.

She paused a few moments too long before answering. "I went back home. Like you told me to."

"Don't lie, Ma."

A long sigh crackled over the line. "Flights are very expensive.

I couldn't get a good fare till next week. Don't be so angry with me, Jo."

"I'm not angry. I actually need your help with something."

I could count on one hand the number of times I'd asked my mother for help as an adult. She was plainly eager to be needed. Halfway through my list of items, she stopped me so she could grab a pen and write it all down. "Okay, start over . . ." I went through it again from the top. I could see each item gleaming in my imagination as I described it. I kept all my diving gear in a storage closet next to the laundry room. I had opened the door only once since returning from Florida, to dump everything inside as a tide of impotent rage swelled within me. I regretted that now. What happened to Aldo wasn't my scuba equipment's fault. My equipment had kept me alive long enough to find the exit. I owed it my life.

Mom read her list back to me. "Good?"

"Good. Thank you." In this case I knew there'd be no follow-up questions. It was an unspoken arrangement Mom and I had settled on years ago. My professional life was a dim moon distantly orbiting her home world. Jellyfish were as weird and distasteful to her as tax law was to me.

I had gotten what I wanted. It was time to hang up. Instead I sat down at Nadia's kitchen table, staring at that photo of her and Roger on the refrigerator while I waited for my mother to fill the silence. I wanted my gear, yes, but that was not the only reason I'd called. Talking with Tony about Aldo on Memorial Day had loosened something in me. I was finally ready to broach the subject with my mother. There was no one on Shattering who both knew him and knew how the loss of him had nearly destroyed me.

The words foamed in my throat. To speak the truth aloud felt like it would snip the last threads tethering me to a rational planet. Though I knew Mom was still at my place, I pictured her sitting in her own living room in Indiana, on the sofa with the nubby green fabric that had always scratched my arms and legs as a child. She still lived there in the house where I'd grown up, still walked daily past the spot in the kitchen where she'd found my father unresponsive on the floor. How did she do it? Aldo had died a thousand miles from Shattering, yet the entire ocean ached with the memory of him.

"Are you still there?" Mom asked.

"I'm here," I said. Then I told her about the *yōkai* that had been stalking me since that night in the lantern room.

Mom listened without interrupting. I said more than I meant to. Once unleashed, the words took on new life, chewing through me with a terrible hunger. I told her about the *yōkai*'s silence and the sound of the water rolling off it, how it had led me right to the tentacle on the beach, and my bargain with the snake in the cave.

When I was done, I felt raw and exhausted. My eyes stung. I caught a teardrop before it rolled off my jaw, and studied the shimmering bead balanced on the tip of my finger, thinking of the tiny but deadly *Malo kingi*. The really frightening thing about *Malo kingi* and all the Irukandji jellyfish was the delayed onset of symptoms following a sting. A person might walk around for hours, fooling you into thinking they were fine, only to be abruptly incapacitated by cramping, vomiting, and a powerful certitude in their impending death. Not for nothing were Irukandji known as the doom jellyfish—their venom stripped away your sense of hope. Grief was like that, too. It left only dread for what was to come.

Mom cleared her throat. I wondered if this confession had been too much, even for a woman who was crazy about ghost stories. Then she said, in a tone so casual we might've been discussing the weather, "*Yōkai* aren't always bad guys, you know."

I swiped the back of my hand across my eyes. "They were bad in every story you ever told me!"

"That's because you liked the scary stories. You were a very strange child. You used to get mad at me if the stories weren't scary enough. But the truth is, in some versions, *yōkai* are friendly. Like what-do-you-call-them. The angels who look out for you."

"Guardian angels?"

"Right. They protect you from sickness. They keep you from doing dangerous things." She paused. "After Dad died, I used to see him around sometimes."

I sat up straighter, the back of my neck prickling. "You never told me that."

"Of course not. You would've tried to put me in a nursing home!"

"Come on, Ma, no I wouldn't have."

But I might have thought she was crazy. I might have started ignoring her phone calls, resentful at how her jagged, crazy grief scratched at the neat boundaries of my logical world.

"Where did you see him?"

"In the garden. I would look up from washing the dishes and see him out the window, just walking around, looking at the plants."

"Did he ever speak to you?"

"Oh, no. He was never a big talker. You remember how he used to say I talked enough for both of us?"

"He only said that once. But you never let him forget it."

"No, I did not."

I thought I could hear Mom smiling, too.

Anyway, she went on, despite his silence, it was plain that Dad wanted something from her, and after a few weeks of glimpsing him through the window, she finally went outside and was surprised to discover how badly the garden had deteriorated in his absence. The weeds and bugs had taken over. Something had dug a tunnel beneath the fence and chomped through all the lettuce. The ruin swelled and strengthened around her until it seemed, Mom said, like a malicious *oni* from the old bedtime stories, a hungry, shapeless thing that was funneling my father's memory into its mouth.

Mom gathered her courage. The very next day, armed with a spade in one hand and a spray bottle of Dad's homemade insect repellent in the other, she charged into the garden and attacked! The demon called up reinforcements: The beetles seethed, the crabgrass sprouted clawed feet that stretched deep into the earth. But Mom's will was strong. For seven days and seven nights she battled in the heat and the rain, scratches and bugbites flaming up her arms—

"Ma . . ."

"Okay, maybe it wasn't so long. The point is that I won. I took back the garden from the monster. This is an inspiring story."

I declined to point out that my father—the devout Buddhist and pacifist—would've surely taken issue with the combative tone and glorification of conquest in this "inspiring" tale.

"All Dad wanted was to see his garden cleaned up," said Mom. "And then he went away, onto the next thing. Whatever that was.

So find out what your *yōkai* wants and give it to him. Treat him with respect. Then maybe he'll go away, too."

She said it the way she delivered all life advice, as if it were obvious and I was astonishingly dumb for not getting there on my own. Except I had gotten there on my own. I was well on my way to giving the *yōkai* what it wanted: *Thumbs-down. Descend.* It wanted me back in the water. But for what purpose? Was it a benign guardian angel who would protect me from Clementine, or a vengeful demon who wanted me drowned?

It was the same conundrum as with jellyfish. You didn't know which were deadly and which were harmless until someone got stung.

"When will you visit next?" pressed Mom. "It's been almost a year since you came home."

I opened my mouth to dispute her, then realized she was right. I had last visited over Fourth of July. We went to the town fireworks display, then stayed up late watching *Everybody Loves Raymond* reruns. We had a shared affinity for feel-good white family sitcoms, the kind with dopey jokes and audience laughter that shrieked into the room. She fell asleep in Dad's old recliner with her mouth open, snoring like a chainsaw.

"Soon," I said. "I just have some work I need to finish first."

"You need a vacation. Come visit. Bring your friends. Oh wait, I forgot—no friends, just jellyfish." She laughed. "Do you remember?"

I remembered. They were my words, uttered in response to my parents' instruction that I invite some friends to my ninth birthday party. No friends, I had insisted. Just jellyfish. My father had been alarmed by my budding misanthropy, but Mom, who had an odd sense of humor, thought it was funny. On the day of my birthday, she took me out of school early and drove me to the Indianapolis Zoo, where I spent a blissful hour with my face pressed to the glass of the jellyfish exhibit. In later years, she'd grow to find my obsession annoying and scold me for not having more normal hobbies, but for that day—that single beautiful memory shining out of childhood's murk like the glowing bell of a deep-sea jelly—I was enough.

"How about a *girl-friend*?" said Mom, carefully enunciating the unfamiliar word.

I flushed and glanced at my phone, as if expecting to discover someone else's name on the screen. "I don't have one of those, either."

"Too bad," said Mom. "Well, maybe someday."

There was a stretched-out silence as we both contemplated this new territory we found ourselves in: the olive branch she'd extended me, whether I was going to accept it.

"I love you, Ma," I said finally, and this, too, sounded strange to my ears. We weren't an emotive family, and while I did love my mother and felt certain she loved me back in her imperfect way, neither of us was in the habit of blurting it out loud like the families in our sitcoms.

But Mom responded quickly, as if this were a call-and-response we played often. "I love you, too."

The Test

As destructive fishing practices deplete major fish stocks, jellyfish entice as a source of sustainably caught seafood. You could be forgiven for assuming an animal that's 95 percent water offers little in the way of nutritional value, but once again, jellyfish surprise: Low in calories but high in protein and antioxidants, they have been consumed in Asia for centuries, and jellyfishing as an industrial practice is gaining ground worldwide.

> **AA:** "Take of my body and eat from it," said the Jellyfish Lord.

Though I'd known about the moving barrier for over a week, now that it was common knowledge, the whole island felt tainted. The air was thicker. People moved in slow motion and spoke in the hushed tones you used at the bedside of a sick person. My skin crawled with a constant, low-grade claustrophobia. I wanted off Shattering like never before, but even if everything worked out the way we hoped, what was I going back to?

A couple of days after signing Ha-Yun's contract, I mustered up the courage to call Elijah. He was quiet as I feebly explained my decision to "pursue an opportunity elsewhere," and he went on being quiet so long I wondered if the line had disconnected. Then came the sigh: long, crackly, exhausted. Elijah's theme song.

"You know the research division never made us any money. I was willing to keep it going, to keep you around. You really cared about Seaheart, or you seemed to."

"I did," I insisted. "I do! It's just—"

"Things change." He sounded so wistful. I would've preferred anger. How could I convey to him this wasn't what I wanted?

I saw my messy office at Seaheart, the staff room with its water-ringed table, the gift shop whose shelves teemed with stuffed clownfish, branded magnets, and unisex T-shirts no one ever bought. I saw my lab, invitingly dim and quiet, where I'd lost hours tending to my jelly babies, the one place I'd found comfort after Aldo died.

But Aldo had hated Seaheart. He'd been nagging me to leave the aquarium for months, like it was a freeloading girlfriend tying me down. Aldo had wanted me to work with him, at the bioengineering company. I'd never get to do that now. But I could pick up where he left off.

"Things change," I agreed, and Elijah sighed again.

I tried to put the conversation out of my mind. There was plenty else to focus on. Emmett's scheme for Clementine was well underway. Daily prep sessions were held out at the lighthouse museum, in one of the second-floor rooms off-limits to the tourists, which entailed Emmett bickering with two other men about their remote detonation device while I pored over the lighthouse keeper's logbooks. It was a pointless exercise; Sylvia knew those books better than anyone and had already told me her father mentioned seeing scarlet lights only the one time. But there was something in that historical account, brief and vague though it was: a warning, another clue that itched at the back of my skull. I wanted to either prove Clementine hadn't been responsible for Augustus Steele's death, or understand how she had done it, but the logbooks yielded no answers—just pages upon pages of mundane details about maintenance and inventory, tides and storms, that I squinted at until my eyes burned.

When the prep sessions wrapped up, I returned the logbooks to their display case and ventured down the perilous staircase to the shoreline in search of the *yōkai*.

In light of the conversation with my mother, I wanted to know what this thing was up to before I got in the water again. I scrambled over algae-slick rocks and hopped between tide pools. I scanned the cliff face for a ledge where a long-limbed figure might be perched, swinging its flippered feet. I summoned my courage and faced the water, taking in that unbroken expanse of gray blue stretching out and out until it met the false seam of the horizon. But now that I was actually seeking it out, the *yōkai* apparently had no interest in me. Had I appeased it with my decision to dive? Was that all it had ever wanted from me?

The tourists mostly stuck to the bluff, where the bird-watching was better. But one bright and windy day about a week after the town hall meeting, I arrived on the beach to discover someone had beaten me there. I descended the staircase, keeping my eyes on the small figure standing close to the waterline. As I watched, the stranger stooped, extending a hand toward something at her feet.

"Hey!" I cried, hurrying toward her. Though Tony was telling all the visitors not to touch anything on the beach, I feared these warnings wouldn't have any impact. I had felt the pull of Clementine's tentacle. I had seen my own fingers floating inches away, undeterred by the knowledge of what had happened to Roger.

But this tourist had only been reaching for a rock, which she flung into the surf as I approached, unleashing a spout of foam that caught the light and glittered. She turned and faced me—a thin, college-aged Black girl whose short pink locs perfectly matched the fanny pack sagging at her waist.

"Oh, hey," she said, squinting at me through the sunlight.

"You've got a better chance of seeing birds from up there."

Her eyes followed my finger up to the bluff before snapping back to my face. She was wrong to me like how all the tourists were wrong, but there was something else about this stranger, a kind of overeagerness I wanted to distance myself from on instinct.

"Are you a local?" she asked curiously.

I didn't know how to answer that. "Sort of."

She seemed not to clock my evasiveness, her stare now roving across the rocks and the shiny tide pools tucked between them.

"This is where it happened, right?" she said. "Where that guy got stung?"

There was hunger in her voice, and it sent fury blazing through me. Who did this outsider think she was, coming here to rubberneck our tragedy?

"He's not just *a guy*, okay? His name is Roger Alvarez. He has a wife here on the island. He's in the hospital. He could die at any minute."

The girl went on blinking, seeming neither rebuked nor annoyed.

"I think you should go," I said. "Stop poking around before you get yourself hurt."

The words sounded vaguely threatening in a way I hadn't intended and couldn't back up. I had no authority to tell a paying visitor what they could and couldn't do.

"Okay, then," the girl said, slowly and without hostility, as if humoring me.

I watched her recede up the beach, throwing the occasional look behind her to see if I was still there. I lingered for another hour, so alert to the nosy tourist's potential return, I didn't notice the rising tide until it was lapping at my sneakers.

• • •

Five days before the full moon, my awaited packages arrived at Nadia's house. The breath puffed out of me in an awed sigh as I stroked all my scuba gear: the vestlike BCD configured exactly how I liked it, my mask with its orange silicone skirt, my weight belt and waterproof torch and the dive knife Aldo had given me, still sharp. My mother had done an excellent job packing, as I'd known she would, dutifully wrapping each item in several sheets of newspaper.

The Nematoskyn was foreign and awkward by comparison. The prototypes came in three generic sizes, and even the smallest one didn't fit right, baggy at the crotch and too tight around the shoulder blades. I practiced shimmying the suit over my calves and thighs and torso in Nadia and Roger's living room, Nadia watching silently from the couch. The cool, glossy fabric felt weirdly alive as it adjusted to my every movement. Pulling on the accompanying gloves and hood, I was fully encased inside my borrowed, sting-proof skin.

Nadia leaned in to brush the silky sleeve of the Nematoskyn. Despite the suit's thickness, I could feel her fingers gliding over my shoulders and down my arms, pressing, assessing. "How does it work?"

"I'm not totally sure." Ha-Yun's company wasn't divulging much, for fear of inspiring competitors. "I know it's got three layers. The top one has this slippery stuff woven into it, to keep the stinger cells from adhering."

"Isn't there any way to test it?" A rare wobble of uncertainty had entered Nadia's voice. Roger's accident had eroded some of her optimism. I looked at her, phone sealed in her fist as it was 24/7 in case the hospital called, and saw the face of a woman terrified she was going to lose someone else.

"It has been tested," I assured her gently. "Over and over again, with a dozen jellyfish species, including the ones with deadly stings. It'll work." Defending the Nematoskyn against Nadia's fears had the effect of making me feel more confident. Ha-Yun was annoying, but she was brilliant. And Aldo had been involved in the design, too.

"My gear, on the other hand . . ." I faced the slashed-open packages still cluttering the hallway where I'd opened them. "It's been sitting in storage," I admitted. "I should do a dry run before—before the big night."

It wasn't really my equipment that I was worried about. Even collecting dust in a closet for seven months, it was more reliable than I was. Machines broke down in expected ways, and usually it was simple enough to repair or replace them.

Minds were a different matter. A mind frayed unpredictably and then stitched itself poorly together, fooling you into thinking it was healed.

"Isn't it more of a wet run?" Nadia asked with a weak attempt at a smile.

• • •

The next morning, I bundled everything into a big brown suitcase Nadia had loaned me and dragged it down to the dock, where Tony was waiting. I hadn't seen her much since the town hall meeting. I knew she was still swamped running the B and B, yet she'd agreed right away to accompany me on my practice dive. I was grateful for her steadying presence as *The Phantom Maiden* lurched into the Gulf. I thought I'd been building up my confidence during the hours I spent on the beach, but I saw now that being near the water was nothing like being on it, unbalanced by every bump and swell.

Tony took us around to the glossy waters of the smuggler's cove. She cut the motor, and the surrounding sounds intensified. The light smack of the water against the hull, the squeal of some gulls I couldn't see. Aldo had always filled our predive safety checks with his wisecracks and chatter. It felt wrong to be doing any of this without him.

Tony stripped off her sweats and T-shirt, revealing a black one-piece swimsuit. Before I had the time to properly appreciate the curves of her exposed skin, she vaulted over the side of the boat and into the water.

A massive splash surged upward, raining droplets onto my arms and face. Tony unleashed a yelp as her head popped out of the water. "It's fucking freezing in here!" She cackled and dove back down, her feet slipping under, smooth as a mermaid's snapping tail. She was a natural. A deranged thought crashed into me: I could happily watch Tony backstroke lazy circles around *The Phantom Maiden* for the rest of my life.

But she wasn't going to let me get away with that, and that was another reason I was glad she was here.

"C'mon, *Jo-Ness*," she called teasingly, splashing water at me. "Haven't got all day!" Her face softened as I shuffled toward the side of the boat, feeling massive and awkward in all my equipment. "You can do this," she said, with such serene confidence I had no choice but to believe her.

So I tucked the regulator into my mouth and pitched backward into the water.

It wasn't a graceful entry. Bubbles seethed in a blinding froth. My arms flailed, seeking handholds that weren't there. I was wildly out of practice. I felt the thinness of my protective equipment as I'd never felt it before. There was so little keeping any of us from death down here. A mask. A hose. A tank. I was holding my breath—an absolute no-no while diving—but I was terrified the air supply that had worked flawlessly on the boat would fail me underwater.

I had made this happen. I volunteered to get in the water with Clementine, I haggled for the Nematoskyn, I asked my mother to ship my equipment.

I made myself suck in a tiny bit of air. Then another.

I opened my eyes and blinked as my surroundings swam into focus, illuminated by soft beams of sunlight straining through the cloudy water. I was only a few feet down, but it felt the way diving always did, as if I'd wiggled through a wormhole and entered a new corner of the universe. Bubbles tickled my face as they spun upward to meet the surface. The cove was shallow at this point. Looking down, I could just make out an old lobster trap where it had come to rest against the substrate, its ropes billowing like severed braids.

As the initial shock of my entry faded, I became aware of the cold pressing in on me. Tony was right: It was fucking freezing. The Nematoskyn was designed for tropical waters and would be no help warding off the Atlantic's chill. But there was a warm, untouchable calm unfurling inside me. For the first time since arriving on Shattering Point—maybe for the first time since losing Aldo—I felt as if I'd come home.

Tony swirled into view. Some trick of the watery light made her tattoos come alive, the honeybees flitting down her forearms, the blimp floating up her left bicep. Her hair fanned out around her head like a jellyfish's tendrils. My heart soared, opening up a tiny space for something other than fear.

Tony's eyes were opened to slits. She smacked a palm against my shoulder and then took off. *Tag, you're it.*

As she dolphin kicked into the murk, my vision tunneled: It was too much like my final glimpse of Aldo before he was swallowed by the silt-out.

I followed, frantic, desperate to keep her in my sight. But my equipment was for diving, not swimming. Even rising to gulp air every few seconds, Tony was faster than me. The seabed slanted away as the cove deepened. Every second took us closer to open water. I kept almost catching her; she kept shooting away like a fish. She was playing a game, and I felt like I was dying.

Finally, I gave up, surfaced, and pulled the regulator from my mouth.

"Enough!"

Tony, who was ten or so feet ahead of me, paused at the sound of my voice and turned, water streaming from her hair.

We made our slow way back to the boat. She clambered aboard first and helped me out of the water. I stripped off my mask and held it, tracing my thumb around the silicone skirt.

"Sorry. I thought you were having fun." Tony draped a fluffy bath towel around my shoulders and rubbed my arms until I stopped shivering. "I take it your gear worked all right?"

I nodded and touched her knee, to show I wasn't angry. Everything had gone exactly as it should've. I had dived, and no disasters had befallen me. The *yōkai* hadn't even shown up. I was starting to feel more convinced I really had banished it forever.

Tony grabbed her own towel and joined me on the floor of the boat. "I'm coming with you on your night dive."

I felt a leap of what was either excitement or fear. "Is that a good idea?"

"Someone's got to make sure Emmett doesn't blow you up. And if your magic suit fails, you're not gonna want to wait to get back to shore for medical attention. Better if I'm right there on the boat."

"Thank you," I said. And I meant it.

But what I was thinking was that if my magic suit failed, there was nothing anyone could do to help me.

Strawberry Moon

One of the most tragic consequences of disavowing an entire class of organisms is that we delay—or entirely miss—the discovery of their full potential in this world. Jellyfish's undulations help transport nutrients through the water column. Their mucus could be deployed to collect and break down toxic chemicals. Jellyfish venom is being studied for its ability to stunt the growth of cancer cells. Better understanding the conditions that cause jellyfish blooms is a way of better understanding our changing oceans, and what, if anything, can be done to reverse the damage.

> **AA:** I take your point. But this raises a thorny question: Must a species be useful to be worthy of survival? Is that a message we want to send? Don't all living, breathing things have the right to go on living and breathing?

> **AA:** Except sea turtles. Fuck those guys.

The day of the full moon dawned gray and drizzly, but by evening the haze had pulled back. Wisps of cloud skidded high in the sky, urged along by a steady breeze.

The smuggler's cove would serve as our base of operations for the evening. At quarter to seven, Tony pulled up outside Nadia's house in the junky gold car to transport me and my suitcase full of scuba gear. Her red medical bag was in the trunk, along with a square yellow device I recognized as a portable defibrillator.

"You're going to electrocute me with that thing," I said.

Tony smiled wryly. "Obviously I'll dry you off first."

The way she was talking like she was definitely going to have to resuscitate me wasn't exactly reassuring.

I added my suitcase to the trunk and stood there looking at our combined gear, wishing we were headed anywhere else. In just a few hours, I'd be helping to destroy Clementine. I knew I had to do it. For Nadia, for Tony, for Roger, who deserved to have his family by his side. But that didn't mean I had to feel good about any of it.

As usual, Tony somehow knew just what was going through my head.

"Things die, Jo," she said quietly, "so that other things can live. It's not nice, but it is natural."

I looked at her. She seemed sad, but resolved. If Tony could reach her peace with this decision, then I could, too.

The trunk closed with a snap. Then someone was screaming.

We both started as Nadia sprang onto the porch. She was crying and waving around her cell phone. I was so prepared for bad news that it took me several seconds to process what she was shouting: "He's awake—he's awake! Roger's awake."

Tony and I raced into the house. We found Nadia in the kitchen, where the cell signal was strongest. The room was a mess. Roger was the clean one, and in his absence, Nadia and I were living like slobs. She'd planted her elbows on the table, hunched over a plate with a congealed slab of half-eaten casserole on it, her phone pressed to her ear with both hands.

"What's going on?" asked Tony. She slid into the chair next to Nadia. "Is he off the ventilator? Can he talk?"

"They've been weaning him off the medication," Nadia whispered. "But they didn't expect him to come around so quickly. The nurse said she'd never seen anything like—Roger! Rog!" Her voice hitched with an excited sob. "It's me, baby. How are you feeling? I'm here with Jo, and Tony—" She quieted, her grip around the phone tightening. I could make out the muffled stream of a low voice on the other end.

Nadia looked up at me. "He wants to talk to you."

"To *me*?"

"Put it on speaker," ordered Tony.

Nadia complied, fingers trembling.

"Uh—Roger?" I said uncertainly, bending over the phone. "It's Jo. How are—?"

"*Joooo!*" Roger's voice exploded out of the speaker, making us all jump. Nadia quickly lowered the volume, but he continued to bellow as if we were standing on opposite ends of a soccer field. "Jooo! I figured it out! Everything is *connected*. You, me, Nadia, the trees, your grandma, this hospital tray." There was a rattling clang of what I could only assume was the tray hitting a wall. "We're all cradled inside a giant gold hammock. I've been brought close enough to see the individual strands. I was freed but I'd rather be trapped. I've seen and been seen and it comes back to me now in dreams, millions of glowing strands tying us all together—"

"What sort of drugs is he on?" asked Tony wonderingly.

Roger was still babbling, but at a distance now. Someone had pried the phone away. A different voice started talking—calm, official-sounding, one of Roger's doctors. Nadia took the call off speaker, her face pale.

My legs felt unsteady. I dropped into a chair.

"It's good," Tony whispered. "He's talking. He remembers who you are."

I nodded. But privately I worried Roger might have suffered brain damage.

Nadia went on listening to the doctor, interjecting with a question every now and then.

"We can't stay," added Tony. She was looking out the window, at the lengthening shadows in Nadia and Roger's backyard. The sun would set within the hour. With darkness came Clementine.

I stood and pressed my hand onto Nadia's shoulder. She reached up and squeezed my fingers, distracted. I wanted her to put down the phone, just for a second, look me in the eye, wish me luck. Something.

"We'll see you later," I murmured.

She nodded vaguely. I followed Tony back to the car.

• • •

Roger's awakening felt like an omen for my dive, though I couldn't tell whether it was good or bad. The cove was full of people tonight, only a handful of whom were directly involved in the mission to kill the giant jellyfish. The rest were spectators, gathered in anticipation of celebrating their freedom from Clementine. A campfire burned in the clearing beneath the trees. Someone strummed a guitar. The cheerful music chewed through me like acid, and the campfire's smoke seemed to singe every particle in my lungs.

Emmett Beckendorf waited on the floating dock. His boat, *Calypso,* sat low in the water, loaded down with the barrels of explosives, all looped together by a rusty chain. A crane and winch had been mounted in the stern, ready to lower the chain into the water. Tony secured her medical bag and the defibrillator in an under-seat locker, then strode over to the campfire to share the good news about Roger. I knelt to open Nadia's suitcase. I'd already inventoried my gear twice, but I had the urge to go over it all again—touching every item, a closed loop of preparation that never culminated in taking any action.

There was one new addition: the tiny microphone that would sit inside my full-face mask and communicate via a wireless transmitter to the surface unit on *Calypso*, which resembled a blocky, old-fashioned radio. This was how I would cue Emmett to cue the land team to start the countdown on the barrels as soon as Clementine was in position.

"You've got to talk slowly," Emmett said to me as I fiddled with the strap-mounted earpiece. "The pressure fucks with the transmission."

"I've used underwater comms before." I didn't add that it had only been one time on a research dive in grad school, and the speech distortion had been so severe as to render the divers incomprehensible. But the technology had come a long way since then.

Forced to accept that everything was ready to go, I closed the suitcase and stowed it aboard *Calypso*. Then I felt a hand come down on my shoulder. It was Tony.

"We have a problem," she said.

She led me toward the mouth of the tunnel, where the problem stood looking around with interest at the festivities. It was the tourist I'd scolded on the beach, the one who'd been so fascinated by Roger's accident. Tonight she wore a dark jacket and the same pink fanny pack, her hands fidgeting at her sides.

"Jo, meet Shanel Sawyer," said Tony. "She said she already knows who you are."

"I didn't recognize you the other day at first," said Shanel eagerly. "You're Dr. Ness. I saw you speak at a conference last year. You were part of a panel on aquaculture's impact on jellyfish blooms."

I inwardly cursed the smallness of the jellyfish world. I remembered the panel, if not this young woman's face among the audience members.

"I'm a graduate student at the University of New Hampshire," Shanel said. "Their biological oceanography program. I'm about to start my second year."

"Great," I said. "Fantastic." I squeezed at a headache stirring between my eyes. I glanced at Tony, whose mouth had gone flat like she was either very annoyed or suppressing a laugh. "Let me guess. You saw the news story about the guy who got stung and thought you'd come out here to get a firsthand look?"

"I have a Google alert set up for stings in New England." Shanel rocked on her heels, seeming proud of her ingenuity. "It's not every day a sting puts someone in the hospital. I got curious. I'm planning to do my thesis on the envenomation mechanism of *Physalia physalis*—"

"The Portuguese man-of-war. That's not what we're dealing with here."

"You know what the animal is, then?"

"She's . . . a new species. I hope to know more soon."

It was the wrong thing to say. Excitement flared in Shanel's eyes. It was the same type of excitement that appeared in Aldo's eyes when he talked about venom, the same one that tolled noisily through me when I got to see a jellyfish. It was a blind nerdy fascination, a real force of nature, and there was no reining it in once it got started.

"No," I said. I had a full-blown headache now.

"I haven't even asked anything!" protested Shanel.

"No, you can't come with me. No, I don't need an assistant or an intern or a dive buddy. No, this won't be the subject of your thesis."

"I have relevant experience!" Shanel's voice cracked with desperation. "I have a bachelor's in marine science, I'm PADI certified, I can drive a boat. Two years ago I interned at a lab in Washington with a toxinologist studying jellyfish venom—"

My headache stopped in its tracks. Everything stopped.

"You interned with Aldo Antunes at the Chapman Marine Station?"

Shanel nodded. "Do you know him?"

Shanel Sawyer. Now the name tingled at the edge of memory. I heard it in Aldo's voice. Two years ago . . . Yes, I remembered: Aldo and I had met up for a wreck dive in South Carolina. The 250-foot World War II freighter was slouched on an offshore ledge and encrusted in a thick layer of barnacles. Beards of algae rippled from the drooping bow. Sand tiger sharks nosed along the starboard side, drawn by the hordes of baitfish that bunched and swirled around us, so thick at times they blocked visibility like a massive eddy of silver leaves.

It was an excellent dive. After, we dropped our gear at the motel and went to eat at a diner. Aldo loved American diners. The greasier, the better. He claimed the first restaurant he ever patronized in this country was a diner with checkered floors where they served all-day pancakes and milkshakes the size of his head. While we were eating, his phone rang. You were never really on vacation when you had a whole lab to run. Aldo talked loudly through a mouthful of biscuits and gravy. "No, no. Those are the old samples. I don't know, what did Shanel say? Well, ask her. She basically runs the place."

"Call him," challenged Shanel. Her voice had regained its boldness. She'd misinterpreted the stillness in my face as a sign she was winning me over. "Call Aldo and ask him if I'm reliable. He'll vouch for me. He wrote one of my grad school references."

"I can't call him," I said. "He's dead."

Shanel's shoulders sank. "I'm sorry. I didn't know. How did—?" Seeming to decide against this line of questioning, she shook herself and regrouped: "You got here first. And you have more experience than I do. This animal is your discovery. You should get to be first author. But why not bring me on as your second?"

"Because I'm trying to protect you."

"From what?" She sounded as annoyed as I was.

I looked helplessly at Tony, who grimaced. What could either of us say to persuade her to stop snooping? The truth? Would she believe us? And if she did, would it just stoke her curiosity more? Tony had tried to warn me away from Clementine, and look how that turned out. Aldo only respected people who were as stubborn as he was. If Shanel was as good a researcher as he'd thought, she wasn't going to be easily deterred. And I couldn't deny that her showing up here, now, felt prescient. Important. For weeks I'd wanted to talk to Aldo about Clementine. Maybe talking to his former intern was the next best thing.

I exhaled slowly. "Come with me."

"Jo," warned Tony as I stepped toward Sylvia Steele's tucked-away cabin and Shanel, grinning, followed. "There's no time—"

"I'll only be a few minutes," I said.

Fortunately, Sylvia wasn't around to balk at the invasion as we walked through the wood-paneled passage toward the sewing room where Nadia was once imprisoned. I checked to make sure the brass key was still hanging on its nail to the left of the door. Shanel claimed the rocking chair, and I settled onto a kelp-colored ottoman. The grad student maintained an awed silence, though little flares of interest twitched all over her face as I recapped everything that had happened since I arrived on Shattering Point a month ago: Clementine's surfacing last fall, her apparent power to create an invisible barrier around the island, Roger's encounter with the rogue tentacle, and the barrier's recent movement toward shore, necessitating Emmett's plan to end the giant jelly once and for all. I worried it would take ages to get through, but the story, for all its drama, turned out to be a short one. There were too many gaps and mysteries. There was still so much we didn't know.

I waited for Shanel to brush me off or laugh or ask me if I was taking any drugs. Instead, her face twisted into an expression of bewilderment, she said, "And after all that you've learned, you're just going to blow Clementine up?"

I flinched. "Believe me, it's not what I want, either. I'm open to other suggestions if you have them." I recognized the hopeful lie in these words: It was too late. Emmett had the other islanders' support. He was going through with this plan whether I played a role in it or not.

Shanel thought for a minute, then unzipped her fanny pack and withdrew a compact black camera. "Depth rated up to one hundred and thirty feet."

"I told you. This animal doesn't film well."

"You've never tried to capture her underwater," Shanel pointed out. "Maybe it'll be different. It's worth a try, isn't it? If your giant jellyfish doesn't exist after tonight, at least there will be some record."

She passed the camera to me, and I looped the lanyard around my wrist.

Then I stood, and Shanel stood, too, looking at me expectantly.

"Now what?" she asked.

"Now I ask you to promise me you won't try and get a peek at Clementine tonight, and you lie and say you won't."

Shanel smirked, not even trying to playact innocence. "What's the harm? You're getting rid of her anyway."

"We don't know what's going to happen," I reminded her. "Killing Clementine could make the barrier disappear, or it could do nothing, or it could cause some new awful scenario we haven't thought of. We shouldn't make assumptions."

Shanel nodded. I wasn't fooled for a second. She was too much like Aldo, too much like me. The minute we parted, she'd be racing up to the bluff, seeking a glimpse of Shattering Point's sea monster before she was gone from this world forever. A month ago, I might not have cared. People made dumb choices—what did that have to do with me?

But something had shifted in me after Roger was stung. I no longer felt responsible just for Clementine's fate, but for the fate of every person who set foot on this island.

I smiled briefly at Shanel, and then—moving at a speed that surprised even myself—I lunged into the hall, slammed the door, and locked it.

Shanel cried out. The doorknob jiggled but didn't give as she twisted it from inside.

"I'm sorry!" I called through the door, slipping the key back onto its nail. "It's better this way. Please just trust me. I'll touch base with you after the dive. Uhh. Thanks for the camera?"

I retreated back up the passage, cringing at the sound of Shanel's protests and the door creaking as she tested her weight against it. On my way out of the cabin, I nearly ran into Sylvia, who swelled like a bullfrog when she saw me traipsing out of her house.

"There you are. What the hell do you think you're—?"

"You might hear some banging and shouting coming from your sewing room. Just ignore it, okay?"

Sylvia looked for a moment as if she was going to whack me with her walking stick. Then weariness overcame her. She shook her head. "I don't even want to know what that's about."

* * *

The sun hadn't set yet, but the patches of sky between treetops were twice as dark as when I'd gone into the cabin with Shanel. Sylvia walked with me down to the boathouse, where a crowd was gathered. The summery atmosphere had given way to an air of uncertainty. The islanders chorused *good luck* and *go get her* as Tony and I boarded *Calypso* and Emmett started the engine. I scanned for Nadia's face, but she hadn't made it. Was she still on the phone with Roger's doctors? Had it slipped her mind that I was doing this for her? For us?

Sylvia hefted her walking stick into the air, offering us a salute. Then she was a shadow shrinking into the night as Emmett guided us away from the dock and out of the sheltered inlet, into open water.

Panic spread its icy feelers through my guts the farther we got from shore. Tony touched her fingers lightly to my back, and I felt a borrowed courage surging into me. I had done this before. I could do it again. The full moon had risen over the bluff—rose-colored, massive, lurid, like something stolen from another galaxy.

"My gran used to call it the strawberry moon," said Tony. "First full moon of the summer."

We stood clustered around the barrels, bearing silent witness to this alien face hovering in blank judgment above us.

I was already wearing the Nematoskyn. The excess fabric bunched around my thighs as I squatted and opened the suitcase again.

I had always liked night dives. They were peaceful, the way

caves were peaceful, but there was a greater sense of possibility in open water. The world seemed simultaneously small—reduced to the corridor of brilliance shed by a flashlight—and indescribably vast, as you swung that corridor and carved out new sight lines through which the spectral mass of a big fish might suddenly swerve, sending the thrill of discovery shooting through you.

When I pointed my flashlight over the side of *Calypso*, the water threw the beam back at me, and I had a brief, crazy vision of cracking my skull against the surface, as if back-rolling into concrete.

Tony, who'd been inside the cabin talking to Emmett, reemerged as I parked my butt on the gunwale, the air tank dangling off the side of the boat.

"Land team's in position. Emmett wants you to try going down about twenty feet."

At least this time I knew what to expect. The water opened its arms to me, and I fell right through them.

I descended slowly, the cold seeping through my suit. When the dive computer on my wrist read twenty feet, I tipped my head back to study the bottom of *Calypso*, reduced to a scoop of greenish shadow with the anchor chain plunging into deeper darkness.

My fins stirred through water thick with murk. The moon, big as it was, couldn't reach its light more than a few feet down. A translucent slip of a fish skidded past. I tried to train my torch on it, but it was gone as fast as I'd registered the movement.

Static crackled through my earpiece, followed by Emmett's voice: "Testing one, two. Josephine, do you copy?"

"I copy." My mask had wedged the mic into a weird position, closer to my nose than my mouth. "If you can hear me, go ahead and lower them."

A minute passed before the first barrel broke the water, sending a ring of ripples reverberating across the surface. I watched from below as the chain unraveled, swallowed into the blackness untouched by *Calypso*'s lights. The first barrel was followed a moment later by another, and another—a line of deadly explosives disappearing one by one into darkness. For the first time since entering the water, I shivered. The whole setup struck me as archaic and evil-looking, like some kind of ancient underwater torture device. Any one of these barrels could spell Clementine's end. Or my own, if I wasn't careful to get out of range.

The chain tightened and stilled. The trap was laid. Now all we needed was our giant, doomed jellyfish.

Descent

In the vastness of the sea, it's easy for even the biggest organisms to stay hidden. It wasn't until 2012 that the giant squid was filmed live in its natural habitat. What other colossal invertebrates still lurk undiscovered in the layers where sunlight never reaches?

> **JN:** They never found out why you survived that snakebite. No genetic abnormality, no quirk of the blood. But you carried the answer inside you. The body always knows the truth. What happens to the truth when the body is gone? I should've had you donated to science, medical mystery that you were, but I couldn't bear the thought of a roomful of scalpel-wielding strangers in scrub suits and surgical caps leering at you through plastic face shields. I wanted to keep you where I could keep an eye on you. I see that was selfish now. I see that grief makes a person selfish.

Clementine was in no rush to make an appearance. We waited for an hour aboard *Calypso*, the lighthouse beam oscillating over our heads and the strawberry moon tracing its slow arc across the sky. Emmett sat huddled inside the cabin with a crinkled paperback that looked like it had been rained on and allowed to dry more than once. Tony joined me where I sat tucked beneath a tarp in the stern.

"What do you think Shanel's doing right now?" I asked. I'd told Tony about barricading the grad student in Sylvia's sewing room. It had seemed like the right decision at the time, but I felt a creeping shame as I relived her indignant cries following me down the hallway.

"Probably making you a scarf," said Tony.

I snickered, then stopped as my thoughts pivoted to Roger, his rage and relief when we'd finally found Nadia unharmed in Sylvia's house. I shouldn't give his ramblings on the phone any credence. He'd clearly been out of his mind. Yet slivers of his deranged monologue kept cutting into me. *We're all cradled inside a giant gold hammock . . . I was freed but I'd rather be trapped.*

"Do you think Roger's going to be all right?" I asked softly.

"I think the worst of the danger has passed," said Tony.

I nodded, hoping she was right. I'd shed all my gear but the Nematoskyn, and I could feel the warmth of Tony's arm where it was wedged against mine, just like that afternoon in the bird hospital.

I wondered what I wanted from Tony, what she wanted from me. Only now was it dawning on me that there was a version of the future where tonight was the last time we were together. Insane circumstances had thrown us into one another's lives. What happened once those circumstances were gone? Nadia and I had a shared past to pick up from. It was different with Tony. We barely knew each other. I fretted at the possibility that whatever we'd shared in the last few weeks had been nothing more than a diversion, born of a total lack of other options.

The tarp crinkled as Tony adjusted her legs beneath it. "Did you ever play that game as a kid where you spun the globe, and wherever your finger landed was where you had to live?"

I smiled. "All the time."

"I used to keep a list. Fribourg, Switzerland. Adelaide, Australia. Aswân, Egypt."

"You must've landed in the ocean a lot, too."

"No one counts when they land in the ocean, Jo. You get to spin again."

"Speak for yourself." Finding my fingertip placed on the blue part of the globe had always been the most exciting outcome. I would race to my reference books, eager to discover which species of jellyfish would be my next-door neighbors.

"And now?" I prompted. "I know you want to visit your mom, but what about after?"

Tony was quiet for a minute. "I just want to live somewhere that's not surrounded by ocean."

"I'm from Indiana. Cornfields, strip malls. Not a speck of salt water in sight."

"What a dream," said Tony. In the harsh glow of *Calypso*'s deck lights, I could see her jaw working, as if she were chewing on her next words, sampling their flavor. "If we can get off Shattering, maybe you can take me there."

My heart fluttered. It was a massive if. *If* we were able to kill Clementine. *If* the jellyfish's death made the barrier disappear.

But Tony's if was also a door, swinging open onto a world where I took her to my hometown to meet my mother; where we ate lunch at the new Vietnamese restaurant that had once been the crummy pizza parlor where I'd waited tables, painstakingly counting my tips so I could put a portion toward my first set of scuba gear; where we strolled through my father's garden, and I regaled Tony with the tale of how my mother had once fought a malicious demon there, and won.

A world where, as I'd promised Nadia, everything would be okay.

"I'd like that," I told Tony.

She smiled, then wrinkled her nose as the air between us abruptly soured. "Do you smell that?"

I did: a sweet-sour reek like flowers wilting into a vase of rancid water.

Both my feet had fallen asleep. I stamped the feeling back into them as I shimmied into my gear again. *Calypso*'s stern and side lights cut out. The darkness closed around us and was fended off by the steady pulse of the lighthouse beacon every few seconds.

A silhouette emerged from the cabin. "It doesn't like the boat lights," said Emmett, his voice simultaneously frail and too loud. The whole world had fallen silent. Even the slap of water against the hull was distant.

It was a silence such as the priest had never heard before, as if their little boat had sunk right into the grave.

"Don't get any closer than you have to," said Tony, handing me Shanel's underwater camera so I could tighten the lanyard around my wrist. Was Tony the blind priest unknowingly transporting me to my fate, or was Emmett? I felt a sudden panic at the thought that we'd broken the rules by bringing an extra person into my mother's story. "And make sure you're clear of those explosives before you give the signal . . ." The lighthouse beam slashed across her face, which looked drained and uncertain.

I wanted to say something to her, something heartfelt and meaningful. But the words stalled in my throat. I told myself there would be time after.

"See you soon," I managed.

And for the second time that night, I back-rolled into the frigid Atlantic.

I stuck near the barrels as I descended, a temporary measure to help orient myself. It was never easy to maintain a sense of direction underwater, and this was doubly true in darkness. If I strayed too far from the boat, I might not find my way back.

I kept my eyes pinned to the speckled darkness beneath my fins. Clementine would be easy to see if she was fluorescing. If not, she could be almost invisible—a translucent blob I wouldn't see until we collided.

A tinny voice spoke in my ear: "Are . . . hear . . . good?"

"Hello? Can you say that again?"

"Jo . . . hear us?"

"It's weak, but I can hear you."

No reply. I was just going to have to trust that the signal was working well enough. Returning to the surface now risked missing Clementine altogether.

I searched myself for fear and found only its absence: a cool sense of surrender. I wondered if this was what Aldo had felt as the needle on his pressure gauge touched zero. I'd played out his final moments in my head a hundred times, ultimately deciding, for the sake of my own sanity, that his death had been peaceful, like going to sleep.

Now I felt a stupid certainty creeping up on me: Aldo was down here somewhere. Not the *yōkai* that had borrowed his body, or the giant snake that had stolen his voice. The *real* Aldo. This was where I would finally find him, in the vast, open darkness where Clementine was lurking.

The constant movement of the nearest barrel swaying on its chain was starting to gnaw at my calm. I hated those barrels. I felt stalked by them, pinned hungrily in their sights. I exhaled and sank a little lower, watching *Calypso* dissolve into the gloom. According to my dive computer, I was thirty feet down, but it felt like a whole universe separated me from Tony and Emmett.

My dive light shivered, blinking off and then on again. I froze. It would be very bad to be adrift down here without a light source.

There was a spare flashlight in the pocket of my BCD—small beamed, intended for up-close inspection, but a whole lot better than nothing. I reached for it and froze again. Just like the night in the lighthouse, I was convinced I had imagined it until I saw it a second time: a red glow thudding in the depths like a great, watery heartbeat.

I abandoned my search for my backup torch and fumbled for Shanel's camera instead, managing to switch it on just as hundreds of tentacles whirled from the depths in a glowing, synchronized unraveling.

I'd witnessed this display from shore, but to be in the water with it—surrounded by it—was a completely different experience. The light was so bright I had to fight the urge to close my eyes. My torch hadn't died, but it may as well have, reduced to a pinprick in that wash of brilliance.

Every feeling that wasn't amazement drained out of me. I forgot about the barrier, the plan, the explosives, Nadia, Tony. I even forgot about Aldo. Clementine floated freely in the water, a serpentlike stalk towing a curtain of ribbon-thin tendrils. On the far end of the stalk, in place of anything approximating a head, a dozen gelatinous blades undulated like a garden of sea fans. Swimming bells: These were the rudder-like organs that provided the propulsive power for this massive animal, allowing her to maneuver through the water column.

Clementine shifted, flexed, and fluttered, a luminous and alien dance. The jellyfish wasn't reeling me down into the ocean's darkness like the monster that ensnared the widow. She seemed almost dormant, curled and drifting with the current. A bundle of tentacles reached out and tenderly stroked the last barrel.

Static hissed in my ear. "Jo . . . clear . . . now?"

The barrel rocked on its chain as Clementine swirled around it. I couldn't escape the feeling that the giant jelly knew exactly what she was doing: playing with danger, flirting with fate.

I tried to speak. Now was the moment. The solution to Shattering Point's jellyfish problem might be seconds away. It was the problem I'd come all this way to solve. We would never know unless we tried it. Now was the moment to give the signal to blow this beautiful sea monster into a thousand pieces of slimy, jelly confetti.

Clementine's tentacles furled upward, drawing my eyes up the chain to a vaguely human figure. I knew even before picking out the shape of long, swaying legs terminating in two lime-green flippers that it was him.

Aldo hung suspended vertically fifteen feet below the surface, the jellyfish's bioluminescence passing over him in pulsating waves. No bubbles lifted from his regulator. He was statuesque. Godlike. Clementine sprawled below him, now pulsing a placid maroon. My thoughts turned, absurdly, to Norm Sloan and Betty the German shepherd, the loyal old dog sitting on her haunches, awaiting her master's word to attack.

"Jo . . . clear?" the voice persisted.

Aldo's gloved hand lifted. Instead of curling his fingers and tipping his thumb downward into the signal the *yōkai* had given me on the beach, he simply held his palm out to me, as if in a ghostly pantomime of a high five.

The meaning was unmistakable. You didn't have to be a diver to understand.

"Negative," I said—shouted—into the microphone in my mask. I had enough sense to push back from the chain, just in case my message got misunderstood or ignored. "Don't blow the charges. I repeat: *Do not blow the charges.*"

The words had barely left my mouth when Clementine's tentacles slid away. The rudders kicked into action, and the whole glowing form was hauled shoreward, out of range of the deadly barrels.

The relief that melted through me was pure and fleeting. Had I really just done that? Doomed myself and all the other islanders? Doomed Tony?

I looked for Aldo, but he was gone, too. *Stop*, he'd told me. *Halt*. And I had. But that couldn't be it, could it?

I chased after them. It wasn't a choice. I chased after Aldo and Clementine like an eye blinking to dislodge a piece of grit. It was instinct, neutral and unthinking—not my own instinct, but the jellyfish's. *Clementine* was moving *me*, and I was powerless to resist her.

The gap between us closed gradually. Shanel's camera was

still clutched in my gloved hand. Or was it? I was having a hard time tracking my body. Thoughts of the breakers slamming me into the rocks skittered across my mind and vanished. As she neared shore, Clementine rotated so that her tendrils grazed the surface. Jellyfish tentacles weren't capable of high-level sensory perception like an octopus's arms, yet watching her stroke the air-water interface, it was impossible not to think of a clever animal testing the limits of its prison.

The tendrils stretched out, pulling up just short of my body. A white-hot flash of fear returned me to myself as I remembered Roger convulsing in the shadow of the lighthouse. I panicked and descended, and the seabed rose to meet me, a Martian landscape sprinkled with more abandoned lobster traps.

My feet touched the substrate, releasing two small puffs of silt, and the world collapsed into a tight corridor: I was in the cave, blinded, alone.

Directly above, Clementine had transformed into a layered, shimmering canopy woven of scarlet light. Even at this distance, she was too large to capture in a single shot. I raised the camera to my face and panned until the viewfinder was centered on Aldo, a dark stain blotting the creature's glow like the hard curve of the moon eclipsing the sun.

I ascended, my heart thudding against the embrace of the Nematoskyn, which clung to me now like a cold sheet of plastic wrap. When I entered the circumference of Clementine's glow, the chill left me. My eyes throbbed hotly in their sockets, my skin burning with fever.

I was close enough now that Clementine had only to drop her

skirt of tentacles and I'd be completely enfolded in grasping stingers.

Aldo and I hovered feet away from each other. How many times had we held a position just like this as we hung out in a safety stop, letting the nitrogen ooze from our tissues? A happy ache filled me. I thought I'd rocket right through the surface like a champagne cork. At long last, we were together, in the water where we'd always felt at home.

But I couldn't see his eyes. His goggles threw the red light back at me.

I reached for him, half expecting him to shy away, but he held still as I removed his mask.

The face staring back at me was a blank plane of mottled flesh, devoid of features. No mouth whose corners lifted in a shit-eating grin. No heavy black eyebrows squatting on his forehead. No dusting of stubble that always came back within hours of shaving. No eyes. It was a face only in the barest sense of the word, sculpted by someone who had little idea what human faces looked like.

I recoiled. This wasn't Aldo. This was only the copy.

Only the ghost.

Dread shot through me. My mother was wrong. The *yōkai* was not my guardian angel. The trap for Clementine had turned into a trap for me—one I'd willfully blundered into because I'd needed to convince myself I could see him again, talk to him one last time.

And now a dancing wave of tentacles was rippling toward me, and I was numb. Like the men who'd tried to poison Clementine in Lawrence's video, I couldn't move if I tried. The jellyfish held me right where I was, hands still extended toward the *yōkai*. I felt simultaneously tiny and massive. I was me and not me. I was a particle of marine snow gently falling to the seabed, and I was the whole ocean that surrounded it.

Clementine's tentacles grazed my left shoulder, and time contracted: I imagined the long thread of the stinger firing from its chamber, a microscopic harpoon evolved to launch on contact. But there was no answering spray of pain down my arm. The tentacles slipped across me like gummy strands of seaweed.

Ha-Yun's magic suit was working.

I tried fluttering my fins, and my feet cooperated. Clementine had released me, intent on snaking her long tendrils down to the seafloor. A moment later, I saw why: A section of the reaching tentacles went rigid, exactly like a fishing line tensing with a freshly hooked catch. A small, stunned, unlucky thing was reeled up toward the central stalk. Clementine was hungry.

In the few seconds I'd been distracted, the *yōkai* had changed location, blinking out like a dead bulb and reappearing near where the unfortunate fish had vanished. What was it doing up there? A billowing veil of glowing tentacles separated us, limiting my view. I waited anxiously for the *yōkai* to dive down and exact whatever demon vengeance it had lured me here to carry out, and the longer I went on waiting—Clementine spearing and reeling more meals for herself, my ticking regulator a constant reminder of my fast-dwindling air supply—the more the conviction grew in me that nothing was going to happen.

Maybe I had painted myself as the cursed heroine in a story that didn't belong to me. Maybe I'd been wrong to think the *yōkai* was stalking me, trying to hurt me. Maybe my mother and I had both been wrong to think its presence had anything to do with me at all.

It wasn't my guardian angel. But maybe it was Clementine's.

I paused to check my tank pressure and make sure my gloves were pulled tight over the sleeves of the Nematoskyn, leaving no skin bared.

Swimming through those tentacles was like traversing a forest of illuminated, hanging vines. Clementine didn't try to stop me, but she didn't make a path for me, either. The heat intensified, until my skeleton was on fire, each bone hot and malleable as a piece of steel plucked from a blacksmith's forge. I saw myself being thinned and stretched into a new shape. A new kind of human.

I lost my sense of direction. I couldn't tell up from down. Clementine closed herself around me, tentacles compressing into a sheer and glowing wall.

Something black and thin entered my field of vision. The tentacles swirled around it, testing it: the hose of the *yōkai*'s detached regulator, swinging freely through the water.

I followed the length of the hose, letting it lead me up and out of the forest until I was once more level with the *yōkai*. Only a few feet down from the surface, we were right up against Clementine's central stalk where the tentacles grew tough and bristly. The glow was still hot against my face, but I felt myself coming back to myself—enough to wonder about the specialized organs for reproduction and digestion that must lurk somewhere along the length of this gelatinous tube.

The *yōkai* pointed lazily at its own chest.

Watch me.

So I did. I watched as it pressed Clementine's stalk with splayed fingers like a person leaving their impression in wet concrete.

Instantly, Clementine shape-shifted again, fanning out, every tentacle sprawled. From the top of the lighthouse, it must've appeared as if a giant, shining spiderweb was spreading across the surface. It was an intimidating display, showcasing the full size of the jellyfish, which was big enough to mummify a dozen people in her whipping tendrils and still have some to spare.

Yet as she swelled, Clementine was growing more diffuse. More vulnerable. Like a spiderweb, she was mighty and delicate. The bigger she grew, the frailer she became. Queasiness rocked me at the thought that Clementine might tear herself to shreds, and me with her.

Because with every inch of length she gained, I could feel the agony twinned inside my own body. Ligaments stretched. Lungs straining. Hairs singed and plucked from my arms and legs.

In desperation, I reached into the bristly place where the *yōkai* had stuck its hand, as if there were a button there that could switch off this self-destructive unfolding.

Clementine stopped, but pink light continued to blister off the jellyfish's tensed, stilled form. I moved in wonder along the outstretched stalk, passing between the tendrils now frozen into torpid cords—less like navigating a forest, more like exploring the guts of a massive stringed instrument blasted open for my viewing.

And with this view, I could see now the hard, foreign bumps twitching on every tentacle, copies of the lesion I'd dissected in Tony's kitchen. Clementine was covered in them. The *yōkai* sped up, and I kept pace: Clementine couldn't hold herself like this forever. But like the endless caverns of my dream, the stalk went on and on, lurching left and then right, curving up and plunging down, dragging me on a journey that I had accepted would not end in Aldo but would necessarily end, one way or another, as all journeys did.

Hours seemed to pass before I glimpsed the rudders shining out of the gloom. They billowed gently, each one a bulbous swimmer treading water to help the jellyfish maintain her position. The *yōkai* had blinked out again and reappeared in front of me, as if to be certain I saw it, and I did: The tentacles nearest the swimming bells were ghost white and lacy, as different from the taut, scarlet tendrils I'd just passed through as an empty hearth from a crackling fire.

When I grazed one with the tip of a gloved finger, it broke off like a shriveled leaf.

The jellyfish shuddered and shrank away from me, curling herself tight again. The *yōkai* went with her, its edges blurring into the red glow, and in the final image of its drooped head and listless, dangling arms, I thought I caught a current of real sadness, as if the ghost were already mourning.

* * *

My tank pressure was as low as I'd ever let it get. It was time to get out of the water, and fast. The current I hadn't been aware of resisting on my shoreward journey sailed me out to meet *Calypso* in a matter of seconds. The world had turned back on. The cold of the Atlantic sank through the Nematoskyn, and the water slapped upward in choppy peaks that bashed me from side to side as I surfaced and popped the regulator from my mouth, gulping cold, salty air.

The darkness had me disoriented. I had surfaced at *Calypso*'s bow. I struck out for the stern, where a tall silhouette was hanging off the side of the boat. I waved and yelled, and the lighthouse beacon found me at the same moment as Tony's flashlight, two beams—one near and weak, one powerful and distant—swinging their brilliance across my face. I lifted my hands to shield my eyes.

A cry of alarm went up. I felt the swirling gush of movement in the water before I saw tentacles uncoiling beneath me.

Clementine had followed me back to the boat.

Senescence

Size isn't everything. Bigger doesn't always mean more dangerous when it comes to jellyfish. *Mnemiopsis leidyi*, also known as the sea walnut, is a tiny particle of destruction, eating its way through fish populations in the Black Sea. *Malo kingi* is no bigger than your thumbnail and possesses one of the most potent venoms in the world.

The issue with giant jellies isn't that they're more venomous. It's that their sheer size guarantees sustained contact with a high number of stinging cells. Giant jellies overwhelm.

AA: Insert *Jaws* music here.

The jellyfish floated beneath *Calypso*, still corkscrewed into her protective spiral, bathing the boat's underside in a red glow. Tony had dropped or lowered her flashlight. The boat was an island of darkness except for its panel of small blue deck lights.

The current had nudged me farther into open water. The air reeked of rotten flowers. The smell must've been unbearable from the boat. The drippy view through my mask made the whole scene blurry and unreal, but I wasn't about to remove any gear with Clementine so close.

From my perspective, she was docile, graceful, disinterested, the way jellyfish always appeared to be—at least until you blundered into their stingers. But from the boat, it must've looked as though they were surrounded. Every time the lighthouse beam passed over *Calypso,* I got another snapshot of panicked figures scurrying across the deck.

I wanted to shout at them to calm down and not make any sudden moves. Clementine was a night feeder: She would retreat to the depths soon enough. But even if I'd been close enough for them to hear me, I wasn't confident I could speak. My fever had returned, coexisting now with a bad case of whole-body shivers.

A distant boom rolled through the water. The force of the explosion shoved me farther from the boat. Emmett must've told the land team to blow the charges. But it was exactly as he had feared: We'd missed our window. Clementine was out of range, too close to the boat for even the topmost barrel to wound her.

A mechanical grumble cut through the night as *Calypso*'s stern lights blazed to life. When the explosions failed, Emmett had started the engine, perhaps hoping to scare the animal off.

It had the opposite effect.

Clementine's glow brightened until it was the hue of fresh blood. The chills fell off me. I was, abruptly, burning. I stripped off my mask and the Nematoskyn's hood, lost to every instinct but the one screaming at me to cool down before I burst into flames. I had shut my eyes without meaning to, and as they inched painfully open, they took in a scene that looked like it had come straight out of one of Margo's *Monster in Motion* paintings.

Calypso was gone, entombed inside the bright slithering mass of Clementine's tentacles. The jellyfish was either trying to board the boat or sink it. The tendrils oozed across the deck and slapped searchingly against the cabin where Emmett was concealed, and when the windows didn't yield, they quested doggedly on, squirming toward the figure pinned against the gunwale, cut off from the safety of the cabin, nothing behind her but water and darkness.

Tony. The memory of her name freed something in me. My fever dimmed to a clammy but bearable warmth. I replaced my hood and mask and approached, fighting the current, already ragged with exhaustion, fueled by nothing but a hopeless urgency like the one that had come over me in the cave. I had to reach her before . . . before . . .

The ends of this ultimatum stuttered out. The lone figure tucked into the stern of the boat caved at the knees as a single glowing coil brushed her calf. If she emitted a sound, I didn't hear it. The night fractured into a starburst of panic. I remembered the circlet of angry red blisters on Roger's hand. How long did Tony have before the venom took hold? Three minutes? Less? I closed the remaining distance between *Calypso* and me and bobbed helplessly at the starboard side, too weak to haul myself aboard with so much heavy gear strapped to my back.

Clementine shifted around me, tentacles unreeling and plopping back into the water with a series of tiny splashes. Her interest in the boat had waned as quickly as it had arrived. I felt angry, betrayed—I had never felt that way about a jellyfish before. I watched, livid, as Clementine twirled and gracefully sank.

When I looked back at *Calypso*, a dangling hand had appeared. Emmett had left the cabin, grunting now as he dragged me aboard.

I was tired and freezing but I forced myself to unbuckle my harness and crawl over to Tony, where she lay prone in the stern.

"Tony, are you okay?" My teeth chattered violently. Emmett trudged over with a flashlight. Her eyes were clamped shut, rolling beneath their lids.

"Did it get her?" he asked.

"Her leg—"

I tore off my gloves and set a hand against her sternum. Tony's breathing seemed fine, but what did I know? She was the one who knew what to do in an emergency.

Emmett leaned over us and swiped his light across the water. "It's still down there. Biding its time . . . What *happened*? Why did you tell us to wait?"

There were good lies that could've put him off, but my frazzled mind could only cobble together some semblance of the truth. "I couldn't do it, Emmett. Killing Clementine isn't the right move. Not for her, not for us—"

Even in the patchy lighting, I could see the outrage rippling across his face like a storm system.

His furious reply was stayed by Tony, who emitted a throaty groaning interspersed with syllables that never quite coalesced into language.

I looked up at Emmett. "Get us out of here."

He cursed, then raced back to the cabin.

• • •

It was a quick journey back to the cove, offering no chance to gather my thoughts or prepare my next move. I had dried off with one of the towels from my bag, and my fingers and toes blazed as the feeling shot back into them.

Emmett scooped Tony up from the floor of *Calypso* and deposited her on the floating dock.

"What happened?" Sylvia stood by the boathouse, precisely where we'd left her. "I heard the explosions. Did you do it? Is it dead?" She broke off when she saw Tony, her expression unreadable. I had no idea how much time had passed since we left. A bank of clouds blotted out the strawberry moon, and the lighthouse beam couldn't be seen from the cove. The night's darkness was unending. Daybreak was a hundred years away.

Emmett unloaded Tony's medical bag and the portable defibrillator, but none of us made a move toward either of them. It wasn't clear what she needed. She was breathing, and her heart was beating. She just wasn't responding. It was as if she'd been placed in a trance. I rolled her pant legs up to her knees, searching for welts. The skin there appeared smooth and unbroken. Was it possible Clementine hadn't gotten her? But I had seen it with my own eyes.

More figures were dashing down the beach toward us with flashlights. One of them was Nadia. The sight of her crumbled whatever resolve had been keeping me upright. I fell into her arms and wept.

The small crowd gathered in a loose ring around Tony until Sylvia shooed them back.

"What happened?" the old woman repeated.

"She sabotaged us!" bellowed Emmett, jabbing a finger at me. "I told you she couldn't be trusted. She's a complete lunatic. We never should've let her come here. She wants that thing alive, even if it kills all of us. Just look what happened to Tony—"

"Would you please shut up?" snapped Nadia, her arms still wrapped around me.

Emmett's words sank through me like slow gut punches. He wasn't wrong. If I had followed the plan and told him to blow the charges at the right time, the giant jelly might not have been in any condition to attack the boat, or sting Tony. And because of what the *yōkai* had shown me, I knew now that my moment of mercy had been as pointless as it was selfish.

Someone in the crowd asked whether there were enough explosives to try again tomorrow night.

"It doesn't matter," I said. My mouth tasted like blood. I realized belatedly that I'd bitten my tongue. Someone had released Shanel Sawyer from the sewing room. I saw the grad student bullying her way toward the front of the crowd, trying to get a peek at what was going on.

I lifted myself out of Nadia's arms and said it again, so everyone could hear: "It doesn't matter what you do anymore, okay? Clementine isn't just sick. She's dying."

A long beat of silence greeted this pronouncement.

"How can you be sure?" asked Sylvia.

I described the frozen-over tendrils drifting like drowned limbs at the end of Clementine's stalk. There was a word for it: senescence—the cell deterioration that came with age. Inflammation and dysfunction, decreased resistance to stress and disease. Humans gained wrinkles and lost their hair. Octopuses grayed, shrank, and stopped eating. In jellyfish, deterioration occurred so quickly that there usually were no visible symptoms—just an empty tank with a floating smear of mucus where there had once been a lively, pulsating creature.

But Clementine was bigger and bolder. A survivor, clinging to life.

My thoughts were slippery with exhaustion. I had no idea whether I was making any sense. I kept my eyes on Tony as I talked, suffering a small death in the seconds-long pause after each one of her exhalations, returning to life when she inhaled again.

"Do you mean to tell me," said the lobsterman Lawrence Fleming slowly, "that we've been trying to kill this beast for months, and it's been dying on its own the whole time?"

There was a deep irony here that Aldo would've loved: the hubris of humans trying to manufacture the inevitable.

"How much longer does it have?" demanded Emmett.

I shook my head. "A few weeks, a month?" There was no way to be certain. I felt again the crackly give of Clementine's rotted tentacle as it had broken off in my hand. "But not long," I said quietly.

An excited murmur moved through the crowd as the people near the front relayed this news to the ones standing farther back. Hope was shining in Nadia's eyes. She looked like her old, radiant self again. I had given her that, but it brought me no joy. Didn't they understand? The jellyfish's time had come, and it might just prove to be ours, too. Everything had been for nothing. I had risked Tony for nothing.

My thoughts stopped whirling when she emitted another groan. There was no time to contemplate my grim realization, no time to convince the islanders their relief was unfounded.

"Tony . . ." I bent over her again. The onlookers fell silent. In the joined beams of their flashlights, I saw her eyes were open, her expression slack and dreamy.

"What's she saying?" whispered Nadia.

I leaned down until I could feel Tony's breath against my ear.

"I saw it."

I drew back and looked at her, torn between relief that she was talking sensibly and terror that it was only a short reprieve. "Saw what?"

"Everything." Tony smiled and closed her eyes.

The Colony

Marine animals have adapted to jellyfish stingers in a variety of ways, but first prize for ingenuity goes to the nudibranch, or sea slug. These colorful, soft-bodied mollusks steal and repurpose nematocysts for their own use, storing the stinging cells in pouches along their backs and deploying them later against their own predators. We feeble humans can only dream of such defenses.

AA: Ahem. The Nematoskyn??

JN: Call me when your magic suit lets me grow stinging cells.

An impossible sunrise broke over the tree line, flooding the sky with peach and gold. I sat on the front porch of the gray bungalow overlooking Retreat-by-the-Sea, clasping a mug of coffee between my hands, long since cooled. The yard behind the B and B was cloaked in shadow. I could just discern the outline of a fox skulking around the patio furniture, lowering its snout every few seconds to snuffle in the wet grass.

Fox spirits were a type of *yōkai,* I recalled: wily shape-shifters with a feathery plume of extra tails. I turned to see if Nadia had also noticed the visitor, and found her curled up in Tony's porch swing, eyes closed, one limp hand dangling above the splintered floorboards. She'd insisted on staying the night, alternating shifts of watching over Tony while she slept. The patchwork of tiny naps I'd pieced together over the past few hours should've had me exhausted, too. Instead I felt blisteringly awake in a way that had nothing to do with caffeine. Scenes and sensations from my dive with Clementine kept coming back to me. Every time I dozed off, I was in the water again.

The fox looked up and then bolted, its sharp ears picking out the creak of the bungalow's front door as it opened.

Tony stood barefoot in a tank top and flannel pajama pants, her hair damp and flattened from the shower. Spying Nadia asleep on the porch swing, she pressed a finger to her lips and beckoned me inside.

"How are you feeling?" I asked as Tony shut the door softly behind me.

"Never better," she said, sounding like she was getting tired of answering the same question. It was true that she seemed perfectly fine. Within a half hour of her giant jellyfish encounter, she was walking around, dazed but lucid, brushing off everyone's concerns with Tony-like breeziness. She retained only a vague memory of what had befallen her aboard *Calypso,* but insisted Clementine hadn't stung her.

I had my doubts. I kept thinking about *Malo kingi* and Irukandji syndrome. What if the sting was having a delayed effect? Just because Clementine's venom had felled Roger within minutes didn't mean it would work like that on everyone. Aldo was a testament to how toxins affected people in different ways.

Sensing my skepticism, Tony tugged up the hem of her pajama pants, and for the fifth time now, I bent and examined the unbroken skin of her calf where I'd seen Clementine's tentacles make contact.

"You see? Nothing."

"It doesn't make any sense," I said.

"Maybe Clementine wasn't in a stinging mood."

"A jellyfish stinging isn't like a dog biting," I countered. "It's not a choice. It's more like a chemical reaction. The stinging cell should've been triggered on contact."

"You said she's dying. Maybe she's too weak to sting."

"She could sting Roger when the tentacle wasn't even connected."

"Jo," said Tony, lips twitching, "do you want me to have been stung?"

"Of course I don't want that!" I knew she was joking, but the question kicked up a flurry of defensiveness. "When I thought she had gotten you, I was so—it was like I couldn't—" The memory of the distress was so near, I floundered after words to describe it.

I was still crouched on the living room floor. Tony hitched me into a standing position, her arms tight around my waist. We lingered like that for a minute, and I had the dreamy sensation I was underwater again, only this water was warm and gently insistent, pushing us more closely together.

Tony looked down at me, her expression troubled. "I felt you," she said.

"Excuse me?"

"When I fainted or whatever. I didn't remember until now. I had a weird dream."

"About *strands*?" Now I was joking, but Tony's forehead creased like she'd forgotten all about Roger's phone call.

"Strands . . . yeah, maybe. I was thinking of them more like threads."

"Are you serious?" I asked.

"There was one for every person on the island. I picked one and followed it back to you, and when I opened my eyes, there you were."

"How did you know which thread belonged to me?"

"I just did." Tony shook her head. "It's hard to explain."

Before I could summon an appropriate response to this latest weirdness, Nadia shuffled into the house, rubbing her eyes. Her bleariness evaporated when she saw Tony and me still wrapped around each other.

"O-ooh," she said with a delighted gasp. "Oh my gosh! This is so—but how long have you guys been—?"

"Chill out, Nadia," said Tony.

Nadia could not chill out. She squealed and bounced, shaking my arm. "I'm so happy for you, Josie!"

I flushed with pleasure—as much to receive Nadia's blessing as to discover I didn't need it.

Tony looked like she was trying not to smile. "I see you've already helped yourself to coffee. I've got a whole bed-and-breakfast's worth of breakfast if you guys want to join the tourists for their goodbye feast. I'm kicking them out," she said, in response to my raised eyebrows. "It was way too easy for Shanel to follow us out to the cove last night."

"But what about the business?" asked Nadia with concern.

Tony shrugged. "There are more important things than the business. Besides, now that we know it'll just be a short-term thing . . ." She trailed off, and my stomach clenched. I had filled Tony in on Clementine's senescence, and for as much as she thought the jellyfish was a magnificent animal, I knew there was a part of her that was relieved. No more choices to make, no more plans to argue over. In a week, a month, life on Shattering could go back to normal. Or so the islanders believed.

I let them believe it. For once in my life, I didn't want to be the buzzkill. At least not until I had proof.

I needed to talk to someone who wouldn't be so easily placated by Clementine's imminent death. Who still itched to understand the jellyfish's awful power.

Someone like Aldo.

• • •

Tony said Shanel was staying in Rhode Island, but when I walked into the B and B, the grad student was already awake, sitting at the dining room table by herself. She had her head bowed over a tablet, so engrossed in whatever she was reading that she didn't see me until I'd slid into the chair beside her.

"How are you?" I asked, because we had to start somewhere.

"Great." Shanel closed the case on her tablet and looked at me coolly. "I love being locked in a stranger's house all night."

"I'm sorry. Is that what you want to hear?"

I wasn't sorry, especially given my new concerns about what Clementine's death might really mean. If Shanel had had her way last night, she would've been trapped here with the rest of us, perhaps doomed like the rest of us.

I took out the waterproof camera she'd loaned me and set it on the table: a peace offering.

I'd looked through the footage once already and found it to be predictably disappointing—Clementine glowing like a cartoon light bulb, her magnificence muted to a vague impression of glowing threads floating in the dark—but Shanel gawked over the camera's little screen, all her rancor forgotten, her already protuberant eyes widening until they seemed at risk of bursting from their sockets.

"I can't believe you were down there with her. I wish I had been—"

"Do you?" I challenged.

Shanel's foot jiggled against the floor. The video had undammed a surge of excited energy, and she couldn't seem to sit still. "No," she conceded reluctantly. "You were right. I don't want to be stuck here. But I'm still jealous you were able to get this close to her."

The footage reached its end, revealing no trace of the *yōkai*. If Clementine was reduced by the camera's capture, her guardian angel was erased entirely.

We pored over that final still of the jelly's dead tentacles. It wasn't much of a shot, but at least the contrast was obvious. They looked like a puddle of sludge stuck to the end of that glowing body.

Shanel released a pained sigh. "So she really is dying. I guess that makes your job easier."

I felt my doubts sliding around inside me, oil-slick. "The thing is . . . I'm not sure that it does. We know the barrier is connected to Clementine, right? And we know that Clementine is dying.

What if the barrier is shrinking *because* Clementine is dying? What if when the jellyfish dies, the barrier doesn't poof out of existence—it just collapses completely, and we'll be like—like—"

"Like fish turfed out of the aquarium," offered Shanel, frowning. "Caught on the wrong side of the glass."

I nodded. "I went out past the barrier once before, and it almost killed me. I don't think any of us could survive it."

She leaned back, tapping her knuckles against her lips. I had seen Aldo do the exact same thing when he was thinking hard. Had she absorbed some of his mannerisms during her internship? I'd never thought about all the little things I must've picked up from him over the years.

The words just fell out of my mouth: "What was it like working with Aldo?"

If Shanel was surprised by the sudden change in topic, she hid it well. "Were you two close?"

"We went to grad school together." I would leave it at that. But Shanel was smart: I could tell by the way her expression softened that she knew there was more to the story.

"He was a good supervisor," she said after a pause. "He gave me lots of independence."

"You can tell me the truth."

"I am. I respected him."

"But?" I didn't want the pity and the platitudes. I craved a true snapshot of the man Aldo Antunes had been: a good man and a brilliant researcher, but also pigheaded and erratic. For all his charm, he was hard to get along with. We had that in common.

Shanel hesitated. "He wasn't the most organized."

"Oh, come on. He was a complete disaster." File boxes teetering all over his office, an Outlook inbox with thousands of emails unread. How he managed to get any funding was a mystery. He could hardly sit long enough to scarf down a sandwich, let alone write a grant.

Shanel gave an uncertain smile.

"What else you got?" I asked.

"I guess he could be kind of unreliable. Asking me to complete a task, and then coming in a few hours later, like, *Why are you doing that? I need you over here doing this* other *thing*."

"Pain in the ass," I said, smirking.

"He was moody, too." She was warming up to the conversation, grinning. "I mean, most of the time he was fun to be around, and he clearly had a lot of enthusiasm for the work. Then, for no reason at all, he'd shut down. Shut you out. This one night I stayed at the lab late, waiting for some samples to finish. I heard a sound coming from down the hall. I thought an animal had gotten in. But it was Aldo. He was in the storeroom . . ." She broke off.

My heart jackhammered against my ribs. "What was he doing?"

"He was—he was crying."

Shanel lowered her eyes. I got the sense she hadn't meant to tell me this part of the story. I couldn't think of any response, so I replayed my dive footage from the beginning, watching the blur that was Clementine while my mind spiraled far away.

Of course I had known Aldo was subject to dark moods that swirled out of nowhere like summer storms, but I couldn't recall ever witnessing him cry. What had upset him that night? Why hadn't he called me? What other secrets had he been keeping?

Those were my real questions, but instead I asked Shanel, "Did he see you?"

She shook her head.

"You didn't go in to ask what was the matter. You didn't try to help him. You just left him to deal with his pain. Alone."

"He was my boss!" cried Shanel. "It wasn't my place. I didn't want to embarrass him. I figured he went in there because he wanted to be alone." She took a large breath and blew it out of her nose. "I don't like this. Speaking ill of the dead. It's not right."

Suddenly I felt bad for cornering her into this conversation, making her feel responsible for the misery of a man she'd barely known. I wanted to distribute some of my guilt so it would weigh me down a little less, but this girl wasn't the right person to bear it. No one was.

"You're not speaking ill of him," I said. "You're just talking about who he was. The good, the bad, the inexplicable."

She still wouldn't make eye contact with me. She'd reopened her tablet and was staring at it again. I saw she was reading an article about *Physalia physalis*, the Portuguese man-of-war. An image of the striking animal dominated the screen, its shimmery blue bladder bobbing on the surface while reams of knotted, dark purple tentacles dangled below.

"For your thesis?" I guessed.

Shanel skated a chewed fingernail down the screen, tracing the line of a tentacle. "It's beautiful, isn't it?" She sounded like a parent cooing over an infant. Half a million stings along the Atlantic coast annually, and all she saw was loveliness. I could appreciate why Aldo had liked this girl.

"It is," I agreed.

"Technically I should say *they're* beautiful," amended Shanel, "since the man-of-war is colonial."

I knew what she was getting at. True jellyfish like the moon jelly and the lion's mane were scyphozoans. Shanel studied hydrozoans, some of which resembled jellyfish in their appearance. But a great many hydrozoans were in fact floating colonies consisting of multiple organisms, all performing a specialized purpose, all working for the welfare of the whole. Not an *it*, as Shanel put it, but a *they*. Aldo had studied the venom from both groups.

I spun the tablet around so I was looking at the article right-side up. I'd seen man-of-wars before, both in photos and in real life—they were notorious for washing up on beaches, sometimes hundreds of them at once, a minefield of stingy blue balloons stranded by a strong wind.

But looking at the photo on Shanel's tablet, I had the strange feeling that I was seeing this animal for the first time.

A prickly sensation gathered in the back of my neck and spread. I raised my hands and stared at them. I rotated them, slowly splaying the fingers, then lifting them up in the air, as high as they could reach.

"Um—Dr. Ness?" said Shanel, politely but with concern. "Are you all right?"

"Shanel—what would happen if a colonial unit were to detach from the colony?"

"It would die," she said bluntly. "The members of a colony are entirely interdependent. They can't survive on their own."

The prickly sensation moved down my arms. Previously incomprehensible shapes were merging into focus. I thought back to Clementine unfurling in the water last night, extending herself until she was stretched tight as a rubber band about to snap. It was a sensation I'd felt before, I realized now: when Roger and I had tried to leave the island on *The Phantom Maiden*. I'd mistaken it for a panic attack. I knew it now for what it was: the pain of a body pulled past its natural limits.

I lowered my arms. Shanel was still looking at me quizzically.

"Hear me out for a second," I said. "What if Clementine is colonial like your man-of-war, except she's figured out how to . . . incorporate us, somehow? Make us a part of her colony? The barrier isn't a physical wall we can't push past. It's just the limit of how far we can stretch!"

That excited buzzing was echoing between my ears, making it hard to tell whether I was shouting.

Shanel's eyes had widened to comic proportions again. "How is that possible?"

I had no idea. But the question to answer right now wasn't how. It was why.

"Every unit in a colonial animal performs a purpose," I said. "So why would Clementine evolve to pull humans into her colony? What purpose are we all serving?"

Shanel's nervous energy had gone into overdrive. She bounced to her feet, knocking her chair onto the floor behind her. "Protection," she said breathlessly. "Self-preservation."

I nodded eagerly. It was a genius trick. What better way for an animal to fend off the planet's most vicious predator than by attaching their survival to its own? Anyone who glimpsed Clementine became a part of her and was therefore restrained from doing violence against her.

"If you're right," Shanel whisper-shouted, leaning forward with her hands planted on the table, "this is the most highly evolved colonial organism in the world!"

The shared wonder pulsed between us like a live thing. I had five blissful seconds to enjoy it before crash-landing back into the world of selfish pragmatism. I'd come here hoping Shanel could talk me out of my suspicions. Instead, we had a theory to confirm them. It had never felt so lousy to be right.

I groaned and dropped my head into my hands. "Then we really are screwed." I looked up at Shanel, who stared down at me, her delight fast curdling into an expression of dismay as she, too, made the connection. "Clementine's colony is collapsing. If she goes, who's to say we don't go down with her?"

• • •

We met Nadia and Tony as they were walking down the hill to the B and B.

"Breakfast can wait," I said.

On the bungalow's front porch, Shanel and I repeatedly interrupted each other as we tried to explain our theory—how witnessing Clementine's light somehow caused the islanders to become intertwined with her body, a body that pulled its constituent parts closer as it failed. Nadia looked awestruck, Tony disturbed.

"That's why she didn't sting you," I told Tony. "Jellyfish can't sting themselves!"

"Technically," said Shanel, lifting a finger in the air, "Clementine is something other than a jellyfish. Same phylum, different class—"

"We can suss out the terminology later," said Tony. "After we figure out how to save ourselves."

I led the way into the kitchen. A puff of chilled air gasped out of Tony's freezer when I opened the door. With gloved hands, I extracted the bag-wrapped package I'd placed there on Memorial Day and peeled back the layers. Clementine's tentacle looked like a string of graying meat past its sell date, bearded with a fuzz of ice crystals. Shanel couldn't take her eyes off it. All my sins and strangenesses were forgiven in light of this ultimate souvenir.

"Oh wow," she murmured. "Is this really—? Wow, wow, wow."

"Do you think you can get it back to your lab today?" I asked.

She bobbed her head yes.

"I want to know what sort of infection she has," I said. "And I want to know how her bioluminescence works. That seems to be the key to how she pulls people in, so it might be the key to separating from her."

Nadia had folded herself into the corner by the stove, staying well back from this thing that had nearly killed Roger. But as Tony and Shanel bustled off with the tentacle to figure out how to package it for its journey to New Hampshire, she sidled forward and set her hand on my arm.

"I'm sorry, Josie. You were right not to want to kill Clementine. If we'd actually managed to blow her up last night—we might not even be here right now."

"You didn't know," I said. "*I* didn't know for sure until this morning."

"You had an instinct," she said solemnly. "I should've trusted it. I won't make that mistake again."

It felt good to have Nadia back on my side. I could only hope

I was making the right decision again now. It killed me to relinquish Clementine's tentacle to Shanel. I wanted to be the one cutting off a sliver of it, dousing it in chemicals, studying it beneath a microscope until its cells danced behind my eyelids.

But I had finally accepted I would have to put my territoriality aside. Our real task on Shattering Point was just beginning, and I couldn't carry it out on my own. Aldo had trusted Shanel, and so I would, too.

Loophole

Where do jellyfish live? When it comes to geography, once again, jellyfish aren't picky. They have been documented in oceans across the world, in waters deep and shallow, swarming along coastlines and drifting in the vast deserts of the open sea. Warming oceans may only serve to expand their range, increasing the likelihood of jellyfish-human encounters where they have historically been rare.

AA: Are you ready to greet our gelatinous new overlords?

JN: Born ready.

I woke the next morning disoriented, with no idea where I was. It wasn't until I rolled over and saw Tony flopped face down on the bed beside me that I remembered Nadia's insistence that I spend the night here at the bungalow. The three of us had been out late, on the bluff by the lighthouse, sharing a beach towel we'd spread over the grass. Clouds had blocked all but the thinnest drizzle of starlight, just enough to give shape to the silhouettes slowly amassing on the bluff behind us. Eight, ten, twelve, twenty—when I saw all those people there, I worried another execution scheme was afoot here on Clementine's second night, but it turned out the islanders had come for the same reason we had: They wanted another look.

Now I let my eyes flutter shut, trying to relive the scene's tragic beauty in the early-morning peace: Nadia's head on my shoulder, Tony's arm around my waist, the rotten smell of an ending, and the sudden dissolution of it all as Clementine appeared, spectacular in her decay, silencing the breakers and the sound of my breathing, suspending every one of us in that red and dying light.

She was still alive. We were still alive. If Shanel could at least identify what ailed Clementine—and if we could then learn how to strengthen her—it might grant us a reprieve in which to figure out how to separate ourselves from the colony permanently. For the time being, I was going to have to let that be enough.

Then the sound came again, and I opened my eyes, realizing what had woken me: Someone's hand was smacking the bungalow's front door.

Tony awoke as I was dressing, and together, we hurried down the hall to confront the visitor.

It was Nadia, panting as if she'd sprinted here.

"I'm sorry to wake you—"

"Is it Roger?" I asked, fearing the worst. Nadia had video chatted with him only yesterday. He'd seemed tired, she said. Weak. The doctors told her it would take a while for him to fully recover. But he hadn't been babbling anymore. I had thought we were in the clear.

"No," said Nadia. "But it's—there's been—" She braced a hand against the doorframe. "You've got to see it yourself."

Tony and I followed Nadia down the hill toward Beach Street, and as we neared the western shore where Pamela had dropped me off in the fog a million years ago, I was met with one of the stranger sights I'd encountered on Shattering Point.

Three people stood side by side on the narrow dock: goateed Nico, Emmett Beckendorf, and Sylvia Steele. They held identical poses, hands flattened against the air in front of them like mimes testing the bounds of an imaginary box. As I watched, Emmett snaked his arm forward and then recoiled as if bitten. Sylvia and Nico copied the gesture, their movements gracefully out of sync and mirrored in the long shadows thrown onto the dock before them. I felt like I was witnessing a dance performance, and the audience was the seagulls, shrieking their glee as they hopped and squabbled on the far end of the dock.

No one said a word as Tony, Nadia, and I approached. Nico stepped back, ceding his spot on the dock. Despite the mild morning air, I saw that he had sweated through his T-shirt. Sandwiched between Sylvia and Emmett, I lifted my hand and took my place in the dance.

To the naked eye, I touched nothing, yet I could feel the air resisting, my fingers buzzing with an electric tingle not unlike a mild jellyfish sting. When I backed off, the feeling vanished. Forward and back, forward and back. I teetered on the edge of that invisible boundary, acclimating to the subtle but definite difference.

I leaned farther, until the electric sensation spread up to my shoulder, searing through flesh, muscle, and bone. I retracted my arm, equal parts fascinated and terrified, and inspected the skin for abrasions. There were none. My arm felt achy, as if from overuse.

I tensed my hands and released them. I had expected this, but not so soon. Shanel had barely been off Shattering twenty-four hours.

"When did it happen?"

"This morning," said Sylvia. "Nico was on guard duty . . ."

"It moved in so fast, I almost didn't make it back in time." Nico was ashen, shaky. "I thought it was going to keep coming in. But then it just stopped. Right there." He pointed. "Like it got tired."

Tony nudged me aside. It was her turn to play chicken with the barrier. I watched her sink in up to her shoulder, lurching at the moment when discomfort turned to pain.

Emmett rounded on me. "You said it was dying."

"She is!"

"Not fast enough. We're trying again. We've got one night left, one barrel left—"

"You can't do that." My mind was spinning. Sylvia had a far-off look in her eyes as she laid a hand against the barrier, no doubt thinking of her grandfather, Augustus Steele, whose fate now hovered inches from us all.

I seized Emmett around his muscled forearm. "You can't do that," I repeated, working to keep my voice steady, "because you'll make things worse."

I launched into the explanation of Clementine's colony. Tony and Nadia tried to back me up, but we were talking all over each other, not making any sense.

"You have no idea what you're talking about," Emmett snarled, shaking off my hand.

"And if *you* manage to blow her up, we'll all die!" I shouted.

"Quiet—both of you," ordered Sylvia. Her moment of reverie

had passed. She scowled as she shifted her flinty eyes back and forth between Emmett and me. "I don't know which of you is right. And it doesn't matter, because the first thing we've got to do before we test any more theories is make sure people are safe."

An evacuation was in order. Everyone who lived or worked along this stretch of Beach Street needed to move farther inland. That included Nico—still white-faced, scurrying off to close up the ice cream parlor—and Tony, to whom Nadia quickly extended an invitation to crash at her and Roger's place. The pair hurried back to the bungalow to pack. Emmett stayed behind to monitor the barrier, and I ducked into Retreat-by-the-Sea to call Shanel. The grad student didn't answer. I left a panicked voicemail, asking her to get in touch ASAP.

I paced around the B and B, willing Shanel to call me back. The place was empty. Tony had followed through on her plan to kick out the remaining tourists. I thought I'd feel relieved now that the outsiders had taken their weirdness and departed. Instead, moving between those vacant rooms, spotting the occasional stray item that had been left behind—a pair of sunglasses on the mantel, a partnerless polka-dot sock on the bathroom floor—I felt itchy with a sense of helplessness I could do nothing to quell.

I worried it had been a mistake to entrust Clementine's tentacle to Shanel. She understood colonial organisms better than I did, but she was still a resource-poor graduate student I barely knew. I'd been so starstruck by her connection to Aldo, and I'd let it get in the way of my better judgment.

What I ought to have done was consult someone with money and equipment and access to a team of experts.

Ha-Yun Kim's bioengineering company was headquartered in San Francisco. It was just past six in the morning on the West Coast. I found her phone extension in her email signature. Her voicemail kept timing me out; it took three separate messages to blunder through the whole story.

"I need you to send someone out here. Lives could be at stake. Call me as soon as you get this."

I sounded crazy. Would she dismiss me, or was mine the type of crazy that worked for her?

Now I was awaiting not one but two callbacks. I stepped onto the front porch, phone clenched in my fist, to discover chaos had descended over Beach Street, doors slamming, people tugging dogs or lugging suitcases or yelling at each other or just milling around numbly like they had no idea what to do. I wondered what any of this felt like to Clementine. What were we to this giant colonial animal? Distant appendages, shot through with occasional twitches and flutters? Or something more like the remoras that suctioned themselves to the sides of larger fish—minor, unshakable annoyances along for the ride?

What did Clementine feel when I shifted in my seat, when I swallowed a mouthful of food or laughed or got drunk or had a panic attack?

Could she feel me now?

I took a deep breath, and my lungs inflated politely. The rudimentary machine of my heart ticked away inside my chest.

Emmett Beckendorf was a point of stillness amid the flurry of activity, standing stiff-armed midway up the dock. The more I stared at him, the more he looked like a madman facing off against an approaching tsunami.

I was not going to be able to talk him out of trying to kill Clementine again tonight. Tony and Nadia were on my side, but we were still only three voices backing a theory so far-fetched a reasonable person could easily dismiss it. The kid, Sidney—he would believe anything if it meant Clementine didn't have to die. But a child's endorsement wasn't going to make the difference here.

I needed to cultivate support among the adults. And I knew just the Clementine-loving empath to start with.

The flowers in Norm Sloan's fairy-tale garden danced daintily in the wind. I slammed the Celtic Green Man knocker into the door, six, eight, ten times. A minute passed, and no one appeared. I tried the knob and was surprised when it turned, admitting me into a shadowed foyer.

"Hello?"

I shuffled inside, peering around a coat stand draped with a fleece jacket. The house appeared to be deserted. Maybe the Sloans had already packed up and relocated to the home of a friend who lived farther inland. Still I crept around like a burglar, fearful the dog would lunge around a corner and clamp her jaws into my arm. I poked my head into the kitchen, then the living room. I walked down the hall to Margo's studio, which looked exactly as it had last time, minus the artist herself. Lipstick-smudged teacups rested on every surface. There was a canvas propped on an easel facing away from me. I took a hesitant step toward it, wondering if it could be the portrait Margo had started of me and the *yōkai*, before reminding myself I wasn't here to look at art.

The next room was the master bedroom, also empty. But light leaked from behind an adjoining door that had been left ajar.

I tried to push it open, but something was in the way. I pressed my eye to the gap and felt the rattle of alarm in my stomach before I fully processed what I was seeing.

I managed to wedge my way inside the bathroom, which was plastered in hideous floral wallpaper. Margo Sloan was slouched on the floor in front of the sink. Her ginger wig was lopsided, her forehead blotchy and cold to the touch.

I reached for my phone. There was no service. I would have to race to the bungalow to get Tony . . .

But Margo was already sitting up, squinting at me with a groggy smile.

"Oh. Hello, dear. Have you come for your next portrait session? I'm afraid it'll have to wait." She cast a reproachful look around the little room, whose air was sour with the stench of vomit and sweat. "I have not been well," she said wisely.

I helped her stand. Beneath the baggy sleeve of her blouse, Margo's arm felt as snappable as a dry twig. She shook me off and leaned into the mirror, pursing her lips and straightening her wig.

"Should I get Tony?" I asked.

"There's no need to make a fuss. I must've gotten dizzy and fallen down, is all. Good thing I've got the cushioning to protect from that sort of thing." Margo gave her bottom a fond pat.

"Where's Norm?" I asked.

"How should I know?"

She stepped back from the mirror and tried to move past me into the hall. A spell of weakness nearly capsized her. If I hadn't swooped in and curled my arm around her waist, she would've fallen again.

We clung together in the doorway. "What do you need?" I stammered. "Maybe a glass of water, or—?"

"Some fresh air," said Margo, "would be lovely."

The ocean breeze was life-giving, washing away the bathroom's stink. I could feel Margo shaking as she held on to my arm. Norm had said she had a stomach bug the day of the Memorial Day cookout, but that was weeks ago now. How long did stomach bugs last? What if she had some kind of infection that wouldn't go away on its own? I remembered Tony's words from that night in the kitchen: *Eventually, someone's gonna get really sick and not be able to get past the barrier to reach the treatment they need.*

Beach Street maintained the atmosphere of an evacuation zone. I saw Nico trying to coax a stubborn little dog into a car, a lobsterman gazing sadly at his front door. Margo barely seemed to register her neighbors' distress. Her eyes were pinned to the shore ahead. Her strides lengthened as we walked farther from the house, and her grip on my arm loosened.

Emmett was still on the dock. Someone had provided him with a folding chair. He was staring at that stretch of nothing where the air thickened as if it were a gripping television program, but he turned his head when he heard our footsteps.

"News?" he asked, his gaze swinging between Margo and me.

"We're just going for a walk," I said.

Emmett looked at Margo closely. He could tell something was off.

The artist shuffled forward, squinting, fingers still resting on my arm.

"Clementine's barrier started moving," I explained, realizing her sickness might have kept her out of the loop. "That's why everyone's packing up. You and Norm should probably—"

"Careful," warned Emmett as Margo extended a hand.

I watched her fingers pet the air as if it were a skittish animal she was trying to win over. I watched her lean forward slowly, and now the animal was something slick and huge and hungry, intent on swallowing her whole.

"Margo—" I began uneasily.

A pleasant sigh sailed out of her, the sound you'd make as you slid into a hot bath. Then Margo Sloan strode right past Emmett's folding chair and down the dock.

My first instinct was to reach out and pull her back to the safe zone, but I couldn't. The barrier repelled me like an electric shock. Emmett had had the same impulse; we both yelled as we were pushed backward, Emmett almost wobbling into the ocean.

I steadied him, and we held on to each other, staring disbelievingly after Margo's blurry figure as she proceeded down the dock, becoming less real by the minute.

• • •

Cars were abandoned. Doors gaped open. Crates and suitcases cluttered the curb. The evacuation was on pause as the islanders flocked to the western shore to lay eyes on the miracle themselves: Margo Sloan had passed harmlessly through the barrier and was perched on the far edge of the dock with her legs dangling and her back to us, indifferent to our shouts and cries. It was as if she'd been sucked into another dimension. As if she'd already left us behind.

"Maybe she can't hear us?" suggested Nadia.

"No way, man. That bitch is ignoring us. Margo!" bellowed Tony. She picked up a stone from the grass and chucked it. It fell short of Margo by fifteen feet. "Goddamn it. Isn't there anyone who can—?"

"No one," said Sylvia.

With Roger still in the hospital and the tourists departed, there was nobody left on Shattering who hadn't seen Clementine, nobody who could pass through the barrier and demand Margo tell us what was going on.

Emmett paced in tight circles with his hands balled into fists. "You're sure she didn't say anything?" he asked me for the tenth time.

"She wasn't feeling well. She wanted some fresh air."

"I thought she looked different."

"She wasn't feeling well," I repeated, annoyed.

But I knew what he meant. There had been something different about Margo—a thinned-down quality, as if she'd been drained of a vital substance. I had attributed it to her illness, but maybe it was the same wrongness I'd observed in the tourists, the inverse of what I'd noticed in all the other islanders, like Margo's familiar face had been replaced with an impostor's mask.

The crowd pressed closer. Vanquished hopes had been rekindled here at this final hour. Everyone wanted to try to mimic Margo's escape. Emmett rammed the barrier with his shoulder. Tony kicked it. Nadia poked it. Sidney went with an enthusiastic high five. No one could get through. As I was shoved away from the dock, I glimpsed a lone figure separating from the crowd and trudging up Beach Street, trailed by an unleashed German shepherd.

I followed Norm at a distance. The Sloans' front door remained unlocked. I could hear Betty's collar jingling somewhere inside the fairy-tale garden. I walked right into the house and into the kitchen, where Norm was washing his hands at the sink.

He started when he saw me. "What the heck do you think you're doing in my house? Get out, get out!" He flapped a dish towel at me—yellow cloth patterned with tiny shapes that could have been hummingbirds or bumblebees.

I held my ground. "Aren't you mildly curious about how your wife was able to stroll right through the barrier?"

"Just like Margo to find some loophole," Norm grumbled. "Always has to stand out. Always has to be the special one."

"She wasn't special. She was sick."

He turned away from me, banging things together on the counter. I scanned the kitchen. No shards of glass today. The spotless room felt more suited to surgery than cooking. Every bit of food had been tucked out of sight except for a basket of apples on the table, so red and shiny they could've been props.

"You said she had a stomach bug. Had she eaten anything unusual the last few weeks?" I asked.

Norm's shoulders stiffened. He didn't answer. It was like he was hoping if he ignored me, I'd go away.

He wasn't going to get rid of me that easily. Margo Sloan had gotten off the island *without* killing Clementine. And I needed to know how now, today—before the colony collapsed further, before Emmett could unwittingly try to destroy us all again tonight.

"What about that tea she's always drinking?" I pressed. "She said it was homemade. Do you know what's in it?" Could it be that Margo had ingested some rare plant that held the key to freeing us all from Clementine's grasp? Could it possibly be that simple?

"No."

"Where does she keep the tea leaves? I need to see—"

"*No!*" Norm shouted this word with such passion, it gave me pause. I couldn't wrap my head around his resistance. He hated me. Fine. I hated him, too. But the risks posed by the barrier were bigger than any petty animosity we felt toward each other. How could he not see that?

I was silent long enough that Norm darted a glance over his shoulder, checking to see if I was still there. We locked eyes, and I saw on his face an expression as surprising as it was familiar, because I'd seen it in the mirror every day for the last eight months as I beat myself up over what I'd done to Aldo.

Norm Sloan looked guilty.

A suspicion reached toward me. I pushed it aside, and it nosed its way back, more insistent. "You did something."

Norm clenched his jaw. "Did not."

I crossed the kitchen floor, and Norm took a step back, holding the dish towel in front of himself like a shield.

"You tried to kill her," I said.

"You're out of line." A vein throbbed in his forehead, but his voice shook. He was a bad liar.

A muted outrage built in me slowly. I had the feeling I was experiencing all this from a very great height. I stepped closer, and Norm shrank against the counter. His eyes skittered left, then right, seeking an escape route.

"It didn't kill her," I said. "It did something else. Something you didn't intend. I need to know what you used."

"You're wrong. I never—"

A row of steel canisters was perched on the countertop, rotated to display their prim labels: *Coffee. Flour. Sugar.* My hand shot out of its own accord. Norm winced as a canister struck the floor and opened, scattering white grains across the geometric tile.

"Do you want the barrier to crash in and kill you in your sleep?" I didn't recognize my voice. All my frustration, confusion, and helplessness had tapered down to a sheer point, aimed at this small, selfish man sulking in front of me. "It's happened before. That's what's at stake here. You can forget about your plants and your dog and your house. Margo got out. And she's going to be the only one unless we know exactly how you did it."

Now the color had gone from Norm's face. He looked blanched and sickly. Betty had heard me yelling and was whining at the door.

"She bleached my orchids," said Norm quietly.

"What?" My pulse was still singing in my ears.

"My prizewinning orchids. I'd been cultivating them for two years. My babies." Norm's voice was thick, his eyes big and watery. "We fought one night. And she went into the garden, and she—she—"

I couldn't believe it. The guy was actually crying. He blinked and the tears spilled free, tracing twin paths down his pouchy cheeks.

"Margo Sloan, Shattering's famous artist. Fun gal, unpredictable, quirky. That's how everyone thought of her. No one knew what she was like behind closed doors." He grimaced and wiped the tears away. "She was a monster."

"Show me what you used," I said.

Norm hesitated a moment longer before going to the door.

"Down, girl. Heel."

Betty obeyed him, trotting at her master's side as he led us to the garden, the solution, the poison that could save us all.

The Armory

And who are we who study these maligned and slimy creatures? What punishing childhoods drove us to seek refuge in the stringy, stingy beasts of the sea? If once our numbers were tiny, jellyfish research has witnessed its own bloom in the last two decades. Now we swarm annually over university lecture halls and conference centers, trade barbs, and disband, leaving no trace of our gathering—not so much as a smear of toxic mucus on the floor.

Do we do it for money? Do we do it for fame? Do we do it to self-medicate undiagnosed personality disorders? Our precise motives remain unknown, yet as time passes and our population continues to swell, one fact seems undisputed: We jelly lovers are here to stay.

AA: Bracing for your disapproval . . .

JN: I love it.

I stood outside the Sloans' house, swishing it through the air like a magic wand: a green stem clustered with purple, trumpet-shaped flowers. It looked harmless, something you'd spy growing on the side of the road and briefly admire before moving on with your life and forgetting about it forever.

Poison was like that. Camouflaged. We handled household cleaners, passed mushrooms squatting in the grass, berries plump and shining, a snake snoozing by the hose. All it took was a second's bad judgment—a momentary misidentification—for the innocuous to turn deadly. Or else a little accident: a hand slapping around the back of a kitchen cabinet for the cinnamon and meeting the mandibles of a startled brown recluse spider instead. This covert nearness was one of the things that had fascinated Aldo about toxins. We were all of us, every day, surrounded by substances that could kill us.

In my other hand, I squeezed the repurposed jam jar that contained the dried petals of the purple flower, which Norm had been crushing and slipping into Margo's tea for the past three weeks. Had she noticed a faint new bitterness clinging to the back of her tongue as she guzzled the tea down? There was no way to know what had or hadn't occurred to her in retrospect, whether she was even aware she'd been poisoned at all.

Down the street, the islanders were still clustered around the dock, trying their luck with the barrier. As I watched, two figures separated from the crowd and hurried up Beach Street toward me, Nadia jogging to keep up with Tony's longer strides.

"The mail boat came," said Nadia breathlessly. "That must've been what Margo was waiting for. She got on board and left."

"She's *gone*?" I said, startled.

"Yeah. Can you believe that?" said Tony with disgust. "Not saying a word to any of us, not even trying to help . . ." Her eyes lowered to the toxic flower and the jam jar I was still holding. "What have you got there?"

Distractedly, I related how Norm had been spiking Margo's tea. The story felt like old news to me already, but Tony made a slight choking noise, and Nadia looked like she might be sick.

"Oh my god. I knew he was a jerk, but *this*?" Tony ogled the Sloans' house, where I imagined Norm was cowering, waiting for a pitchfork-wielding mob to come get him.

"I don't understand," Nadia said faintly, looking from the jar back to the dock where Margo had vanished. "How was she able to do it?"

I shook my head. Again the question was not *how* Clementine had released Margo, but *why*. For all her power, Clementine was still a cnidarian, a model of minimalist efficiency. Cnidarians did nothing without a purpose.

What was Clementine's purpose?

The same as all of ours, I thought: She was trying to survive.

I shook the flowers in their jar. "We can't kill Clementine," I said, "but we can kill ourselves."

"Excuse me?" Tony wore an expression like she really thought she'd heard me wrong. Even Nadia looked alarmed.

"Not really kill ourselves," I amended. "Just weaken ourselves enough to trick her into thinking we're dying. Clementine has a defense mechanism. Like how a sea star can shed an arm to get away from a predator. If she senses we're dragging the colony down, she'll release us. Lose the part, save the whole."

A breeze rolled up the street from the water, coaxing a jangling music from somebody's wind chimes. I could tell by the smell of it that a storm was moving in. Nadia wrung her hands. Tony took the jam jar from me and squinted at it.

"I believe you, Jo," she said slowly. "But you're gonna have a hard time selling anyone else on this latest theory."

She was right. From the other islanders' perspectives, I had already screwed up twice. I'd sabotaged Emmett's execution scheme, and then I'd given everyone artificial hope by proclaiming it was simply a waiting game. I'd made assumptions. I'd been wrong. What little credibility I'd possessed with these people was gone.

What would Aldo do? Crazy, fearless Aldo, who sought nobody's permission. *A man must make sacrifices for science.*

It was so obvious, I smiled. "That's why I need to replicate it. A controlled experiment. Small amounts, ingested next to the barrier so we can know right away if it's working."

"You're talking about drinking poison." Tony sounded almost angry. "Intentionally."

"I'm talking about severing this animal's hold on us for good."

"There has to be another—"

"There's no time!" I looked at Nadia. "I need you to trust me."

Her face had gone pale. She glanced at Tony, who was shaking her head vigorously from side to side.

When Nadia looked back at me, I could finally sense it: the warm hum of sameness vibrating between us. I recognized her as the girl I'd come to know and care for eleven years ago, but also on that deep, uncanny level that bound me to everyone on Shattering. It felt like I'd known Nadia for ages, in the geologic sense, like we'd evolved over millions of years together.

I felt the click of her jaw as it opened.

"Okay, Josie," she whispered. "Just tell us what you need."

• • •

The sky hanging above the Gulf was stained the color of a bruised plum. Emmett Beckendorf was once more the lone watchman, now standing on the dock with the tensed posture of a man ready to bolt at any second. While Tony, Nadia, and I were gathering the materials for our experiment, the barrier had crawled in by another five feet, stranding his folding chair and scattering the islanders who'd still been trying to copy Margo's escape.

"Take a break," Tony told Emmett.

His eyes moved from her to Nadia to me. He looked wrung out, past the point of caring.

"Thanks," he grunted, and departed without looking back.

I watched him hurry up Beach Street, which was empty now but for a few people still jamming items into their cars. The evacuation was nearly complete. In the distance Sylvia Steele, recognizable by the third limb of her walking stick, prowled back and forth, goading stragglers to hurry up.

The first clap of thunder rolled across the water as Nadia passed me the travel thermos we'd prepared at her house—jasmine tea spiked with half a teaspoon of the toxic dried flowers. A tiny dose, and a fraction of what Norm had been giving Margo. With any luck, that would be enough, and we'd never have to find out how I reacted to a bigger quantity.

Tony remained skeptical. "I still don't like this," she said. "I looked up this flower of yours. It contains a chemical they use in medicine to counteract tachycardia. It could stop your heart."

"It didn't stop Margo's," I said. "I'd like to think I'm at least as hale and hardy as she is."

Nadia was wearing a bright yellow raincoat that lit her up like a splash of sun. I knew she was worried, too, but she still managed to smile as she sat down cross-legged on the dock beside me. "I want you to know, Josie," she said seriously, "I think you're really brave."

"I think you're really stupid," said Tony.

"Bottoms up," I said. There was no point in waiting any longer. I tipped tea into the thermos lid and drank it down, tasting nothing but jasmine.

I waited for something to happen. I felt almost giddy. It was easy to imagine Aldo right here beside me, cheering me on while the toxins moved purposefully through my bloodstream. He would've loved everything about Shattering Point—its remoteness and mystery, its strange insular people, Clementine and her secrets, Shanel and her snooping—but this scene would've pleased him more than anything. Poison was Aldo's claim to fame. Through poison he'd practiced defying the odds, defying the limitations of his own anatomy. Now I was using it to defy Clementine's.

"How do you feel?" asked Nadia.

"Fine."

Five minutes had passed in silence. Tony was sulking on a bench. Still the rain held back, roiling in the black bellies of the clouds. I reached toward the barrier, wincing as the strain nipped through my fingers.

"I think I need more," I said.

Nadia helped me add a pinch of the dried flowers, and I drank another lidful of the tea.

I sprawled out on the dock, starfishing my limbs and looking up at the sky. Nadia lay down next to me.

"What do you think Margo's up to?" she asked.

"Drinking martinis on the mainland. Toasting her freedom." The truth was I couldn't really imagine Margo doing anything off Shattering. Her existence was tied to this place. But she had said she'd been planning to move away, to Portland, with her sister. Somewhere out there was another woman with Margo's blue eyes and empathic superpowers.

I stretched out my foot and tapped the barrier with the tip of my sneaker.

"More," I said.

Sweat popped out on my forehead and under my arms. A heavy cramping feeling started high in my gut and spilled downward. I braced my hands against my abdomen and breathed slow and deep, picturing my *Aurelia aurita* flaring its umbrella-like body through the water, tufted oral arms swaying.

Nadia embarked on a steady stream of nostalgic chatter, to distract me or herself.

Did I remember Professor Hano's five hundred kanji? *Now. Fire. Person. Mouth. Rain.*

Did I remember driving into town for the hot-air balloon festival, and discussing how someone really ought to make one designed like a jellyfish?

Did I remember when the power transformer blew during that thunderstorm, plunging Gladstone's campus into darkness, and some kid handed out glow sticks, and we wore crowns of light in our hair and bangles of light stacked on our arms while we gobbled all the ice cream from my mini fridge before it could melt, and the burn of disappointment when the electricity came back on?

I was amazed by how clear her recollections were from that time sealed on the other side of a decade. As she narrated these memories—her voice unspooling like an enchanted thread that drew me along its length into a shared dream—I saw the person I was then flutter into focus, and all the people I'd imagined I could become. Before my dad died. Before my career. Before the winds of misunderstanding blew Nadia and me apart. Before Aldo and losing Aldo. Before Clementine lashed us all together, like sailors lashed to the mast of a sinking ship.

But it wasn't all doom and desperation. I had come to Shattering Point a solitary human, armored up against the world. Guilt-ridden over Aldo's death, hiding from my mother, clinging to a dead-end job, terrified of the water that had always welcomed me. Alone. Clementine had changed all of that. I could feel the gentle hook of her behind my sternum now, as familiar and insistent as a heartbeat. This twitch of life lived inside Nadia, too. And Tony and Sylvia, Sidney and Norm, Emmett and Nico. I had never felt so expansive, so loved.

"Do you remember our constellation?" asked Nadia. We were lying on our backs on the roof of the science building, stars budding the blackness overhead.

No. We were on the dock on Shattering Point in the middle of the day. I focused on the texture of the damp boards beneath my spine, trying to remind myself what was real.

Nadia's arm rose to my left, her fingers tracing an invisible map through the air. "What was it called?"

"*Stygiomedusa.*" I burped and tasted bitter jasmine.

The center of my forehead opened, and more memories

swirled out. Nadia surveying me appreciatively in our Japanese classroom: *Wanna share a brain?* Nadia pitching her shoes off the rooftop. Aldo spreading his arms as he presided over his fans in the sports bar. Aldo dropping to a knee, presenting me with my dive knife as if it were an engagement ring. I hadn't loved him the way my mother wanted, but I had loved him all the same.

Then I saw memories that weren't mine to see. A curly-haired boy weeping into a stuffed gorilla. A gangly teenager shouting into a gangly man's face. My body was long and low to the ground. I scented the child's blood as he approached, felt the echoing slap of his footfalls. I struck, and my fangs met sweet flesh. I didn't stick around to see little Aldo fall or hear him cry out for his mother.

Voices. A round thing materialized and clarified into Tony's face. A wall of mottled glass rose above her head, higher and higher, thickening and curving until it closed over us like a snow globe. Clementine's barrier rippled with curlicues of scarlet light. It was still there. I was still here.

I struggled to sit up. "More."

"No." Tony was tight-lipped with fury. "That's enough. This isn't working. We have to try something—"

I snatched the thermos from Nadia and drank the remainder of the tea.

My stomach heaved. The skies finally opened, but the rain didn't touch me. All discomfort fled as I soared bodiless above the clouds. I tucked my glossy wings and plunged down, down, into the familiar water.

My feathers thinned and lengthened into a curtain of swaying tendrils. I felt the useless blood siphoning out of me as the poison crawled through my veins, lighting me up from the inside until I glowed like Clementine.

"Is it happening?" someone asked. Another face, hovering inches from mine. A kind face I knew, or had once known, when I was a person who knew such things.

I reached up and touched the smooth skin of her jaw. "I really did love you, you know."

"Josie." Nadia's voice dimmed. What remained of the daylight dimmed. "Can you hear me? Are you—?"

* * *

I swam through the flooded tunnels with purpose. Nothing could stop me now. A guideline was in my hands, leading me not out but deeper. The snake whispered nearby, serenading me with false promises I ignored. It had nothing to offer me I couldn't find on my own.

The tunnel widened, narrowed, and widened again. It became a chute climbing upward. My hand moved instinctively to add air to my BCD. That was when I discovered I wore no gear but the Nematoskyn, which had transformed into a perfect fit.

The chute opened into a vast cathedral-like space, suffused in rippling blue light. Stalagmites lifted from the floor, and stalactites dripped from the ceiling, giving the impression I was standing in the opened maw of a toothy beast.

The Armory. I got to see it after all.

Floating amid the forest of rock was a familiar figure in black neoprene. He waved at me the way you wave at a friend you've been expecting who's turned up just a little late.

Aldo emitted a little *umph* of discomfort as I crashed into him.

The momentum of the impact pushed us out into the chamber, where we came to rest against another stalagmite. Apart from his dive suit, he didn't have his gear on, either. He looked calm and refreshed, not at all like the drowned thing the rescue divers had brought to the surface.

I touched the curve of his cheekbone, the black fuzz of his beard. I would've opened his mouth and counted his teeth if he hadn't laughed and swatted my hands away.

Aldo's eyes searched my face. "What did you in?"

"Poison," I said.

"Seriously?" He tipped his head back and studied me. Impressed. "Who'd you tick off bad enough to get poisoned?"

"I did it to myself. It's a long story." And it was a story that didn't matter. Because I was here with Aldo, at last, the *real* Aldo. No more riddles and shadows lurking in the corner of my eye. No more ghosts.

I looked around the Armory, which seemed to go on forever. The light had no clear source, shifting and sliding like the light that spilled from the tanks at Seaheart.

"How did you end up here?" I asked. "What really happened to you in the cave?"

"It was the snake. It came back for me." Aldo shrugged. "I always knew it would."

"You ran out of air."

"That was after."

"You ran out of air looking for me," I persisted. "You hallucinated the snake while you were hypoxic."

Aldo rolled his eyes, and his next words leaked out of him in a sly whisper: "*Control freak.*"

"What!" I shouted, affronted. "I'm just trying to understand what happened!"

"I'm telling you what happened. You're trying to make it your fault, because then you could've prevented it. Your error in judgment, mine, the spirit of a nasty serpent I pissed off two decades ago—who cares?"

"I care."

"Then I highly suggest dying. Great way to end your worries."

I frowned. "You mean I'm not—?"

"I don't think so." Aldo squinted at me and shook his head. "Not yet. But come! We're running out of time." He bunched his legs and sprang sideways off the edge of the stalagmite, coasting out to the far end of the Armory.

I followed clumsily. My limbs were getting heavier by the second. Aldo was right. I was just a visitor in this realm. The thought depressed me.

The stalagmites grew taller, their tips meeting the stalactites plunging down from the ceiling, forming rocky pillars that tapered in the middle like hourglasses. Aldo halted, his neck craned back. Stretched above him, looped between and around the pillars like the web of a giant spider, was a labyrinth of knotted golden strings. Roger's hammock.

"Strands." I inhaled sharply. "Threads."

"I've been thinking of them as cords," said Aldo. "There's one for each of you." He flutter kicked up to the hammock and plucked a cord like a guitar string. It emitted no sound, but I felt the tension and release thrum deep inside me, a sensation poised at the juncture where pleasure turned to pain. "This one's yours. I've been using it to keep an eye on you. I can send things through it sometimes. It's blurry," he confessed. "Like writing with your eyes closed."

I wondered now if the *yōkai* wasn't a *yōkai* at all, but a message eroded by time and distance. The faint imprint that the pen leaves on the next page in the notebook.

I joined Aldo at the hammock. Unlike him, I had to stir my feet and fan my arms to keep from sinking. The cords were subtly different up close, thick and slender, ridged and smooth. I reached for one that radiated the deep orange hue of a harvest moon.

It was as Tony had said: I just knew.

The edges of the cave furled into blackness. I was still here, but I was also *there*, on the western shore of Shattering Point. Someone had moved me out of the rain, beneath the broad leafy overhang of a maple tree. My shirt was gone. Tony moved in slow motion, securing two wires to my chest with white stickers. Nadia stood nearby, shaking.

Wait, I thought. *One more minute.*

Tony jolted as if she were the one who had been shocked.

I dropped my hand, and my vision cleared. I was back in the cave. I had bought myself some time, but how long?

"Bird Girl," said Aldo, smiling.

"Her name's Tony."

"I like her. She's good for you. Nice and laid-back. You need someone like that around now that I'm gone."

"I want to be good for her, too," I said. "What if I screw up?"

"Oh, you will. No doubt about that."

"Thanks."

"But she'll forgive you," said Aldo. "You need someone around like that, too."

I reconsidered the hammock. Except for its shape, it really didn't seem like a hammock at all. It was more like an animal, humming with life. "What am I supposed to do here?"

Aldo handed me the same dive knife he'd given me for Christmas.

"Can I cut them all?" I asked.

He shook his head. "Sorry, just your own."

I looked at the cord he'd designated as mine: thick and fibrous, the color of rust. "If I slice through this—"

"You'll be free," said Aldo.

"And you'll be gone."

"I'm not really here. You're just hallucinating me while you're hypoxic." I glowered, and Aldo smiled merrily. "See? Doesn't feel nice having your reality questioned, does it?"

It didn't. I made a mental note to try to stop doing that in the future.

A slice of my reflection hovered in the titanium blade. The cord trembled, as if it knew what was coming.

"A favor, before you go?" said Aldo.

I looked up. "Anything."

"Get me out of that fucking sea turtle."

Now I smiled. "I'm sorry. Is there someplace you'd rather be?"

"I don't care, as long as it's dramatic. Scatter me in the mouth of an active volcano. Or take me down to the Mariana Trench."

"I'll get right on that."

I expected the sharp knife to glide through the cord. Instead I had to hack at it like a tough string of meat. Sinew by sinew, it peeled slowly away. I felt no pain, but there was the same queasy feeling I'd had cutting through Clementine's tentacle on the beach, as if it were my own body I was slicing into.

"Goodbye!" called Aldo, though as the cord snapped and its light died and I dropped like a stone toward the Armory's floor, he remained there, suspended above me, still solid, bathed in the hammock's golden glow. I was the one who was leaving.

* * *

The first thing I became aware of was a bumpy surface beneath my back. My attempts to lift my leaden eyelids were unsuccessful. It was quiet, until the volume turned on, and then it was horribly loud: waves rushing, a seagull shrieking, the clamor of voices right above my head.

I managed to open my eyes a crack and immediately wished I hadn't. Borne on the wash of daylight was all the pain the darkness kept back. A hot froth boiled up my throat. Someone wrenched me onto my side as I started retching up a mud-colored liquid.

I closed my eyes and settled back. I felt good now, clean and safe and empty.

"Jo."

I groaned.

"Jo!"

I opened my eyes. Sunlight pressed murkily through the branches of the maple tree. The grass steamed. Shattering Point looked as if it had just risen from a bath.

Tony's face hung inches above mine. "I am going to kill you."

"She doesn't mean that!" Nadia dropped to her knees beside me, her face wet with rain or tears, and pressed her lips to my forehead. "That was so scary. We thought you were gone. How do you feel now?"

She helped me sit up and put my shirt on. I glanced back at Tony. She was packing up the portable defibrillator, not looking at me.

"I'm sorry." I was talking to Tony, but it was Nadia's hand I reached for. "I feel fine now. Honest." An overstatement. My stomach ached, and the area inside my chest crawled with a tight, itchy feeling. "I feel . . . light," I said. It was an echo of the feeling that took hold of a diver when they hit the water, and natural buoyancy took over, and all that heavy scuba gear became instantly weightless.

I looked behind me. The tree obstructed my view of the dock.

"How do I look?" I asked, recalling the change in Margo.

"The same," said Tony, but she still wasn't looking at me.

Nadia helped me to my feet. Together, the three of us walked through the wet grass and onto the dock. The clouds directly above still threatened rain, but out over the Gulf they were flat and white and lazy. The storm was moving east.

I squinted. I didn't see anything out of the ordinary, but I wasn't sure whether to trust the vision I'd had of Clementine's barrier made solid. Nadia and Tony held back as I pressed onward, the boards creaking underfoot.

I kept walking, straight to the end of the dock, until there was nothing in front of me but ocean. The tide was in. The water lapped at the pilings. I breathed in the rusty-smelling sea air, relishing the power of my puny human lungs.

I had done it. I had passed through the barrier like it was nothing. Goodbye, Clementine. Goodbye, Aldo. I stretched my arms in front of me, and they looked like my arms always had—same smattering of freckles, same network of blue veins.

Behind me, someone was shouting, and I felt my shoulders tense. I knew now why Margo hadn't responded to any of our hails. It felt like terrible luck to turn around. I had cheated something, like Aldo with his snake. To even cast a glance over my shoulder risked reeling me back.

"Don't you fucking dare!"

That was Tony. She and Nadia formed a duo of overlapping cries buffeting my spine.

My view of the Gulf swirled down to a keyhole of beckoning light. I was hovering at the mouth of the cave, minutes from my escape. But there wasn't really any question of what to do, was there? I had left someone behind once before. Aldo's death wasn't my fault. I understood that now. I also understood that loss wasn't really about a person's death. It was about your life, and what you were willing to live with moving forward.

Clementine remembered me. I was the ghost now.

I took a last deep breath, turned, and strolled back down the dock to see what could be done for my friends.

Turritopsis dohrnii

Nothing lasts forever. Except jellyfish.

It was the wrong time of year to be in Portland.

Hordes of people thronged the cobblestoned streets, peering into shop windows and bending to inspect the lobster roll prices chalked onto sandwich boards outside every restaurant. The breeze swirling between orange brick buildings smelled like an unappetizing combination of seafood and sunscreen. I was out of practice: with cities, with traffic, with crowds. Just over two weeks had elapsed since I'd successfully severed myself from Clementine, but only now that I'd returned to civilization could I finally appreciate the island's appeal of being so far removed.

A long queue had formed outside a kiosk advertising whale-watching tours. I stared at the logo pasted to the side of the stall—a silhouette of an airborne humpback—wondering if this company could've been around when my parents embarked on their failed search for whales over thirty years ago. I was tempted to buy a ticket. For as much time as I'd spent on and in the water,

I'd never been up close with a whale. And there was something nice about imagining I was following in my parents' footsteps. My life had taken such a different track from theirs, it was rare for our experiences to overlap.

"Earth to Jo!" Tony waved at me from the other side of the queue, her voice pitched in an annoyed way that indicated she'd been trying to get my attention for several seconds.

I squeezed through the crowd to join her. She wore a baggy-sleeved striped T-shirt over gray Bermuda shorts, a nondescript baseball cap spun backward on her head. It was the kind of outfit that looked like it could've been assembled from a lost and found, but on Tony, it radiated tomboy glamour. I curled a finger through one of her belt loops, and she permitted herself to be lightly rocked from side to side, her annoyance already fading and a smile taking its place.

"Any luck?" she asked.

I consulted my phone, which was opened to Google Maps. I'd yet to get the fractured screen repaired, but at least we'd returned to the universe of reliable cell service.

"We should be close. It says it's just here, off Market Street."

Tony frowned. "I think we should bag it. Middle of the day on a Sunday? Odds are good she's out running errands or something. And our flight leaves in—"

"Jo, Tony! Over here!" Now it was Nadia waving at us from beneath the overhang of a coffee shop.

We reconvened on the sidewalk: me, Tony, and Nadia. Roger stepped out of the shop a moment later, rattling the ice cubes at the bottom of a coffee drink. He'd been discharged from the hospital last week and still had the run-down look of a recently ill person, the sleeves of his T-shirt flapping around arms that were noticeably thinner. The last thing he remembered from Memorial Day was making coleslaw in his kitchen. He had no recollection of getting stung by the tentacle, or calling me on the night of the dive, insisting when Tony teased him about his "magic hammock" that she was exaggerating. I thought he wasn't giving himself enough credit. *Everything is connected.* Roger had been trying to tell me about Clementine's colony. I still didn't know how, but he really had figured it out.

Nadia looped her arm through his, and I thought of how much it had once bothered me to see the two of them together, how little it bothered me now.

"I found the road," she said. "It's just this way." She pulled Roger into an alley, and Tony and I followed.

The crowd thinned as we left Old Port behind. Snatches of the waterfront appeared between buildings. We plodded uphill, going slowly for Roger, who was still regaining his strength, until we reached a cluttery neighborhood shaded by elm trees. A basketball thudded pavement somewhere out of view. Nadia, who'd taken charge of Google Maps, led us to a row of town houses with periwinkle siding and rapped smartly on number 7.

The door opened almost immediately, as if the occupant—a short, older white woman with oversize rainbow glasses clinging to the end of her nose—had been lingering just inside, waiting for us.

I launched into my prepared speech: "Good afternoon, ma'am. We're sorry to bother you. My name is Josephine Ness. We flew in yesterday from Shattering Point, and we were wondering if—"

The stranger dismissed the rest of my explanation with a cheerful flick of her wrist. "Oh, I know who you are. Madge said you'd be coming around. She's always going on about those islanders of hers." She had the same carrying voice as her sister. Tony and I traded glances, and I knew she was also dwelling on the phrasing: *those islanders*. Evidently you could take a person off Shattering, but you couldn't take Shattering out of a person. "The name's Kath. Come in, come in. She's just in the sunroom."

Kath ushered us down a short hallway and into a glassed-in porch off the back of the house. Patio furniture had been shoved to one side, the better to accommodate an easel and drop cloth and chest of clear plastic drawers stuffed with art supplies. Margo Sloan had wasted no time setting up her studio. The artist herself stood with her back to us, apparently intent on something in the shaded backyard. There was a moment of awkwardness when no one seemed to know how to get her attention. The scene so closely resembled how we'd seen her last, on the dock that Friday morning two weeks ago when she'd left us all behind. Then Kath shouted, "Madge! Guests!" and Margo whirled, her long skirt billowing and paint globules scattering from her brush onto the drop cloth.

She took her time greeting each of us, wrenching Roger's and Tony's heads down in order to plant kisses on their cheeks. I was relieved at how happy our visit seemed to make her. Considering the circumstances surrounding her departure, it hadn't been a given that Margo would want to see anyone from Shattering. Norm hadn't resisted giving Tony his sister-in-law's address in Portland; now that it was common knowledge he'd poisoned his wife, the man had succumbed to unprecedented meekness. But though Tony had left message after message on Kath's answering machine, she never actually got through to either of the sisters.

That, plus the difficulty in tracking down the right neighborhood, had made me start to wonder whether Norm had deceived us with a fake address and phone number after all.

Margo hugged me, then framed her hands around my face, regarding me like a work in progress on one of her easels. "Josephine, dear. You're looking well. Your aura is positively glowing."

"You're looking well, too, Margo."

Tony supplied the subtext: "You know, for someone who was almost poisoned to death."

Roger grimaced. The plan had been to proceed gently, but that wasn't Tony's style. She looked at me and shrugged.

Margo smiled faintly and suggested we sit down for a cup of tea.

Tony and I extracted five patio chairs from the corner of the sunroom and dragged them out into the grass. It was pleasant under the trees, if a little humid. The pounding of the basketball had been replaced with birdsong and the steady hum of insects. Margo pinched the coiled handle of her teacup in three fingers and sipped primly. I recognized the citrusy smell of her homemade blend. How could she bear to drink the stuff, still? I expected to have an aversion to jasmine for the rest of my life.

"So you know what Norm did to you?" asked Roger. Nadia had filled him in on all the wild events that had transpired while he was recovering, and now he was watching Margo drink her tea with a nauseated expression.

"Of course, dear. I'm not a complete idiot." Margo set down her teacup and patted her mouth with a napkin. "It didn't dawn on me till after I'd left the island. Sometimes you need to get away from people in order for their true colors to be revealed."

"You don't sound mad," observed Nadia. She took a cautious sip of her tea, probably out of a desire not to appear rude. Tony kept her hands curled around the arms of her chair.

"I was, at first. Positively livid! But then I thought, *Oh, what's the point?* He did me a favor in the long term, getting me off that island. And if he hadn't poisoned me, I'd've poisoned him at some point. Marriage," declared Margo, "is *not* for the faint of heart."

There was a beat in which we all absorbed this disturbing moral. I saw Nadia and Roger lock eyes across the table as the joint and silent pledge unfolded between them to never let themselves become so miserable as the Sloans. Even I had to admit that for all their problems as a couple, it was pretty difficult to imagine Nadia or Roger poisoning each other.

"I did call him after I got to Portland," added Margo. "I couldn't quite resist the urge to give him a piece of my mind. And I needed someone to ship me my things. Lord knows I won't be setting foot on Shattering again."

"Why's that?" I asked.

She gave me a look as if it should be obvious. "We've been granted a reprieve, dear. That's all. Our monster is still devoted to us. Never think for one moment that Clementine has let us go."

For a second the humidity parted. I felt a chill slink out of the shadows beneath the trees.

Margo took another drink of her tea. "What my soon-to-be-ex-husband did *not* tell me is how the rest of you were able to get off the island. So, go on! How is it you managed to leave Shattering?"

I let the others tell the story. I was sick of it by now. I'd already had to tell it four times. Twice to Shanel—on the first round, she was too amazed to interrupt; on the second, she stopped me approximately every seven seconds to ask a question. Then Ha-Yun Kim, intrigued by my unhinged voicemails, called me back to demand the full story. The very next day, she set up a video call with the rest of her research team so we could go over it all again. She threw a temper tantrum when she learned the only existent piece of Clementine currently resided in a lab at the University of New Hampshire in the hands of some random graduate student.

"Make her an offer she can't refuse," I'd said, already smiling at the thought of the brilliant engineer strong-armed into negotiating with Aldo's stubborn protégée.

Of course, there was only one thing Shanel wanted, and that was to be involved in all things Clementine. In exchange for surrendering the coveted tentacle, she would be a paid collaborator on our research. Already Ha-Yun's mind was on fire with product ideas inspired by the most highly evolved colonial organism on the planet, and if I was ambivalent about this ruthlessly utilitarian approach, I also accepted it as the price of getting the resources I wanted: Ha-Yun had named me principal investigator of Project Clementine, with an entire budget line designated for my research. What sort of sickness had finally felled Shattering Point's sea monster, who'd never resurfaced that third night in June? Was she really as old as Sylvia Steele thought? What was the mechanism that let her pull people in? Was it something to do with her bioluminescence, that bloodred light that had moved through all of us, calling out to us in a language we didn't speak yet implicitly understood?

Those were the questions that interested me now, but Margo

Sloan deserved her answers, too. Nadia took the lead, describing how after I passed through the barrier, the islanders had gone, in her words, "a little crazy."

"That's putting it lightly," snorted Tony. "Picture a group of fifty people running around all looking for things that could *almost kill* them."

"Oh, my," said Margo, pressing her fingers to her lips. "But why didn't everyone just use the flowers, if you knew they worked?"

"Too risky. After what happened to Jo, no one wanted to ingest something that might stop their hearts. We were all trying to think of the Goldilocks solution: not so mild it wouldn't fool Clementine, not so strong it would actually finish us off."

"It was the strangest brainstorming session I've ever been part of," said Nadia, shaking her head. "Who knew people were so, um, creative?"

"There's a killing impulse inside each of us, dear," said Margo warmly. "So what did everyone end up trying?"

"I skipped an insulin dose," replied Nadia. "Simple as that. And to think I'd been so careful with my supply since arriving on the island . . ."

"Stabbed myself with an EpiPen," said Tony, flashing a thumbs-up.

"*Everyone* got off the island?" said Margo, her big blue eyes swiveling between each of us.

"Not everyone wanted to leave—for some people it's their home, and always will be," said Nadia. "But everyone *can* leave now. We've all separated from Clementine. The barrier is gone. Clementine is gone, too. That's what matters."

There was a definitiveness to her concluding statement that I didn't want to challenge.

The talk turned to lighter subjects: the series of portraits Margo was working on for her first art show in the city; Tony's recent visit home to see her mom, who was in remission and reassuringly committed to her old project of despising every one of her daughter's life choices; our little group's upcoming trip to Indiana. My mother had been overjoyed to learn that not only was I making time for a visit, I was actually bringing *real human friends* with me. She'd cleaned the house top to bottom twice already and would surely do so a third time before our plane touched down in Indianapolis.

"Speaking of which." Tony tapped her wrist, where a watch would be if she wore one. "We still need to grab our stuff from the Airbnb before our flight."

The house felt colder after sitting outside. We walked back up the hall to the front door, where Kath intercepted us—"But you must stay for lunch!"—and Margo took advantage of the delay to grip my arm and steer me down a side passage away from the group. We entered a room that was just a maze of suitcases and boxes, a bed jammed in the corner like an afterthought. Margo navigated the mess with ease, still dragging me behind her. We arrived at a pile of canvases leaning against the windowsill. Before I had time to process my rising sense of foreboding, I was staring at the finished portrait of the *yōkai* and me.

My stomach dropped, but it was only from surprise. There was nothing horrifying about this painting. It showed a woman perched on a chair, hands open and resting on her thighs. A few strands of dark hair had slipped from her ponytail to dangle beside her slightly protuberant ears. Her chin was up, head angled as if listening. Her expression looked troubled—the face of someone perpetually elsewhere, lost in a stream of fast-moving thought.

Behind her stood a man. One gloved hand was curled over the back of the chair, a hair's breadth from the woman's shoulder. He was clad in a black diving suit, but his face was maskless, bared. It was a face I remembered well. The eyes were cast down at the woman, the lips quirked upward in a half smile as if he were already entertained by whatever ridiculous thing he was about to say to rescue her from her own head.

The figures' background was intentionally blurry. If not for the chair, they could've been anywhere. In a library, in a lab, underwater, or hurtling through outer space.

"It's for you. A gift," said Margo. "I've been working on it every day since Norman sent me my belongings. I only put on the finishing touches last night. That's how I knew you'd be here today. It was the right time for you to receive it."

I didn't know what to say. My throat felt blocked by a complex storm of emotions. Regret. Sorrow. Wonder. Joy. All this time I'd thought it was the *yōkai* Margo had glimpsed that morning, but it turned out the real Aldo had managed to make an appearance after all.

"Thank you," I said finally.

Margo beamed, seeming positively thrilled that her artwork had moved me to tears.

I tried to picture where in my apartment I'd hang it. Probably above my mantel for now, near that sea turtle urn full of ashes I still needed to scatter. Before the end of next month, I'd be closing up my lab at Seaheart and relocating to San Francisco. I found I wasn't dreading the change as much as I'd anticipated—probably because Tony had commented offhandedly that there were some pretty good veterinary programs in that area. We could both use a new place to start over.

I heard Tony's voice calling me from the hallway. We really did need to make our way to the airport. But now that we were alone, I couldn't resist asking Margo about one more thing.

"What did you mean when you said Clementine hadn't really let us go?"

Margo laid a hand against her sternum. "I can feel her here, still. She's different now, but not dead."

I nodded. I'd talked about it with Tony, and she'd admitted she felt it, too: a phantom limb sensation, the cramp of something severed but still living. Sometimes it was in the ends of our toes. Other times it was more like a murky malaise that crawled across the skin without settling. We hadn't spoken about this feeling to any of the others. It felt too cruel to suggest so soon after our miraculous escapes from Shattering that as long as any of us was alive, Clementine's colony lived on.

"Sylvia showed me something her grandfather wrote eighty years ago," I said. "About an animal that glowed red on the water. She thought that meant Clementine had been alive for decades. I didn't think it was possible at first; how could she have gone so long without someone seeing her? But I've been thinking about it, and, well—have you heard of *Turritopsis dohrnii*, the immortal jellyfish? When it reaches the end of its lifespan and its body starts to deteriorate, it reduces itself and returns to the polyp stage. Almost like if a person could avoid death by returning to infancy and then regrowing."

"How awful!" cried Margo. "To be wrenched away from an ending and back to a beginning, over and over . . . You really think that's what's happening to poor Clementine?"

"It's only a theory." But if it were true, and Clementine was still out there somewhere, invisible to human eyes, biding her time as a tiny stalk that would one day evolve into another full-size medusa, what did that mean for Tony and me and the rest of the islanders? When the colony re-formed, would those of us who'd drifted too far from Shattering simply drop where we stood like limbs hacked off at the joint? Or would it be a gentler summons, a sweet ache like homesickness gradually calling us back to the island and to each other?

Margo rested her hand on my shoulder. "Take some advice from me, dear. Don't cling to your mortal tether. Let an ending be an ending. It's better for everyone when people exit with grace."

We returned to the hallway. The sisters gathered in the door and waved to us as we traipsed down the front path. Roger and Tony walked ahead, bickering about the shortest route to the Airbnb. I probably should've shared their stress over making our flight on time, but I couldn't bring myself to muster any worry. The summer day was so fine, and the past, for once, felt comfortably distant.

Regardless of Clementine's intentions for me, I knew I wasn't done with Shattering Point. After I'd learned everything I could from the diseased tentacle, now preserved in formalin and awaiting me in my new lab in San Francisco, I would push Ha-Yun to send Project Clementine into the field, where it had all started, to see what could be seen beneath the shadow of the lighthouse. I still had a Clementine case study to add to my book, and though Aldo wouldn't be cowriting this final chapter, I had a feeling it would've been his favorite part.

But first, a vacation with my friends.

Nadia, who'd hung back to walk alongside me, pointed to the canvas I was carrying tucked under one arm. "What's that?"

I flipped the painting around. She took it and smiled. "Margo did this for you? That's a great likeness, Josie." She flitted a fingertip over Aldo's face. "Who's the guy behind you? I don't recognize him from Shattering."

"His name's Aldo Antunes. He was my best friend."

Nadia's smile flickered—perplexed that she hadn't heard of this important person, or else reacting to my use of the past tense and the loss it implied.

"It's okay," I assured her. "Really." I took the painting back and squeezed her hand. "I'll tell you all about him on the plane."

Acknowledgments

The Jellyfish Problem is as much a book about the power of community as it is a book about a giant jellyfish. In that vein, thanks are due to the community of individuals who helped this novel come to be.

First, to my amazing agent, Sarah Burnes, who found me in the wilds of Twitter and believed in this book when it was just a few weird chapters.

To Amanda Bergeron and Randi Kramer for thoughtful edits that expanded my understanding of Shattering Point and of Jo, and to the whole team at Berkley for helping *The Jellyfish Problem* meet its readers.

To Emily Osborne for a beautiful cover that perfectly captures the spirit of this book.

To Aru Menon for early enthusiasm and astute feedback.

To Alex Baron, Christian Emmanuel, Jennifer Ng, and Julieta Vitullo for their suggestions and encouragement.

To my Wild Writing Group: Lauren Bajek, Yume Kitasei, Nicholas Russell, and Sameem Siddiqui. It was during our Pittsburgh retreat that *The Jellyfish Problem* really started to take shape.

A second shout-out to Yume for being the best beta reader I could ask for. I look forward to commiserating with you on all our future projects.

To the Hartwick College Wandersee Scholar-in-Residence program for funding book purchases and a research trip to Maine, and to Samrat Upadhyay and Alexander Weinstein for their early endorsement of this project.

To all my friends and supporters at Hartwick, especially Steph Carr, Libby Cudmore, and Brad Fest.

Clementine is a fictive sea monster, but on my journey toward creating her and thinking through Jo's career, I'm grateful to have been guided by so many informative texts, especially:

Spineless: The Science of Jellyfish and the Art of Growing a Backbone by Juli Berwald

The World Is Blue: How Our Fate and the Ocean's Are One by Sylvia Earle

Stung! On Jellyfish Blooms and the Future of the Ocean and *Shapeshifters: The Wondrous World of Jellyfish* by Lisa-ann Gershwin

Becoming a Marine Biologist by Virginia Morell

Below the Edge of Darkness: A Memoir of Exploring Light and Life in the Deep Sea by Edith Widder

My gratitude also goes to Cheryl Jones, for sharing her scuba know-how, and to Abby Tripler, who provided friendship, ocean expertise, and countless hours watching nature documentaries on Netflix.

Jo's story about the *ayakashi* is my own invention but borrows elements from "The Story of Mimi-Nashi-Hōichi" by Lafcadio Hearn. My knowledge of Japanese folklore was additionally influenced by Michael Dylan Foster's *The Book of Yokai: Mysterious Creatures of Japanese Folklore*.

This book is dedicated to my mother despite her dislike of water, because I can't imagine being the writer or person I am without her. Thanks, Mom, for three-plus decades of your love, strength, and humor. (And sorry about all the water.)

Finally, to Korra: We met as Clementine was achieving her final form. Thank you for holding all the faith so I could hold all the doubts. Thank you for your love.